ANCIENT TRADITION AND CONTEMPORARY
EXPERIENCE
MINGLE TO CREATE AN UNFORGETTABLE
COLLECTION
OF AUTHENTIC NATIVE AMERICAN STORIES

The Old Marriage
by Debra Earling

A schoolgirl, Louise, fights to escape the seduction, aided by witchcraft, of a threatening boy, Clarence Yellow Knife, in a tale of superstition, sexuality, and tribal lore.

The Bingo Van
by Louise Erdrich

Contemporary reservation life and the dreams of a young man, Lipsha, revolve around the local bingo game, a broken romance, lost chances . . . and a tattoo of a running black pony.

Aunt Parnetta's Electric Blisters
by Diane Glancy

Dark humor and folklore are interwoven in the delightfully captured dialect of Aunt Parnetta and her husband, their reservation home, and a refrigerator that has a life of its own.

Turtle Lake
by Gloria Bird

The rape of the land by logging companies, tribal beliefs and the spooky experiences of Tapete, a young Northwest Indian, and his slow-witted brother-in-law create a story with chilling impact.

. . . AND MORE STORIES THAT CELEBRATE
THE SOUL, THE
SPIRIT AND THE DREAMS OF TODAY'S
NATIVE AMERICANS

Novels by Craig Lesley

RIVER SONG

WINTERKILL

TALKING LEAVES

❖❖❖❖

CONTEMPORARY NATIVE AMERICAN SHORT STORIES

❖❖❖❖

Introduced and Edited by
Craig Lesley

Associate Editor,
Katheryn Stavrakis

A LAUREL TRADE PAPERBACK

A LAUREL TRADE PAPERBACK
Published by Dell Publishing
a division of
Bantam Doubleday Dell
Publishing Group, Inc.
666 Fifth Avenue
New York, New York 10103

Interior design by Nancy Field

ISBN: 0-440-50344-2

Printed in the United States of America

Published simultaneously in Canada

October 1991

10   9   8   7   6   5   4   3   2   1

???

ACKNOWLEDGMENTS

The following selections in this anthology are reproduced by permission of the authors, their publishers, or their agents:

"Deer Woman" by Paula Gunn Allen © Paula Gunn Allen, 1991. Reprinted by permission of the author.

"Turtle Lake" by Gloria Bird © Gloria Bird, 1991. Reprinted by permission of the author.

"Swimming Upstream" by Beth Brant © Beth Brant, 1991. Reprinted by permission of the author.

"Going Home" by Joseph Bruchac © Joseph Bruchac, 1991. Reprinted by permission of the author.

"A Visit from Reverend Tileston" by Elizabeth Cook-Lynn: Reprinted from *The Power of Horses and Other Stories* published by Arcade Publishing (a subsidiary of Little Brown and Company). First appeared in *Blue Cloud Quarterly*.

"Queen of Diamonds" by Michael Dorris: Reprinted from *A Yellow Raft on Blue Water* reprinted with permission from Henry Holt and Company. Also appeared in *The American Voice*.

"The Old Marriage" by Debra Earling © Debra Earling, 1991. Reprinted by permission of the author.

"After Celilo" by Ed Edmo © Ed Edmo, 1991. Reprinted by permission of the author.

"Humming of the Stars and Bees and Waves" by Anita Endrezze © Anita Endrezze, 1991. Reprinted by permission of the author.

"The Bingo Van" by Louise Erdrich: Reprinted by permission; © Louise Erdrich. Originally in *The New Yorker*.

"The Way It Was" by Tina Marie Freeman-Villalobos © Tina Marie Freeman-Villalobos, 1991. Reprinted by permission of the author.

"Aunt Parnetta's Electric Blisters" by Diane Glancy first appeared in *Trigger Dance* published by the University of Colorado. Reprinted by permission of the author.

"High Cotton" by Rayna Green from *That's What She Said*, published by Indiana University Press. Reprinted by permission of the author.

"The Flood" by Joy Harjo first appeared in *Grand Street*. Reprinted by permission of the author.

"Northern Lights" by Joy Harjo first appeared in *The American Voice*. Reprinted by permission of the author.

"Taking Care of Business" by Kathleen Shaye Hill: first apperaed in *Backbone: A Journal of Women's Literature*. Also appeared in *The Stories We Hold Secret*, published by Greenfield Center.

"Aunt Moon's Young Man" by Linda Hogan first appeared in *Missouri Review* and *Best American Stories* published by Houghton Mifflin, 1989.

"The Pebble People" by Roger Jack first appeared in *Earth Power Coming* from Navajo Community Press. Reprinted by permission of the author.

For Katheryn Ann Stavrakis
and our daughters, Elena and Kira

I wish to thank Damaris Rowland and Leslie Schnur at Dell Publishing for their help initiating this anthology and seeing it through to completion. Gale Miller, Claudia O'Driscoll, LaVonne Ruoff, Kathleen Sands, and Elizabeth Woody deserve credit for their suggestions and support.

CONTENTS

❖❖❖

Introduction

I like my stories to speak about lives that are usually not
found in American literature. I believe this speaking gives
something back to the people whose lives have given me
the energy and the need to write our stories. *

LINDA HOGAN

When Damaris Rowland and Leslie Schnur, of Dell Publish-
ing/Laurel Books, approached me about the possibility of doing
an anthology of contemporary Native American short fiction, I
was delighted with the prospect, because I felt publication of
such a collection by one of the major houses was long overdue.
While the general reading public knows the highly acclaimed
novels of many outstanding Native American writers, the wonderful variety and quality of short fiction hasn't been as well
known, except by those who keep up with the small press and
literary publications where much of the short fiction has appeared over the past ten years. Happily, I believe that's changing,
and I saw this new anthology as an opportunity to reacquaint
fiction readers with works of established writers as well as to
introduce lesser-known and new writers. In addition, I wanted
readers to rediscover the enduring values in contemporary Native
American literature: respect for the land and tribal elders, a sense
of history and tradition, awareness of the powers inherent in
storytelling, and a closeness to the spiritual world.

* Best American Short Stories of 1989 (Boston: Houghton Mifflin), 1989.

Much of mainstream society has overlooked similar values during decades of shopping malls, high-tech gadgetry, and junk bond greed. However, many people are now searching for the values and traditions inherent in Native American literature because these nourish the soul. Moreover, people are beginning to realize the value of the earth itself. If we are to survive, the earth needs protection and healing. As Barry Lopez has noted, "Landscape is the culture that contains all human cultures." For centuries, Native people have tried to live in harmony and balance with nature, and the voices of their writers continue to carry that message forward.

However, the stories here in no way reflect a "romantic" view of nature or contemporary Native American life. Change is the rule rather than the exception, and enormous stresses operate on the culture and the individual. Frequently, the characters are torn between two worlds. Families are wrenched by displacement, alcoholism, spouse or child abuse. Remarkably, the characters manage to survive in spite of overwhelming odds. And as these voices attest, they survive with courage, and dignity, and humor.

When I was growing up along the Columbia River near Celilo Falls, the great salmon fishery, the Native people celebrated the spring salmon runs with a feast. While Chief Tommy Thompson and the elders led the ceremony, the "first foods"— salmon, spring roots, and berries—were shared among tribal members and visitors. After everyone had eaten the food together, they could eat separately throughout the season. Salmon bones were returned to the river, ensuring the salmon's return. In my mind, the feast emphasized closeness to the river and natural cycles, as well as the importance of elders and traditions.

The Dalles Dam destroyed Celilo Falls in 1957 even as a series of dams on the Columbia inundated Native fishing villages. Many people moved away from the river, their livelihood destroyed, their culture shattered. The dams also decimated the salmon runs until the returning salmon fell to less than one-tenth of pre-dam levels. But in spite of the changes, some people remained close to the river, and through tribal efforts, more salmon began returning. Year after year, the feast continues at Celilo Village each spring, and now similar feasts occur on the Klickitat River and at Simnasho on the Warm Springs Reservation. One realizes that around the country, Native people are following similar ceremonies, which are growing in number and importance.

The people returning to these festivals have witnessed enormous changes and many hardships, but they have survived, in part because they have never completely lost touch with the old values, or the voices of earth and water.

The stories in this collection speak to these enduring visions and values.

❖❖❖

As a board member of the Northwest Native American Writers Association, I have been aware of the quality fiction and poetry coming from the NNAWA. So I began by asking the NNAWA members to submit or recommend fiction for consideration. Elizabeth Woody, for example, had written a terrific book of poems, *Hand into Stone,* which I admired and which received an American Book Award from the Before Columbus Foundation. I knew she was writing fiction as well. When I attended one of her readings, she included the impressive short story "HomeCooking," and I was amazed to see one of my students crying during the reading. At the conclusion of the reading Elizabeth handed me the story. "This one's for the new anthology," she said.

At the same time, I wrote and called people across the country for help and suggestions. Approaching poets whose work I've admired for years, I asked, "Are you working on any fiction?" And I began reading through the literary magazines and small press publications.

Three groups of writers emerged: those who are widely publicized and recognized; those who have been writing for a number of years but whose audiences are smaller because their works appear in literary magazines and small press publications; those who are "new" writers—just beginning their fiction writing careers.

This anthology includes all three groups. I am particularly happy to introduce a large number of new writers and new stories. But all these stories gave me many pleasurable hours of reading and editing, and I was pleased to discover even more talented writers than I had anticipated. Furthermore, I hope this collection will encourage readers to seek out other works of fiction, poetry, and nonfiction by these contributors.

I admire good writing; I enjoy a good story; I love to be surprised by something I haven't seen before—a remarkable character, a wonderful image, an unusual turn of phrase. As I read submissions for this anthology, my idea was simply to choose the best stories I could find and let the themes emerge from the works themselves.

In 1980, I was fortunate enough to take a fiction workshop with Raymond Carver, and I remember how he stressed that good fiction made us aware of how other people live and would often contain small details or observations that revealed important things about their lives. It's something I always think about as I work on my own fiction. As I read these stories, I kept an eye open for these telling details and I hope the readers will too. For example, in Debra Earling's story "The Old Marriage," the heroine, Louise, buries the rattlesnake rattles Clarence Yellow Knife has slipped into her hand on the hillside and marks them with three red rocks so she can stay away from them, because she knows the rattles have a dangerous power. But her slowness in burying them also reveals that she has been influenced by the power already.

In Greg Sarris's story "How I Got to Be Queen," Alice, the sister who holds the family together, sprinkles sugar on the children's peanut butter sandwiches so they will eat them. And in Michael Dorris's story "The Queen of Diamonds," the teenage girl Ray looks at paint samples and concludes how the different colors match the mixed blood members of her family: "Once, in a hardware store, I found our exact shades on a paint mixtone chart. Mom was Almond Joy, Dad was Burnt Clay, and I was Maple Walnut." These are the kinds of vivid details and observations that bring fiction to life.

Another goal I kept in mind was to include a number of humorous stories. Native American writing, storytelling, song, and gossip are rich with humor. I wanted to pass that on. Also, as Fiction Editor for *Writers' Forum* over the past eight years, I have come to realize how rare humorous stories are. As a result, I was delighted to encounter a number of stories I considered truly funny. Tom King's "A Seat in the Garden" contains humorous allusions to the Hollywood movies that exploit Indian angles. The gardeners in the story, who encounter a ghostly Indian in their plot, decide maybe they have planted on an ancient Indian burial ground, something they've seen in the fright movies. Their descriptions of the Indian are funny too, because they say he looks like Jeff Chandler and Victor Mature. The old "westerns" featured Mature and Chandler frequently cast as Indians. In the story's neat reversal, three old Indian men who collect bottles to "save the earth" have the last laugh by serving as "interpreters" for the figure in the garden. They say he demands a bench be constructed there, but they use the bench themselves to rest during their rounds of bottle collecting.

Gerald Vizenor provides satiric humor with his "trickster" figure Luster Browne, or Lusterbow, from "The Baron of Patronia." The traditional trickster figure is lusty and adventuresome, adaptable as a coyote, and usually brings change or chaos to the people. Vizenor's Luster is just such a character. Petty and spiteful government bureaucrats (exactly the type all too often sent to reservations) give him a worthless parcel of land, but he flourishes, nonetheless. Eventually, he forms a partnership with Novena Mae Ironmoccasin, an orphan raised by Benedictine sisters. At age fifteen, Novena Mae "created a wild Stations of the Cross on fourteen wounded trees behind the mission, and then she retreated to the hardwoods." Here she is attracted to Luster, and ten children result from their union.

Luster's zest for life is apparent not only in his procreation but also in his joyous shouting about love and flowers in the various "panic holes" on his land. He teaches his children and even the mongrel dogs Chicken Lips and White Lies to do the same.

Another trickster, more of a cosmic type, who pokes fun at William Buckley, appears in Carter Revard's "Never Quite a Hollywood Star."

In Gloria Bird's "Turtle Lake," two ice fishermen begin telling "Stick Indian" and "Sasquatch" stories. After a while, their own storytelling scares them and they race across the lake in pell-mell fashion, seeking safety. Their humorous retreat is nicely balanced with ambiguity. Perhaps the men have been frightened only by their words, but one fisherman believes the legendary Stick Indians came when they heard their name spoken aloud.

Sorcery and witchcraft add a more somber tone to this collection. Today, sorcery remains strong among many tribes. As I worked on my novel *River Song*, consulting with medicine people about current practices, I learned that many sorcerers hold the rattlesnake power—strong and also dangerous. In Debra Earling's provocative and haunting "The Old Marriage," Clarence Yellow Knife comes from rattlesnake people, which seems to give him a hold over Louise, the object of his bizarre affection. Encounters with Clarence evoke in her visions of snakes, and she seems unable to break free of his power. In Anna Walters's "Bicenti," witchcraft appears in a car turned upside down, a large dog slaughtered on another car's roof, and a dark man who "contorted his face into grotesque masks" and "mimed an unearthly performance, contorting his body beyond the bounds of human ability."

Many stories incorporate traditional myths. Paula Gunn Allen's "Deer Woman" provides an excellent example of a contemporary story that weaves in mythological elements. Two men go out "snagging"—looking for women—at the stomp dance, but eventually encounter two beautiful and mysterious women who take them to the land of "little people," Thunder, and the deer. Even as the women are transformed into deer people, the men's lives become changed—one meets an early death because he told forbidden secrets. Contemporary details of Winnebago motor homes and San Francisco's BART system contrast with the supernatural and surreal elements in this evocative story.

Anita Endrezze alternates parts of a Yaqui myth with the

main narrative in "The Humming of Stars and Bees and Waves," as an old woman seeks a cure for her blindness in a cave populated by Spider Woman's descendants.

In reading these stories, I was pleased at the number of unforgettable characters, especially the women. Of her prizewinning story "Aunt Moon's Young Man," Linda Hogan notes, "I love Aunt Moon. For me, she is one of the courageous heroes and adventurers I have seldom seen in stories." Indeed she is! The irrepressible Aunt Moon provides the nosy villagers with cures and remedies, endures their jealous gossip after she attracts a handsome young man to her home, and flourishes with her newfound love. At the same time, she teaches the story's young narrator to love all creatures and regard herself as beautiful.

Courage of another kind is evident in Beth Brant's "Swimming Upstream," in which a recovering alcoholic just manages to avoid the bottle after learning of the accidental drowning of her son. Her salvation comes as a kind of vision when she watches salmon leaping a falls and imagines one salmon's destiny to be associated with her son's.

In Greg Sarris's story, "How I Got to Be Queen," the narrator Alice is a remarkable character, the kind readers will hope to see again in his forthcoming works. Younger and wiser than her troubled sister Justine, Alice is the glue that holds together an otherwise scattered family. Her grumbling over responsibilities and chores cannot conceal her generosity, and when neighborhood thugs threaten Justine, Alice seizes that moment to demonstrate her courage.

In this collection, many narrators' voices are so striking that the reader recalls the strengths of the Native American oral tradition. I once heard Stanley Elkin remark that a writer should use first person only if the voice is strong enough to reach out and seize the reader by the throat. These voices are that strong but shrewd as well—knowing a great deal about their worlds and sharing that knowledge with such intimacy that the reader participates in the work. Rayna Green presents such a storyteller in "High Cotton," one whose tale is so wonderfully strange that the reader suspects it arises from an actual family story passed between relatives. The circumstances surrounding the drunken uncle's "salvation and dedication to Jesus" and the long-suffering aunt's revenge create a humorous tour de force.

Lipsha Morrissey, the marvelous narrator of Louise Erdrich's "The Bingo Van," makes enough shrewd observations to fill a novel. One concerns charging money for his healing powers: "You know how it is about charging. People suddenly think you are worth something. Used to be, I'd go anyplace I was called, take any price or take nothing. Once I let it get around that I charged a twenty for my basic work, the phone at the bar rang off the hook." Later, Lipsha uses some of his visionary power to win at bingo.

Michael Dorris's Rayona, the unforgettable narrator of "Queen of Hearts" is funny, savvy, and wise beyond her fifteen years. After she discerns that her distraught mother is planning an automobile accident in the small park where her father proposed, Rayona notes: "This is the destination she threatens whenever she's depressed, but she never actually goes." Every observation Rayona makes is exactly right, and readers will be pleased that her voice continues in A *Yellow Raft in Blue Water*.

Hard times and illness are inescapable in these stories, too. Clem, the central character in Mary TallMountain's "Snatched Away," sees a tied gunnysack bundle come floating down the Yukon River. "Baby. Throwed away," explains Andy, his native friend. "When baby comes out, maybe he got bum leg, maybe no leg, or he come out wrong, head mashed. Women say he's no good, tie him up, dump him over riverbank." Andy also talks about the smallpox that afflicts his people, and the tuberculosis. After Andy's death, Clem faces losing his own children to adoption when the doctor discovers his wife has TB.

Alcoholism and other diseases take their toll, but the stories contain magnificent healings as well. Set, the Kiowa artist in N. Scott Momaday's "She Is Beautiful in Her Whole Being" has a spiritual sickness. "Yes I am sick," he says. "I have been sick for a long time, but I hope to be well and strong. I can be well and strong with Grey's help—she knows how to help me." And Grey, the Navajo woman who becomes his wife, performs a traditional healing that strengthens Set and prepares him for his destiny.

Bigmouth, a rabid wolf, attacks the boy One Spot in an unforgettable episode from Jim Welch's award-winning novel *Fools Crow*. The boy's death seems certain, but he is saved by the tremendous healing powers of Fools Crow, who chants:

> *I take heart from the sacred blackhorn.*
> *Where I walk, the grasses touch my feet.*
> *I stop with my medicine.*
> *The ground where my medicine rests is sacred.*

Overall, the marvelous healings contained in these stories should remind the readers of the powers and magic inherent in the process of storytelling itself.

And the storytelling goes on. Fourteen of the stories in this anthology are new; many previously published stories have had very limited circulation. As the biographical notes indicate, the prizes and awards received by these contributors are most impressive: American Book Awards from the Before Columbus Foundation; Best American Short Story selections; National Book Critics' Circle Awards; PEN Awards; Pulitzer prize. But most important are the stories themselves. While I've selected a few to highlight in the introduction, I know the reader will recognize the importance of each selection and seek out the storytellers' other works—past, present, and future.

> I think the storyteller in Indian tradition understands that he is dealing in something that is timeless. He has a sense of its projection into the past. And it's an unlimited kind of projection. I am speaking, I am telling a story, I am doing something that my father's father's father's father's father's father's father did. That kind of understanding of the past and of the continuity in the human voice is a real element in the oral tradition. And it goes forward in the same way. I am here and what I am doing is back here and it will be here. *

* N. Scott Momaday, *SunTracks* (University of Arizona Press, 1976).

PAULA GUNN ALLEN

❖❖❖

Deer Woman

TWO YOUNG MEN were out snagging one afternoon. They rode around in their pickup, their Ind'in cadillac, cruising up this road and down that one through steamy green countryside, stopping by friends' places here and there to lift a few beers. The day was sultry and searing as summer days in Oklahoma get, hot as a sweat lodge.

Long after dark they stopped at a tavern twenty or thirty miles outside of Anadarko, and joined some skins gathered around several tables. After the muggy heat outside, the slowly turning fan inside felt cool. When they'd been there awhile, one of the men at their table asked them if they were headed to the stomp dance. "Sure," they said, though truth to tell, they hadn't known there was a stomp dance that night in the area. The three headed out to the pickup.

They drove for some distance along narrow country roads, turning occasionally at unmarked crossings, bumping across cattle guards, until at length they saw the light of the bonfire, several unshaded lights hanging from small huts that ringed the danceground, and headlights from a couple of parking cars.

They pulled into a spot in the midst of a new Winnebago, a Dodge van, two Toyotas, and a small herd of more battered models, and made their way to the danceground. The dance was going strong, and the sound of turtle shell and aluminum can rattles and singing, mixed with occasional laughter and bits of talk, reached their ears. "All right!" Ray, the taller and heavier of the two exclaimed, slapping his buddy's raised hand in glee. "Gnarly!" his pal Jackie responded, and they grinned at each other in the unsteady light. Slapping the man who'd ridden along with them on the back, the taller one said, "Man, let's go find us some snags!"

They hung out all night, occasionally starting a conversation with one good-looking woman or another, but though the new brother who had accompanied them soon disappeared with a long-legged beauty named Lurine, the two anxious friends didn't score. They were not the sort to feel disheartened, though. They kept up their spirits, dancing well and singing even better. They didn't really care so much about snagging as it gave them something to focus on while they filled the day and night with interesting activity. They were among their own, and they were satisfied with their lives and themselves.

Toward morning, though, Ray spotted two strikingly beautiful young women stepping onto the danceground. Their long hair flowed like black rivers down their backs. They were dressed out in traditional clothes, and something about them—something elusive—made Ray shiver with a feeling almost like recognition, and at the same time, like dread. "Who are they?" he asked his friend, but Jackie shrugged silently. Ray could see his eyes shining for a moment as the fire near them flared suddenly.

At the same moment, they both saw the young women looking at them out of the corners of their eyes as they danced modestly and almost gravely past. Jackie nudged Ray and let out a long slow sigh. "All right," he said in a low, almost reverent voice. "All right!"

When the dance was ended, the young women made their way to where the two youths were standing, "Hey, dude," one of them said. "My friend and I need a ride to Anadarko, and they told us you were coming from there." As she said that she gestured with her chin over her left shoulder toward a vaguely visible group standing across the danceground.

"What's your friend's name?" Ray countered.

"Linda," the other woman said. "Hers is Junella."

"My friend's name's Jackie," Ray said, grinning. "When do you want to take off?"

"Whenever," Junella answered. She held his eyes with hers. "Where are you parked?"

They made their way to the pickup and got in. It was a tight fit, but nobody seemed to mind. Ray drove, backing the pickup carefully to thread among the haphazardly parked vehicles that had surrounded theirs while they were at the dance. As he did, he glanced down for a second, and thought he saw the feet of both women as deer hooves. Man, he thought. I gotta lay off the weed. He didn't remember he'd quit smoking it months before, and hadn't had a beer since they'd left the tavern hours before. The women tucked their feet under their bags, and in the darkness he didn't see them anymore. Besides, he had more soothing things on his mind.

They drove companionably for some time, joking around, telling a bit about themselves, their tastes in music, where they'd gone to school, when they'd graduated. Linda kept fiddling with the dial, reaching across Junella to get to the knob. Her taste seemed to run to hard-core country and western or what Ray privately thought of as "space" music.

She and Linda occasionally lapsed into what seemed like a private conversation, or joke; Ray couldn't be sure which. Then, as though remembering themselves, they'd laugh and engage the men in conversation again.

After they'd traveled for an hour or so, Linda suddenly pointed to a road that intersected the one they were on. "Take a left," she said, and Ray complied. He didn't even think about it, or protest that they were on the road to Anadarko already. A few hundred yards further, she said "Take a right." Again he complied, putting the brake on suddenly as he went into the turn, spilling Junella hard against him. He finished shifting quickly and put his arm around her. She leaned into him, saying nothing, and put her hand on his thigh.

The road they had turned onto soon became gravel, and by the time they'd gone less than a quarter of a mile, turned into hard-packed dirt. Ray could smell water, nearby. He saw some trees standing low on the horizon and realized it was coming light.

"Let's go to the water," Linda said, "Junella and I are kind of traditional, and we try to wash in fresh running water every morning."

"Yeah," Junella murmured. "We were raised by our mother's grandmother, and the old lady was real strict about some things. She always made sure we prayed to Long Man every day. Hope it's okay."

Jackie and Ray climbed out of the truck, the women following. They made their way through the thickest of scrub oak and bushes and clambered down the short bank to the stream, the men leading the way. They stopped at the edge of the water, but the young women stepped right in, though still dressed in their dance clothes. They bent and splashed water on their faces, speaking the old tongue softly as they did so. The men removed their tennis shoes and followed suit, removing their caps and tucking them in the hip pockets of their jeans.

After a suitable silence, Junella pointed to the opposite bank with her uplifted chin. "See that path," she asked the men. "I think it goes to our old house. Let's go up there and see."

"Yes," Linda said, "I thought it felt familiar around here. I bet it is our old place." When the women didn't move to cross the shallow river and go up the path, the men took the lead again. Ray briefly wondered at his untypical pliability, but banished the thought almost as it arose. He raised his head just as he reached the far bank and saw that the small trees and brush were backed by a stone bluff that rose steeply above them. As he tilted his head back to spot the top of the bluff, he had a flashing picture of the small round feet he'd thought he'd seen set against the floorboard of the truck. But as the image came into his mind, the sun rose brilliantly just over the bluff, and the thought faded as quickly as it had come, leaving him with a slightly dazed feeling and a tingling that climbed rapidly up his spine. He put on his cap.

Jackie led the way through the thicket, walking as rapidly as the low branches would allow, bending almost double in places. Ray followed him, and the women came after. Shortly, they emerged from the trees onto a rocky area that ran along the foot of the bluff like a narrow path. When he reached it, Jackie stopped and waited while the others caught up. "Do you still think this is the old homestead?" he quipped. The women laughed sharply, then fell into animated conversation in the old language. Neither Ray nor Jackie could talk it, so they stood waiting, admiring the beauty of the morning, feeling the cool dawn air on their cheeks and the water still making their jeans cling to their ankles. At least their feet were dry, and so were the tennies they'd replaced after leaving the river.

After a few animated exchanges, the women started up the path, the men following. "She says it's this way," Linda said over her shoulder. "It can't be far." They trudged along for what seemed a long time, following the line of the bluff that seemed to grow even higher. After a time Junella turned into a narrow break in the rock and began to trudge up its gradual slope, which soon became a steep rise.

"I bet we're not going to Grandma's house," Jackie said in quiet tones to his friend.

"I didn't know this bluff was even here," Ray replied.

"It's not much farther," Junella said cheerfully. "What's the matter? You dudes out of shape or something?"

"Well, I used to say I'd walk a mile for a camel," Jackie said wryly, "but I didn't say anything about snags!" He and Ray laughed, perhaps more heartily than the joke warranted.

"This is only time I've heard of Little Red Riding Hood leading the wolves to grandma's," Ray muttered.

"Yah," Linda responded brightly. "And wait'll you see what I'm carrying in my basket of goodies." Both women laughed, the men abashedly joining in belatedly.

"Here's the little creek I was looking for," Junella said suddenly. "Let's walk in it for a while." Ray looked at Jackie quizzically.

"I don't want to walk in that," Jackie said quickly. "I just got dry from the last dip." The women were already in the water walking upstream.

"Not to worry," Junella said. "It's not wet; it's the path to the old house."

"Yeah, right," Ray mumbled, stepping into the water with a sigh. Jackie followed him, falling silent. But as they stepped into what they thought was a fast-running stream of water their feet touched down on soft grass. "Hey!" Ray exclaimed. "What's happening?" He stopped abruptly and Jackie ploughed into him.

"Watch it, man," the smaller man said. He brushed past Ray and made after the women who were disappearing around a sharp turn.

Ray stood rooted a moment, then hurried after him. "Wait up," he called. His voice echoed loudly against the cliff.

As Ray turned the corner he saw Linda reaching upward along the cliff where a tall rock slab leaned against it. She grasped the edge of the slab and pulled. To the men's astonishment it swung open, for all the world like an ordinary door. The women stepped through.

Ray and Jackie regarded each other for long moments. Finally, Ray shrugged and Jackie gestured with his outspread arm at the opening in the cliff. They followed the women inside.

Within, they were greeted with an astonishing scene. Scores of people, perhaps upward of two hundred, stood or walked about a green land. Houses stood scattered in the near distance, and smoke arose from a few chimneys. There were tables spread under some large trees, sycamore or elm, Ray thought, and upon them, food in large quantities and tantalizing variety beckoned to the men. Suddenly aware they hadn't eaten since early the day before, they started forward. But before they'd taken more than a few steps Linda and Junella took their arms and led them away from the feast toward the doorway of one of the houses. There sat a man who seemed ancient to the young men. His age wasn't so much in his hair, though it hung in waist-long white strands.

It wasn't even so much in his skin, wrinkled and weathered though it was beneath the tall crowned hat he wore. It was just that he seemed to be age personified. He seemed to be older than the bluff, than the river, than even the sky.

Next to him lay two large mastiffs, their long lean bodies relaxed, their heads raised, their eyes alert and full of intelligence. "So," the old one said to the women, "I see you've snagged two strong young men." He shot a half-amused glance at the young men's direction. "Go, get ready," he directed the women, and at his words they slipped into the house, closing the door softly behind themselves.

The young men stood uneasily beside the old man who, disregarding them completely, seemed lost in his own thoughts as he gazed steadily at some point directly before him.

After maybe half an hour had passed, the old man addressed the young men again. "It's a good thing you did," he mused, "following my nieces here. I wonder that you didn't give up or get lost along the way." He chuckled quietly as at a private joke. "Maybe you two are intelligent men," He turned his head suddenly and gave them an appraising look. Each of the young men shifted under that knowing gaze uncomfortably. From somewhere, the ground, the sky, they didn't feel sure, they heard thunder rumbling. "I have told everybody that they did well for themselves by bringing you here."

Seeing the surprised look on their faces, he smiled. "Yes, you didn't hear me, I know. I guess we talk different here than you're used to where you come from. Maybe you'll be here long enough to get used to it," he added. "That is, if you like my nieces well enough. We'll feed you soon," he said. "But first there are some games I want you to join in." He pointed with pursed lips in the direction of a low hill that rose just beyond the farthest dwelling. Again the thunder rumbled, louder than before.

A moment later the women appeared. Their long, flowing hair was gone, and their heads shone in the soft light that filled the area, allowing distant features to recede into its haze. The women wore soft clothing that completely covered their bodies, even their hands and feet. It seemed to be of a bright, gleaming cloth that reflected the light at the same intensity as their bald heads. Their dark eyes seemed huge and luminous against skin that somehow gave off a soft radiance. Seeing them, both men were nearly overcome with fear. They have no hair at all, Ray thought. Where is this place? He glanced over at Jackie, whose face mirrored his own unease. Jackie shook his head almost imperceptibly, slowly moving it from side to side in a gesture that seemed mournful, and at the same time, oddly resigned.

Linda and Junella moved to the young men, each taking the hand of one and drawing him toward the central area nearby. In a daze Ray and Jackie allowed themselves to be led into the center of the area ringed by heavily laden tables, barely aware that the old man had risen from his place and with his dogs was following behind them. They were joined by a number of other young men, all wearing caps like the ones Ray and Jackie wore. Two of the men carried bats, several wore gloves, and one was tossing a baseball in the air as he walked. Slowly the throng made their way past the tables and came to an open area where Jackie and Ray saw familiar shapes. They were bases, and the field that the soft light revealed to them was a baseball diamond.

The old man took his place behind first base, and one of the young men crouched before him as a loud peal of thunder crashed around them. "Play ball!" the old man shouted, and the men took up their places as the women retired to some benches at the edge of the field behind home plate where they sat.

The bewildered young men found their positions and the game was on. It was a hard-played game, lasting some time. At length, it reached a rowdy end, the team Jackie and Ray were on barely edging out the opposition in spite of a couple of questionable calls the old man made against them. Their victory was due in no small measure to a wiry young man's superb pitching. He'd pitched two no-hit innings and that had won them the game.

As they walked with the other players back toward the houses the old man came up to them. Slapping each on the back a couple of times, he told them he thought they were good players. "Maybe that means you'll be ready for tomorrow's games," he said, watching Jackie sharply. "They're not what you're used to, I imagine, but you'll do all right."

They reached the tables and were helped to several large portions of food by people whose faces never seemed to come quite into focus but whose goodwill seemed unquestionable. They ate amid much laughter and good-natured joshing, only belatedly realizing that neither Linda nor Junella was among the revelers. Ray made his way to Jackie, and asked him if he'd seen either woman. Replying in the negative, Jackie offered to go look around for them.

They agreed to make a quick search and rendezvous at the large tree near the old man's house. But after a fruitless hour or so Ray went to the front of the house and waited for his friend, who didn't come. At last, growing bored, he made his way back to the tables where a group had set up a drum and were singing lustily. A few of the younger people had formed a tight circle around the drummers and were slowly stepping around in it, their arms about each others' waists and shoulders. All right! Ray thought, cheered. "49's." He joined the circle between two women he hadn't seen before, who easily made way for him and smoothly closed the circle about him again as each wrapped an arm around his waist. He forgot all about his friend.

❖❖❖

When Ray awoke the sun was beating down on his head. He sat up, and realized he was lying near the river's edge, his legs in the thicket, his head and half-turned face unshielded from the sun. It was about a third of the way up in a clear sky. As he looked groggily around, he discovered Junella sitting quietly a few yards away on a large stone. "Hey," she said, smiling.

"How'd I get here?" Ray asked. He stood and stretched, surreptitiously feeling to see if everything worked. His memory seemed hesitant to return clearly, but he had half-formed impressions of a baseball game and eating and then the 49. He looked around. "Where's Jackie and, uh—"

"Linda?" Junella supplied as he paused.

"Yeah, Linda," he finished.

"Jackie is staying there," she told him calmly. She reached into her bag and brought out a man's wristwatch. "He said to give you this," she said, holding it out to him.

Ray felt suddenly dizzy. He swayed for a moment while strange images swept through him. Junella with no hair and that eerie light; the one that was some pale tan but had spots or a pattern of soft gray dots that sort of fuzzed out at the edges to blend into the tan. The old man.

He took a step in her direction. "Hey," he began. "What the hell's—" but broke off. The rock where she sat was empty. On the ground next to it lay Jackie's watch.

❖❖❖

When Ray told me the story, about fifteen months afterward, he had heard that Jackie had showed up at his folks' place. They lived out in the country, a mile or so beyond one of the numerous small towns that dot the Oklahoma landscape. The woman who told him about Jackie's return, Jackie's cousin Ruth Ann, said he had come home with a strange woman who was a real fox. At thirteen, Ruth Ann had developed an eye for good looks and thought herself quite a judge of women's appearance. They hadn't stayed long, he'd heard. Mainly they packed up some of Jackie's things and visited with his family. Ray had been in Tulsa and hadn't heard Jackie was back until later. None of their friends had seen him either. There had been a child with them, he said, maybe two years old, Ruth Ann had thought, because she could walk by herself.

"You know," Ray had said thoughtfully, turning a Calistoga slowly between his big hands, a gesture that made him seem very young and somehow vulnerable, "one of my grandma's brothers, old Jess, used to talk about the little people a lot. He used to tell stories about strange things happening around the countryside here. I never paid much attention. You know how it is. I just thought he was putting me on, or maybe he was pining away for the old days. He said that Deer Woman would come to dances sometimes, and if you weren't careful she'd put her spell on you and take you inside the mountain to meet her uncle. He said her uncle was really Thunder, one of the old gods or supernaturals, whatever the traditionals call them."

He finished his drink in a couple of swallows and pushed away from the table we were sitting at. "I dunno," he said, and gave me a look that I still haven't forgotten, a look that looked somehow wounded and yet with a kind of wild hope mixed in. "Maybe those old guys know something, eh?"

It was a few years before I saw him again. Then I ran into him unexpectedly in San Francisco a couple of years ago. We talked for a while, standing on the street near the Mission BART station. He started to leave when my curiosity got the better of my manners. I asked if he'd even found out what happened to Jackie.

Well, he said that he'd heard that Jackie came home off and on, but the woman—probably Linda, though he wasn't sure— was never with him. Then he'd heard that someone had run into Jackie, or a guy they thought was him, up in Seattle. He'd gone alcoholic. Later, they'd heard he'd died. "But you know," Ray said, "the weird thing is that he'd evidently been telling someone all about that time inside the mountain, and that he'd married her, and about some other stuff, stuff I guess he wasn't supposed to tell." Another guy down on his luck, he guessed. "Remember how I was telling you about my crazy uncle, the one who used to tell about Deer Woman? Until I heard about Jackie, I'd forgotten that the old man used to say that the ones who stayed there were never supposed to talk about it. If they did, they died in short order."

After that, there didn't seem to be much more to say. Last time I saw Ray, he was heading down the steps to catch BART. He was on his way to a meeting and he was running late.

GLORIA BIRD

❖❖❖

Turtle Lake

HE CHILL should have disappeared with the winter's early thaw beneath the warm *takakutsya*, the Chinook that blew like a hand over the arched backs of hills. The summer came in blazing yellow and dust over the reservation land of sage, yarrow, and cheat grass in its usual near drought. Tapete drove the back roads, willing the heated landscape to enter him, his truck skimming the washboard roads on turns, leaving a dust trail as thick as smoke behind him. He traveled the way back home, gripping the steering wheel with icy hands—his eyes shining like obsidian.

He entered north Reservation Road, passing the old logging road that forked at Cottonwood Ridge, the hunting grounds that were respected as communal territory. As with other families who owned property there, they built no home in those woods, left trees untouched, and land unfenced. He passed the turn to his sister's place knowing that Sissy and her husband, Sklemucks, had temporarily moved home. When Sissy had married the boy Sklemucks, the one who never grew up, people said it was because she probably couldn't have children of her own. Tapete's suspicions were confirmed by her on his last visit—that it was the boy's *simiakia*, that which belongs to a man, and the fact that he would always do whatever she told him to. Sklemucks, the boy who hunkered and lolled on his feet like a bear, whose hair grew shaggy and hung in his face, who laughed easily and whose heart was good, Tapete knew, could be counted on to not stray from home.

❖❖❖

Last winter, when he had come home for the holidays, he and Sklemucks had gone to Turtle Lake to do some ice fishing. Sissy wanted to use the truck, and dropped them off on her way into town. They arrived late morning. The air was chilled, and their breath became clouds as it left their mouths. They piled two bald tires on the thick ice to burn for warmth, dug holes through the ice with a hand ax, and lowered their lines in. Sklemucks liked to talk. He rolled the words around in his mouth like chew, Tapete thought. His voice was loud, and his laugh even louder. They had each caught five or six of the stocked browns when the fish quit biting. Maybe the soft and orange-fleshed fish heard Sklemucks and were scared away, he thought.

"Tapete, what kinda grub we got? I'm getting hungry," Sklemucks said. He didn't wait for an answer. As he stood, the shift of his weight caused the ice to creak and moan beneath him. "Haw-a-a-a-aw!" he laughed, motioning with his lips in the direction of the ice moan. "Better watch out, Big Foot is coming," he said.

"Big Foot, my ass. It's Sklemucks—not Sasquatch," Tapete said. "Two big ugly Indians!"

"Haw-a-a-a-aw" echoed from Cayuse, and spread itself thin over the lake in the cold air like fog.

"Oh yeah?" Sklemucks said. He picked up the branch he had used to stir the ice in his fishing hole, and began walking toward Tapete, holding the stick straight out in front of him. He made motions like he was jacking off and laughed. He reached the sack lunch Sissy had packed for them, and fumbled through its contents rattling the paper.

Tapete was hungry too, but didn't want to eat too soon. "Where'd Sissy go in town?" he asked. He tried to guess how long they had been fishing, and how much longer it would be before she returned for them.

"K mart," Sklemucks said. He was stuffing a sandwich into his mouth. He continued talking and chewing at the same time. "You know women," he said.

"Man, I hope she buys you some odor eaters!" Tapete said. He waved a gloved hand in front of his nose for emphasis. Sklemucks had received the bear grease as a gift, and had rubbed his work boots with it to make them waterproof. The stuff was rancid. Tapete knew that his sister made Sklemucks keep his boots on their back porch because of the odor, and that their dogs kept trying to steal the boots.

"You know what they say the skunk smells?" Sklemucks asked. He answered his own question, leaning closer to Tapete. "His own hole," he whispered. He pointed at Tapete, laughing his raucous laugh.

"Ah, shit," Tapete said. He set his pole down on the ice. "Pass me the bag," he told Sklemucks. He knew he had better get his share before Sklemucks finished it all off by himself. Tapete reached for the bag and pulled out a sandwich. He took a big bite, chewing slowly. The shoreline had changed since he was a child. There once were cattails for three feet around the edge of the lake. The old dock was made of several slender poles tied with rope; it was gone now. The boat ramp area was the only cleared spot just below the road, and the road wasn't paved. Now, the dirt road went farther into the trees and opened to an improved picnic area: two picnic tables, a garbage can, and a barn-red outhouse.

"Remember all the turtles?" he asked. Tapete envisioned the giant snappers walking the dirt road lifting their legs high. At one time there had been turtles all over the roads, and they had all come out of Turtle Lake. There were smaller painted turtles, too. The kind with bright orange patterns on their stomachs, each one different from the other.

"Yeah," Sklemucks said. "Whatever happened to them?"

"Logging trucks."

Sklemucks scratched his head.

"The *suyapi* came in and rushed the tribe into full-scale logging back in the fifties," Tapete said.

"I remember my dad talking about it," Sklemucks said. "Said some of the mountains are naked up on top now. He says it's a bad thing what happened."

"In those first years of logging the most precious timber was lost—the tallest, oldest trees," Tapete said. He moved back to his blanket and sat down. He absently pulled at the wire of his fishing pole feeling for signs of tension at the other end. "For a while, things were pretty good around here. Everyone had work. I remember Dad drove one of those trucks, and Sissy and I had new clothes and shoes. Dad bought that pickup new, the one that's sitting in their yard now."

"It's that old?" Sklemucks said.

"He won't part with it for nothing. It was his first and only brand-new rig. He just keeps telling me to fix it up, that it's a valuable antique now."

"Haw-a-a-a-aw!"

"The logging company was in town, of course, and the Indians worked for them. The tribe got a small percentage of the profits, but nothing like they should have: a hundred dollar per capitas at Christmas for a while, that was all. Those *suyapi* already knew how long it would take to get out all the old growth. By the time the tribe took over, the price for timber dropped."

"We got the post plant," Sklemucks offered.

"That loses money. No one wants to buy fence posts or sawdust," Tapete said. He was surveying the white landscape that surrounded the perfect circle of Turtle Lake. The hills were forested grassland. He picked out ponderosa pine, Douglas fir, lodgepole pine, a few scattered western larch, and the dark green tamarack hung with the moss that reminded him of the fringed loose-fitting shawls the women danced in.

"Ever go up on Cayuse?" Sklemucks said.

"No. You?" Tapete said.

"You remember Enos, that old geezer who used to live on Blue Creek Road?"

"The old guy with the horses, right?" Tapete said.

"Yeah, that's the one. We went with him once to round up some strays. He was missing a special horse, his favorite. It wasn't broke in yet and was still pretty wild. We went out all one day looking for it. We camped out that night in the foothills. I remember we were all rolled up in our sleeping bags and our fire was nearly burned out. We started hearing noises coming from above us, and I almost shit my pants! Haw-a-a-a-aw!" Sklemucks shook the hair from his face rearing his head like a horse does.

Tapete looked over at Sklemucks. Tapete wondered if Sklemucks was telling him the truth. His raised and half-moon-shaped eyebrows made him appear permanently curious. Tapete smiled. "What kind of noise?" he said.

"It almost sounded like coyotes, but there's no coyotes around there. I scooted closer to my dad and started to say something, but he shushed me. I could tell he was listening too because his head popped up and was tilted to one side. Whatever it was circled around the camp all night, and I don't think I slept."

"Stick Indians," Tapete said, joking.

"That's what Enos told me and Dad the next day, too. We never found the horse. 'Stick Indians probably got it,' Enos said." Sklemucks was digging little circles into the snow with his stick.

"Did you smell anything?" Tapete said.

"What do you mean?"

"Stick Indians are supposed to smell real bad. Didn't your dad tell you that?"

"Enos said he felt like someone was watching us, and we kept hearing things behind us all the way back. Didn't see anything—too many trees."

"I remember my grandpa and my *tupi'ya*'s brother used to tell stories about Stick Indians. They talked about smelling them —that's how you knew they were around. One time Grandpa said that they went out the next day and found all the junk cars in the yard overturned. The Stick Indians did it—they're strong too. When I was a kid those stories sure used to scare me." Tapete could feel his skin prickle and goose bumps spreading across his back under the thermal shirt and down vest he wore.

He felt exposed sitting out in the middle of the lake. He stood up.

"Gets spooky out here, enit?" Sklemucks said as if reading his thoughts.

"It's getting cold" was all Tapete said.

"Do you think the old folks made up those stories just to scare us kids with?"

"I know the old people talked about them and I think they believed in them, but I never heard anyone ever say they actually saw one. Maybe there used to be Stick Indians—but not anymore." Even as Tapete said this to Sklemucks he was not altogether certain of anything.

"What about the picture that guy took over on the coast," Sklemucks said, "and the footprints?"

"Sasquatch?" Tapete said. "That's not the same thing, but don't tell the anthropologists that."

"The what?" Sklemucks was squinting up at Tapete.

"*Suyapi.*"

"You know what I think?" Sklemucks said.

"What?"

"I think Stick Indians are spirits."

Tapete wanted to change a subject that was becoming uncomfortable. Maybe Sklemucks was right. He could believe in spirits easier than ten-foot-tall Indians who still lived back in the woods. "How about let's get our gear to shore, huh? Sissy should be coming back soon. We can get another fire going on shore."

"Spooked?" Sklemucks teased. A piece of his third sandwich fell out of his mouth and made him laugh even louder than before. "Ha-ha! haw-a-a-a-aw!"

"Yeah," Tapete said, "looking at you."

They gathered up their things and, for a change, Sklemucks stayed quiet. Tapete suspected that Sklemucks was a little spooked himself. They pulled up their fish, and just as Tapete bent to pick up the bag and his blanket, a loud crack beat itself against the cliff and back to their ears. He looked at Sklemucks and could see fear mask over his face turning him white. He knew flight would follow. They could hear the ice cracking at the other end of the lake and moving toward them fast. It sounded like lightning.

"Holy shit!" Sklemucks yelled. "Let's get outta here!" He was already running toward shore, carrying nothing.

Tapete followed, clutching everything he could carry. The blanket hung down in front of him as he ran; he stepped on it and fell. The fall, at least, propelled him skidding in the right direction. He felt ice scraping like pebbles against his cheek. His thoughts came as disjointed frames of pictures. Sklemucks at first seemed far away and small, and then he became as large as the trees surrounding the lake. Tapete tried to measure the distance between himself and where Sklemucks bent forward, his hands resting on his knees. He was trying to catch his breath, the mountain of his outline made him appear like a bear in the shadows of the trees. Tapete thought he could hear the rasping of Sklemucks's breath, and thought he could smell salami. Tapete scrambled to his feet, snatching up the bag with one hand and stuffing the fish into it with the other. He grabbed his pole and ran, leaving the blanket behind.

Tapete reached the shore at full speed, and Sklemucks caught him to break his fall. They both spun around in time to watch the upheaval of ice around the place where they had been fishing. The fishing holes seemed to turn inside out, all the ice caving in and swallowing up the still burning tires. He looked at Sklemucks, who was squinting toward the other end of the lake at the place where the crack started. Tapete followed his gaze. "Did you see something?" he asked.

Sklemucks didn't answer. They heard a loud whack of something *big* hitting the ice and breaking though to water, but they couldn't tell where it was coming from. The sound echoed off the cold air and hills and seemed to come from every direction at once. They listened to the rock and splash of ice hitting ice for a long while before it grew silent again. Neither of them spoke for a few moments.

"I didn't see anything," Tapete finally said.

"Neither did I," Sklemucks said. "What do you think it was?"

"Don't ask." Tapete's toes were cold, and his cheek stung. He kicked loose pine cones from the thin snow beneath the trees, and ripped off a piece of the bag to start a fire. He dug beneath the snow to the layers of pine needles. Beneath the first layer of wet ones he found the light brown dry needles that would burn. He placed some in the shape of a teepee over the crumpled paper, and lit it. Sklemucks rattled the inside of the bag for more food, oblivious to Tapete and the fire-making.

◆◆◆

Driving through the heat and dust, Tapete spotted the pitched roof of his folks' house from the road. In the noonday sun, the tar paper reflected the heat and shone silver. He slowed his truck to make the turn onto their driveway. The soft mounds and holes that gathered scarce rainwater, he knew, would rock his truck like a boat in an ocean of grasshoppers. He shifted into first gear arranging his thoughts and sorting the words he would use to explain his coming home. It was no use. He did not know how to explain, but even if he found himself unable to say anything, Tapete knew they would understand more than he did. They would be glad to see him and to have him home. He pulled his truck next to the woodpile and the shed that housed his father's antique truck. He thought he saw the large outline of Sklemucks standing behind the screen door. Tapete killed the engine, expecting to hear the screen door opening and slamming shut as Sklemucks came out to greet him. When he didn't hear anything, he turned toward the house. There was no one there.

He stepped out of his truck and walked ankle-deep in grasshoppers to the house.

He entered his mother's kitchen just as she was putting more wood into the stove. He took the slim kindling from her hands.

She smiled a greeting at him wiping her hands on her apron. She watched as he slid the pieces of wood into the firebox of the stove and replaced the burner to the stovetop. Sissy was sitting at the table and she squealed hello to him as he entered. Both his mother and sister came to hug him. "I knew you would come home," his mother said.

"Where's Dad and Sklemucks?"

He sat down at the table next to the stove.

"In town," his mother said. "They went in to the Trading Post and are swinging by to pick up Sklemucks's old man on the way back."

"Is anyone else here?"

"No," Sissy said. "Why?"

He leaned back into his chair and turned to his mother, who was dishing him a bowl of stew from the pot simmering on the stove. He watched two pieces of corn on the cob roll into his bowl followed by potatoes, and bits of green and orange. By its smell he knew it wasn't deermeat. She placed the bowl in front of him, and he realized how hungry he was.

"We are going to talk with the old man about 'cleaning out' Sissy and the boy's house. Get rid of whatever it is that has been bothering them."

Tapete knew what she meant. He looked across the table at Sissy, wondering what had been going on. He bit into a hot piece of potato and rolled it around his mouth to cool it off.

"I told Mom and Dad about what happened with you guys out at Turtle Lake last time you were here, and what a hard time I had getting back to pick you two up again," Sissy said.

Tapete remembered that as soon as they had climbed into the cab of the truck, Sklemucks had started to tell Sissy about his fall. "You shoulda seen ol' Tapete here trying to ice-skate on his face! Haw-a-a-aw!"

"Asshole here started talking about Stick Indians so loud that he woke them up!" Tapete had said. He caught the worried expression that crossed his Sissy's face as he told her this, but she didn't say anything.

All the way home Sklemucks had talked and laughed. At first he repeated the fall, telling different versions of it to amuse himself. "Tapete got his legs stuck in his skirt and fell down. Haw-a-a-aaw!" he laughed. "You shoulda seen his eyes bug out—like this," he said. Sklemucks had opened his own eyes wide, trying to draw the corners of his mouth down, smiling. "Haw-a-a-aw!" he screeched. "Owl eyes!"

He kept it going until Sissy finally told him, "That's enough, Sklemucks, do you hear me?"

It wasn't a question; but Tapete noticed that she was trying to keep from laughing.

Now, his mother sat down next to him with a cup of coffee and asked, "Have things been bothering you too?"

He shook his head slowly. "Not exactly," he said, filling his mouth with the warm stew. He did not know how to begin. "I feel cold all of the time, and can't seem to get warm."

"You know how Sklemucks is—" Sissy said. "He forgot all about it the next day. Springtime we noticed that the dogs started barking a lot at nights, and they started whimpering to the door—as if I would let them in! Then we started hearing things on the roof, almost like squirrels running across the roof, but it was heavier. The next day we would go out and look around, but never found anything. I could tell Sklemucks was getting pretty scared after a while—so was I. As soon as the mud dried on the roads we moved back here."

It was all this simple, Tapete realized. His mother sat sipping her coffee and he knew she was thinking about what he had just told her. People knew what they knew. His mother's eyes were on him.

"We had to wait for you," she said.

He realized that it was what he knew all along.

BETH BRANT

❖❖❖

Swimming Upstream

ANNA MAY spent the first night in a motel off High-way 8. She arrived about ten, exhausted from her long drive—the drive through farmland, bright autumn leaves, the glimpse of blue lake. She saw none of this, only the gray highway stretching out before her. When she saw the signs of a motel she stopped, feeling the need for rest. It didn't matter where.

She took a shower, lay in bed, and fell asleep, the dream beginning again. Her son—drowning in the water, his skinny arms flailing the waves, his mouth opening to scream but no sound coming forth. She, Anna May, moving in slow motion running into the waves, her hands grabbing for the boy and feeling only water run through her fingers. She grabbed and grabbed but nothing held to her hands. She dove and opened her eyes underwater and saw nothing. He was gone. She dove and grabbed, her hands connecting with sand, with seaweed, but not her son. He was gone. Simon was gone.

Anna May woke. The dream was not a nightmare anymore. It had become a companion to her. A friend, almost a lover, reaching for her as she slept; making pictures of her son, keeping him alive while recording his death. In the first days after Simon

22

left her, the dream made her wake screaming, sobbing, arms hitting at the air, legs kicking the sheets, becoming tangled in the material. Her bed was a straitjacket, pinning her down, holding her until the dream ended. She would fight the dream then. Now she welcomed it.

During the day she had other memories of Simon. His birth, his first pair of shoes, his first steps, his first word "Mama," his first book, his first day of school. Now that he was dead, she invented a future for him during the day. His first skating lessons, his first hockey game, his first reading aloud from a book, his first . . . But she couldn't invent beyond that. His six-year-old face and body wouldn't change in her mind. She couldn't invent what she couldn't imagine. The dream became the final video of her imagining.

She hadn't been there when Simon drowned. Simon had been given to her ex-husband by the courts. She was unfit—because she lived with a woman, because a woman, Catherine, slept beside her, because she had a history of alcoholism. The history was old. Anna May had stopped drinking when she became pregnant with Simon, and she had stayed dry all those years. She couldn't imagine what alcohol tasted like after Simon came. He was so lovely, so new—the desire for drink evaporated every time Simon took hold of her finger, or nursed from her breast, or opened his mouth in a toothless smile. She had marveled at his being, this gift that had come from her own body. This beautiful being who had formed inside her, had come with speed through the birth canal to welcome life outside her; his face red with anticipation, his black hair sticking straight up as if electric with hope, his little fists grabbing, his pink mouth finding her nipple and holding on for dear life. She had no need for alcohol—there was Simon.

Simon was taken away from them. But they saw him on weekends, Tony delivering him on a Friday night, Catherine discreetly finding someplace else to be when his car drove up. They still saw Simon, grateful for the two days out of the week they could play with him, they could delight in him, they could pretend with him. They still saw Simon, but the call came that changed all that. The call from Tony saying that Simon had drowned when he fell out of the boat as they were fishing. Tony sobbing, "I'm sorry. I didn't mean for this to happen. I tried to save him. I'm sorry. Please Anna, please forgive me. Oh God, Anna, I'm sorry, I'm sorry."

So Anna May dreamed of those final moments of a six-year-old life. And it stunned her that she wasn't there to see him die when she had been there to see him come into life.

Anna May stayed dry but she found herself looking into cupboards at odd times. Looking for something. Looking for something to drink. She thought of ways to buy wine and hide it, taking a drink when she needed it. But there was Catherine. Catherine would know and Catherine's face, already so lined and tired and old, would become more so. Anna May looked at her own face in the mirror. She was thirty-six and looked twenty years older. Her black hair had gray streaks she hadn't noticed before. Her forehead had deep lines carved into the flesh, and her eyes—her eyes that had cried so many tears—were a faded and washed-out blue. Her mouth was wrinkled, the lips parched and chapped. She and Catherine were aged and ghostlike figures walking through a dead house.

Anna May thought about the bottle of wine. It look on large proportions in her mind. A bottle of wine, just one, that she could drink from and never empty. A bottle of wine—that sweet, red kind that would take away the dryness, the wrinkled insides of her. She went to meetings but never spoke, only saying her name and "I'll pass tonight." Catherine wanted to talk, but Anna May had nothing to say to this woman she loved, who slept beside her, who shared the same dream. Anna May thought about the bottle of wine. The bottle, the red liquid inside, the sweet taste gathering in her mouth, moving down her throat, hitting her bloodstream, warming her inside, killing the deadness.

She arranged time off work and told Catherine she was going away for a few days—she needed to think, to be alone. Catherine watched her face, the framing of the words out of her mouth, her washed-out eyes. Catherine said, "I understand."

"Will you be all right?" Anna May asked of her.

"I'll be fine," Catherine said. "I'll see friends. We haven't seen our friends in so long, they are concerned about us. I'll be waiting when you get back. I love you so much."

Anna May got in the car and drove up 401, up 19, over to 8 and the motel, the shower, the dream.

Anna May smoked her cigarettes and drank coffee until daylight. She made her plans to buy the bottle of wine. After that, she had no plans, other than the first drink and how it would taste and feel.

She found a meeting in Goderich and sat there, ashamed and angered with herself to sit in a meeting and listen to the stories and plan her backslide. She thought of speaking, of talking about Simon, about the bottle of wine, but she was afraid they would stop her or say something that would make her stop. Anna May didn't want to be stopped. She wanted to drink and drink and drink until it was all over. "My name is Anna May and I'll just pass." Later, she hung around for coffee, feeling like an infiltrator, a spy, and a woman took hold of her arm and said, "Let's go out and talk. I know what you're planning. Don't do it. Let's talk." Anna May shrugged off the woman's hand and left. She drove to a liquor outlet, *vin et spiriteaux*, "Don't do it." She found the wine, one bottle, that was all she'd buy. "Don't do it." One bottle, that was all. She paid and left the store, the familiar curve of the bottle wrapped in brown paper. "Don't do it." Only one bottle. It wouldn't hurt and she laughed at the excuses bubbling up in her mouth like wine. Just one. She smoked a cigarette sitting in the parking lot, wondering where to go, where to stop and turn the cap that would release the red, sweet smell of the wine before the taste would overpower her and she wouldn't have to wonder anymore.

She drove north on 21 heading for the Bruce Peninsula, Lake Huron on her left, passing the little resort towns, the cottages by the lake. She stopped for a hamburger and without thinking, got her thermos filled with coffee. This made her laugh, the bottle sitting next to her, almost a living thing. She drank the coffee, driving north along 21, thinking not of Simon, not of Catherine, but thinking of her father. Charles, her mother had called him. Everyone else had called him Charley. Good old Charley. Good-time Charley. Injun Charley. Charles was a hard worker, working at almost anything, construction being his best and favorite. He worked hard, he drank hard. He attempted to be a father, a husband, but the work and the drink took his attempts away. Anna May's mother never complained, never left him. She cooked and kept house and raised the children and always called him Charles. When Anna May grew up, she taunted her mother with the fact that *her Charles* was a drunk and why didn't she care more about her kids than her drunken husband? Didn't her mother know how ashamed they were to have such a father, to hear people talk about him, to laugh at him, to laugh at them—the half-breeds of good-old-good-time-Injun-Charley?

Anna May laughed again, the sound ugly inside the car. Her father was long dead and, she supposed, forgiven in some way by her. He was a handsome man back then and her mother a skinny, pale girl, an orphan girl, something unheard of by her father. How that must have appealed to the romantic that was her father. Anna May didn't know how her mother felt about the life she'd had with Charles. Her mother never talked about those things. Her mother, who sobbed and moaned at Simon's death as she never had at her husband's. Anna May couldn't remember her father ever being mean. He just went away when he drank. Not like his daughter, who'd fight anything in her way when she was drunk. The bottle bounced beside her as she drove.

Anna May drove north and her eyes began to see the colors of the trees. They looked like they were on fire, the reds and oranges competing with the yellows and golds. She smoked her cigarettes and drank from the thermos and remembered this was her favorite season. She and Catherine would be cleaning the garden, harvesting the beets, turnips, and cabbage. They would be digging up the gladioli and letting them dry before packing the bulbs away. They would be planting more tulips because Catherine could never get enough of tulips. It was because they had met in the spring, Catherine always said. "We met in the spring and the tulips were blooming in that little park. You looked so beautiful against the tulips, Simon on your lap. I knew I loved you."

Last autumn Simon had been five and had raked leaves and dug holes for the tulip bulbs. Catherine had made cocoa and cinnamon toast and Simon had declared that he liked cinnamon toast better than pie.

Anna May tasted the salt tears on her lips. She licked the wet salt, imagining it was sweet wine on her tongue. "It's my fault," she said out loud. She thought of all the things she should have done to prevent Simon's leaving. She should have placated Tony, she should have lived alone, she should have pretended to be straight, she should have never become an alcoholic, she should have never loved, she should have never been born. Let go! she cried somewhere inside her. Let go! Isn't that what she learned? But how could she let go of Simon and the hate she had for Tony and for herself? How could she let go of that? If she let go, she'd have to forgive—the forgiveness Tony begged of her now that Simon was gone. Even Catherine, even the woman she loved, asked her to forgive Tony. "It could have happened when he was with us," Catherine cried at her. "Forgive him, then you can forgive yourself." But Catherine didn't know what it was to feel the baby inside her, to feel him pushing his way out of her, to feel his mouth on her breast, to feel the sharp pain in her womb every time his name was mentioned. Forgiveness was for people who could afford it. Anna May was poverty-struck.

The highway turned into a road, the trees crowding in on both sides of her, the flames of the trees almost blinding her. She was entering the Bruce Peninsula, a sign informed her. She pulled off the road, consulting her map. Yes, she would drive to the very tip of the peninsula and it would be there she'd open the bottle and drink her way to whatever she imagined was there. The bottle rested beside her. She touched the brown paper, feeling soothed, feeling a hunger in her stomach.

She saw another sign—SAUBLE FALLS. Anna May thought this would be a good place to stop, to drink the last of the coffee, to smoke another cigarette. She pulled over onto the gravel lot.

There was a small path leading down onto the rocks. Another sign: ABSOLUTELY NO FISHING. WATCH YOUR STEP—ROCKS ARE SLIPPERY. She could hear the water before she saw it.

She stepped out of the covering of trees and onto the rock shelf. The falls were narrow, spilling out on various layers of rock. She could see the beginnings of Lake Huron below her. She could see movement in the water going away from the lake and moving toward the rocks and the falls. Fish tails flashed, catching lights from the sun. Hundreds of fish tails moving upstream. She walked across a flat slab of rock and there, beneath her in the shallow water, salmon slowly moving their bodies, their gills expanding and closing as they rested. She looked up to another rock slab and saw a dozen fish congregating at the bottom of a water spill—waiting. Her mind barely grasped the fact that the fish were migrating, swimming upstream, when a salmon leapt and hurled itself over the rushing water above it. Anna May stepped up to another ledge and watched the salmon's companions waiting their turn to jump the flowing water and reach the next plateau. She looked down toward the mouth of the lake. There were other people, like her, standing and silently watching the struggle of the fish. No one spoke, as if to speak would be blasphemous in the presence of this. She looked again into the water, the fish crowding each resting place before resuming the leaps and the jumps. Here and there on the rocks, dead fish, a testimony to the long and desperate struggle that had taken place. They lay, eyes glazed, sides open and bleeding, food for the gulls that hovered over Anna May's head. Another salmon jumped, its flesh torn and gaping, its body spinning and hurtling until it made it over the fall. Another one, its dorsal fin torn, leapt and was washed back by the power of the water. Anna May watched the fish rest, its open mouth like another wound. The fish was large, the dark body undulating in the water. She watched it begin a movement of tail. Churning the water, it shot into the air, twisting its body, shaking and spinning. She saw the underbelly, pale yellow and bleeding from the battering against the rocks, the water. He made it. Anna May wanted to clap, to shout with elation at the sheer power of such a thing happening before her. She looked around again. The other people had left. She was alone with the fish, the only sound besides the water was her breath against the air. She walked further upstream, her sneakers getting wet from the splashing of the fish. She didn't feel the wet, she only waited and watched for the salmon to move. She had no idea of time, of how long she stood waiting for the movement, waiting for the jumps, the leaps, the flight. Anna May watched for Torn Fin, wanting to see him move against the current in his phenomenal swim of faith.

Anna May reached a small dam, the last hurdle before the calm waters and the blessed rest. She sat on a rock, her heart beating fast, the adrenaline pouring through her at each leap and twist of the fish. There he was, Torn Fin, his last jump ahead of him. She watched, then closed her eyes, almost ashamed to be a spectator at this act of faith, this primal movement to get to the place of all beginning—only knowing he had to get there. He had to push his bleeding body forward, believing in his magic to get him there. Believing, believing he would get there. No thoughts of death, no thoughts of food, no thoughts of rest, no thoughts but the great urging and wanting to get there, get *there.* Anna May opened her eyes and saw him, another jump before being pushed back. She held her hands together, her body willing Torn Fin to move, to push, to jump, to fly! Her body rocked forward and back, her heart beating madly inside her breast. She rocked, she shouted, "Make it, damn it, make it!" The fish gathered at the dam. She rocked and held her hands tight, her fingers twisting together, nails scratching her palms. She whispered, "Simon. Simon." She rocked. She rocked and watched Torn Fin's fight to reach his home. She rocked and whispered the name of her son into the water, "Simon. Simon." Like a chant, "Simon. Simon. Simon," into the water, as if the very name of her son was magic and could move the salmon to their final place. She rocked. She chanted. "Simon. Simon." Anna May rocked and put her hands in the water, wanting to lift the fish over the dam and to life. Just as the thought flickered through her brain, Torn Fin slapped his tail against the water and jumped. He battled the current. He twisted and arced into the air, his great mouth gaping and gasping, his wounds standing out in relief against his body, the fin discolored and shredded. With a push, he turned a complete circle and made it over the dam.

"Simon!" Torn Fin gave one more slap of his tail and was gone, the dark body swimming home. She thought . . . she thought she saw her son's face, his black hair streaming behind him, a look of joy transfixed on his little face before the image disappeared.

Anna May stood on the rock, hands limp at her sides, watching the water, watching the salmon, watching. She watched as the sun fell behind the lake and night came closer to her. She walked to the path and back to her car. She looked at the bottle sitting next to her, the brown paper rustling as she put the car in gear. She drove south, stopping at a telephone booth.

She could still hear the water in her ears.

JOSEPH BRUCHAC

❖❖❖

Going Home

LOOK, TOMMY, down there in the valley. Look at all those little houses. Look at how they are all like little boxes, those houses in that little town of theirs. They always like to build in the valleys, those white people." The new Ford van rolled along the thruway as Jake Marsh pointed with one long brown finger out the window, the Indian accent coming out from between lips held carefully unmoving. The half smile of Trickster was on his face, a can of ginger ale in his other hand.

Behind the wheel, Tom Hill shook his head and laughed silently. "Yes," Tom said. "Yes."

"Oooh, Tommy, maybe there is a college in that town. Yes, there is a college there. Maybe it is the college where Sonny is going to school. We are always sending money to him at school. He has been in college for a long time now."

"Twelve years," Tom said, coughing.

"He always writes to us for money. He is a good boy. He is doing well in the college. Someday we will go and see him. All of us will go and see him. If he ever tells us where the college is."

"All of us," Tom said. "All hundred and twenty of us."

"Yes, Tommy, we will go for his graduation ceremony and have a giveaway. We will give away many blankets. Then he will

31

come home. They say at the agency they have a good job for him. Janitor. That will be a good job for an Indian boy with a college degree. It will have vacation time with pay."

"Retirement benefits," Tom said, keeping his face straight.

"Tommy, you know he has a girl at the college. But he won't tell us about her. I think maybe she is white."

"She is white."

"Yes, with a little boy. About six years old now."

"She's on the East Coast, too. She's up working for *Notes.*"

"Ah-hah," Tom said. He shifted his hands on the wheel and pointed with his lips at the sign that read REST AREA. Jake shook his head and they passed the turnoff without slowing down. "There wasn't anything for us in that prison," Tom said. "It was so far out in the desert it cost wives and girl friends more than thirty dollars just to come and visit. It was called a rehabilitation center. A training center. For rehabilitation they would have us dig holes and then fill them up again. And for training they had us build walls. Long stone walls. They looked like the Great Wall of China, except they were only about three feet high, the walls we built. They had us build them at the base and up the side of the mountain that rose behind the prison. That mountain was beautiful. It was the best thing there. You could feel its breath blowing over the camp. But there was nothing for us inside Fort Grant, especially for the Indians. So we asked to be allowed to have a sweat lodge. There were sweat lodges in the other prisons, but none at Fort Grant, even though we had more than twenty Indians and we all knew we needed it. Damn."

"Right rear tire," Jake said.

Tom pulled the van over to the side of the road. The flat tire went *wha-that wha-that* on the pavement and then growled into the gravel. Both men got out and stretched. They walked up the side of the grassy bank and sat down. It was a crisp day in early September. The air was sweet to breathe as the taste of well water. Jake leaned on one elbow to look closely at a small plant.

"It says I should pick it," he said.

"Your uncle was the medicine man," Tom said. He looked at the plant. They were both smiling, but Jake pulled the small

plant up and wrapped it in his handkerchief, leaving a little tobacco on the ground where a few grains of gravel had come up
with the roots. They walked back to the van and began to change
the tire. They worked with the slow ease of men who had spent
years doing that sort of thing. When they were done, they spat,
wiped their hands on the seats of their jeans, and got back in.

Jake sat behind the wheel. He started the engine. "What did
you do next?" he said. He slipped the van into gear.

"First we did it their way. We went to the prison chaplain
and asked him to be our sponsor. There was only one chaplain
for all faiths—Methodist, Baptist, Catholic, Jewish, Mormon,
even the Black Muslims. He was a Catholic priest from Boston,
Father Malley. So thin we used to say he was scared to cross his
legs for fear he'd cut his knees. Father Malley said it was not
possible. That was when Harold Buffalo spoke up. 'Sir,' he said,
'there is going to be a sweat lodge here. When something like
that is going to happen you can't stop it.' "

"Did they interpret that as a threat?"

"They interpreted that as a threat." Tom smiled and looked
out the window. "Ten miles," he said, reading the sign. "First
they thought of transferring him out. Then they thought maybe
that was what he wanted them to do. He'd asked to be trans-
ferred from Fort Grant twice before and been refused. Finally
they decided to restrict his privileges and not let him take rec
with everyone else. Harold didn't mind, though. He started running by himself every day. First he ran a mile every day. Then he
ran two miles. By the time they decided it hadn't been a threat
and let him back into population, he was running ten miles a
day. He had been a Green Beret and knew a lot about survival in
the desert. Maybe that was why they'd been worried about him.
Everybody in Arizona remembered the Fox."

"I heard about the Fox in Nevada," Jake said. "Another
Green Beret."

"He escaped from Florence. He was in for killing four men,
two of them police. He knew they'd never give up on trying to
catch him, but he didn't even try to get to Mexico. He just
stayed out in the desert near the prison. Nights he'd sneak into

the camps of the men hunting him and steal food. He even climbed back over the wall into the prison and left his calling card for them, right where the captain would step in it the next morning. It took them a long time to catch the Fox, but they say they finally did. Trapped him in a box canyon and shot him to pieces. But none of the prisoners ever saw his body. Some say he just stayed out there or finally did make it to Mexico. So they kept a close eye on Harold because they remembered the Fox. But all he did was just run, further and faster every day, around and around inside the fence." Tom pulled out a pack of Camels and shook two cigarettes loose. Jake took one, then lit both with his lighter. The smell of the tobacco was strong. Blue smoke filled the inside of the van. Jake jerked his head to the right and Tom nodded. They pulled off onto the exit.

A state police car was parked near the toll booths. Tom opened the glove compartment and slid the automatic pistol out without looking at it, his eyes held straight ahead. He put the gun between his legs and covered it with his red handkerchief. They stopped at the toll booth.

Jake smiled at the fortyish woman with dark hair in the booth. She looked as if her feet hurt, but she smiled back.

"Hi, chief," she said.

"Indians get to use this road free, don't they?" Jake said.

"You tell that to the people at the other end when you got on?" she said. She showed her teeth in a wide smile. "That's a nice ring you got there. Make it yourself?"

"They didn't give me any ticket and I did make the ring. You like it?"

"I like turquoise. Blue is a good color." She waved them on. "Have a nice day."

They turned onto the four-lane that led into the city.

"I think," Tom said, "the state cop in that car wasn't really sleeping. I think he was watching which way we were going."

"They aren't stupid these days," Jake said. "I'm sure he saw us take eighty-one south, right?"

"Right. No one is following us, though."

Jake looked into the rearview mirror. He swung the blue van

to the left, crossed over the divider in the center of the road with a bump, swerved, and steered back into the northbound lane. He took the next exit. It led to the smaller road, which bypassed the city. "Unless they already got a chopper watching us, we're okay for a while," he said.

"What happened next," Tom said, "was that one morning Harold Buffalo was just gone. They found his pillows stuffed under his blankets. Even the bloodhounds couldn't pick up his scent. They looked everywhere for him and couldn't find him. He was gone that day and all that night. But the next morning when we looked up to the top of the peak above the prison, just at dawn, we saw the light of the fire and the smoke rising. It took them most of the morning to get up there. They found him sitting in front of the fire, just where he sat to pray and greet the dawn. 'It's a good day,' he said. Then he said, 'There is going to be a sweat lodge at Fort Grant.' " Tom leaned out the window and looked up, then back. "All clear," he said. He took two more cigarettes from his pack, lit both, and handed one to Jake.

"*Niaweh*," Jake said.

"Everybody had seen that fire of Harold's. By now reporters had come from Tucson and they'd seen the smoke, too. So the guards hardly beat Harold up at all before they brought him back down and took him to the warden. When he got to the warden's office, Harold told the Man he knew how to get out anytime he wanted to. He could get out without anyone seeing him. He could teach other people how to do it, too. In fact, there were already nineteen others who knew how to do it. That was what he told the warden. Then he told him they needed a sweat lodge. Three days later, we had our first sweat at Fort Grant."

They were on a little highway on the other side of the city now. They turned onto an even smaller, winding road, which led down through the hills. On all sides the vegetation was thick. A rabbit ran in front of them and Jake slowed the blue van down. A raccoon walked across their path. To their right a roadside dump sprawled. Car bodies and garbage were piled by the roadside.

"Indian recycling station," Tom said. He took the crushed ginger ale can from the litter bag and tossed it out. It spun through the air and bounced off the cracked enamel side of an old G.E. refrigerator.

"If I was a state cop," Jake said, "I would set up a nice little roadblock at the edge of the reservation. Maybe around the next corner where this runs back into the state road." He pulled the blue van off the road and put on the emergency brake.

Tom took the duffel bag out of the back of the van and slung it over his shoulder. "Well, they won't have to look far to find this." He patted the blue van. "So long, Big Blue," he said.

"They're going to catch us," Jake said. He had picked up a long stick from the roadside. He was whittling at it carefully with the big knife he had taken from the sheath at his side. The turquoise ring glinted with sunlight as his hand moved with small quick strokes and the keen edge shaved off curls of wood.

"Not before we get to the mountaintop," Tom said. It was impossible to see his eyes behind the dark glasses, but Jake knew they were black and hard and laughing.

"Yes," Jake said. "It is good to go home." Together they walked into the trees.

ELIZABETH COOK-LYNN

❖❖❖

A Visit from
Reverend Tileston

FIFTY MILES from the nearest town of any size, deep in the Bend of the Missouri River where the Dakotapi had made history for generations, lived the Family: Father, a first-born son whose eyes bore the immutable and unspoken agony of his generation, handsome and strong, a cattleman not so much from choice as from necessity; Mother, a fine quill artist, small boned and stout, a woman with one crooked elbow caused by a childhood accident, a good cook, accomplished at the piano, guitar and harmonica, talents she had learned at the government boarding school; Uncle, the Mother's younger brother, a truck driver sometimes, a drunk increasingly often whenever those inexplicable waves of grief washed over him; Grandmother, Grandfather and five children ranging in ages from 3 to 15 years. Uncle's son often lived with the Family as did the Grandmother's half sister and her husband and their two granddaughters. The Family was part of a small community which had reassembled itself at this place after the violent Diaspora and Displacement which was endured by this ancient tribe for several generations, the Family all the more closely knit because of this tragedy of recent history as well as the more practical problem of long distances to the few sparse surrounding towns settled a hundred years before by whites anxious to possess land and become rich. The year was 1935 and this was a place where strangers, though alien and undesirable, even called *to 'ka,* were largely unthreatening and often ignored, and where strange events were witnessed with inexplicable but characteristic tolerance.

From the gravelled road which followed the course of the river, the small three-room frame house in which the Family now lived, built by the U. S. Government for Bureau of Indian Affairs employees in early reservation days and abandoned in later times, looked strangely remote and ageless. It seemed to stare listlessly toward the river's loop, and in winter its long-windowed eyes would be the first to catch a glimpse of the landing of the Canadian geese on the cold shores of the whitened, timeless river. It turned its back on the ludicrously inexpedient pyramid-shaped, steel-roofed ice-house which had once afforded Bureau employees from the East the luxury of iced drinks in the summer as they came to this blistering Dakotah prairie to work "in the Indian Service." The ice-house was abandoned now, also, too big and deep to be of any use to the Family except for the summer drying of the pounded meat and berry patties, *wasna,* which would be laid out upon its roof in the sun. During this drying process the children would be set to fanning the flies away with long willows, a task which held attention a surprisingly brief time. Bored, they would run off in pursuit of more imaginative pastimes only to be called back as soon as Grandmother discovered their absence.

Also at the rear of the house was a large tipi, the color of smoke at the top, streaked with rain, lined with cow hides, comfortable, shaded in late afternoon by the lone pine tree which was, itself, a stranger to the hot plains country of the Dakotah, itself a survivor of the days when Bureau employees lived there. The children imagined that the tree was brought there by a medicine man and was used in his cures but it was not a cedar, just a scraggly pine tree which had barely survived hard times. There was a tall hand pump set in the middle of the yard where Grandmother would kneel to wash the paunch during butchering times and also a corral set some distance away in the tall pasture grass at the foot of a small rise in the prairie landscape. A huge mound of earth covered a man-made cave which was complete with wooden steps and a slanting door which had to be picked up and drawn aside. A very large bull-snake often found refuge from the blistering sun under one of the wooden steps, stretching himself full length in the soft, cool, black earth.

Just beyond the cave was the small, white outdoor toilet, another survivor of former times, a product of imaginative Public Health Service officials who set about dotting Indian reservations with these white man's conveniences during the early part of the century. Across the road from the house a gray stuccoed Catholic church, St. Anne's, sat with a closed, tight-lipped visage as though shielding itself from the violent summer prairie storms which came intermittently, pounding the gravel and the stucco, flattening the prairie grass. To the rear of the church lay the remains of the ancestors in a cemetery which, years later, was said to be occupied by a den of rattlesnakes.

In summer evenings, the air was often still and quiet, heavy with moisture. After a late meal, the quiet deepened. The only sound was Grandmother's soft footsteps as she went back and forth to the kitchen carrying dishes from the table. Her ankle length black dress hid her bowed legs and her head was covered, always, with a black scarf, her long white braids lying on her breast. Every now and then she stopped to wipe her smooth face with a white cloth, breathlessly.

"Grandmother, we should cook outside, tomorrow," said the Youngest Daughter, disheveled and hot, bearing a load too heavy for her to the kitchen.

The mother simply sat, one arm outstretched on the table, the crooked one fanning her face and hair with a handkerchief. For her it had been a long day as she and her sister had spent the afternoon picking wild plums and buffalo berries along the river.

As the evening came on, the children could be heard outside running and chasing one another around the house and yard, trying to touch each other on the back, stretching away, laughing, now and again falling and crashing into the bushes near the pump. The dogs barked loudly. It was a game the boys never seemed to tire of even as the sun started to glow in the west and Uncle went outside to begin his nightly summer ritual of starting a smoke-fire, a smudge, to keep the mosquitoes away for the evening.

"Hoksila kin tuktel un he?" muttered Uncle as he looked around for one of his nephews to help him gather firewood. "He's never around when you need him."

"Go get some of that wood over there by the back porch," he directed his voice toward the hapless Youngest Daughter who wrinkled up her nose, but went, dutifully, to get the wood. Uncle bent down on one knee to place the sticks and dead leaves just right to produce a heavy smoke. He carefully touched a match to the soft underbrush and as the smoke rose he watched, one thumb hooked in his belt. In a few moments smoke filled the air and members of The Family began to gather for the evening.

They might even see man-being-carried in the sky, thought Uncle, and then he could tell a story if the children felt like listening and could stay awake long enough for the stars to show themselves clearly.

When he straightened up, he was surprised to see a small, black sedan some distance down the road, making its way slowly toward them. He kept his eyes on the road to see if he could recognize in the dusk who its occupants were. He stepped up on the porch and lit a cigarette, the match illuminating the fine, delicate bones of his deeply pocked, scarred face.

Holding the match close for a moment, Uncle said, to no one in particular, "A car's coming."

Cars were rarely seen here on this country road this late in the evening.

As Uncle stood watching, he heard church music, faintly at first, and later, blaring, and he realized after a few long moments that it was coming from the loudspeaker positioned on top of the sedan.

"On-ward Christian So-o-o-l-diers," sang the recorded voices of an entire church choir into the quiet evening light as the car came slowly into the river's bend, "with the cross of J-e-e-e-sus going on before."

Uncle stood with the cigarette in his mouth, his hands in his pockets as his brother-in-law came out of the house and sat down on the porch step with a cup of coffee. They watched the car approach and listened to the music, now blaring loud enough to get the attention of the children who stopped running and stood gazing at the strange looking vehicle.

They stood, transfixed, as the car approached slowly and came to a stop. The loudspeaker fell silent as the driver of the sedan parked the car on the side of the road near the mailbox and, with great cheer, stepped from the car, waving and smiling. He was a man of about forty with a broad, freckled face. He was perspiring heavily and he made his way down the short path from the road to the house. Behind him came two women dressed in blue white flowered dresses, brown stockings and flat brown shoes; their faces, like pale round melons, were fixed with broad smiles. They all carried black leather-bound Bibles, the kind with red-tipped pages.

"Boy, it's hot!" said the fortyish, freckled man as he held out his hand in greeting. The Father did not look at him nor did he get up. He put the cup to his lips and sipped coffee quietly, ignoring the intrusion with sullen indifference. Uncle kept his hands in his pockets and with his tongue he shifted his cigarette to the other side of his mouth.

Ignoring what was clearly a personal affront by the two men on the steps, the freckled man said, "Say, that's a good trash burning operation there," turning to the children standing beside the smudge. The children looked first at the smudge and then back at the perspiring man and, silently, they shook hands with him. Grasping the unwilling hand of the Youngest Daughter standing a few feet away, the man, in a loud voice asked, "Is your mommy home, honey?" Nearly overcome with embarrassment she said, "Yeh, she's in there," and gestured toward the door.

"Well," the man said as he turned and walked up the steps slowly, avoiding the Father and the Uncle still mutely positioned there, "we've come a long way with the message of hope and love we've got right here," and he patted the black leather-bound book he carried. As he tapped on the screen door, the Mother appeared and the freckled man quickly opened the door, stepped inside and held it open for the two smiling women who accompanied him to squeeze inside and in front of him.

"I'm Sister Bernice," began the plumper of the two women, "and this is Sister Kate . . . ?" Her voice trailed off as if she had asked a question. When there was no response, she turned to the freckled man and, putting her hand on his elbow she said, "And we're here with Reverend Tileston."

Taking a deep breath, the Reverend said to the Mother in his kindliest voice, "Ma-a'aam, we'd like to pray with you," and there in the middle of the room he knelt and began paging through his Bible, motioning for the women to join him as he knelt. His two companions quickly dropped to their knees and the plump one said to the Mother, "Please pray with us, sister," and the Mother, after a brief, uncertain moment, also knelt. Espying the Grandmother and her half-sister peering at them curiously from the kitchen doorway, the Reverend quickly got up and led them to the middle of the room saying, "Come on with us, Granny, pray with us," and the two old women, too, with great effort, got to their knees. The Youngest Daughter, having followed the astonishing trio into the house, stood beside her grandmother and looked expectantly at the perspiring freckled man as he fell to reading from the leather-bound book:

"With ALL our energy we ought to lead back ALL men to our most MER-ci-ful Re-DEEE-mer," he read. His voice rose:

"He is the Divine Conso-o-o-oler of the afflicted"; Youngest Daughter hung her head copying the attitude of the visitors.

"To rulers and subjects alike He teaches lessons of true holiness,"
the Reverend sucked in air:

"unimpeachable justice and,"
he breathed again,

"generous charity."
The Reverend's voice seemed to fill the cramped little room and

Sisters Bernice and Kate, eyes tightly closed, murmured "Amen" louder and louder with each breath the minister took.

Youngest Daughter glanced first at her Mother, then her Grandmothers who were kneeling shoulder to shoulder, faces impassive, eyes cast to the floor. Then, the Reverend closed the book, raised his arms and recited from memory, PROVERBS:

"Hear O Children, a father's instruction," he shouted. "Be attentive, that you may gain understanding! Yea, excellent advice I give you; my teaching do not forsake."

One of the dogs, hunching itself close to the screen door, began to whine.

The Reverend continued to shout: "When I was my father's child, frail, yet the darling of my mother, he taught me, and said to me: 'Let your heart hold fast my words! Keep my commands, do not forget; go not astray from the words of my mouth.'"

His arms fell and his voice softened as he uttered the last phrase, opened his eyes and looked, unseeing, at the little girl, his gaze moist and glittering. The dog's whine became more persistent, his tone now pitched higher to match the Reverend's and he began to push his nose against the screen door causing it to squeak loudly.

The Reverend Tileston looked into the passive faces of the Mother and the Grandmothers and he said, "The beginning of wisdom is: get wisdom; at the cost of ALL-L-L-L you have," his arm swung dangerously close to the unfortunate dog who flattened his ears and pushed himself closer to the door.

"Get understanding," Reverend Tileston urged. "Forsake her not and she will preserve you; love her, and she will safeguard you; extol her, and she will exalt you; she will bring you honors if you embrace her; she will put on your head a graceful diadem; a glorious crown will she bestow upon you."

The words seemed to roll from his tongue and Youngest Daughter imagined shining crowns placed upon the heads of her Mother and her Grandmothers still kneeling stiffly and impassively. She was thrilled with the sound of the English words though she knew she didn't comprehend their meaning. It was like the time when Felix Middle Tent, the well known Dakotah

orator, made his speeches at the tribal council meeting she sometimes attended with her father, when he used his most eloquent
and esoteric Dakotah vocabulary, oftentimes derisively referred
to by Uncle as "jawbreakers."

As the Reverend's hefty arm again swept the room, the
whining dog lurched backward and fell against a large pail of
buffalo berries which Mother had left on the porch that late
afternoon. Terrified, the dog leapt into the second pail of plums,
scattering them wildly, then he dashed under the porch where he
set up a mournful howl. The boys who had been listening at the
side window fled into the bushes, laughing and screaming.

The Mother and Grandmothers, surprised and shocked at
this turn of events but bent upon retrieving the day's pickings,
swept past the astonished, speechless minister, shouting abuse at
the now thoroughly miserable dog, and the screen door slammed
behind them. Youngest Daughter was left looking into the disappointed faces of the Reverend and his companions. She smiled.

Forced by these circumstances to admit that the spiritual
moment was lost, the Reverend Tileston got to his feet and
ushered Sisters Bernice and Kate out of the house carefully picking a path through the berries covering the porch. He was relieved that the Father and Uncle were nowhere to be seen and he
turned at the last step and made a final effort, saying "Meditate,
Mothers, on the Scriptures, have knowledge of them for they are
the food which sustains men during times of strife."

The women, engrossed in saving the berries, didn't hear
him.

His final proselytical gesture, the attempted distribution of
printed pamphlets, was also ignored.

Their composure now completely shattered, the trio which
bore God's word into this obscure bend in the river found its
way, falteringly, to the sedan, switched on the loudspeaker, and
drove slowly away.

Youngest Daughter looked after them as they ventured
deeper into the curve along the river and the faint echo of
"With the Cross of Jee-e-sus . . ." rang in her ears. After a
moment she went to find Uncle who would tell her a story about

the star people and how the four blanket carriers once helped him find his way home from a long and difficult journey.

She hoped that the Reverend knew about the blanket carriers.

MICHAEL DORRIS

❖❖❖

Queen of Diamonds

I SIT ON THE BED at a crooked angle, one foot on the floor, my hips against the tent of Mom's legs, my elbows on the hospital table. My skirt is too short and keeps riding up my thighs. Mom has earlier spent twenty minutes pulling my long natty hair into a herring-bone braid and has tried to give me beauty magazine tips to improve my appearance—cosmetics to highlight my cheek bones or soften my chin, a blusher that might even my skin tone. I check the clock on the wall. Five minutes till the end of visiting hours. I want to leave but Mom would hit the ceiling and tell me I'm not polite.

We play solitaire on the sliding desk pulled across the foot of the electric bed. With the back moved all the way up and a pillow wedged under her knees, nothing Mom wants is out of her reach. Her round face is screwed into a mask of concentration, like a stumped contestant on *Jeopardy!* with time running out, and her eyes see nothing but the numbers on the cards. She wears her favorite rings, a narrow abalone, an inlaid turquoise-and-jet roadrunner, and a sandcast silver turtle. Dwarfed among them, the thin gold of her wedding band cuts into her finger. She's on her throne, but her mind is with the game.

In the last two hours we have each drunk three plastic glasses of warm ginger ale and Mom has sampled a second lunch, abandoned as the two other women in the room sleep through the afternoon visiting hours. We talk softly to keep our privacy.

Mom turns each trio of cards and slaps them down clean so that only the top one shows. "This time I can feel it," she tells me.

I don't disagree but I could. The last pass through I have seen a two of clubs and a jack of spades hidden below an early ten of hearts. It is only a matter of time until the cards win.

After squaring the deck Mom starts through again. This time she slaps the sets into her palm before she lays them out, and the first face up is the black two. She pegs it onto its ace without changing her expression, but does seem pleased to see the jack.

"Come to Mama," she whispers and matches it to her queen of diamonds. The ten follows suit. "What did I tell you? Nothing to it." Her eyes are large and brown, dull from her morning medicine and from not enough sleep, but they flash with her victory.

I can't help it, her cheat bothers me, but I go along. It's not worth arguing about.

"You're on a roll," I tell her when all fifty-two are distributed, ace to king, in four matching rows. "Now try the other kind, the jump-over."

"I quit when I'm ahead." She pushes the pile in a jumble toward me, finds the button that adjusts her angle, and sinks into a reclining position.

I take the cards, shift my weight, and shuffle, riffle and pat them even. Out of habit, I offer Mom an illegal cut which she ignores, then I pick up the deck and peel off a four of clubs.

"Do you remember how?" Mom asks.

The object of the game is to reduce everything to one stack. You set the whole deck down, one by one, then find a match with the card that comes before, either by suit or number: a six on a six, a spade on a spade. You can find its mate next door or by jumping back two, no more no less. I usually end with about twenty short stacks. This time it's eighteen.

"I never win this," I say, getting up to go.

"You fold too easy. Let me see those cards once . . ." But Mom doesn't move. Something's wrong. She seems suddenly smaller, like she has shrunk in her bed. Her eyebrows relax and she stares up at the ceiling. Her hands go limp at her side. It occurs to me for the first time that this visit to the hospital might be different, that she might really have a disease. I start to reach for the white cord with a button on the end, but Mom snatches it first and puts it under the sheet. She looks over my shoulder and makes like she's trying to smile but can't quite bring it off.

I turn and see my father standing in the doorway. For a big man he's quiet, and I'm always surprised when he appears. He's tall and heavy, with skin a shade browner than mine. He has let his Afro grow out and there's rainwater caught in his hair. His mailman uniform is damp too, the grey wool pants baggy around his knees. At his wrist the bracelet of three metals, copper, iron, and brass, has a dull shine. I've never seen him without it. He looks uncomfortable and edgy in the brightly lit room, and wets his lips.

"How's your Mama doing?"

These are the first words I've heard from him since my 15th birthday six months ago, when he telephoned to say he'd be late to the party.

I stand. I push six feet, taller than any other girl in my school, but I still feel short in front of him.

"Don't you say hello to your father?" Dad asks me.

"Elgin," Mom says behind me. "You didn't need to come visit again."

Again? Mom must have called to tell him she was laid up. There's no other way he could have known because her friends are not permitted to speak to him these days.

"You go on now, Ray," Mom says. "Your Daddy and I have to talk." She has been busy rearranging herself and the bed. The cards have disappeared and the table is pushed off to the side. She's now lying almost flat, with the sheet tucked under her chin. The pillow still supports her knees, though, so she has to lift her head to see us.

"Now don't rush off," Dad says to me. "Let me get a look at you."

He inspects me like a first class package, looking for loose flaps. His eyes measure and weigh, take me apart and put me back together. I wait for him to compliment my height, to say, as he likes to do, that I take after him rather than Mom, who only comes up to my ear even in her highest heels. I expect he'll judge I'm too skinny. But he just shakes his head, half-sad, half-confirmed in some belief.

"I'll see you tomorrow, Baby," Mom says like an order. She's impatient for me to go so she can have Dad to herself, and that makes me curious.

I don't know what she sees in him. She has other boyfriends who call when they promise, pay the check at restaurants, and want to live with us.

"Ray doesn't have to leave, Christine. She's no fool."

Dad's words run along my backbone and make my shoulders tighten. I'm interested in all opinions regarding me that don't have to do with my height or weight. I file away that I'm not a fool, according to my father, who hardly knows me, and stay tuned for what he thinks I'll understand.

Dad reaches into his pants pocket, takes out Mom's beaded keychain, and jiggles it from his fingers. "I'm returning your car."

Mom shakes her head no. "Keep it till I'm ready to come home. Pick me up."

"That takes more than a beat up Volare."

"Is that what you say to a sick woman? It's got new plugs!" Mom says.

"It takes more than new plugs. And anyway, you don't look so sick."

He's right. She looks disappointed, mad. Her chin juts. She props herself on her elbows, bringing her chest close to her knees. Her eyes are narrow slits buried in the fullness of her flushed cheeks.

"Look at the chart. Ask the goddamn doctor. I'm sick enough for him."

Dad tucks the keys in my shirt pocket, together with a green parking lot stub. "Hold these for your mother. A-6. Don't forget."

Mom is ready to explode. Her lips press together in a tight seal and she tries to drag the pillow out from under her legs. She opens her mouth to say something but all that comes out is air. It is as if she has just run a long race and lost. She tries to sit up the rest of the way, to get out of bed, but she's tangled in the sheet, trapped on her back.

"Get the hell out of here." Mom's voice is rough, hard-edged. Her body twists on the mattress. I can tell she hates to be helpless when Dad's so indifferent.

He watches her like she's some stranger. "It's not going to work this time. Just give it up."

"You give it up. You! I don't give nothing up."

Mom is furious, maddened by the snarled bed clothes. One of her rings hooks into a flaw in the sheet and she tries to rip it out, but the material is too tough.

"I'll call you," Dad says, and points a long finger at my chest.

"Go back to your little black girl, then," Mom shouts. "Forget us. Who needs you, anyway." She collapses into the pillows, throws her arms over her face, then stops all movement. She's listening, waiting. She expects Dad to apologize like he always does when things go this far. She's pulled her ace from the hole and bet her whole pot.

Dad watches for a second, then quietly backs out the door. His jaw is set, his wide curved lips are hard, his half-closed eyes look like they're painted on his face.

The two other sick women in the room are awake, and as interested as if they were watching TV. They are old ladies straight off the reservation, their eyes bright and full of gossip, although their bodies are fed with tubes. I can read their thoughts: *That little Indian woman, I don't know what tribe, with a big black man. And a child, a too-tall girl. She looks like him.* They are delighted. They have a story to tell if their children visit that's more interesting than rough white doctors and Indian nurses with boyfriend problems. They look from the door to me to Mom on the bed, and then back at each other. They're tense with alertness.

Mom's breathing is like rain in the night, beating on the windows and blowing the curtains. I don't want to be here when she peeks and discovers Dad is gone, so I leave too, heading for the stairs, away from the elevators where he might be waiting, wanting to explain himself on a slow ride to the first floor.

I open the exit and take the flight up instead of down. I'm not ready to go home. Without Mom the apartment is like a closet packed with our rented furniture. Without her there, I hear noises I never otherwise notice and smell food the neighbors are cooking. I listen to the broken TV, and eat standing up.

In the last year Mom has become a regular customer at IHS. Most of her ailments surface in the middle of the night. She wakes wheezing from too much party or passing out on the top of the covers and the next thing she's back in the ward for tests. The first day in, she calls for a priest, though she never goes to church. She says she's entitled to the Last Rites, that it's part of being in the hospital, that she's earned it by making the first nine Fridays when she was a kid. The doctors tell her if she doesn't slow down she's going to shoot her liver, but she won't take care of herself. "It's just the way I am," she says. She claims she is indestructible.

When she gets home, ready to celebrate the return of feeling good, she tells people she's been to Mexico, that she's a new woman. Not that she fools anybody. Most of them don't care one way or the other, except for Mom's best friend Charlene, who works at the hospital pharmacy and lives in our building. Whenever she sees Mom dressed to go out on the town, she makes some joke about medicine.

"I hear they're giving prescriptions out cheap at the Silver Bullet," she said the last time. Mom just rolled her eyes at Charlene, reminding her to act like I don't understand what they're talking about.

"Don't kid yourself, Christine. The human body can only take so much punishment."

"Punishment! I love it!" Mom sparkled her eyes and, with her fingers, formed a tight curl in the center of her forehead.

And now, here she is, back in the hospital again.

The corridors are quiet for the night. On the top floor a few people in green uniforms pass without noticing me. I could be invisible. For a place full of sick people it's too silent. You'd think the patients would let the world know their troubles, that they'd moan or sigh or yell out. But the ones I see through the open doors of their rooms just lie gazing into space, like they're already dead. I take the down elevator. Dad will be long gone by now, to wherever he goes. Or whoever. Mom said a little black girl, but that's what she accused him of a hundred times before.

"We're the wrong color for each other," I heard Mom tell him a long time ago. "That's what your friends think."

"We may be different shades but look at the blend." Dad's voice had been low, almost singing. He probably wasn't talking about me, but he might have been, since my skin is a combination of theirs. Once, in a hardware store, I found our exact shades on a paint mixtone chart. Mom was Almond Joy, Dad was Burnt Clay, and I was Maple Walnut.

The lobby is deserted, but I know my way around. I follow the yellow line that leads to the room filled with vending machines. Now that I understand what's going on, I don't blame Mom for using the car as bait. I have tried things on Dad, too, before I became no fool: tears, good grades, writing letters, getting him presents. At first every one of them seemed to do the trick. He'd smile or send me a postcard or promise to call tomorrow and then weeks would pass.

One time I even hung around on the route he was delivering. I cut school and stood on the corner at ten o'clock in the morning, listening for the bark of dogs or the sound of banging porch mailboxes. I had it all pictured in my mind. He would be walking along, his head down sorting the letters, and wouldn't notice me until he looked up to cross the street. Then he'd do a double-take, grin, and say he didn't believe it. He'd invite me to share his lunch under a shade tree, and people passing in cars would smile at us, a father and daughter who looked so much alike, having their lunch too early in the morning just because they enjoyed being together.

But Dad was a temp and that meant his track was unpredictable. When the mailman finally came that day, it was a mean-looking woman with red hair and "M" "A" "R" "Y" tattooed on her knuckles.

I buy an ice cream sandwich for dinner. It's so cold that the wrapper is frozen to the cookie part, and I have to pick ragged scraps off the end of my tongue after each bite. I get a drink at the water fountain and wipe my mouth with a paper towel. I think of stopping in to see if Charlene is still in the pharmacy, but it is after five and she is on the eight to four shift.

I take a side door into the parking lot and head across to the bus stop. There are plenty of streetlights burning and not many cars. I pass A-6 and it doesn't take much to see the Volare, missing one taillight, in the Employees Only zone, straddling two spaces. And there, big as life, is a fat candy striper from the hospital trying to jimmy the door.

The car isn't much but I can't stand and watch some teen volunteer smaller than me rip it off. She's busy poking an unbent coat hanger through the crack in the window and doesn't hear me creep up. I hold my breath. I want to take her by surprise. When she sees me, tall and dark in the night, she'll freak. The red and white striped material is stretched to the breaking point across her hips. I give a karate yell, and with all my strength, slap her on the butt with my open palm. She screams louder than me, and just then the door swings open, sending her backwards, and me with her. She's punching with her elbows and hollering like that babysitter in *Halloween*. The car lamp comes on as she turns, her face scrunched into a thin-lipped growl, the coat hanger clutched in her hand like a murder weapon.

It's Mom.

I don't know which of us is more surprised. She has herself squeezed into a red and white uniform but she still wears her slippers and the white ID bracelet with her name and blood type.

Mom recovers first, takes a deep breath, stands and brushes

off her knees. She tosses the coat hanger into the backseat. "You scared the shit out of me," she says, all irritated.

I'm still shaking. I can't get over that it's her and not some maniac.

"Go home, Ray. And, here. I won't be needing this." She hands me her green leather purse, then reaches back and takes out her driver's license.

"What are you doing?" I ask her, coming back to my senses. "Why are you dressed like this?"

"I've had it," Mom says, slamming her hand onto the roof of the car. "First he cheats on me. That's not news. Then he won't keep the car to pick me up. I can read between *those* lines. Then they stash my clothes somewhere so I can't leave the goddamn hospital of my own free will. Now *you* show."

I try to figure out what Mom is so upset about. She and Dad never live together more than a week before they start picking on each other and talking divorce. But they never go through with it. Being married never stops either one of them from doing what they want. It doesn't interfere.

"What's *different?*" I ask her. "Did I miss something?"

"What's different? Goddamn him anyway! And after fifteen-going-on-sixteen years of marriage your father thinks he's in *love*" — she pronounces the word as if it was spoiled fish in her mouth "—with some twenty-two-year-old bubble-head doper named Arletta. *Arletta!*"

I don't react enough to suit Mom, so she sticks her face right under mine and yells at me. "It's common knowledge. She's hanging off him in every bar in town. He might as well take me out and shoot me and get it over with."

In the uniform, two or three sizes too small, Mom looks bursting with strength. Even in the dim light of the parking lot, her eyes shine, and I notice she had brushed her hair and put on makeup.

"Let's go home," I say.

"I'm not going home." She settles herself behind the wheel, points toward my pocket for the keys, and I hand them over. She grips the arm rest and slams the door. "Don't let him have *anything*. Keep it for yourself."

"Hold on," I say and run around the back of the car to the other side. She reaches over to push down the lock but it doesn't work. I get in. "What are you talking about?"

"What I'm talking about," she starts loud, and then takes a deep breath, calms her voice. "What I'm talking about is this: we're broke. We owe two months' back rent on that lousy apartment. My unemployment is expired and I'm tired of finding two-bit jobs. I'm forty years old and my husband wants to ditch me and marry some Arletta. I figure I've wore out my welcome in this world and the only thing I've got that's worth anything is the insurance on this fucking car. So it's going to have an accident and you're going to win the lottery. Kiss me good-bye."

She pushes her cheek at my face but I pull back. Her hand is so tight on the wheel that her rings stand at attention, reflecting the lights in the parking lot. Some of what she says is news to me and some of it isn't. I stay put.

"Don't tell me," I say. "You're going to Tacoma, to the park where Dad asked you to marry him, where I was conceived." This is the destination she threatens whenever she's depressed, but she never actually goes.

"Don't think you're so goddamn smart."

"That's it, though, right?"

"It's one place your father will understand," she says, with a gleam in her eye.

It's a good hour away, even how Mom drives.

"Well, I'm coming, too. I've always wanted to see this park since you talk about it so much."

She turns her head and glares at me. If she could move objects by the force of her eyes, I'd be out, but she can't.

"It's a long walk back." She unclenches her hands and hoists them like claws, then bangs them back onto the steering wheel so hard that the car shakes. She scares herself and that scares me. She glances at me again, dared into actually going through with her plan, but I don't give an inch. I'm tired of convincing her to be reasonable.

She backs out of the lot, and peels onto the street. A few blocks later, she guns the engine, sending the car up the south ramp of Interstate 5. The fingers of her right hand fiddle with the radio dial until she finds a station with a country song that matches her mood, Kenny Rogers' "Coward of the County," but it is just ending and the next one they play is an old Patsy Cline song.

"To hell with that noise," she says and switches it off. We drive for a long while in silence. The highway is wet, and the white and red lights from the cars around us are as bright as rocks under water. The night air smells of wood pulp and rain, and from above comes the sound of jets flying low to land or take off at Sea-Tac. The flat buildings of the Boeing hangers are lit and most of the traffic turns off on the airport exit.

"You'll do all right, Ray," Mom says at last. Her voice is changed, dreamy, like she's telling a story. "This car is good for two thousand. I'm just sorry I lapsed that policy they took on me at the last job."

We keep driving. I think of things to say and then don't say them. I can't very well tell her that everything is great, that our life is so hot, that she is imagining her troubles. Everything she says is true. But she's leaving too much out. Most of the time Mom is off to the races, excited at every chance. She fills out a dozen Publishers Clearing House sweepstakes tickets and then watches for the mail for the news she's won. The future never discouraged her before, since she doesn't think about it from a distance.

"Go to Aunt Ida on the reservation," Mom says. "She liked you. She brought you a doll."

Mom took me to Montana to her brother Lee's funeral when I was too little to remember much. Her mother, who everybody—even Mom—calls Aunt Ida, visited us once in Seattle when I was about eight. I remember her as big and forbidding, a woman who refused to speak English and loved TV. Mom sends her a present every Christmas and makes me sign the card, but they aren't close. Mom always tells me how lucky I am, since *her* mother drives her crazy.

"Aunt Ida wouldn't know me if she fell over me." I wouldn't know her either. I try and think of her face without much luck. I have a scene in my mind of the night she went back home. Mom and I stood by the side of the Trailways, trying to see through the bus windows to where Aunt Ida sat, and I had to keep waving and waving. I looked up at Mom to complain, to say I was tired, and she was biting her lip, like she didn't want Aunt Ida to leave. But she stopped when she noticed me seeing, and we left before the bus did.

"We could both go there," I suggest, thinking maybe that's what Mom wants to hear. Then suddenly I'm terrified she'll agree. The last thing I need is to leave Seattle and be stuck on some reservation with people I don't know.

"Ha!" she says. "I'm not going back *there* alone."

I don't count. Mom means she has to have a husband or at least a boyfriend who is serious enough to put up with the long drive and all her relatives. Mom hasn't been back since she came to Seattle at nineteen, except for that one time.

"Well, if you won't go, why should I?"

She has no straight answer for that. "Look, Ray, don't ask me questions. Start figuring out things for yourself. If I had any answers I wouldn't be here right now."

Tacoma is the next six exits, the sign reads. Mom turns off the highway and takes a ramp that leads to downtown, then twists and turns her way to the park. It's late by now and the place is deserted. The trees are dark blots against the cloudy night sky and in their shade the land is pitch black. Signs appear out of the night, illuminated by our headlights, arrows pointing, falling rock.

"This is as far as you go." Mom pulls the car off onto the pine needles that line the road.

"Forget it," I say. "You're bluffing."

"The hell I am."

"I'm not getting out."

"This is a solo." Mom is rough and knocks me with her elbow as she reaches across and flips the handle on my side. Her arm is hard as a stick. The door falls open. "And after all those

State Farm payments it sure isn't going to be Elgin who collects as next of kin."

"You're just going to dump me here like this? In the middle of nowhere late at night?"

She sits there with her hands in her lap, waiting for me to leave.

"This is the kind of thing that could scar me for life." I use a phrase I've heard on *All My Children*. I'm over my limit with Mom. I can't keep up with her. Ever since I can remember I've been caught up in her ups and downs and all it leads to is this: me sitting in a dented car with a mother convinced she's about to drive herself off a cliff in a public park, just to spite my father, who she's just told she never needed anyway.

"You win," I say. "Go for it. I just hope the policy is paid."

I slam out the door and stand by the car. The night air is chilly and smells of salt water. I look around for anything I can see, but it's too dark. I kick the side with my heavy boot, deepening the dent. I kick it again. Mom glares at me from the driver's seat, her mouth open in shock.

She sits there for a minute, not moving. I think she's changed her mind, but no, she turns the key. The engine catches, then dies. She tries again, pumping the gas pedal with her foot with such force that the car rocks forward. Still nothing. "It's flooded," she announces, and we both wait, pretending to ignore each other. In the distance, on the highway beyond the park, I see the headlights of cars move by, back and forth, out of reach. I count the seconds, slow like you read a pulse, one-and-two-and-three, and when I get to twenty-eight she turns the key again. Not a sound.

"Shit!" Mom says. "Shit, shit, shit, shit, *shit!*"

She gets out of the car on her side, and stamps the ground with her bedroom slipper. She balls her hands into fists and beats them against her forehead.

"He brought me back the car without even gassing it up!" Mom shouts. My anger is nothing compared to hers. She's so mad it almost seems to me that she lights in the dark. But it is only a match flaring for her Kent. "It was full when he took it."

She stomps across the road, stands there for a while, then comes back.

I wait for her to calm down.

Finally she says, "How the hell are we supposed to get out of here?" She is on her second cigarette now and is halfway back to normal.

"I saw an all-night Gulf station near the off ramp."

"That's miles from here! All I'm wearing is a pair of paper slippers."

"I'll go," I tell her. "You stay with the car."

"In the *dark? Alone?* No way, José. There's muggers out here. Anybody could come along. A girl could get hurt."

I wonder if she means her words to be as stupid as they sound. She does. In the glow of her cigarette ash her eyes are ready to laugh. "You wouldn't want anything to happen to your mother," she says. "You could get scarred for life."

I don't know whether I'm ready to make up or not, but she gives me no choice. "Well, there's all that insurance money," I say.

"For the car, you stupid, not for me. For you to get rich, they have to trash the car."

"Somebody already did." We both look. The taillight dangles from the rear fender, spilling a red beam at a funny angle. The dent in the side door has grown from my kick, and the lying, broken gas gauge, illuminated on the dashboard, still points to "F." Hunched onto the side of the road, the Volare looks like a bum down on his luck.

Mom must be thinking the same thing. "This car could use a drink," she says, and finally laughs. It is the kind of noise you make at a bad joke, at a pun. The kind where the air bursts from your mouth like a backfiring far away or a jet breaking the sound barrier in the movies. It's a late-night laugh, a cross between surrender and letting go.

"Walk in the grass," I say. "Spare your feet."

"Just a minute." She reaches into the backseat and comes out with the coat hanger. "Just in case." She slaps it a few times into her palm.

So off we go. Me toting the banged up gas can and Mom padding along next to me, complaining about the dampness of the ground, complaining she is catching a cold, complaining about my father being too cheap to fill the tank of a borrowed car, complaining that with his long legs I walk too fast for her. The red and white uniform shines whenever we cross under a streetlight. I return her purse and she runs the brush through her thick curly hair, but she never stops, never drops back, and by the time we reach the Gulf station she is the first one in, all smiles, ready to charm the sleepy man behind the desk into giving us a lift.

DEBRA EARLING

❖❖❖

The Old Marriage

Perma, Montana 1939

LOUISE'S EARLIEST MEMORY of school was Clarence Yellow Knife. He used to follow her around, a beaver-dark boy with a stinking mouth full of rotting teeth. When they were very young he didn't bother her much. He was too shy and too stupid to actively do anything. But as they got older, it was all the things he did to show Louise he didn't like her that told Louise he liked her too much. He did things most other boys did like lift her dress up at the drinking fountain or pull her hair. But most of the boys were happy to play kickball or look for snakes in the old graveyard. They grew tired of tormenting her. They learned fast she could plow a plumb line punch to the belly or face when they least expected her to. Lester Blackroad even began asking her and Melveena Big Beaver to play Red Rover with the boys. But Clarence refused any friendliness and skulked around the old nun graveyard alone, watching them all from an uncomfortable distance. Louise grew jumpy always looking behind her to find Clarence hunkered in the stickery blue spruce or hugging the cold tether-ball pole, far enough away not to be spotted by simple glances, still close enough to hear all she said. And Clarence bothered Louise in and out of school. At powwows he liked to toss firecrackers through the knot holes in the lower half of the outhouse. He caught Louise once and startled her to standing. She looked down into the dim, stinking toilet hole, down to where she could see one eye framed by a knothole blinking back up at her. Louise ran to find Grandma at the stickgame grounds. She felt ashamed and dirty. When Louise told her Grandmother what Clarence had done the old woman reassured her it was nothing. "If you had pooped on him," she said, "he would have liked it. Nasty thing."

When Louise was eight Clarence began leaving notes in her desk that she stopped showing to others for fear of getting into trouble herself. The words were dark and funny. And when she was alone she said them to herself, sounding out each word carefully like a prayer. "Boner, trapcheeks, poontang, pecker." She told the words to Melveena and they laughed, not sure of the meaning of each word but knowing all the words together spelled out a terrible, grown-up shame. They whispered the words in each other's ears and drew pictures in the dust feeling a strange and giddy new power.

In class Melveena shielded Louise's ear with her damp hands and spoke very fast. "These words are probably more bad than the blood rags my sister has to wash each month." Louise didn't understand what Melveena was talking about, but she nodded anyway. Melveena looked at Louise with a sudden serious face. "Whatever these words mean, Clarence wishes they mean you. My sister says these are the words for making babies and if we say them too much we're going to have one." So they said the words over and over again like a chant until the words became smooth and meaningless, no longer funny or bad, but loose and easy on their tongues like the sound of their own names.

❖❖❖

When Louise was nine Clarence blew a fine powder in her face and told her she would disappear. She sneezed until her nose bled and Clarence gave her his handkerchief. She had to lie down on the school floor and tilt back her head and even then it wouldn't stop. She felt he had opened the river to her heart. The cloth he had given her was wet with her blood. She felt hot and sleepy. Sister Thomas Bernard pulled her up and told her to go to the bathroom and wash her face. Sister pinched the bridge of Louise's nose. Louise kept the handkerchief pressed to her face, embarrassed by all the attention she was getting. She could feel her blood cool in slow streams between her fingers. The back of her head danced with silver stars and she fell back like a snagged fish released again to water.

She woke two days later in warm sunlight. Grandma squeezed her hand as she blinked awake. Louise's hands were cold. "We got this back," Grandma said. She held up the handkerchief that Clarence had given her. It was crumpled stiff and black with her blood. Louise didn't understand at first and then she remembered Clarence standing by as the school nurse lifted her into the car. He shyly asked the nurse for his handkerchief back. And as they pulled out of the school yard, Clarence smiled at Louise and lifted his bloody handkerchief up so she could see all he had taken from her. She remembered how Grandma had told her to stay away from him. He was the son of Dirty Swallow, the rattlesnake woman. Louise asked her grandmother how she had gotten the handkerchief back. How did the old woman manage to snitch back her blood from Clarence Yellow Knife's tight fist, his ugly smile? Grandma didn't answer her. Louise imagined many things and settled on Sister Thomas and her hard thumping knuckles. She wouldn't let the boys play with dead rattlers or poke at the mouths of dead birds with sticks. And she wouldn't let Clarence keep a blood-soaked handkerchief.

Six days later Louise had a dream that followed her from a long night into morning. It was a familiar dream. She heard an Indian voice, neither a man's nor a woman's voice. The voice did not speak to her but to the dream she cupped in her small hands like a million water-colored glass beads.

It is cold. Snakes sleep in deep holes trapped by snow. We tell our stories now. Rattlers are quiet. It is so far back your blood smells like oil in the tongues of your grandmothers. The snow is frozen so hard it can bruise. The snow drifts are razor-edged.

Snow shines like a wet smile. We're locked here. Outside Grandma's house a naked man stands near a red fire. His face the face of a woman smooth and deep-planed. His back is lean with ribs. His hips are narrow.

Flames light high on the roof of Grandma's house. Base-blue tongues of flame burn buckskin tamarack. Black wood dust to white wood ash. The naked man blows through teeth, his cracked lips whistling to fire. His whistle calls a great wind up from snow. Firelight becomes one small candle. It flickers, then fails white, then fails, fails white to smoke. Steady wind scatters white ash to thin choking sheets of hot dust. Snow and timber powder, hot and cold. The man stands before the white stars, the endless snow. He is light left by fire. A blinding white wick neither fire nor snow. His white light is turning to morning.

Louise never asked her grandmother about the handkerchief again. She knew who had brought it back. She remembered stories of her great-grandfather: the secret training rituals of medicine people, sent to find a single pin in a night that pressed to forty below, one pin dropped deep in snow, miles from where they stood shivering and naked. Her grandfather had saved her. Somehow he had picked her blood from the dark hands of Dirty Swallow. And she knew it had been at a great price. She would never talk to Clarence Yellow Knife again.

❖❖❖

When Louise was fourteen Clarence snuck up behind her and slipped a rattler's tail in her hand with the slick skill of a small wind passing. She wasn't sure what to to with it. She stared at it for a long while, then dropped it deep into her pocket hoping it would fall out of the hole she hadn't mended. But the tail became a power she was afraid of, a feeling she had never had before.

"Why didn't you just get rid of that when he gave it to you?" her Grandma asked.

Louise didn't answer. She looked at her feet as Grandma was talking. She didn't know how to tell her Grandma that once the rattle had gotten into her pocket it began moving like the whole snake was still attached. She felt the rattle twitching on her leg, like a new muscle, and was afraid of it in a way that made her strong.

Grandma made Louise bury the rattle on the hill and mark the spot with three red-colored rocks. "That way we can avoid it," she said. Louise took her time burying the rattle. She found the nicest spot on the hill under the shade of a juniper tree. She dug a deep hole that was sweet with the smell of new roots. She carefully wrapped the rattle with a glove she had worn thin to fool it into feeling she was near. Then she covered the hole up as fast as she could with the sweep of her arms and the clawing cup of her hands. She walked away slowly from the small rock mound, pacing her steps, careful not to look back and reveal any desire to stay.

All that night dreams swallowed her. She was falling. Tall grass shot up around her and whispered with heat. Smooth flat rocks near Magpie Hill were shining with sun. She felt the warm breath of her mother and curled down into a dark sleep.

❖❖❖

Louise found a power in ignoring Clarence Yellow Knife. He no longer existed for her. She did not hear or see him. He had less presence for her than the ghost of her sister's dead cat. When he came close behind her from any direction, she sidestepped him and talked as if he weren't there. Her memory of him was a nightmare forgotten in sunlight and denied from dusk to dawn. She stopped hearing the whisper of scales beneath the thin slat steps of Grandma's house. Sleep was good and she began to feel at ease.

She managed to keep distance between them for one year. And when she saw him again she was in the safety of Mulick's store, safe among rows of peanut butter and preserves, crates of fresh eggs. She walked down the main aisle passing him. He said her name as she was heading for the counter and she turned to him and smiled for the first time in years. She had no way of knowing the power she had given him again, not until she saw him from the smoke-stained window as she was leaving. He stood just outside the store, his arms were lank at his sides. Louise watched him for a time but he did not move from his place. He did not leave his long store vigil. Louise had only one nightmare in all the months she denied him. In her dream Clarence was an old man swimming against river water. His shoulders were harnessed, pulling something she could not see. He estimated each swell, each hesitant wave. Watching. She heard the slap of water against the pockets of his body, to rock, to water, to rock. Up from a swell of water, silver as winter rain, he reached for her. He had not gotten her then and he would not get her now. Louise swallowed a deep breath of stale grocery air and stepped outside to face the hot sun and Clarence Yellow Knife.

❖❖❖

There was something about his presence that made Louise think she should not ignore him this time. "Louise," he said, and she stopped to talk to him. She felt his desire in the dense heat of her breasts, a thousand snelled hooks pulled by little sinkers weighed the tips of her nipples, the heavy lobes of her ears. A cold heaviness settled in her lungs like green water. She shifted her feet to brace herself against the son of Dirty Swallow. His presence was odd, like a pressing wind she had to lean into to gain strength.

"You don't talk to me," he said. "Do you hear me talking to you?"

Louise felt something was wrong. She felt heavy on the spot where she stood. She stamped her tongue hard against her front teeth and tried to think of Roger Mullan, his long yellow teeth. His own mother said he could eat apples through a picket fence. She strained to hold the image.

Clarence tugged at the swell in his crotch as he talked to her. She focused all of her attention on moving away from him. He struck a match to a yellow flame on the zipper of his pants, and like an old man, lit a pipe of kinnikinick leaves. His teeth were broken and stained and his breath was bitter. His voice was slow like water moving deep in the channel—pulling her. She knew he wasn't touching her, but the rasp of his swollen tongue pulled at her left breast. She turned to him and he was grinning. He knows what I am thinking. His watching was dark. Around the brown hub of his eyes the whites rimmed yellow as if they'd been boiled. She felt an urge to move closer to the bitter smell of him, a strange urge she didn't understand, like the feeling she had to look very close into the small dead mouths of animals. She knew she would cross the highway again for a closer look at a bone-broken deer, to see and smell the heavy bowels bubbling with maggots. And she knew, she would move closer to Clarence.

"Louise," he whispered. Her name was thick on his tongue. She could feel a wet heat rising from his collar. Louise leaned forward and snaked her tongue out to touch the fat lobe of his ear. He tasted sour with old body salt. He pressed his cheek to hers leaving a damp imprint. Louise pulled back. She would not kiss him. He smelled different up close, like onions and warm earth and the sweet, burning lime that covered everything unclean. He crooked his head toward her, a fat robin listening for lunch.

❖❖❖

The back of her head felt tight, as if every pore had shut down and closed. Louise tried not to look behind her. She breathed in slowly and listened. The wind was still. She imagined her head was smooth as the translucent round moon rising high above their heads.

And like the moon she sees all around them. The fields are brittle with weeds. Below her she sees Clarence Yellow Knife smaller than a hummingbird, his tiny heart beating down the thin, thin walls of his heart. One hundred yards from him, Mulick's store hides neatly stacked cans of soup, vegetables, baskets of penny candy. He can no longer touch her. The thought makes her breathless as clouds. She looks down over the sun-silver hills and begins to see something moving. She sucks her breath full of wind. She sees the root cellar of her great-grandmother, the hill mound of round rocks weathered smooth by rain, and deep inside the cellar, the fat rattler that has out-smarted her family for years is hiding behind fruit jars, and gun-nysacks of jerky, leaving them the pale ghost peel of himself that grows longer and longer each year. She sees the hiding snakes in all their places.

In the damp shade of Grandma's woodpile a slim rattler is sleeping. She sees the Urseline school and all the snakes in the field close to the playground. Lorraine Small Salmon, just five years old, turning jump rope while close to the tips of her shoes a brown rattler is humming. She sees her sisters chasing each other toward and away from the bottomland where the tender-fanged mouths of one hundred snakes wait in the weeds. She sees a fisherman she doesn't know, vulnerable as his sunburned pate, at the Jocko surrounded on all sides by brown rocks and rattlesnakes thick as lichen. She sees the dead snake the boys have hung on the cross of the French nun's grave. She sees the snakes on the road, sliced and smashed by passing cars, their eyes filled with the hard, black backs of flies, and beyond them more snakes. She sees the milk-white eyes of a thousand August rattlers. She sees Dirty Swallow walking toward Grandma's rain-blistered door. Behind her rattlesnakes trail like a wedding train.

From a great distance she heard Clarence Yellow Knife say, "Marry me." Louise stepped back from him to leave. The air was clean and hot. A sudden wind snapped her dress tight to the lean backs of her legs. She shielded her watering eyes from the grit of dust. He never stopped watching her, and for one small moment, she felt bad for him and bad for herself. She could hate him enough to pull him inside of her, to melt his bones to water. She turned from him and began to run. She dropped her small bag of groceries to run faster, to run home, more afraid of Dirty Swal-low in her grandmother's house than any field or road rattler.

Her grandmother's place was closed up for the afternoon. The windows were glazed with white sun. The door was quiet. She could see the narrow shade line below the eyes, the twitch-ing tails of swallows hiding from heat. She felt a dull-fisted warmth in her throat and she tried to swallow. She stepped care-fully through the knee-deep sage, lifting her skirt up from the small snags of cheet grass. She could see the last edge of bush grass, the scuff-smooth cow trail that led around the pond toward home. There was a rhythm of water moving slowly around the creek. She thought of rainbow trout, their dense eyes watching, the scales ringing along their backs as they bit up toward the small white wings beyond water. There was a pause in the reed grass as a deep breeze pulled a small cloud of dust toward a higher place. The red-winged blackbirds were quiet. She looked closer at the bloated cottonwood roots that stretched to the pond edge. A slow current writhed silver and then green in the sleeping shade. She threw a rock toward the pond, saw a sudden lap of water, then more waves, the smooth familiar wiggle parting grass, crackle of weeds, small hiss. She had come to know the language of August fields, the slow thin weave at the roots of grass. Snakes.

Louise remembered another time looking down on her Grandma's small house in the huckleberry summer after her mother had died. She remembered listening outside the open kitchen window to her Grandma talking about the choices of men, of bad medicine and the power of the old marriage. And as a young girl standing barefoot to summer, she saw somewhere a skin bag, dark with the oil of many hands, curling round the singed tips of her hair, a heavy black smoke rising white from his teeth, Clarence his heart drum leaving, his breath inhaling her blue, blue heart. And she thought, smiling, of how she had dreamt that night of running the weed-tight ridge of their house with a braided whip of her dead mother's hair, the small licks of dust turning to stars behind her.

ED EDMO

❖❖❖

After Celilo

'M NOT SURE what it was that caused my going. Maybe youthful exuberance. I'd like to think it was the quest for knowledge and creativity. Lightning was my guide, and the moon was my protector as I stood by the road, sticking my thumb out to the world. It was the spring of 1964, when all the glories of high school football were over and there was only the dull future facing me. As I looked to the Columbia River, I remembered the many times I had gone there. The river was a welcome friend that never had to be called in for supper.

❖❖❖

Celilo Falls attracted white tourists. Tourists in baseball caps, straw hats, pith helmets. Some were bald-headed. Tourists came to the falls to watch Indians fishing off of scaffolds. Tourists with sunglasses hanging from their sunburnt necks; their knobby knees bulging from beneath Bermuda shorts. They handed us silver quarters to pose with their children and their grandchildren. I liked to get next to a little white girl. If she was afraid, I'd move closer to her and when she would get tears welling in her eyes, I'd reach out and grab her and giggle. You know, being next to a real Indian is really a frightening experience! The river was calming. I'd watch the soothing current and see the sun reflect off the silver waves.

In 1957, the government built The Dalles Dam and flooded us Indians out of our traditional fishing places. We didn't want to be flooded out, but they called it progress. I remember that they held meetings in people's houses. Then we Indians would talk about our future and wonder what would happen to us. It was a hard time.

My father had seen the plans at The Dalles Chamber of Commerce and he tried to warn the people at Celilo. But the people only teased him and called him an ol' Chinaman because my father didn't wear braids like the other Indian men of the village. When the engineers began leveling the earth to make a new right-of-way for the Union Pacific Railroad, the Indians of the village saw that the government meant to do as they had planned. Many remembered that when Bonneville Dam was built in the 1930s, the Herman Creek Indians were forced to move but not compensated for any of their fisheries or their homes.

My father organized the Indians at Celilo Village to meet on a regular basis. We didn't want the government just to move us out and not compensate us for any of the fishing or our houses. My father wrote to Senator Neuberger of Oregon, who introduced a bill in Congress to have the government pay us for our fisheries and buy us new houses. At the time we were negotiating the amount of payment. The chief's son said, "You should pay us fifty dollars for every board in our drying sheds, because this is our way of life." The government man got angry and told us Indians that we should accept their "fair" offer, and that if we didn't, he would go to the judge at Wasco County and have our land condemned and bulldoze everything without paying us anything.

When the workmen finished surveying at the end of the day, some of us boys would pull out the stakes from the ground, fill the holes, and make a small fire out of the stakes. Others would climb the cliffs and shoot BB guns at the big dump trucks as they hauled dirt. We would laugh when a driver stopped his truck. In our own small way, we tried to stop the dam.

Finally, when we were moved out, we had to burn our house. I had to choose what to take and what to leave to get burned up. Just as Dad started the fire, I ran back into the house to get my bedside stand. It was an old commode. Later I was to get it refinished and it became an antique. We watched with mixed happiness and sadness as the old house went up in flames. We were to get a new house across the river.

We moved into an all-white community—Wishram, Washington. After a year of fighting, my brother and I were accepted into school. One time a little white girl got mad at me for some reason. She spit on me and told me to go back to where I came from. I couldn't go back because there was a freeway where my house used to stand. I couldn't understand why she said that.

I grew up in tough times. I learned how to escape into books and I knew the library. I was not hurt by the characters in the books. I could pick and choose from a world that accepted me and didn't put me down because I was an Indian or came from a poor village.

◆◆◆

It was a bright sunset as I stood on the north side of the Columbia River and a blue car stopped.

"How far you goin'?" a young man asked.

"Portland," I said hopefully.

"Get in," he said.

He handed me a cigarette. The car ride was filled with country and western music and chitchat. We crossed the Hood River Bridge and drove west. He said that he was only going as far as Cascade Locks. I was glad for the ride. He dropped me off at the freeway exit.

"Good luck," he exclaimed.

"Thanks, man!" I replied.

The sun had almost set and it was almost dark. I began to get scared. A cop might be looking for a runaway from a small town.

Headlights shone on me as a car pulled over. I saw it was a pickup. I got to the side. I peered in and a tall black man sat behind the steering wheel.

"Get in, kid," he commanded.

I hesitated, but he asked wearily, "Do you want a ride or not?"

I got in and we made small talk until we got to Portland. He drove me to the east end of the Burnside Bridge where the transients and homeless stayed and dropped me off.

"Walk across the bridge, kid, an' you'll find your people." He said it matter-of-factly.

I thanked him and began walking across that bridge.

ANITA ENDREZZE

❖❖❖

The Humming of Stars and Bees and Waves

LONG AGO, there was a spirit woman and her name was *Yomumuli*.* She made the earth:

> *the rippling grasses gone swaying into the*
> *   wind*
> *the scarlet mountains floating in clouds*
> *   of tiny blue birds.*

And the day was divided into astonished animal faces, and the night was a fountainhead of stars and the slumber of river turtles.

(Since that time, the papery husks of stars have fallen into the seas and mothers have grown older. Rosa is a woman who talks to herself. Although she doesn't remember the first creation, she does remember the birth of her only child, a son named Natchez.)

* Note: Yomumuli means "enchanted bee" in Yaqui.

74

She made the people and put them in a village. And in the middle of the village was a Talking Tree that hummed like bees.

(When Natchez was little, Rosa talked to the coyotes and ravens and flowers. But now she is old and can't see very well.

I wonder, she thinks, if my dreams can tell me how to make my eyes better. She knows that her tribe believes in dreams, but since she's *half-Yaqui*, she doesn't know if the dreams believe in her. Still, she begs for a dream that would speak healing words.)

The tree spoke a sacred language. No one could understand. Not the youngest. Not the wisest or bravest or strongest. Not even the oldest.

(Rosa wakes one morning and remembers a dream that tells her to enter a cave. Grandmother Spider Woman tells her to bring cedar, tobacco, and corn. No walkie-talkie. No flashlight. No strings or bread crumbs to mark the path. Just blind faith.

And so, when the moon is yellow and the mist low under the dark apples . . . when the fields are gold and dry with rows of stars shining on the tassels . . . when the horizon is lilac and the mountains to the west are blue-black, Rosa ties the bag with the offerings around her waist and hikes up the trail to the old caves. The caves are usually there, but legends have it that they sometimes disappear. Rosa is not sure what to expect, so she mutters to herself as she walks.

The back of her neck is hot and sticky, even though the air is cooling and rising from the valley. The trail gets steeper and narrows to one foot in front of the other. She puts one hand on her knee in order to propel herself forward on the steepest parts and prays the rest of her will follow.

"Damn stupid thing to do," she mumbles. She's a little worried about bears, even though one of her husbands had been a bear spirit. That's how she saw her men: this one, a bull, that one a St. Bernard. At least talking would scare away a bear now; she is too old for such foolishness.

Finally, she rounds the curve of the mountain. Her heart is

beating fast. The cave opens in front of her like a huge toothless mouth. She can feel the cold, musty air push out toward her. The floor of the cave is rough, littered with angular rocks.

She's a small woman with bony knees and with one shoulder slightly higher than the other, but her skin is surprisingly smooth for her age and her hair is still thick. She waits until her heart calms down, then pretty soon, it's getting dark outside. She might as well go in.

I hope I know what I'm doing, she thinks. She walks with her hands stuck out in front of her. She can hear water rushing to her left: a swift stream. "Don't let me die in here," she prays.)

When *Yomumuli* returned from her creating, she shook off the images of shimmering feathers and jungle greens and small monkey faces and loosened her fingers from speckled granite and purple-spiked sea urchins and brushed off the coral sands from her memory and listened to her children.

They were worried: they had been given something sacred and not understood it. Some argued that the holy is never understood.

(Rosa listens. The stream has a voice and it chants: *earthbowl* and *duskwomb*. The walls have a voice that says: *terra-cota hands* and *eyes of clay*.

Rosa feels the presence of tiny spider women, sitting with their spindly legs crossed. Minerals drip drip, funnels of teeth-like spikes, vaginal and wet. The spider women unlid their thousand eyes and reach out, sticky fingerlings, silken threads slivering the cracks of deeper darkness. The threads anchor on Rosa, the outworlder. The voices are those from the void: *terra marina, terra noche*. In Rosa's ears, she hears the bullroar and raw rushing out of a water drum.

My own body is full of minerals, she thinks, and thousands of her cells echo the stratification of the earth. She isn't lost.)

Yomumuli puts her cheek to the Talking Tree and listens to the humming voice.

(Rosa is a stone woman. She is a stone fish swimming through a river of turquoise. A half-blind fish, finny and leaping, to the rhythm of a shadowless current.

When she was a young woman, she liked men. She still likes men, but none of them will look at her. When she was young, she needed a cane to walk sometimes. Her sight was good; now it's cloudy in one eye, and life's so lame that she doesn't need a cane.

Often, life is beyond understanding to her. There's more than blood in her veins now. There's a longing for more life, more stories, more kisses.

She remembers her own grandmother who lived alone for forty-six years after her husband died, celebrating his birthday with flowers in front of the silver-framed photo, and yearly visits to the cemetery. Now Natchez has a baby and Rosa sleeps alone, her husband of thirty years dead for some time. She remembers his nightly whispers to her before they fell asleep. One of his favorite sayings was: "Life has no guarantees.")

Yomumuli heard what the tree was saying. She turned to look at her people and spoke, shrugging a cloud from her shoulder: I'll tell you what the tree says, but you must promise to believe me!

(Rosa trips and falls to her knee. There's blood and a sharp pain. "Shit," she moans. She feels old, old as the clay shards in the lap of earth, old as the curled fetus shapes in red clay graves, skin wrinkled over thin ribs and around, faces of grief. *Terra recepta. Corpus terra.*

"I'm not crazy," she repeats to herself. "I'm here for a reason. I know what I need, to see, but not how to do it."

Inching forward, her knee throbbing, she feels the walls narrowing. The stream widens into a pool: she can hear the stillness in the center and the rushing out near her feet.

The spider women throws a ball of moony webs up into the air and a soft light fills the cave's inner heart.

"So, now what do I do?" asks Rosa.

"Do you believe in us?" click the spider women.)

Of course! of course! And so the people listened: the tree told the animals how to live . . . that the deer should eat grass and the puma eat the deer. Then it spoke about the future when men from a far country will come and everything will change. There will be new laws and new death and a great metal snake with smoke plumes will race across the land. When the people heard this, they became afraid.

(Being half-Yaqui isn't easy, Rosa thinks. You have to believe that trees and rocks and birds talk and you have to have faith in glass-walled elevators and voices that are transmitted from space. Then there's panty hose that assumes your shape and dreams that struggle to shape your awareness.

Long ago, Rosa got real tired of shape-changing: being Indian with Indians and white with whites. As she got older, she became less afraid and howled like a coyote in heat whenever she damn well felt like it. From the ceiling of the cave, tree roots hang down in a gnarled nest. The cave seems to be breathing.

"I believe," whispers Rosa.)

Some didn't believe *Yomumuli*. So she left, with her favorite river rolled up under her arm, walking north, her feet like two dark thunderclouds.

(Rosa thinks about her white mothers, their names rolling off her tongue like pearls: Jean, Ann, Yohana, Marija, Barbara, Ana, Margareta, Elizabeth, Sussie, Giuliana, Anna, Orsola, Felicita. And her Indian mothers: Estefana, Charlotta, Empimenia, and others whose names were lost, unwritten, but remembered in a certain flash of eyes. Names of grandmothers who still sing in the blood.

Rosa feels Grandmothers' eyes all around her. She sees with

their eyes. She sees the pond, its water clear as air. The elements are transmutable.)

And some of the people went to live in the sea, their whale songs tubular and roiling, boom-echo and deep in the interior seas of their throats, longing and sounding all in a moaning song, floating up to the spume moon.

(Rosa turns to the cave walls. Clay. She pulls a chunk out and rolls it in her hands, forming a ball. Little clay baby. Cave naval, lodestar, and motherlode. She pinches it into a rough bowl. With her thumbs she shapes it, smooths it.

Quickly, she fills the bowl with pond water. A sip. It tastes like metal and semen and breast milk. It is sour and sweet and musty and white and black and red and yellow.)

And some became flying fish, ringing the waves, sparkling, and others became the singers of the sea, with their long hair and rainbow skin. They say if you're lost at sea, these creatures will help you because they remember the time when we were all one.

(Rosa unties her bag of offerings and puts the tobacco in the bowl. The cedar chips to the right, the corn to the left. Fumbling a bit, she pulls out a book of matches and carefully lights the tobacco. A thin hand-like shape of smoke rises.

She thanks her family. She thanks her guardian spirits. She thanks her own strength. She thanks the creator.

The Grandmothers sing: *ebb and return, web and wheel, smoke and water, the void has wings, we sing and reel. Spinner and spinal songs, spiraling, symphonic and symbiotic, sightless but full of visions: we Grandmothers, we dreamers.*

The singing stops and Rosa gathers the strands of webs into a little ball. She puts it into her weak eye. The tobacco has burnt itself out. She lights the cedar chips. No fire, but sweet and piercing. Then she scatters the corn on the floor.

Her insight is blooming. It is becoming a way of seeing.

Sparkling eyes, whirlwinds of nerves. A visible cortex. Quartz quadrants. Four corners of wind and gates into seeing. She crosses the earth, she crosses the sky.)

And some of the people descended into the earth and became jointed: jet-black or red. These little ant people who live in the sand will also help you if you are lost.

(She took the clay bowl and pressed it back into the cave wall.)

For they also remember the time when we were all one.

(Rosa stands and feels the darkness fall around her, but she can see. Her white moon-eye, her shedded-snake-skin-eye, her winter-worn leaf eye: gone the thickening curtain, gone into the thoughts of the spider women. In and spin. Filaments of eyes.

There are cedar trees floating in the air and the faces of those she has loved waver delicately in front of her. She is seeing with her heart.

She feels the pain burning away. Its the pain of learning to let go. *Que será, será*. Sierra Rose is the name of the daughter she never had. *Let go*. Her husband's hands hugging her in the morning. *Let go*. Her little son saying, "I'll always stay with you." *Let go*. Herself thinking: I never want another friend; they all leave or die and it hurts too much. *Let go. Let go*.

Her eye is clear. There is no division between the worlds of seeing and believing.

Rosa is ready to leave. She knows there is confusion outside and the noise of cars honking in the night. But there are also stars with no room for self-pity. Rosa ties a lace on her Reeboks and turns around.)

Those who stayed in the village grew taller and taught their children how to face the future.

(She walks quickly toward the cave entrance, which has a lesser denseness of dark. Then she sees the moon seeping out of the fat wheat heads. It's full and yellow.

In the valley, she hears the cottonwoods shaking under the force of their water-filled roots. The bees are sleeping, dreaming of heavy black clouds booming over gold-white fields and sheet-lightning flashing into a hot and crinkly air.

And the ravens are dreaming of circling in a chickory-blue sky. Twirly seeds of yellow star-bursts fall in floating circles to the earth. Rosa feels the circles growing inside her, as if she were a tree of immense dawns.

Taking a deep breath, she smiles to herself, thinking of her son and her new granddaughter. "I'm not useless," she says firmly, "and I'm not alone."

As she brushes the dirt from her clothes, she spares one last look at the cave. Its darkness, its blindness, had terrified her. It was the blindness of death, the conception of nothing.

Now she begins the way back. In the distance, the sky is luminous with the lights of the city, a city that may turn into thin air, for it also remembers the time when we were one.

And the people who live there are like enchanted trees, with bones for branches and eyes for leaves. If they listen, they can hear the humming of stars and bees and waves.

These are my ancestors, my future.

LOUISE ERDRICH

❖❖❖

The Bingo Van

WHEN I WALKED into bingo that night in early spring, I didn't have a girlfriend, a home or an apartment, a piece of land or a car, and I wasn't tattooed yet, either. Now look at me. I'm walking the reservation road in borrowed pants, toward a place that isn't mine, downhearted because I'm left by a woman. All I have of my temporary riches is this black pony running across the back of my hand—a tattoo I had Lewey's Tattoo Den put there on account of a waking dream. I'm still not paid up. I still owe for the little horse. But if Lewey wants to repossess it, then he'll have to catch me first.

Here's how it is on coming to the bingo hall. It's a long, low quonset barn. Inside, there used to be a pall of smoke, but now the smoke-eater fans in the ceiling take care of that. So upon first entering you can pick out your friends. On that night in early spring, I saw Eber, Clay, and Robert Morrissey sitting about halfway up toward the curtained stage with their grandmother Lulu. By another marriage, she was my grandma, too. She had five tickets spread in front of her. The boys each had only one. When the numbers rolled, she picked up a dabber in each hand. It was the Earlybird game, a one-hundred-dollar prize, and nobody had got too wound up yet or serious.

"Lipsha, go get us a Coke," said Lulu when someone else bingoed. "Yourself, too."

I went to the concession with Eber, who had finished high school with me. Clay and Robert were younger. We got our soft drinks and came back, set them down, pulled up to the table, and laid out a new set of tickets before us. Like I say, my grandmother, she played five at once, which is how you get the big money. In the long run, much more than breaking even, she was one of those rare Chippewas who actually profited by bingo. But, then again, it was her only way of gambling. No pull-tabs, no blackjack, no slot machines for her. She never went into the back room. She banked all the cash she won. I thought I should learn from Lulu Lamartine, whose other grandsons had stiff new boots while mine were worn down into the soft shape of moccasins. I watched her.

Concentration. Before the numbers even started, she set her mouth, snapped her purse shut. She shook her dabbers so that the foam-rubber tips were thoroughly inked. She looked at the time on her watch. The Coke, she took a drink of that, but no more than a sip. She was a narrow-eyed woman with a round jaw, curled hair. Her eyeglasses, blue plastic, hung from her neck by a gleaming chain. She raised the ovals to her eyes as the caller took the stand. She held her dabbers poised while he plucked the ball from the chute. He read it out: B-7. Then she was absorbed, scanning, dabbing, into the game. She didn't mutter. She had no lucky piece to touch in front of her. And afterward, even if she lost a blackout game by one square, she never sighed or complained.

All business, that was Lulu. And all business paid.

I think I would have been all business too, like her, if it hadn't been for what lay behind the stage curtain to be revealed. I didn't know it, but that was what would change the order of my life. Because of the van, I'd have to get stupid first, then wise. You see, I had been floundering since high school, trying to catch my bearings in the world. It all lay ahead of me, spread out in the sun like a giveaway at a naming ceremony. Only thing was, I could not choose a prize. Something always stopped my hand before it reached.

"Lipsha Morrissey, you got to go for a vocation." That's what I told myself, in a state of nervous worry. I was getting by on almost no money, relying on my job as night watchman in a bar. That earned me a place to sleep, twenty dollars per week, and as much beef jerky, Beer Nuts, and spicy sausage sticks as I could eat.

I was now composed of these three false substances. No food in a bar has a shelf life of less than forty months. If you are what you eat, I would live forever, I thought.

And then they pulled aside the curtain, and I saw that I wouldn't live as long as I had coming unless I owned that van. It had every option you could believe—blue plush on the steering wheel, diamond side windows, and complete carpeted interior. The seats were easy chairs, with little headphones, and it was wired all through the walls. You could walk up close during intermission and touch the sides. The paint was cream, except for the design picked out in blue, which was a Sioux Drum border. In the back there was a small refrigerator and a carpeted platform for sleeping. It was a home, a portable den with front-wheel drive. I could see myself in it right off. I could see I *was* it.

On TV, they say you are what you drive. Let's put it this way: I wanted to be that van.

Now, I know that what I felt was a symptom of the national decline. You'll scoff at me, scorn me, say, What right does that waste Lipsha Morrissey, who makes his living guarding beer, have to comment outside of his own tribal boundary? But I was able to investigate the larger picture, thanks to Grandma Lulu, from whom I learned to be one-minded in my pursuit of a material object.

I went night after night to the bingo. Every hour I spent there, I grew more certain I was close. There was only one game per night at which the van was offered, a blackout game, where you had to fill every slot. The more tickets you bought, the more your chances increased. I tried to play five tickets, like Grandma

Lulu did, but they cost five bucks each. To get my van, I had to shake hands with greed. I got unprincipled.

You see, my one talent in this life is a healing power I get passed down through the Pillager branch of my background. It's in my hands. I snap my fingers together so hard they almost spark. Then I blank out my mind, and I put on the touch. I had a reputation up to then for curing sore joints and veins. I could relieve ailments caused in an old person by a half century of grinding stoop-over work. I had a power in myself that flowed out, resistless. I had a richness in my dreams and waking thoughts. But I never realized I would have to give up my healing source once I started charging for my service.

You know how it is about charging. People suddenly think you are worth something. Used to be, I'd go anyplace I was called, take any price or take nothing. Once I let it get around that I charged a twenty for my basic work, however, the phone at the bar rang off the hook.

"Where's that medicine boy?" they asked. "Where's Lipsha?"

I took their money. And it's not like beneath the pressure of a twenty I didn't try, for I did try, even harder, than before. I skipped my palms together, snapped my fingers, positioned them where the touch inhabiting them should flow. But when it came to blanking out my mind I consistently failed. For each time, in the center of the cloud that came down into my brain, the van was now parked, in perfect focus.

I suppose I longed for it like for a woman, except I wasn't that bad yet, and, anyway, then I did meet a woman, which set me back in my quest.

Instead of going for the van with everything, saving up to buy as many cards as I could play when they got to the special game, for a few nights I went short term, for variety, with U-Pickem cards, the kind where you have to choose the numbers for yourself.

First off, I wrote in the shoe and pants sizes of those Morrissey boys. No luck. So much for them. Next I took my birth date and a double of it—still no go. I wrote down the numbers of my grandma's address and her anniversary dates. Nothing. Then one night I realized if my U-Pickem was going to win it would be more like *revealed*, rather than a forced kind of thing. So I shut my eyes, right there in the middle of the long bingo table, and I let my mind blank out, white and fizzing like the screen of a television, until something formed. The van, as always. But on its tail this time a license plate was officially fixed and numbered. I used that number, wrote it down in the boxes, and then I bingoed.

❖❖❖

I got two hundred dollars from that imaginary license. The money was in my pocket when I left. The next morning, I had fifty cents. But it's not like you think with Serena, and I'll explain that. She didn't want something from me; she didn't care if I had money, and she didn't ask for it. She was seventeen and had a two-year-old boy. That tells you about her life. Her last name was American Horse, an old Sioux name she was proud of even though it was strange to Chippewa country. At her older sister's house Serena's little boy blended in with the younger children, and Serena herself was just one of the teen-agers. She was still in high school, a year behind the year she should have been in, and she had ambitions. Her idea was to go into business and sell her clothing designs, of which she had six books.

I don't know how I got a girl so decided in her future to go with me, even that night. Except I told myself, "Lipsha, you're a nice-looking guy. You're a winner." And for the moment I was. I went right up to her at the Coin-Op and said, "Care to dance?," which was a joke—there wasn't anyplace to dance. Yet she liked me. We had a sandwich and then she wanted to take a drive, so we tagged along with some others in the back of their car. They went straight south, toward Hoopdance, off the reservation, where action was taking place.

"Lipsha," she whispered on the way, "I always liked you from a distance."

"Serena," I said, "I liked you from a distance, too."

So then we moved close together on the car seat. My hand

was on my knee, and I thought of a couple of different ways I could gesture, casually pretend to let it fall on hers, how maybe if I talked fast she wouldn't notice, in the heat of the moment, her hand in my hand, us holding hands, our lips drawn to one another. But then I decided to boldly take courage, to take her hand as, at the same time, I looked into her eyes. I did this. In the front, the others talked among themselves. Yet we just sat there. After a while she said, "You want to kiss me?"

But I answered, not planning how the words would come out, "Our first kiss has to be a magic moment only we can share."

Her eyes went wide as a deer's, and her big smile bloomed. Her skin was dark, her long hair a burnt-brown color. She wore no jewelry, no rings, just the clothing she had sewed from her designs—a suit jacket and pair of pants that were the tan of eggshells, with symbols picked out in blue thread on the borders, the cuffs, and the hem. I took her in, admiring, for some time on that drive before I realized that the reason Serena's cute outfit nagged me so was on account of she was dressed up to match my bingo van. I could hardly tell her this surprising coincidence, but it did convince me that the time was perfect, the time was right.

They let us off at a certain place just over the reservation line, and we got out, hardly breaking our gaze from each other. You want to know what this place was? I'll tell you. O.K. So it was a motel—a long, low double row of rooms, painted white on the outside, with brown wooden doors. There was a beautiful sign set up, featuring a lake with some fish jumping out of it. We stood beside the painted water.

"I haven't done this since Jason," she said. That was the name of her two-year-old son. "I have to call up my sister first."

There was a phone near the office, inside a plastic shell. She went over there.

"He's sleeping," she said when she returned.

I went into the office, stood before the metal counter. There was a number floating in my mind.

"Is Room 22 available?" I asked.

I suppose, looking at me, I look too much like an Indian.

The owner, a big sandy-haired woman in a shiny black blouse, noticed that. You get so you see it cross their face the way wind blows a disturbance on water. There was a period of contemplation, a struggle in this woman's thinking. Behind her the television whispered. Her mouth opened, but I spoke first.

"This here is Andrew Jackson," I said, tenderizing the bill. "Known for setting up our Southern relatives for the Trail of Tears. And to keep him company we got two Mr. Hamiltons."

The woman turned shrewd, and took the bills.

"No parties." She held out a key attached to a square of orange plastic.

"Just sex." I could not help but reassure her. But that was talk, big talk from a person with hardly any experience and nothing that resembled a birth-control device. I wasn't one of those so-called studs who couldn't open up their wallets without dropping a foil-wrapped square. No, Lipsha Morrissey was deep at heart a romantic, a wild-minded kind of guy, I told myself, a fool with no letup. I went out to Serena, and took her hand in mine. I was shaking inside but my voice was steady and my hands were cool.

"Let's go in." I showed the key. "Let's not think about tomorrow."

"That's how I got Jason," said Serena.

So we stood there.

"I'll go in," she said at last. "Down two blocks, there's an all-night gas station. They sell 'em."

I went. O.K. Life in this day and age might be less romantic in some ways. It seemed so in the hard twenty-four-hour fluorescent light, as I tried to choose what I needed from the rack by the counter. It was quite a display; there were dazzling choices— textures, shapes. I saw I was being watched, and I suddenly grabbed what was near my hand—two boxes, economy size.

"Heavy date?"

I suppose the guy on the late shift was bored, could not resist. His T-shirt said "Big Sky Country." He was grinning in an ugly way. So I answered.

"Not really. Fixing up a bunch of my white buddies from Montana. Trying to keep down the sheep population."

His grin stayed fixed. Maybe he had heard a lot of jokes about Montana blondes, or maybe he was from somewhere else. I looked at the boxes in my hand, put one back.

"Let me help you out," the guy said. "What you need is a bag of these."

He took down a plastic sack of little oblong party balloons, Day-Glo pinks and oranges and blues.

"Too bright," I said. "My girlfriend's a designer. She hates clashing colors." I was breathing hard suddenly, and so was he. Our eyes met and narrowed.

"What does she design?" he said. "Bedsheets?"

"What does yours design?" I said. "Wool sweaters?"

I put money between us. "For your information, my girlfriend's not only beautiful but she and I are the same species."

"Which is?"

"Take the money," I said. "Hand over my change and I'll be out of here. Don't make me do something I'd regret."

"I'd be real threatened." The guy turned from me, ringing up my sale. "I'd be shaking, except I know you Indian guys are chickenshit."

I took my package, took my change.

"Baaaaa," I said, and beat it out of there. It's strange how a bashful kind of person like me gets talkative in some of our less pleasant border-town situations.

I took a roundabout way back to Room 22 and tapped on the door. There was a little window right beside it. Serena peeked through, and let me in.

"Well," I said then, in that awkward interval, "guess we're set."

She took the bag from my hand and didn't say a word, just put it on the little table beside the bed. There were two chairs. Each of us took one. Then we sat down and turned on the television. The romance wasn't in us now for some reason, but there was something invisible that made me hopeful about the room.

It was just a small place, a modest kind of place, clean. You could smell the faint chemical of bug spray the moment you stepped inside. You could look at the television hung on the wall, or examine the picture of golden trees and a waterfall. You could take a shower for a long time in the cement shower stall, standing on your personal shower mat for safety. There was a little tin desk. You could sit down there and write a letter on a sheet of plain paper from the drawer. The lampshade was made of reeds, pressed and laced tight together. The spread on the double mattress was reddish, a rusty cotton material. There was an air-conditioner, with a fan we turned on.

"I don't know why we're here," I said at last. "I'm sorry."

Serena took a small brush from her purse.

"Comb my hair?"

I took the brush and sat on the bed, just behind her. I began at the ends, very careful, but there were hardly any tangles to begin with. Her hair was a quiet brown without variation. My hand followed the brush, smoothing after each stroke, until the fall of her hair was a hypnotizing silk. I could lift my hand away from her head and the hair would follow, electric to my touch, in soft strands that hung suspended until I returned to the brushing. She never moved, except to switch off the light and then the television. She sat down again in the total dark and said, "Please, keep on," so I did. The air got thick. Her hair got lighter, full of blue static, charged so that I was held in place by the attraction. A golden spark jumped on the carpet. Serena turned toward me. Her hair floated down around her at that moment like a tent of energy.

❖❖❖

Well, the money part is not related to that. I gave it all to Serena, that's true. Her intention was to buy material and put together the creations that she drew in her notebooks. It was fashion with a Chippewa flair, as she explained it, and sure to win prizes at the state home-ec. contest. She promised to pay me interest when she opened her own shop. The next day, after we had parted, after I had checked out the bar I was supposed to night-watch, I went off to the woods to sit and think. Not about the money, which was Serena's—and good luck to her—but about her and me.

She was two years younger than me, yet she had direction and a child, while I was aimless, lost in hyperspace, using up my talent, which was already fading from my hands. I wondered what our future could hold. One thing was sure: I never knew a man to support his family by playing bingo, and the medicine calls for Lipsha were getting fewer by the week, and fewer, as my touch failed to heal people, fled from me, and lay concealed.

I sat on ground where, years ago, my greats and my great-greats, the Pillagers, had walked. The trees around me were the dense birch and oak of old woods. The lake drifted in, gray waves, white foam in a bobbing lace. Thin gulls lined themselves up on a sandbar. The sky went dark. I closed my eyes, and that is when the little black pony galloped into my mind. It sped across the choppy waves like a skipping stone, its mane a banner, its tail a flag, and vanished on the other side of the shore.

It was luck. Serena's animal. American Horse.

"This is the last night I'm going to try for the van," I told myself. I always kept three twenties stuffed inside the edging of my blanket in back of the bar. Once that stash was gone I'd make a real decision. I'd open the yellow pages at random, and where my finger pointed I would take that kind of job.

Of course, I never counted on winning the van.

I was playing for it on the shaded side of a blackout ticket, which is always hard to get. As usual, I sat with Lulu and her boys. Her vigilance helped me. She let me use her extra dabber and she sat and smoked a filter cigarette, observing the quiet frenzy that was taking place around her. Even though that van had sat on the stage for five months, even though nobody had yet won it and everyone said it was a scam, when it came to playing for it most people bought a couple of tickets. That night, I went all out and purchased eight.

A girl read out the numbers from the hopper. Her voice was clear and light on the microphone. I didn't even notice what was happening—Lulu pointed out one place I had missed on the winning ticket. Then I had just two squares left to make a bingo and I suddenly sweated, I broke out into a chill, I went cold and hot at once. After all my pursuit, after all my plans, I was N-6 and G-60. I had narrowed myself, shrunk into the spaces on the ticket. Each time the girl read a number and it wasn't that 6 or 60 I sickened, recovered, forgot to breathe.

She must have read twenty numbers out before N-6. Then, right after that, G-60 rolled off her lips.

I screamed. I am ashamed to say how loud I yelled. That girl came over, got the manager, and then he checked out my numbers slow and careful while everyone hushed.

He didn't say a word. He checked them over twice. Then he pursed his lips together and wished he didn't have to say it.

"It's a bingo," he finally told the crowd.

Noise buzzed to the ceiling—talk of how close some others had come, green talk—and every eye was turned and cast on me, which was uncomfortable. I never was the center of looks before, not Lipsha, who everybody took for granted around here. Not all those looks were for the good, either. Some were plain envious and ready to believe the first bad thing a sour tongue could pin on me. It made sense in a way. Of all those who'd stalked that bingo van over the long months, I was now the only one who had not lost money on the hope.

❖❖❖

O.k., so what kind of man does it make Lipsha Morrissey that the keys did not tarnish his hands one slight degree, and that he beat it out that very night in the van, completing only the basic paperwork? I didn't go after Serena, and I can't tell you why. Yet I was hardly ever happier. In that van, I rode high, but that's the thing. Looking down on others, even if it's only from the seat of a van that a person never really earned, does something to the human mentality. It's hard to say. I changed. After just one evening riding the reservation roads, passing with a swish of my tires, I started smiling at the homemade hot rods, at the clunkers below me, at the old-lady cars nosing carefully up and down the gravel hills.

I started saying to myself that I should visit Serena, and a few nights later I finally did go over there. I pulled into her sister's driveway with a flourish I could not help, as the van slipped into a pothole and I roared the engine. For a moment, I sat in the dark, letting my headlamps blaze alongside the door until Serena's brother-in-law leaned out.

"Cut the lights!" he yelled. "We got a sick child."

I rolled down my window, and asked for Serena.

"It's her boy. She's in here with him." He waited. I did, too, in the dark. A dim light was on behind him and I saw some shadows, a small girl in those pajamas with the feet tacked on, someone pacing back and forth.

"You want to come in?" he called.

But here's the gist of it. I just said to tell Serena hi for me, and then I backed out of there, down the drive, and left her to fend for herself. I could have stayed there. I could have drawn my touch back from wherever it had gone to. I could have offered my van to take Jason to the I.H.S. I could have sat there in silence as a dog guards its mate, its own blood. I could have done something different from what I did, which was to hit the road for Hoopdance and look for a better time.

I cruised until I saw where the party house was located that night. I drove the van over the low curb, into the yard, and I parked there. I watched until I recognized a couple of cars and saw the outlines of Indians and mixed, so I knew that walking in would not involve me in what the newspapers term an episode. The door was white, stained and raked by a dog, with a tiny fan-shaped window. I went through and stood inside. There was movement, a kind of low-key swirl of bright hair and dark hair tossing alongside each other. There were about as many Indians as there weren't. This party was what we call around here a Hairy Buffalo, and most people were grouped around a big brown plastic garbage can that served as the punch bowl for the all-purpose stuff, which was anything that anyone brought, dumped in along with pink Hawaiian Punch. I grew up around a lot of the people, and others I knew by sight. Among those last, there was a young familiar-looking guy.

It bothered me. I recognized him, but I didn't know him. I hadn't been to school with him, or played him in any sport, because I did not play sports. I couldn't think where I'd seen him until later, when the heat went up and he took off his bomber jacket. Then "Big Sky Country" showed, plain letters on a bright-blue background.

I edged around the corner of the room, into the hall, and stood there to argue with myself. Would he recognize me, or was I just another face, a customer? He probably wasn't really from Montana, so he might not even have been insulted by our little conversation, or remember it anymore. I reasoned that he had probably picked up the shirt vacationing, though who would want to go across that border, over to where the world got meaner? I told myself that I should calm my nerves, go back into the room, have fun. What kept me from doing that was the sudden thought of Serena, of our night together and what I had bought and used.

Once I remembered, I was lost to the present moment. One part of me caught up with the other. I realized that I had left Serena to face her crisis, alone, while I took off in my brand-new van.

I have a hard time getting drunk. It's just the way I am. I start thinking and forget to fill the cup, or recall something I have got to do, and just end up walking from a party. I have put down a full can of beer before and walked out to weed my grandma's rhubarb patch, or work on a cousin's car. Now I was putting myself in Serena's place, feeling her feelings.

What would he want to do that to me for?

I heard her voice say this out loud, just behind me, where there was nothing but wall. I edged along until I came to a door, and then I went through, into a tiny bedroom full of coats, and so far nobody either making out or unconscious upon the floor. I sat on a pile of parkas and jean jackets in this little room, an alcove in the rising buzz of the party outside. I saw a phone, and I dialled Serena's number. Her sister answered.

"Thanks a lot," she said when I said it was me. "You woke up Jason."

"What's wrong with him?" I asked.

There was a silence, then Serena's voice got on the line. "I'm going to hang up."

"Don't."

"He's crying. His ears hurt so bad he can't stand it."

"I'm coming over there."

"Forget it. Forget you."

She said the money I had loaned her would be in the mail. She reminded me it was a long time since the last time I had called. And then the phone went dead. I held the droning receiver in my hand, and tried to clear my mind. The only thing I saw in it, clear as usual, was the van. I decided this was a sign for me to get in behind the wheel. I should drive straight to Serena's house, put on the touch, help her son out. So I set my drink on the windowsill. Then I slipped out the door and I walked down the porch steps, only to find them waiting.

I guess he had recognized me after all, and I guess he was from Montana. He had friends, too. They stood around the van, and their heads were level with the roof, for they were tall.

"Let's go for a ride," said the one from the all-night gas pump.

He knocked on the window of my van with his knuckles. When I told him no thanks, he started karate-kicking the door. He wore black cowboy boots, pointy-toed, with hard-edged new heels. They left ugly dents every time he landed a blow.

"Thanks anyhow," I repeated. "But the party's not over." I tried to get back into the house, but, like in a bad dream, the door was stuck, or locked. I hollered, pounded, kicked at the very marks that desperate dog had left, but the music rose and nobody heard. So I ended up in the van. They acted very gracious. They urged me to drive. They were so polite that I tried to tell myself they weren't all that bad. And sure enough, after we had drove for a while, these Montana guys said they had chipped in together to buy me a present.

"What is it?" I asked. "Don't keep me in suspense."

"Keep driving," said the pump jockey.

"I don't really go for surprises," I said. "What's your name, anyhow?"

"Marty."

"I got a cousin named Marty," I said.

"Forget it."

The guys in the back exchanged a grumbling kind of laughter, a knowing set of groans. Marty grinned, turned toward me from the passenger seat.

"If you really want to know what we're going to give you, I'll tell. It's a map. A map of Montana."

Their laughter got wild and went on for too long.

"I always liked the state," I said in a serious voice.

"No shit," said Marty. "Then I hope you like sitting on it." He signalled where I should turn, and all of a sudden I realized that Lewey's lay ahead. Lewey ran his Tattoo Den from the basement of his house, kept his equipment set up and ready for the weekend.

"Whoa," I said. I stopped the van. "You can't tattoo a person against his will. It's illegal."

"Get your lawyer on it tomorrow." Marty leaned in close for me to see his eyes. I put the van back in gear but just chugged along, desperately thinking. Lewey was a strange kind of guy, an old Dutch sailor who got beached here, about as far as you can get from salt water. I decided that I'd ask Marty, in a polite kind of way, to beat me up instead. If that failed, I would tell him that there were many states I would not mind so much—smaller, rounder ones.

"Are any of you guys from any other state?" I asked, anxious to trade.

"Kansas."

"South Dakota."

It wasn't that I really had a thing against those places, understand; it's just that the straight-edged shape is not a Chippewa preference. You look around you, and everything you see is round, everything in nature. There are no perfect boundaries, no borders. Only human-made things tend toward cubes and squares—the van, for instance. That was an example. Suddenly I realized that I was driving a wheeled version of the state of North Dakota.

"Just beat me up, you guys. Let's get this over with. I'll stop."

But they laughed, and then we were at Lewey's.

◆◆◆

The sign on his basement door said "COME IN. " I was shoved from behind and strapped together by five pairs of heavy, football-toughened hands. I was the first to see Lewey, I think, the first to notice that he was not just a piece of all the trash and accumulated junk that washed through the concrete-floored cellar but a person, sitting still as any statue, in a corner, on a chair that creaked and sang when he rose and walked over.

He even looked like a statue—not the type you see in history books, I don't mean those, but the kind you see for sale as you drive along the highway. He was a Paul Bunyan, carved with a chain saw. He was rough-looking, finished in big strokes.

"Please," I said, "I don't want . . ."

Marty squeezed me around the throat and tousled up my hair, like friendly.

"He's just got cold feet. Now remember, Lewey, map of Montana. You know where. And put in a lot of detail."

I tried to scream.

"Like I was thinking," Marty went on, "of those maps we did in grade school showing products from each region. Cows' heads, oil wells, those little sheaves of wheat, and so on."

"Tie him up," said Lewey. His voice was thick, with a commanding formal accent. "Then leave."

They did. They took my pants and the keys to the van. I heard the engine roar and die away, and I rolled from side to side in my strict bindings. I felt Lewey's hand on my shoulder.

"Be still." His voice had changed, now that the others were gone, to a low sound that went with his appearance and did not seem at all unkind. I looked up at him. A broke-down God is who he looked like from my worm's-eye view. His beard was pure white, long and patchy, and his big eyes frozen blue. His head was half bald, shining underneath the brilliant fluorescent tubes in the ceiling. You never know where you're going to find your twin in the world, your double. I don't mean in terms of looks— I'm talking about mind-set. You never know where you're going to find the same thoughts in another brain, but when it happens you know it right off, just like the two of you were connected by a small electrical wire that suddenly glows red-hot and sparks. That's what happened when I met Lewey Koep.

"I don't have a pattern for Montana," he told me. He untied my ropes with a few quick jerks, sneering at the clumsiness of the knots. Then he sat in his desk chair again, and watched me get my bearings.

"I don't want anything tattooed on me, Mr. Koep," I said. "It's a kind of revenge plot."

He sat in silence, in a waiting quiet, hands folded and face composed. By now I knew I was safe, but I had nowhere to go, and so I sat down on a pile of magazines. He asked, "What revenge?" and I told him the story, the whole thing right from the beginning, when I walked into the bingo hall. I left out the personal details about Serena and me, but he got the picture. I told him about the van.

"That's an unusual piece of good fortune."

"Have you ever had any? Good fortune?"

"All the time. Those guys paid plenty, for instance, though I suppose they'll want it back. You pick out a design. You can owe me."

He opened a book he had on the table, a notebook with plastic pages that clipped in and out, and handed it over to me. I didn't want a tattoo, but I didn't want to disappoint this man, either. I leafed through the dragons and the hearts, thinking how to refuse, and then suddenly I saw the horse. It was the same picture that had come into my head as I sat in the woods. Now here it was. The pony skimmed, legs outstretched, reaching for the edge of the page. I got a thought in my head, clear and vital, that this little horse would convince Serena I was serious about her.

"This one."
Lewey nodded, and heated his tools.

❖❖❖

That's why I got it put on, that little horse, and suffered pain.
Now my hand won't let me rest. It throbs and aches as if it was
coming alive again after a hard frost had made it numb. I know
I'm going somewhere, taking this hand to Serena. Even walking
down the road in a pair of big-waisted green pants belonging to
Lewey Koep, toward the So Long Bar, where I keep everything I
own in life, I'm going forward. My hand is a ball of pins, but
when I look down I see the little black horse running hard, fast,
and serious.

I'm ready for what will come next. That's why I don't fall on
the ground, and I don't yell, when I come across the van in a
field. At first, I think it is the dream van, the way I always see it
in my vision. Then I look, and it's the real vehicle. Totalled.

My bingo van is smashed on the sides, kicked and scratched,
and the insides are scattered. Stereo wires, glass, and ripped
pieces of carpet are spread here and there among the new sprouts
of wheat. I force open a door that is bent inward. I wedge myself
behind the wheel, which is tipped over at a crazy angle, and I
look out. The windshield is shattered in a sunlight burst, through
which the world is cut to bits.

I've been up all night, and the day stretches long before me,
so I decide to sleep where I am. Part of the seat is still wonderfully upholstered, thick and plush, and it reclines now—permanently, but so what? I relax into the small comfort, my body as
warm as an animal, my thoughts drifting. I know I'll wake to
nothing, but at this moment I feel rich. Sinking away, I feel like
everything worth having is within my grasp. All I have to do is
put my hand into the emptiness.

TINA MARIE VILLALOBOS

❖❖❖

The Way It Was

I COULD HEAR Grandma in the other room coughing like she always does in the morning. I pulled the old quilt up higher on my shoulders to shake off the morning chill. Our bedrooms were really just one room separated by an old wool blanket. I liked that because it wasn't scary like a room that's all by itself. Besides, that way we could see each other when we said good night. Grandma lit her cigarette and set her lighter down on the fruit box by her bed. Then she coughed some more.

Somebody was making noise in the kitchen, rattling around pots and pans or something. I couldn't go back to sleep.

Smoke from the woodstove drifted into the bedroom. I had to hurry up and find my robe. If I peed the bed, Grandma would be mad at me. I found it on the floor under the bed. I grabbed it and ran for the door. The floor was icy on my bare feet, and I was glad that Grandma had left her shoes by the front door. I put the big old tattered shoes on and made my way outside to the outhouse—just in time.

When I got back I went to the kitchen and Aunt Linda pumped water on my hands. I cupped the water and washed my face. Grandma called from the bedroom: "Tina . . . Tina! . . ."

"What, Grandma?" I answered as I ran into her room.

"Can you bring Grandma some coffee, like a good girl?"

"Sure" I said.

I was nervous, but proud. I was nervous because I was afraid I might spill the coffee and make a mess, and burn myself. I was proud because I knew that Grandma must think I'm getting to be a pretty big girl now, if I can carry hot coffee all by myself.

I ran back into the kitchen and told Aunt Linda that Grandma wanted me to bring her a cup of coffee. Aunt Linda said that it wasn't quite done yet, and she would take it in to Grandma as soon as it finished perking. She told me to go outside and play while I still had time. I wanted to wait for the coffee instead. At last it was done! Aunt Linda poured it into a mug and fixed it up with cream and stuff, just the way Grandma liked it. She handed it to me and I walked real careful, keeping my eye on the coffee as it wiggled around and tried to spill out on my hands. I wanted to be quick about it too, so Grandma wouldn't think I was piddling around. I smiled. I made it all the way in there without spilling any. I handed the cup over to Grandma. She smiled back at me, and I let out a sigh of relief. She took a sip of her coffee, then a drag off her cigarette. Then she coughed some more.

"Thank you," she said. "Tina, do you want a cup of coffee too?"

My eyes must've gotten big with surprise. Grandma laughed.

"Well, do you, or don't you?"

"Yeah! I do!" I ran back to the kitchen and told Aunt Linda that I could have some too. She poured it and I went back and drank my coffee with Grandma.

When Grandma finished her coffee and cigarette, she got up and got dressed. She pulled out some pants and a T-shirt for me to wear, and I put my clothes on too. We went into the kitchen. By now the house was warmed up and the wood floor didn't feel quite so cold on my feet.

Grandma put some milk in a pan on the stove and heated it up. Then she got a bowl out of the cupboard, and made some toast. When the milk was warm, she tore up the toast and put it into the bowl with the milk. She gave it to me with a spoon and told me that I'd better eat my breakfast and get full so we could get ready for work.

When I was done eating, I put my bowl in the sink where Aunt Linda was already pumping the water to heat for dishwashing. She looked mad. I guess she didn't want to mess around with the dishes this morning. She stared down at me and said, "Well, what?"

I said, "I need a glass of water so Grandma can do my hair."

"Whew . . ." she huffed at me.

She got the water and I took it into the front room where Grandma was waiting. Then I had to go into the bedroom and hunt for a comb.

I came back and sat down on the floor between Grandma's legs. Starting at the bottom of my hair, she began taking out my tangles one by one. I started falling asleep because it seemed to take forever.

"Hold your head up straight!"

I woke up then.

"Sorry, Grandma. Are you almost done now?"

"No. You know better than that. We still have to make your braids. All good little Indian girls have nice braids—without tangles—and they sit still so their Grandmas can make them look pretty!"

"Okay," I said.

I sat still while Grandma put the comb in the water and wet my hair down with it. At last my two braids were finished. They were nice and tight and smooth and wet. Grandma told me that I was the prettiest little Indian girl around. I smiled.

Aunt Linda brought in my socks and shoes. My socks were stiff and dry from the clothesline. Grandma put them on me. I hated the socks. My Mom bought them for me and they were way too big. Grandma had to fold them over the end of my toes, just like Mom did before.

"Grandma" I said, "why the heck does Mom buy me these darn ol' socks that hang way down like that? I hate 'em!"

Grandma gave me a mean look.

"Now don't you start off being a little pill today, or else I'll have you stay here with Uncle Neltz."

I stuck out my lip and ruffled my brow.

"What's wrong with you girl? You're lucky to even have socks to go with these shoes. Your Momma worked real hard for you to have 'em, too."

"Grandma . . . I just don't like it because they get all messed up when I walk, and then they roll up under my toes, and I have to take off my shoes and fix it."

Grandma rolled her eyes and shook her head at me.

"Poor little Princess-Rain-in-the-Face. Do you know why your Mother bought your socks too big?"

"No." I felt sad, because I knew Grandma wasn't happy with me now. She didn't even look proud of me at all.

"She bought your socks too big so that they would last you a long time and you could grow into them. Someday these socks will fit you just right, and do you know what?"

"No," I answered meekly.

"When that day comes you'll know that you are getting to be a big girl—because you'll fit these big ol' socks!"

Grandma smiled big at me. I could see her gums. I still hated the socks, but I knew that Grandma was right, so it didn't matter too much anymore. Roy started the old truck up and Grandma put a few biscuits into an old bread sack. We put the moss sacks into the back of the truck under an old board. There were lots of sacks. I knew that we were going to work hard today. I asked Grandma how many sacks there were. She just said, "Lots."

When I woke up we were in the mountains. I yawned and asked where we were. Grandma said, "Don't you ever run out of questions? We are where we've been a million times. Pay attention to where you're going. Someday you'll wind up lost if you don't. We are on Spirit Mountain, that's where we are."

The truck came to a stop in a clearing surrounded by a thick forest. Roy pulled up the break lever, and we all got out.

Grandma took a sack, Linda took a sack, and I took the rest. Roy said he thought he should stay behind and look after the truck just in case someone should come around wanting to steal it, or wreck it or something.

I was glad he stayed there. Whenever he came with us, he always complained about stuff, and that seemed to make everyone feel tired. He got back into the truck, and the rest of us started making our way through the underbrush and into the forest. Grandma asked me if I knew what direction we were headed.

I said, "Yeah, we're goin' up there."

"No, dingy, were headed north."

"Oh . . . north. Hey, that's where Santa Claus comes from! Grandma, do we get to go see Santa when we're done working?"

"No. It's not Christmastime," she said as she laughed.

We came to a patch of trees that were thick with moss and we began to pick. I started wondering about my Mom. I almost started crying.

"What's wrong with you now?" Aunt Linda looked at me like I was being a baby.

"I wonder where Mom is right now," I said with a lump in my throat.

Aunt Linda laughed and told me that my Momma died and the hogs ate her. I laid down on my moss sack and cried.

"Linda!" Grandma said. "You damn well better leave her alone. See what you've caused? Do you think we'll get anything done at this rate?"

Grandma was real mad at Linda, but came over to me and gently lifted me up. She hugged me close to her as I cried. Linda went on picking.

Grandma said, "Tina, you know that your Mother is off working hard in Nevada, trying to get things squared away for you to come and live down there with her. These things take time. Be patient and do your best to be a good girl. Your Momma will be home to get you before you know it." Grandma lifted my chin and wiped my tears. She smiled at me and said, "Besides, we don't even have any damn hogs!" We both laughed.

We were working hard for a long time. Then, it was time to get the biscuits out. We sat down each of us on an empty sack while we ate. The biscuits were cold and filling, but you had to eat them slow or else they'd get stuck in your throat, worse than the lump in your throat when you're about to cry. When we finished we lay down on our backs and looked up at how tall the trees are while we talked.

"Grandma," I said. "How come the trees get that tall and we can't?"

"Just because," she answered.

"But, because why?"

"Hell, I don't know, they just do. Probably to keep some of the sun, wind, and rain off of us."

"Grandma, I sure do like the trees. They look so pretty, and smell so nice . . . and they do nice things for us, too, huh?"

"Yep, Tina, you're right about that. One of the nice things they do for us is give us moss to pick and sell so we can have food in our bellies."

With that we got up and grabbed our sacks and got started again. We ran out of moss where we were, so we had to move on and look for more. Whenever that happened, I would carry Grandma's sack for her as we searched. We walked a long time. Grandma and Linda were way ahead of me. There were so many branches and fallen trees and underbrush, that I had a hard time keeping up. The bag was getting heavy too, but I didn't want to say anything to Grandma because I wanted to help her, and I didn't want her to think I was a baby and leave me home with Uncle Neltz next time.

"Tina . . . *Tina!* Shit, where is she now?" I heard Aunt Linda's voice.

"I'm right here Aunt Linda!" I yelled, "I'm coming Grandma!" I was out of breath, but I ran as best I could, dragging the moss sack with one arm and pushing the underbrush out of my face with my other arm as I went. Grandma looked glad to see me. I was glad too. I was starting to feel scared out there all alone.

"Look over yonder," Grandma said. "There's a nice patch of moss!"

We finished our day up and began to take the sacks back down to the truck. We had to make several trips. When we got down to the truck, Roy was asleep. He woke up and asked Grandma what time it was. She told him it was almost 5:00 P.M. He stretched himself and scratched his belly, explaining that he'd like to help us bring the moss in, and he would, except his back was hurting him too much. So, we did it ourselves.

Roy started the truck up and we turned toward home. Grandma asked me if I knew where I was.

"Yes Grandma, we're on Spirit Mountain, and we're on our way home!"

I woke up when the truck shut off. I sat up and took my head off of Grandma's lap, then looked out the window to see where we were. Agency Store. I asked if I could come in. Grandma helped me down out of the truck. We went inside and Grandma bought some milk and cigarettes. The store man leaned over the counter and looked down at me.

"Tina, your hair's a mess!" He laughed.

I was frowning. He knew I didn't like people saying that about my hair. "It is not!" I scolded him. "My Grandma just braided it for me this morning!"

He laughed some more. Then he said, "Oh, c'mon now, I'm sorry. How about a nice Hershey bar? Will that fix things up?"

"Yes sir! It will!"

Grandma came up from the cooler with the milk.

"Grandma, can I have a Hershey bar? Please."

"I'm sorry, babe, but we don't have the money for extra stuff today. Maybe next time, okay?"

"Okay . . ." I felt kind of sad.

Then the store man said, "Tina, I already told you that you could just *have* this Hershey bar. That was our deal, remember?"

"Is it okay, Grandma?" She nodded. I took the candy bar and said, "Thank you, sir," as we left.

When I got back in the truck, Aunt Linda and Roy looked like they were mad because I got a goodie and they didn't.

Aunt Linda said, "Gee whiz, just look at this kid. She already gets her way. If her Mom had started her in school this year like she could have, then she'd see how things really work. Then she'd have to be just like everyone else."

I thought to myself, Just what is *everyone else* like? "Anybody want a piece of my Hershey bar?" I gave everyone a piece.

We had to stop and check the mail, then we could go home. I wished we were home already. I was so tired. Roy left the truck running, and Grandma went in. Aunt Linda lit a cigarette and the truck got real smoky so I rolled down the window. Grandma came out and stood by the truck with a bunch of letters in her hand. She was talking to Bill Tom, a man that used to be our neighbor. I listened to them talk.

"I'm surprised to see you here," Grandma said. "Are you moving back, or what?"

"Nah, I just still get my mail here in Grand Ronde because I ain't really settled in to anyplace permanent yet. I been stay'n out toward McMinnville with a couple of my old buddies."

"Shit, you ought to think 'bout comin' back. Ain't the same 'round here without you."

"Well, this place ain't the same anyhow—not since they terminated the Tribe. Mind you, I don't need no damn government man tell'n me if I am or ain't an Indian, but it's the people —just look at what's happened to them. It's like they're lost—in their own backyard. Don't matter what happens or what anybody says, I am and always will be a Grand Ronde Indian. Nobody can take that away, not the government, not the law, not anyone!" Bill looked unhappy.

"I know how you feel," Grandma said. "My Mother moved off the reservation before I was ever born, and I 'magine she had her reasons, but I will always be a Modoc—no matter what."

Grandma was real serious. Then she looked at Bill and smiled. "Hey, who knows with these characters anyhow? The damn government never did know whether to shit or get off the pot. Maybe things will work out okay with the Tribe after all. We just have to try our best, and never forget what the old ones taught us. Never forget who we are. Keep our young ones on the right track, and make them feel proud and honored with who they are. We'll get by—we always have, huh?" Grandma smiled and put her hand on Bill's shoulder. He was looking down at the ground and rolling the little rocks around under one of his shoes.

He looked up at her, "Yeah . . . s'ppose so. I best get goin' back to town. Gotta see a fella about a job in a gas station, fix'n tires. So, I'll see ya later."

Grandma got back up into the truck and we headed back home.

As the truck rolled up to the house, the chickens clucked at it and scurried off in every direction. I was glad to get out and stretch. Linda got up in the back of the truck and started handing the moss sacks to us. Grandma and I put them in the shed next to the bailer. At last we were done and could go in the house.

I couldn't wait to get my icky wet shoes off. My socks were all rolled up and soggy.

"Grandma."

"What?"

"Are my toes gonna be this way forever? Look at 'em. They got old."

She raised one eyebrow and looked at me sideways.

"Old?"

"Yeah. See," I held my foot up toward her. "They're all wrinkled up like Uncle Neltz. Grandma, why is Uncle Neltz old —but not Aunt Linda or my Mom?"

Grandma shook her head, then clucked her tongue. "You are a bushel of questions! First of all, your toes are wrinkled up because they've been inside your wet shoes all day. They'll be back to normal in no time. Now then, Uncle Neltz is older than your Mom or Linda because he is your father's uncle, not my son. Okay?"

"Oh . . . Okay. Grandma, where's my Daddy?"

She came up closer and petted my hair, then tucked a loose

strand behind my ear. "I 'magine he's in Willamina," she said softly.

"Well, how come he doesn't come see me?"

"Oh, now . . . I'm sure he would like to, but he's been workin' hard at that Fort Hill Lumber."

I remembered something exciting. "Grandma, did you know that one time my Daddy let me pull on the green chain at his work?"

Grandma's eyes got big with surprise. "He did?" "What a *big* girl! I bet you worked hard, huh?"

"Yes, and I was in my pajamas too!"

We both laughed.

Roy came in carrying the metal washtub.

"Here you go," he said to us. He sat it down in the kitchen. I sat in the chair by the table, while Grandma pumped water into a pot. She started heating it for my bath.

I thumped an empty matchbox across the table.

"Pow!" I shouted. *"Pow! Pow! Pow!"* I thumped it some more and ran around the table.

"Pow!" I shouted. This time the matchbox landed on the floor. Chinook, Uncle Neltz' cat, gave it a big swat, then another. He swatted it clear out the back door.

"Hey you!" I laughed as I ran outside after him.

Uncle Neltz was sitting in the ripped-up recliner outside the door. My matchbox landed by his feet.

"Hi Uncle," I said as I picked it up.

"Blanket Ass!" he blurted out. Then he put his head down.

"What's-a-matter Uncle?" I felt scared. Was he sick? Was he mad?

"Uncle? . . ." I slowly reached up and tugged at his sleeve. He opened his eyes real quick.

"Gut Ah Heil' En Ta' Hsss!" he yelled.

"Grandma!" I screamed. Then he dropped his sack—*boom* —on the porch. Grandma ran out to see what was wrong. I was crying. She took hold of my arms and knelt down in front of me.

"What, Tina? What is it?"

I was having a hard time catching my breath through my tears.

"Uncle . . . (sniff) . . . Uncle . . . Uncle N-Neltz . . ."

"Yes, yes . . . Uncle Neltz *what?*" she said, looking confused.

"Grandma, I came for my matchbox, then I said 'Hi' to Uncle. Then he called me real loud and I came up closer beside him. He yelled Indian words at me and dropped his sack and went back to sleep . . ." I buried my face in Grandma's neck and cried real hard.

"Hey, hey now—hand on. At least tell me what Uncle Neltz said."

I sniffed and wiped my nose on the bottom of my T-shirt.

"Gut Ah Heil' En Ta' Hsss!" I repeated. Then continued to cry. She looked even more confused.

"Neltz! *Neltz!*" She shook him to consciousness.

"Sunzabitches!" he said as he ran his hands through his hair.

"Neltz!" Grandma looked serious. "What did you say to Tina?"

"*What* the . . ." Uncle Neltz looked back and forth at Grandma and me.

"Tina said you talked Indian to her. *What* did you say?"

"Sheeit! I don't talk no Indian. I *said, Get the hell in the house!*" He was mad and he emphasized each word.

"Whew . . ." Grandma huffed.

She took me back in the house by the hand.

"Your bath water's pert' near warm now." She looked tired.

I sat in the chair again. My hands were in my lap and my tear-streaked face drooped down. I watched a little black ant carry a tiny piece of bread crumb across the floor. Grandma started talking. I could hear Roy and Linda talking quietly in the other room, but their voices were muffled and I couldn't understand them.

"Tina, I know Uncle Neltz scared you, but he's not mad at you. He loves you. He's just old and tired, and he's drunk on that damn Mad Dog again!"

"Ahh! Grandma!" I looked up amazed. "How can Uncle drink a dog? 'Specially if 'e's mad?"

"Oh, you don't know shit from shine-ola!" She shook her head and laughed. That made me laugh too.

She pulled the sheet across the wire so nobody could see me, and put the water in the washtub while I took off my clothes. I bent over and touched the water with my hand.

"How is it?" Grandma asked.

"Good," I said, and got in the tub.

She handed me a bar of soap and a washrag.

"Don't forget to wash b'hind them ears, and b'tween them toes too!"

"Okay, I will." I said.

She went in with the others.

I watched my soap float around. I pushed it and pretended it was my boat. I looked over toward the sheet to be sure nobody was coming. I didn't want to be in trouble for playing in the tub.

I saw the little black ant again.

"Hey Mr. Ant," I whispered. "Want to have a ride on my boat?" I put my hand down out on the floor, and the ant crawled on. I held the tiny ant up close to my face so I could get a good look at him. I thought he was cute and fun to watch. He even tickled my hand! I let him crawl onto the soap boat. I watched him there floating around. I wondered where *his* Mom and Daddy were, and if he had a Grandma too.

"Tina!" Aunt Linda scolded me. "Quit playing, and *wash*—the *rest* of us would like to bathe, too, you know!"

"Oh my gosh!" I said. I looked around in the tub frantically.

"What? What did you lose?" she asked.

"It's Mr. Ant. He's gone!"

"Quit goofing around. C'mon, get it done and over with will ya! *Geez!*" She pulled the sheet back across.

I picked up my soap and washrag and started washing myself.

Someone knocked at the front door, and I heard Roy invite them in. I kept washing. I could hear the voices of my Aunt

Dora and my Cousin Billy, and I heard baby Terry crying. Everyone called Terry "Goose." I washed my hair then I was done.

"Grandma! I'm clean now!" I shouted.

She came in and looked me over. Aunt Dora and Billy came in too. Billy was nine months younger than me.

Grandma said I didn't get all the soap out of my hair. Then she rinsed it for me. Aunt Dora said she had to go or she'd be late. She kissed me and Billy, then left. Grandma dried me and gave me clean panties and one of her big ol' T-shirts to wear to bed.

Billy brought over a neat truck to play with. I went over to the woodbox by the stove and found a small square piece of wood. That was my truck. We played for a while, then Aunt Linda said we had to eat.

We had chicken soup. It was warm and good in my tummy. Billy liked it too. Goose had a bottle of milk and then fell asleep.

"Can Billy and Goose sleep here too, Grandma?" I asked.

"Heck yeah! They're gonna spend the whole weekend. How does that grab ya?"

Billy and I grinned at each other. After dinner, I was glad to see my bed, and I couldn't even remember falling to sleep.

"*Hey!* Blanket Ass! Wake up and pee, the world's on fire!"

"M-m-m-m . . ." I yawned. Uncle Neltz was standing in the doorway.

"Well, you awake 'er not?" he asked.

"Uh-huh . . . I am."

"C'mon then, up-n-adam. Your granny wants you to come help her."

"What's she doin'?" I asked.

"She's trying to cook, and she needs you to keep an eye on the baby."

"Can't Aunt Linda?" I whined. I felt so tired, I just wanted to sleep. I yawned again.

"Get yourself up. There's plenty to be done around here. Everyone ought to do their part. You know that!"

"Oh . . . kay . . ." I got up and put my coat on. There wasn't a fire going yet. I was *cold.*

Billy and Roy were still sleeping. Linda was out feeding the animals.

"Morning, Grandma." I hugged her.

"Look out now, don't get underfoot or you'll get burned."

Goose was crying.

"What do I do?" I asked.

"Go be your silly-self, and make him laugh."

He was lying on a blanket on the floor. I started jumping around his blanket like a monkey. Then, I blew on his tummy, like my Mom did to make me laugh. He laughed hard. It sounded so funny, and he looked like a pumpkin, because he had only two teeth.

Grandma fixed up the table with the plates and forks and all that. Then she brought the food. Everyone took their plates in the other room anyway, so they could sit on the couch and eat. Everyone, except me, Billy, and Grandma. We had mashed potatoes, eggs, and meat.

"What kind of meat is this, Grandma?" Billy asked.

"Deer," she said as she picked up Goose.

Billy and I sat down and started eating. It was delicious!

I watched Grandma as I ate.

"Grandma, how come grown-ups chew up the little baby's food, then put it into the baby's mouth for them to eat?"

She took some food from her mouth and fed it to Goose. "Tina, babies are precious little ones," she said. "They are tender like a butterfly, and every bit as nice to look at. But, the butterfly is all grown up, and he can take care of himself. Babies need special care for a long time, so they can grow up strong and wise, and beautiful. Babies don't have teeth to chew their food, so we have to chew it for them. Besides, it's a nice way to love them and help them grow."

I ate some more and thought over what she had said.

"Well, Goose has two teeth," I said.

"So?"

"But Grandma, Goose has two teeth and you don't have *any*, so how come he can't chew up *your* food?"

"Oh brother!" She smirked at me. "It just doesn't work that way."

I finished eating. Grandma asked Aunt Linda and Roy to go lay the moss out flat to dry, so we could bale it. She said that one morning next week we would get to go up to Portland and sell it to a florist shop.

"How long does it take to go to Portland?" I asked. Uncle Neltz said it was about a two-hour drive.

Billy and I put on old tore-up clothes and played in the mud. We played hide-and-seek, and tag. It was a great day. Everyone said they were glad I had a playmate, for a change.

I was excited. The moss was ready to go! Grandma and I were going to Portland—all by ourselves. Aunt Linda had to stay home and so did Roy. Uncle Neltz didn't like to go places. We were both dressed in our nice clothes.

Grandma and I climbed up into the truck and away we went!

We talked a lot. Then Grandma said she could hardly hear herself think. I told her I couldn't hear her either. She rolled her eyes and grinned.

"I know what, Tina, I'll teach you a song, okay? Then we can sing it together. That'll be fun, huh?"

"Yeah. What song?"

"Well, it's an old Indian song that my mother sang to me, and her mother to her. I sang it to your mom, and now, I'll sing it to you. Ready?"

"Sure!"

She seemed to drift off into a daydream. She held her head up proud as she began to sing.

> *Klim uk a Klatawa clase ole Danial*
> *Klim uk a Klatawa clase ole Danial*
> *Klim uk a Klatawa clase ole Danial*
> *Si I cupa clase salli Hee'—aye*
>
> *Where now is good ol' Danial*
> *Where now is good ol' Danial*

Where now is good ol' Danial
Save in the promise land.

I felt proud. Grandma and I looked in each other's eyes. We were both quiet for a long time. We felt each other's thoughts. We were so proud, we almost cried—and we couldn't sing anymore. I laid my head down on Grandma's lap and fell asleep.

I woke up. At first, I was afraid. Grandma wasn't in the truck. I rubbed my eyes and looked around. The truck was parked in front of a cafe. Through the glass I could see Grandma sitting at a table while she had her coffee and cigarette. I looked in the mirror and noticed my braids were crooked. I guess Aunt Linda couldn't do it as good as Grandma. Yuk, I had to go in the place like that too. I went in and sat across from Grandma.

She asked me what I wanted to have. I decided on hot chocolate with lots of whipped cream and little marshmallows. The waitress brought it and I put ice cubes in it so I wouldn't have to wait to drink it. I took a swig.

"Ahhh . . ." I sighed. "This is good!"

"I hope you like wearing that chocolate mustache as much as you like drinking it." Grandma laughed, and I started looking for a napkin.

Our dispenser was empty, so I started looking at the other tables, and along the counter for one. I caught sight of a shiny black purse with pretty white rhinestones on it. The woman was coming from the bathroom.

"Grandma, that purse looks like my Mom—" I looked up at the woman's face. *It was my mother!*

"Mommy!, Mommy!, Mommy!" I squealed, and ran into her arms. We hugged tight. Then we smooched and looked at each other. She had a chocolate moustache, and I had red clown lips. We laughed till we cried. Grandma laughed too.

"How was that for a surprise?" Grandma asked.

"The *very best!*" I said.

I was too excited to talk. So, I finished my hot chocolate and listened while Mom and Grandma talked.

"So, what kind of life have you set up for you and Tina?" Grandma asked.

"Well," my Mom began, "I have a good job in a restaurant during the day, and I work at a tavern at night, and I am the manager of a big old house that was made into apartments."

"Hmmm . . ." Grandma frowned. I could tell she didn't like it. "Sharon, what do you plan to do with my little Princess-Rain-in-the-Face while all this is going on?"

My Mom looked insulted and upset. "Well, I have a baby-sitter for my daytime job—until she starts school, which we live close to, by the way, and the tavern has a bunk set up in back where she can sleep sometimes so we can still be together while I work."

Grandma shook her head and frowned.

"Of all the places on earth—*why* did you choose Sparks, Nevada? How can you do anything there? There ain't half the woods there as there are in Oregon. It's all bullshit. You will lose sight of yourself in the shuffle."

My Mom was quiet for a minute.

"Mother—there are *no* jobs *here,* and I told you before, I need to make a clean break from her F-A-T-H-E-R! We will do just fine. You'll see!"

Grandma looked sad. I was happy—and sad too. I *didn't* want to go, but I *did* want my Mommy.

"Well Sharon, her stuff is in the back of the truck. It's your choice."

My Mom put a fifty-cent tip on the table and we all walked outside. Mom got my stuff, then we walked to a small building beside the cafe.

A bus with a dog on the side of it drove up. The driver opened the door, and it went *whooshhh!* real loud.

Grandma picked me up and hugged me tight. "I love you, Tina, we all do. We'll miss you and your Mom. You be a big girl for Grandma, and keep an eye on your Mom. You best work hard, and mind too—or you'll be in trouble!" She looked at me. Then we cried. Mom did too.

The bus driver yelled, "Klamath Falls! Shasta! Reno! All aboard!"

Mom gave him the taped up cardboard box full of my things. He threw it in the luggage compartment.

We all hugged again, and tried to smile for each other. We couldn't, and we looked so silly trying that we had to laugh.

"I love you, Grandma. Please come visit . . ." I said through my tears.

She put me down, then knelt down in front of me and said, "Have your Momma fix your braids right, and take that clown paint off your face. Okay?"

"I will, Grandma," I said.

She looked at my Mom.

"Good luck, Sharon. If things don't work out—come home."

"Hey there! Excuse me, lady." The bus driver sounded like a mean man. *"Hey—damn it,* lady, I've got a schedule to keep. You going or staying?"

We got on the bus. I sat by the window and waved. I watched Grandma standing by the truck waving back at me, until she looked like a tiny speck. Then all I saw was the miles of bluish-black highway becoming the bus's tail.

DIANE GLANCY

❖❖❖

Aunt Parnetta's
Electric Blisters

Some stories can be told only in winter.
This is not one of them
because the fridge is for Parnetta
where it's always winter.

HEY CHEKTA! All this and now the refrigerator broke.
Uncle Filo scratched the long gray hairs that hung in
a tattered braid on his back. All that foot stomping and fancy
dancing. Old warriors still at it.

"But when did it help?" Aunt Parnetta asked. The fridge ran
all through the cold winter when she could have set the milk and
eggs in the snow. The fish and meat from the last hunt. The
fridge had walked through the spring when she had her quilt and
beading money. Now her penny jar was empty, and it was hot,
and the glossy white box broke. The coffin! If Grandpa died, they
could put him in it with his war ax and tomahawk. His old dog
even. But how would she get a new fridge?

The repairman said he couldn't repair it. Whu chutah! Filo
loaded his rifle and sent a bullet right through it. Well, he said, a
man had to take revenge. Had to stand against civilization. He
watched the summer sky for change as though the stars were
white leaves across the hill. Would the stars fall? Would Filo

have to rake them when cool weather came again? Filo coughed and scratched his shirt pocket as though something crawled deep within his breastbone. His heart maybe, if he ever found it.

Aunt Parnetta stood at the sink, soaking the sheets before she washed them.

"Dern't nothin' we dude ever work?" Parnetta asked, poking the sheets with her stick.

"We bought that ferge back twenty yars." Filo told her. "And it nerked since then."

"Weld, dernd," she answered. "Could have goned longer til the frost cobered us. Culb ha' set the milk ertside. But nowd. It weren't werk that far."

"Nope," Filo commented. "It weren't."

Parnetta looked at her beadwork. Her hands flopped at her sides. She couldn't have it done for a long time. She looked at the white patent-leathery box. Big enough for the both of them. For the cow if it died.

"Set it out in the backyard with the last one we had."

They drove to Tahlequah that afternoon. Filo's truck squirting dust and pinging rocks. They parked in front of the hardware store on Muskogee Street. The regiments of stoves, fridges, washers, dryers, stood like white soldiers. The Yellow Hair Custer was there to command them. Little Big Horn. Whu chutah! The prices! Three hundred crackers.

"Some mord than thad," Filo surmised. His flannel shirt-collar tucked under itself. His braid sideways like a rattler on his back.

"Filo, I dern't think we shulb decide terday."

"No," the immediate answer stummed from his mouth like a roach from under the baseboard in the kitchen.

"We're just lookin'."

"Of course," said Custer.

They walked to the door leaving the stoves, washers, dryers, the televisions all blaring together, and the fridges lined up for battle.

Filo lifted his hand from the rattled truck.

"Surrender," Parnetta said. "Izend thad the way id always iz?"

The truck spurted and spattered and shook Filo and Aunt Parnetta before Filo got it backed into the street. The forward gear didn't buck as much as the backward.

When they got home, Filo took the back off the fridge and looked at the motor. It could move a load of hay up the road if it had wheels. Could freeze half the fish in the pond. The minute coils, the twisting intestines of the fridge like the hog he butchered last winter, also with a bullet hole in its head.

"Nothin we dude nerks." Parnetta watched him from the kitchen window. "Everythin' against uz," she grumbled to herself.

Filo got his war feather from the shed, put it in his crooked braid. He stomped his feet, hooted. Filo, the medicine man, transcended to the spirit world for the refrigerator. He shook each kink and bolt. The spirit of cold itself. He whooped and warred in the yard for nearly half an hour.

"Not with a bullet hole in it." Parnetta shook her head and wiped the sweat from her face.

He got his wrench and hack saw, the ax and hammer. It was dead now for sure. Parnetta knew it at the sink. It was the thing that would be buried in the backyard. "Like most of us libed," Aunt Parnetta talked to herself. "Filled with our own workings, not doint what we shulb."

Parnetta hung the sheets in the yard, white and square as the fridge itself.

❖❖❖

The new refrigerator came in a delivery truck. It stood in the kitchen. Bought on time at a bargain. Cheapest in the store. Filo made sure of it. The interest over five years would be as much as the fridge. Aunt Parnetta tried to explain it to him. The men set the fridge where Parnetta instructed them. They adjusted and leveled the little hog feet. They gave Parnetta the packet of information, the guarantee. Then drove off in victory. The new smell of the gleaming white inside as though cleansed by cedar from the Keetowah fire.

Aunt Parnetta had Filo take her to the grocery store on the old road to Tahlequah. She loaded the cart with milk and butter. Frozen waffles. Orange juice. Anything that had to be kept cool. The fridge made noise, she thought, she would get used to it. But in the night, she heard the fridge. It seemed to fill her dreams. She had trouble going to sleep, even on the clean white sheets, and she had trouble staying asleep. The fridge was like a giant hog in the kitchen, rutting and snorting all night. She got up once and unplugged it, waking early the next morn to plug it in again before the milk and eggs got warm.

"That ferge bother yeu, Filo?" she asked.

"Nord."

Aunt Parnetta peeled her potatoes outside. She mended Filos's shirts under the shade tree. She didn't soak anything in the kitchen sink anymore, not even the sheets or Filo's socks. There were things she just had to endure, she grumped. That's the way it was.

When the grandchildren visited, she had them run in the kitchen for whatever she needed. They picnicked on the old watermelon table in the backyard. She put up the old teepee for them to sleep in.

"Late in the summer fer that?" Filo quizzed her.

"Nert. It waz nert to get homesick for the summer that's leabing us like the childurn." She gratified him with her keen sense. Parnetta could think up anything for what she wanted to do.

Several nights Filo returned to their bed, with its geese-in-flight-over-the-swamp pattern quilt, but Aunt Parnetta stayed in the teepee under the stars.

"We bined muried thurdy yars. Git in the house," Filo said one night under the white leaves of the stars.

"I can't sleep 'cause of that wild hog in the kitchen," Aunt Parnetta said. "I tald yeu that."

"Hey chekta!" Filo answered her. "Why didn't yeu told me so I knowd whad yeu said." Filo covered the white box of the

fridge with the geese quilt and an old Indian blanket he got from
the shed. "Werd yeu stayed out thar all winder?"

"Til the beast we got in thar dies."

"Hawly gizard," Filo spurted. "Thard be anuther twendy
yars!"

Aunt Parnetta was comforted by the bedroom that night.
Old Filo's snore after he made his snorting love to her. The gray-
and-blue-striped wallpaper with its watermarks. The stovepipe
curling up to the wall like a hog tail. The bureau dresser with a
little doily and her hairbrush. Pictures by their grandchildren. A
turquoise coyote and a ghostly figure the boy told her was Running Wind.

She fell into a light sleep where the white stars blew down
from the sky, flapping like the white sheets on the line. She
nudged Filo to get his rake. He turned sharply against her.
Parnetta woke and sat on the edge of the bed.

"Yeu wand me to cuber the furge wid something else?" Filo
asked from his sleep.

"No," Aunt Parnetta answered him. "Nod unless id be the
polar ice cap."

❖❖❖

Now it was an old trip to Minnesota when she was a girl.
Parnetta saw herself in a plaid shirt and braids. Had her hair
been that dark? Now it was streaked with gray. Everything was
like a child's drawing. Exaggerated. The way dreams were sometimes. A sun in the left corner of the picture. The trail of chim-
ney smoke from the narrow house. It was cold. So cold that
everything creaked. She heard cars running late into the night.
Early mornings. Steam growled out of the exhaust. The pane of
window glass in the front door had been somewhere else. Old
lettering showed up in the frost. Bones remembered their aches
in the cold. Teeth, their hurt. The way Parnetta remembered
every bad thing that happened. She dwelled on it.

That cold place was shriveled to the small upright rectangle
in her chest, holding the fish her grandson caught in the river.
That's where the cold place was. Right inside her heart. No

longer pumping like the blinker lights she saw in town. She was the Minnesota winter she remembered as a child. The electricity it took to keep her cold! The energy. The moon over her like a ceiling light. Stars were holes where the rain came in. The dripping buckets. All of them like Parnetta. The *hurrrrrrrrr* of the fridge. Off. On. All night. That white box. Wild boar! Think of it. She didn't always know why she was disgruntled. She just was. She saw herself as the fridge. A frozen fish stiff as a brick. The Great Spirit had her pegged. Could she find her heart, maybe, if she looked somewhere in her chest?

Hurrrrrrr. Rat-tat-at-rat. *Hurrr.* The fridge came on again, and startled, she woke and teetered slightly on the edge of the bed while it growled.

But she was a stranger in this world. An Indian in a white man's land. "Even the ferge's whate," Parnetta told the Great Spirit.

"Wasn't everybody a stranger and pilgrim?" The Great Spirit seemed to speak to her, or it was her own thoughts wandering in her head from her dreams.

"No," Parnetta insisted. Some people were at home on this earth, moving with ease. She would ask the Great Spirit more about it later. When he finally yanked the life out of her like the pin in a grenade.

Suddenly Aunt Parnetta realized that she was always moaning like the fridge. Maybe she irritated the Great Spirit like the white box irritated her. Did she sound that way to anyone else? Was that the Spirit's revenge? She was stuck with the cheapest box in the store. In fact, in her fears, wasn't it a white boar which would tear into the room and eat her soon as she got good and asleep?

Hadn't she seen the worst in things? Didn't she weigh herself in the winter with her coat on? Sometimes wrapped in the blanket also?

"Filo?" She turned to him. But he was out cold. Farther away than Minnesota.

"No. Just think about it, Parnetta," her thoughts seemed to say. The Spirit had blessed her life. But inside the white refrigerator of herself—Inside the coils, an ice river surged. A glacier mowed its way across a continent. Everything frozen for eons. In need of a Keetowah fire. Heat. The warmth of the Great Spirit. Filo was only a spark. He could not warm her. Even though he tried.

Maybe the Great Spirit had done her a favor. Hope like white sparks of stars glistened in her head. The electric blisters. *Temporary!* She could shut up. She belonged to the Spirit. He had just unplugged her a minute. Took his rifle right through her head.

The leaves growled and spewed white sparks in the sky. It was a volcano from the moon. Erupting in the heavens. Sending down its white sparks like the pinwheels Filo used to nail on trees. It was the bright sparks of the Keetowah fire, the holy bonfire from which smaller fires burned, spreading the purification of the Great Spirit into each house. Into each hard, old pine-cone heart.

RAYNA GREENE

❖❖❖

High Cotton

IS EVERYTHING A STORY? Ramona asked her.

It is if a story's what you're looking for—otherwise, it's just people telling lies and there's no end to it. Grandma waited to see how she took that and she started in again, smoothing out the red-checked oilcloth on the kitchen table as she talked. Ramona watched the purple cockscombs she could see through the kitchen door.

You don't have to hear anything, not about the white ones or the red—nothing about any of them, and you can call 'em all lies if you want. In a way, they are all lies just like them Thunder stories Gahno tells you or like the Bible—something that happened too far back for anyone to see and too close for anyone to deny. You listen to her stories much more and you won't want to know the difference. Still, there's always choices. It's like the time Gahno was out in the cotton field—right here at the old home place, just beyond this door. We was just girls, all of us— her and me and Rose and Anna—and there was Poppa, the meanest old German bastard that ever lived. He had us out chopping cotton in the worst heat of the day. He treated Indian and

white alike—you might say just like we was niggers—well, that's
what Anna used to say when she had sense, but some might
dispute that she ever had any at all. Anyway, a big old black
snake run acrost Gaĥno's foot out there in the high cotton. And
she commenced to screaming and run up to the house. Lord, she
throwed down that hoe and hollered loud enough to make us all
run up from the field.
Snake, she hollered, snake.

But Poppa had seen the blacksnake come acrost the field and he
didn't put no store at all in running from snakes. He liked to kill
'em, you know, and nail their skins up on the barn door yonder.

Goddammit, he yelled, you scheisskopf Indin', ain't one ting but
one blacksnake an' he don't hurt you.

That was his way of talking when he got mad and he never could
talk good English anyway. Well, we all commenced to laughing
and screaming at the sight of Poppa all puffed up and Gaĥno
scared to fits—and her no better at English than him any day.
She was so damn mad she about near spit at Poppa.

Jesus no, Jesus no, he maybe not hurt me, but dat damn snake he
make me hurt myself.

And then we all went to laughing like as not to stop—and she
started to giggle too that way she has even now. Poppa swole up
even more like a toad and marched off into the house for
Momma to soothe his hurt feelings, and Gaĥno threw down that
hoe for good. She left Tahlequah and went to Dallas and she
never came back—and I follered her the next year and Rose ten
years later. Poppa never forgive any of us and Gaĥno wasn't even
his kin—but he acted like she was—so he had one heart spell too
many when your Momma married her son. Betrayal was bad
enough, but race mixing was worse. Marrying Indians was a
damn sight worse to him. I guess he thought she'd stay and slave
for him forever just like he thought we would. But he was wrong.

Grandma paused for breath and then stopped, watching Ramona get up and head toward the old ice box near the sink.

I know there's another story here, Ramona said. Are you going to tell it now or should I get you more ice tea to get through it? You want me to doctor yours with some of Baby Dee's finest so you don't get hoarse?

She saw assent in Grandma's eyes so she opened the flour bin where Rose always kept the drinking whiskey—remembering Aunt Anna who always called it her heart medicine when she took it by the tablespoon ten times a day.

It's Rose I want to tell you about—and Will—and that snake wadn't just a side story. Yes, get me some of Baby Dee's good whiskey. It never hurt me nor anybody else who drank it with a clear heart. He got the trick of it from those Cherokee hill climbers you stem from, I'll say that. But your Uncle Will, he was white and he drank white whiskey. It kilt his sense and will and left nothing but feeling. Baby Dee's whiskey makes me want to go file my teeth and whip up on Andy Jackson. Just bring the jar and a bite of that ham on the sideboard, and I'll tell you the real story.

Ramona set the Mason jar of clear liquid in front of her grandmother, with the bowl of rock candy and mint leaves she favored for her particular brew. And she poured herself some into the blue enamel cup she always used when she came down home to Aunt Rose's.

To heart medicine, she said.

God knows it ain't head medicine you need, Grandma told her. You had too big a dose of that from your Daddy—thinking is the family disease.

Honey, your Uncle Will, he was just like that snake, and the Baptist Church, it was like him—they was made for one another. But he was a drinking man, and he was when Rose married him. When he couldn't get whiskey from the white bootleggers, he got it from the black ones. He never drank no Indian whiskey—not like everybody else—'cause he believed they boogered it just like Baby Dee does in truth. And that whiskey made him crazy anyway. He got worse. He didn't have nothing but the whiskey and the whiskey had him. For ten years he poured the whiskey down.

Rose got all the church women to pray and pray over him, week after week, and they kept poor Jesus awake yelling about Will's sinful state. The more they prayed and hollered over him, the more he cussed and drank. And that made them pray more. You know how them prissy Baptist women is, honey—wouldn't say shit if they had a mouthful—and they like to drove everyone to the ginmills and shake dance parlors before long. But everyone was more disgusted with Will. He'd run everybody's patience out, and if he'd been on fire, not a soul would have pissed on him to save him. He raved and carried on when Rose and Bubba took the truck from him—they hid it out in Dadayi's barn over yonder at Lost City—but he stole the tractor and drove it to the bootlegger's anyway.

Well, then one night, he put the harrow on and run that tractor over thirty acres of good lake bottom cotton, and Rose finally pitched a fit. She and Bubba tied that old drunk to the bedposts and left there to piss and shit all over hisself and he done it —they left him for two days and more.

Thirty acres might not sound like much to you now, but it was something then. They tied him to the bed right there in that room yonder and he thrashed and cussed and rolled for three days. He threatened and begged and done damn near everything he could to get them to turn him loose. But Rose's heart had hardened—even to the point of letting her spotless house stink of drunkard's shit. On the third night, he was worse than ever before, yelling and carrying on. And Rose finally come in from the front parlor where she'd tried to sleep these nights while he was cutting up. She come in and stood at the foot of his bed.

Sister, give me just another bite of that ham and some of Gaĥno's bean bread before I go on. I could piece all day on that ham and never set down to a meal. There's nothing like funerals for good eating.

You better hurry with the story or they're all going to be back from the funeral parlor and hear the worst, Ramona told her. I'm going to have just a little bite myself to keep my strength up. I may need a whole ham the way you're going.

Baby Sister, I never knew you to let your strength get endangered. You're both your Grandma's child, that's for certain.

Well, Rose come into the bedroom trying to breathe in the stench and keep from laughing at the old bastard's misery at the same time. She loved seeing him as wretched as she'd been all these years. So she stood at the foot of the bed, all dressed in an old white flannel gown—the same old one she'd worn for ten years and the one she would wear today if they hadn't bought that silly blue town dress just to go to the boneyard. So there she stood in that ruffled white flannel gown, and Will, crazy with having the whiskey took from him, thought it was Jesus come to take him away. He seen the ghosts and boogers of his worst drunk dreams and commenced to bleat and call out to Jesus. Guilty through all the whiskey boldness, he called out to Jesus and begged Him not to take him now.

Jesus, I been bad I know, but I'll be good tomorrow. Jesus, I'm not ready now, but give me another chance to serve you. Jesus, I'll praise your name tomorrow and never take another drop of drink.

Well, sir, he went on like that 'til Rose got tickled and you know what a cut-up she is when she gets provoked. So, she started to laugh for all those ten years of suffering with that drunken worthless farmer, and she begin to shake that white gown and talk to him. So, she made out to him like she was Jesus. Well, if he could give up his sins, she reasoned, why couldn't she take some up since there'd be room left in the emptiness.

Oh, Will, she said, talking deep, I've got plans for you. I need a sober man, a righteous man, a just man. I've got plans for your life, but you'll have to promise me to quit drinking and whoring and treating your good wife so bad.

Oh, Jesus, I will, I will do it, he yelled. Jesus, I'm the one to do it.

Will, she said, waving her arms and standing on tiptoe in the kerosene light—her gown all cloudy and white around her—I want you to come out of that piss and shit, out of the hog wallow you've fallen in, and I want you to preach my word.

Oh, Jesus, he promised, I'm the one.

Well, she damn near kilt herself laughing, but she went on until they was both worn out with it and he promised to preach Jesus' word until he died. When she'd calmed herself, Will was still a-raving about Jesus. But she looked at that piece of stinking flesh on the bed and thought about murder. She picked up the jonny pot from under the bed and tried to break his head with it. She picked up the pissy sheets and tried to strangle him around his turkey neck, and she offered to smother him with the last of her good feather pillows.

But Jesus had him no matter what she done, and he lived and praised her, thinking all the time it was Jesus putting him to the test. And well it might have been. But wanting to kill him so bad and Jesus saving him made her hate the church on the spot. She thought if he did wake up and fulfill his promise to preach, it was a church she didn't want nothing to do with it anyway. Well, the Devil didn't offer her a solution and the little son-of-a-bitch didn't die. So, she took off that white gown and threw it into the bed with him.

It ain't Jesus, you damned old fool, she up and screamed at him, it's your crazy wife and be damned to the both of you.

She boiled up water for the hottest bath she'd ever had and sat buck naked at the parlor pump organ all night, playing every shake dance tune she knew, and she was sitting there when Baby Dee come to start plowing in the morning. She was laughing and singing and happy like he's never seen her, and he couldn't believe his ears when she asked him if he'd ever thought of taking his whiskey-making skills to Dallas. They was gone before Will come to, and when he did, he took her leaving for the punishment he deserved. He cleaned himself up and went right uptown to the preacher to confess his sins and sign up for the Jesus Road.

Rose and Baby Dee went right to Dallas with Gahno and the other Indians that had left before, and that's where we all ended up—that is, until Will died fifteen years ago as sober as when he was born. But she'd had the good time and he'd paid for what he done to her by living a strict and righteous life. She'd takened away the only thing he loved, and ended up making her living selling it.

And Jesus done it all, she would tell people.

There's a white flannel salvation that comes to drunks in the dark and makes 'em change. So she wondered when it would come to her. She got Baby Dee to booger his whiskey too, so wouldn't nobody get saved on it and tot up more souls for Jesus. She used to tell him—we're in the whiskey business, not the salvation business. Jesus looked like an Arab and dressed like a woman and that ain't what we're about. And they'd go on up to the stomp dances in the hills after they'd come back here to live, never drinking one drop of the whiskey they made, 'cause she'd turned Indian just as sure as she'd turned away from Christians, and that would have driven a nail into Poppa's heart too. She always figured, just like Gahno, that snakes was meant to warn you, and she took the warning.

Well, that's the story and there's no end to it. There's more than one thing that will make you hurt yourself and more than one that'll save you.

Jesus, Ramona said.

Yes, Jesus, Grandma said.

There's the picture of Poppa and Will on the wall, where they belong—in stockmen's suits and French silk kerchiefs. And here's the rest of us —you and Momma and Baby Dee and Gahno and me—gone to the Indians or to Dallas or to some of those strange places you favor. Except for Rose, who's laying dead up town. At least we won't have no one preach over her. She can take that comfort. We can just sing and tell lies when they all come back to the house, and the Indians can bury her the right way tomorrow. You and Baby Dee can do it right. Maybe Baby Dee will take a drink of his own whiskey today.

More stories? Ramona asked.

Snakebite medicine, Grandma said.

JOY HARJO

❖❖❖

The Flood

T HAD BEEN YEARS since I'd seen the watermonster, the snake who lived in the bottom of the lake, but that didn't mean he'd disappeared in the age of reason, a mystery that never happened. For in the muggy lake was the girl I could have been at sixteen, wrested from the torment of exaggerated fools, one version anyway, though the story at the surface would say car accident, or drowning while drinking, all of it eventually accidental.

But there are no accidents. This story is not an accident, nor is the existence of the watersnake in the memory of the people as they carried the burden of the myth from Alabama to Oklahoma. Each reluctant step pounded memory into the broken heart, and no one will ever forget it.

When I walk the stairway of water into the abyss, I return as the wife of the watermonster in a blanket of time decorated with swatches of cloth and feathers from our favorite clothes. The stories of the battles of the watersnake are forever ongoing, and those stories soaked into my blood since infancy like deer gravy, so how could I resist the watersnake, who appeared as the most handsome man in the tribe, or any band whose visits I'd been witness to since childhood.

This had been going on for centuries, the first time in my memory I carried my baby sister on my back as I went down to get water. She laughed at a woodpecker flitting like a small sun above us, and before I could deter the symbol, we were in it. My body was already on fire with the explosion of womanhood, as if I were flint, hot stone, and when he stepped out of the water he was the first myth I had ever seen uncovered. I had surprised him in a human moment. I looked aside but I could not discount what I had seen.

My baby sister's cry pinched reality, the woodpecker a warning of a disjuncture in the brimming sky, and then a man who was not a man but a myth. What I had seen there were no words for, except in the sacred language of the most holy recounting, so when I ran back to the village, drenched in salt, how could I explain the water jar left empty by the river to my mother who deciphered my burning lips as shame?

My imagination had swallowed me like a mica sky, but I had seen the watermonster in the fight of lightning storms, breaking trees, stirring up killing winds, and had lost my favorite brother to a spear of the sacred flame so certainly I would know my beloved if he were hidden in the blushing skin of the suddenly vulnerable. I was taken with a fever and nothing cured it until I dreamed my fiery body dipped in the river where it fed into the lake. My father carried me as if I were newborn, as if he were presenting me once more to the world, and when he dipped me I was quenched, pronounced healed. My parents immediately made plans to marry me to an important man who was years older but would provide me with everything I needed to survive in this world, a world I could no longer perceive, since I had been blinded with a ring of water when I was most in need of a drink by a snake who was not a snake, and how did he know my absolute secrets, those created at the brink of acquired language?

When I disappeared, it was in a storm that destroyed the

houses of my relatives; my baby sister was found sucking on her hand in the crook of an oak. And though it may have appeared otherwise, I did not go willingly. That night I had seen my face in the sacred fire, strung on the shell belt of ancestors, and I was standing next to a man who could not look me in the eye. The oldest woman in the tribe wanted to remember me as a symbol in the story of the girl who disobeyed, who gave in to her desires before marriage and was destroyed by the monster disguised as the seductive warrior. Others saw the car I was driving as it drove into the lake early one morning, the time the carriers of tradition wake up, before the sun or the approach of woodpeckers, and they found the emptied six-pack on the sandy shores of the lake. The power of the victim is a power that will always be reckoned with, one way or the other.

When the proverbial sixteen-year-old woman walked down to the edge of the lake to call out her ephemeral destiny, within her were all sixteen-year-old women from time immemorial, and it wasn't that she decided to marry the watersnake, but there were no words describing the imprint of images larger than the language she'd received from her mother's mouth, her father's admonishments. Her imagination was larger than the small frame house at the north edge of town, with the broken cars surrounding it like a necklace of futility, larger than the town itself leaning into the lake. Nothing could stop it, just as no one could stop the bearing down thunderheads as they gather for war overhead in the war of opposites.

Years later when she walked out of the lake and headed for town, no one recognized her, or themselves in the drench of fire and rain. The children were always getting ready for bed, but never asleep, and the watersnake was a story that no one told anymore. She entered a drought that no one recognized as drought, the convenience store a signal of temporary amnesia. I had gone out to get bread, eggs, and the newspaper before break-fast and hurried the cashier for my change as the crazy woman walked in, for I could not see myself as I had abandoned her some twenty years ago in a blue windbreaker at the edge of the man-made lake as everyone dove naked and drunk off the sheer cliff, as if we had nothing to live for—not then or ever. It was beginning to rain in Oklahoma, the rain that would flood the world.

JOY HARJO

❖•❖•❖

Northern Lights

NORTHERN LIGHTS were sighted above Lake Superior as we danced concentric circles around the drums at Ashland, each step bringing us through the freezing. Bells, the occasional sacred flute like wind beneath an eagle, and the drum marking more than time, rather outlining ancestors, a pipeline into the earth to the mother of volcanoes. I noticed Whirling Soldier beneath the garish lights of the auditorium. He trusted nothing, still broke swords with angry gods. His war scars were evident in the way his eyes flinched and burned with gunpowder, from the recurring horror of his decapitated ditchmate draped on the trees, spilled across him. We talked wild rice, modern fiction, and of his daughter who was hitting eighteen, sober after drinking away adolescence, and we were proud to watch her dance by us, her eyes on fire with the intimate knowledge of survival from the abyss. She carried her niece, his granddaughter laughing, to see so many grandmothers, so many relatives.

He had returned from the war, from Wichita with a spirit feather pressed against his heart. The killing wind chaffed his lips. There were no prayers anymore. All he knew was he was leaving Nam, and approaching the destruction of his people by laws.

The northern lights were reminiscent of mercy gathering on the horizon. Sometimes he thought he saw them in Nam, or was it fire from the unseen enemy, which could have come from the Ohio boy in the foxhole next to him, or the gook rattling the bush who appeared as his cousin Ralph, an apparition making an offering of the newest crop of wild rice.

He was killing himself, he thought, each shot rigged his spine to hell. There was no way to get out. He was in it, and knew the warrior code had said nothing about the wailing of children in the dark. The sacrifice reminded him of his mother stuffing wood into the stove, cooking potatoes in the gray before dawn, before she went to clean houses. They never had enough to eat. He always went to find his father, instead of going to school with his sisters, his stomach warm with potatoes and coffee, sometimes fresh deer meat, when they were lucky.

Suddenly he was in Vietnam, a man like his father had been when he had found him floating on ice in the lake. His father had been fishing for redemption when his heart gave out. The empty bottle skudded away, slipped into the river, an epitaph read by fish drinking in the lake.

Under fire the image of his father on ice often took hold through the scope, and his teeth would chatter in the hot, damp jungle as if he were freezing, but he couldn't put his rifle down. And nothing killed the image, kept it from growing on its own. Soon it was spring and the lake thawed and his father sunk to the bottom. Deer stopped to drink. Clouds surfaced in the blue. He made it through summer, was shot clean through, missed the shinbone while flying on heroin making volcanoes of the bush. By then he couldn't see through to the surface of the lake. He was lucky to be able to walk, climb up the muddy bank, make it to Wichita, after the blur of San Francisco, Oklahoma City, on his way home.

In Yuma, in the hangover of a dream of his mother beading a blanket in his honor he tore the medals from his pack and pawned them for a quart. He snuffed his confusion between honor and honor with wine, became an acrobat of pain in the Indian bars of Kansas.

One of those mornings no different from any other except for the first taste of winter, reminded him of the beginning of the world and he imagined his mother wrapping a deer meat sandwich in a plastic bread wrapper. When he opened the door his breath took the form of question marks, imitated clouds over water. His father sat up on the sagging bed, coughed, asked him where he was going. But he didn't hear the question until years later, as he staggered up some state road north of Wichita, with a pint of Seagram's tucked in his pants, the staccato of machine gun still stuttering in his memory.

What must have been the Head Crow laughed from a stiff telephone wire, swung back and forth beneath the sun, blinking his eyes at the sleeping pitiful world. Whirling Soldier muttered, his voice broke off in waves. He wished he had a cigarette. The eye of a dried sunflower reminded him his baby would be two, but she, too, had probably disappeared in the azimuth of forgetfulness.

He unscrewed the cap of his final fix. His last fight did not involve the clockwork of artillery, but a punch that shattered the mouth of a man who looked like his brother. He staggered away from the man who whimpered like a child into the shiny black blood pool, and threw up in the weeds breaking the sidewalk. Suddenly the high winds of violence that chased him from fight to fight found him north of Wichita, at dawn, talking to a spirit who had never been a stranger but a relative he had never met.

I can't tell you what took place beneath the blessing sun, for the story doesn't belong to me, but to Whirling Soldier who gifted me with it in the circle of hope. After the dance, we all ran out onto the ice to see the northern lights. They were shimmering relatives returned from the war, dancing in the skies all around us. It was an unusual moment of grace for fools.

KATHLEEN SHAYE HILL

❖❖❖

Taking Care of Business

THE MORNING OF THE FUNERAL Reeva went upstairs, stepped into her closet, closed the door as she always did and under the dim light of a 25 watt bulb, got herself dressed. Even though it was warm outside, she put on a gray flannel suit and a shocking pink blouse. With a quick wrist she wrapped her hair up and stuck a few hairpins in it.

She had paid a high price for what he'd done. To begin with, she had lived a life of jealousy—resentment, really—directed toward the women she met who had been protected, who'd held on to their innocence throughout childhood. She had lost a good man, a good husband, because she'd never learned what it meant to make love, never known physical intimacy that didn't leave her feeling violated. And now she even seemed to have lost her children. They thought she was crazy. They hadn't said so but she knew it was true. Each time she stepped out of the room she heard them hurriedly whispering, and as soon as she stepped back in they clammed up and acted as if no words had passed between them. They came to visit less and less often and when they did they no longer asked what the graphs and charts on her walls were for. She had been very clever on that issue; she'd kept them color-coded and the only keys were on the lists which she slid under the rug in her bedroom each night. The memos were important, too. They contained the explanations that rounded out her project. These she kept rolled up like scrolls in the ankles of her steel-toed woodchopping boots.

This morning, for the first time, all the facets of what had become her life-project, her reason for being, were united. Still stocking-footed, she laid them out on the bed—the final chart propped on the left pillow, the list underneath, the graph on her pillow and the memos (but only the most recent ones) lined up below it.

❖❖❖

It had taken her a good many years to realize the extent of what he had done to her. Although she'd been paying for it all along, it hadn't been clear just how much she'd paid until five years ago. That's when Jim had left; because, as he'd very gently put it, she just didn't seem to love him the way he needed to be loved. They shared no intimacy, no passion, he said, and now that the kids were grown, they should both be free to seek the kind of love that would fulfill their later years. There were no fights, there was no cruelty, and all along she had known he was right. Even before he brought it up, she'd known there was something wrong with her. Another kind of man would have used the word "frigid" but Jim didn't have that in him. It didn't matter, though, because the hurt in his eyes and the agony she felt couldn't have been worse if he'd chopped up her heart and served it on that night's salad plate.

She knew it was too late with Jim, but the desperate sorrow got her to that woman psychologist and in a matter of months they'd dredged up her past, waded through it and finally set it aside. At least that's what her goodhearted counselor thought. Only Reeva knew better. As hard as she tried, she just couldn't accept the past and move beyond it in the way that White woman wanted. And even though the counselor was good and kind and sensitive, she seemed unable to understand the double-damage a White man could do an Indian girl. It wasn't that she didn't care; she just didn't understand that his Whiteness made a difference. After a few months Reeva got tired of trying to teach her. Instead, she went along with her, said the things the counselor was able to accept, and, afterward, turned to her graphs, charts, memos and lists.

Every night after work she'd come home, fix dinner, call her mother, then go upstairs and work on the project. It hadn't been easy at first. There had been no words, no way of pinning down those feelings, those memories of night after night spent waiting and never knowing. So it started with the lists of words: fear/ isolation/ violation/ denial/ recrimination. Those were the first words, there were many to follow.

Then there were the memos. A description of a memory or emotion was written on a memo for each word. Like the "F" memo for "fear" : "Every night, not knowing if he'd be there or not. No more baby dolls; it was flannel from here to there. And tucking the blankets in tightly, so tightly I could hardly breathe. Then pushing the bed against the wall and sliding in under those tight, tight covers and laying up hard against the wall and listening to every sound. When I was almost asleep they'd turn the radio off downstairs and I'd wait, as I knew he'd wait, for her to go to sleep. Sometimes I'd hear him, hear the stairs creak, and I'd know he was creeping up those stairs. It was scary to know how much like a rodent, a nightcreature, he was. So I'd close my eyes and wait and breathe heavy like I thought sleep sounded. If I cried or whimpered or said 'please, don't,' he'd say 'shut up or I'm going to tell your mother on you.' Some nights I'd hear him when he wasn't there. I'd peek out of the corner of my eye expecting to see his pasty-white body, dressed in nothing but freshly bleached undershorts, scampering across the linoleum to my bed. But there was nothing. No one. And I knew I was getting crazy." That was fear.

On the chart, fear was olive-green because every time he touched her, each time his corpse-colored fingers pried inside the elastic of her pajamas or between the buttons on her nightgown, she wanted to throw up. Now, each time she woke up at night, scared, still hearing him even though all of this was thirty years past and her house was four miles from his, she took that wide-tipped felt marker and added a horizontal stripe of olive-green to the bottom of the long, broad, "F" column on her chart.

Each word had its own column and she did her best, really put a lot of thought into deciding just what color was appropriate. The hardest was "H," the "hate" column. That color turned out to be sludge-brown. She could think of nothing more appropriate for the hate she felt than the color of the sludge in the bottom of Klamath Lake, because he'd done to her what the White farmers and ranchers had done to her tribe's beloved lake. The color had been hard to find in a wide-tipped felt marker, but it was worth the search that took her all the way to Portland because it was exactly right.

Reeva looked across the chart one last time and admired the murky, muddled colors for the chance they'd given her to visualize the anguish.

She turned to the graph. The line of it was her gauge of happiness. She couldn't remember before age four so that's where it started. The line was above the minimal-happy point until she was eleven, two years after her mother had married him. He was a little strange but he was good to her mother as her own father had not been and, even though he was White, her younger brothers found it easy to call him Daddy.

Reeva and Lani, her best friend, had a lot of silliness together that eleventh year. It was great fun changing into women and when they showered or changed clothes they laughed at how funny their breasts were; how different they looked than the round, lightly marked momma-breasts of their mothers. They had giggled themselves senseless over their bodies and they could hardly wait to grow up and nurse their own babies. But all of that changed. He changed it. That's when he started coming around, poking and prying, and she hated him and she hated her breasts and she never wanted babies anymore.

At sixteen, she tried to tell her mother—only once—what he'd been doing, how he'd been messing around with her. But Momma couldn't believe it. Maybe she just loved him too much. At different times she tried to tell her brothers too, but they seemed not to have heard. Each time they just started talking about something else. The funny thing about it was that all of them, in their odd little ways, seemed to have thrown her, not him, out of their lives.

Then Jim came along and got her away from him so she let him have her. But she never could get herself to nurse those babies.

Reeva let out a long, deep sigh and it filled the room with heavy air. She chastised herself for being self-indulgent. After all, her mother had just died. Her mother had loved that man and, in his own way, she supposed, he must have loved her mother. He'd taken care of Momma all those years and had been a good father to her brothers. That counted for something; at least at the time.

Well, today would be the end of that. She had waited all these years and today he was going to be the one to pay. She was tired of wearing his shame. Let him see how comfortable he was dressed up in it. She reached under her mattress and pulled out the speech. It had taken hours to write. She no longer needed the lists, the graphs, the charts and memos. Once Momma was safely in the Earth, once they had all gathered in Momma's home after the final meal in her honor, once everyone had eaten their dessert and finished their coffee, Reeva was going to make a toast. "This," she would start out, raising a glass of wine high into the air, "Is to pay tribute to the goddamn son-of-a-bitch who robbed me of my childhood, who stole my sensuality before I even knew I had it." Then she would go into detail. She would tell each thing he had done to her. Like how he'd threatened her with Momma, knowing Reeva couldn't bear to face the answer if Momma had to make a choice between him and her. But death had removed that fear. Now, without having to worry about Momma, she'd tell everything. Even how she'd cried and begged and prayed and neither he nor the Creator had listened or cared.

Already, she could picture the faces of the folks at the house. Some would stand there with their mouths hanging open. Some would get indignant and leave. Her kids might try to shut her up in order to protect "their Grandpa." But she wouldn't listen.

One way or another, she'd get it said and they'd all just have to listen up. All of them would pay for the fact that when she had needed it—when she, too, had been young and sweet and vulnerable—no one had cared enough to protect her.

❖❖❖

Reeva was unable to cry. Momma was gone, forever, but no matter how hard she tried she couldn't cry.

They'd finished the final meal at the church and only the closest friends and family members were at Momma's house. His family was there, as were her aunts and uncles, the people who'd known her since childhood, her kids, her ex-husband Jim, her brothers, sisters-in-law, nieces and nephews. A fine audience.

The first glass of wine was to take the edge off, the second to steel her nerves. She looked around at the solemn faces, at the half-finished plates of dessert, half-full cups of lukewarm coffee. No one else was drinking wine today, but she didn't care, didn't give one damn. She'd brought her own. She kept scouring the room with her eyes and now, they landed on him. He was sitting all alone in that recliner Momma'd bought one Father's Day. There he was; sniveling away, whining how life wasn't worth living anymore. Reeva downed the little bit of wine left in her glass and let the dry-edged flavor bite into her tongue for a moment. If he thought life wasn't worth living now, just give her a half-hour.

She refilled the glass in the kitchen, this time sipping it very slowly. People were milling around now but none of them spoke to her. For a long while she watched him. He was a homely little man, ugly and frail. He'd die soon. It showed all over him. He knew it, too—that showed as well. Her kids were hovering over him now, patting him on the back, holding his hand. Giving him the kind of tender care they had never been able to give her. On second thought, maybe she'd never been able to give them that kind of tenderness either.

She looked at him again and he was watching her. He held his hands out toward her. "Daughter," he said. "My daughter . . ." There were great salty tears rolling out of his sad, bloodshot eyes. She turned away and went back to the kitchen to pour what was left of the bottle into her glass.

On re-entering the living room she glanced around at the plates once more. They were all empty. Her moment had come. Reeva cleared her throat and stood up. She was no longer invisible to the group, all heads turned to her. Her eyes had become weapons. She looked at him and he winced. It was clear that he didn't recognize the woman she'd become. In his sorrow and old age, they both knew that he had become the vulnerable one.

Very slowly, she raised the half-empty glass into the air. Her eyes swept the room, skimming over each brown or white face, each pair of worn, painfilled eyes that raised to meet hers. *Their pain*—she had forgotten all about THEIR PAIN. She paused for a moment, but knew nothing except to forge ahead. After all, there the glass was, dangling from her hand, high up over her head. She let her eyes settle on him once. "This," she said—just as she had planned, raising her glass even higher—"this is to pay tribute," she coughed, cleared her throat, looked about, and accidentally saw Momma's portrait above his chair. "This is to pay tribute to the memory of my mother, a woman who suffered but endured, whose only strengths were love and patience. May the Ancestors be watching over her as she travels to the After-World."

Nobody said anything. Nobody even had a glass to toast with. Someone murmured "amen" but mostly they just stared, dumbfounded. Finally, her brothers came to her and each put his arms around her, holding her close. Then Jim came and hugged her. She sank into his arms in a way she'd never been able to sink before. Her children came next and each of them held and kissed her. Finally the gathering cleared and he was standing there. It was just the two of them. He reached out to her, put his arms around her and said, "Thank you, daughter. Thank you." Reeva let him pull her close although she felt her back tighten up in the old way. He held her as tightly as his weak old arms could hold her.

She pulled back and took a long look at his little rodent face. Life had, indeed, given him the face he'd deserved all along. She smiled then leaned into him, putting her lips right next to his ear. "I'm not your daughter," she whispered. "Don't call me that again. And don't think I've forgiven or forgotten the childhood you robbed me of. Your funeral is next. If you ever so much as cross me, you'll pay for it then."

She didn't need to look at him again. His silence and the limp way his arms fell to his sides made it clear that he knew she meant business.

Reeva pulled her shoulders up, took a deep breath and turned to the roomful of people. She smiled, thanked each one of them for coming and said she needed to go home and have some time alone now.

They smiled back and nodded their heads as if they understood.

LINDA HOGAN

❖❖❖

Aunt Moon's Young Man

THAT AUTUMN when the young man came to town, there was a deep blue sky. On their way to the fair, the wagons creaked into town. One buckboard, driven by cloudy white horses, carried a grunting pig inside its wooden slats. Another had cages of chickens. In the heat, the chickens did not flap their wings. They sounded tired and old, and their shoulders drooped like old men.

There was tension in the air. Those people who still believed in omens would turn to go home, I thought, white chicken feathers caught on the wire cages they brought, reminding us all that the cotton was poor that year and that very little of it would line the big trailers outside the gins.

A storm was brewing over the plains, and beneath its clouds a few people from the city drove dusty black motorcars through town, angling around the statue of General Pickens on Main Street. They refrained from honking at the wagons and the white, pink-eyed horses. The cars contained no animal life, just neatly folded stacks of quilts, jellies, and tomato relish, large yellow gourds, and pumpkins that looked like the round faces of children through half-closed windows.

"The biting flies aren't swarming today," my mother said.

She had her hair done up in rollers. It was almost dry. She was leaning against the window frame, looking at the ink-blue trees outside. I could see Bess Evening's house through the glass, appearing to sit like a small, hand-built model upon my mother's shoulder. My mother was a dreamer, standing at the window with her green dress curved over her hip.

Her dress was hemmed slightly shorter on one side than on the other. I decided not to mention it. The way she leaned, with her abdomen tilted out, was her natural way of standing. She still had good legs, despite the spidery blue veins she said came from carrying the weight of us kids inside her for nine months each. She also blamed us for her few gray hairs.

She mumbled something about "the silence before the storm" as I joined her at the window.

She must have been looking at the young man for a long time, pretending to watch the sky. He was standing by the bushes and the cockscombs. There was a flour sack on the ground beside him. I thought at first it might be filled with something he brought for the fair, but the way his hat sat on it and a pair of black boots stood beside it, I could tell it held his clothing, and that he was passing through Pickens on his way to or from some city.

"It's mighty quiet for the first day of fair," my mother said. She sounded far away. Her eyes were on the young stranger. She unrolled a curler and checked a strand of hair.

We talked about the weather and the sky, but we both watched the young man. In the deep blue of sky his white shirt stood out like a light. The low hills were fire-gold and leaden.

One of my mother's hands was limp against her thigh. The other moved down from the rollers and touched the green cloth at her chest, playing with a flaw in the fabric.

"Maybe it was the tornado," I said about the stillness in the air. The tornado had passed through a few days ago, touching down here and there. It exploded my cousin's house trailer, but it left his motorcycle standing beside it, untouched. "Tornadoes have no sense of value," my mother had said. "They are always taking away the saints and leaving behind the devils."

The young man stood in that semi-slumped, half-straight manner of fullblood Indians. Our blood was mixed like Heinz 57, and I always thought of purebloods as better than us. While my mother eyed his plain moccasins, she patted her rolled hair as if to put it in order. I was counting the small brown flowers in the blistered wallpaper, the way I counted ceiling tiles in the new school, and counted each step when I walked.

I pictured Aunt Moon inside her house up on my mother's shoulder. I imagined her dark face above the yellow oilcloth, her hands reflecting the yellow as they separated dried plants. She would rise slowly, as I'd seen her do, take a good long time to brush out her hair, and braid it once again. She would pet her dog, Mister, with long slow strokes while she prepared herself for the fair.

My mother moved aside, leaving the house suspended in the middle of the window, where it rested on a mound of land. My mother followed my gaze. She always wanted to know what I was thinking or doing. "I wonder," she said, "why in tarnation Bess's father built that house up there. It gets all the heat and wind."

I stuck up for Aunt Moon. "She can see everything from there, the whole town and everything."

"Sure, and everything can see her. A wonder she doesn't have ghosts."

I wondered what she meant by that, everything seeing Aunt Moon. I guessed by her lazy voice that she meant nothing. There was no cutting edge to her words.

"And don't call her Aunt Moon." My mother was reading my mind again, one of her many tricks. "I know what you're thinking," she would say when I thought I looked expressionless. "You are thinking about finding Mrs. Mark's ring and holding it for a reward."

I would look horrified and tell her that she wasn't even luke-warm, but the truth was that I'd been thinking exactly those thoughts. I resented my mother for guessing my innermost secrets. She was like God, everywhere at once knowing every-thing. I tried to concentrate on something innocent. I thought about pickles. I was safe; she didn't say a word about dills or sweets.

Bess, Aunt Moon, wasn't really my aunt. She was a woman who lived alone and had befriended me. I liked Aunt Moon and the way she moved, slowly, taking up as much space as she wanted and doing it with ease. She had wide lips and straight eyelashes.

Aunt Moon dried medicine herbs in the manner of her parents. She knew about plants, both the helpful ones and the ones that were poisonous in all but the smallest of doses. And she knew how to cut wood and how to read the planets. She told me why I was stubborn. It had to do with my being born in May. I believed her because my father was born a few days after me, and he was stubborn as all get out, even compared to me.

Aunt Moon was special. She had life in her. The rest of the women in town were cold in the eye and fretted over their husbands. I didn't want to be like them. They condemned the men for drinking and gambling, but even after the loudest quarrels, ones we'd overhear, they never failed to cook for their men. They'd cook platters of lard-fried chicken, bowls of mashed potatoes, and pitchers of creamy flour gravy.

Bess called those meals "sure death by murder."

Our town was full of large and nervous women with red spots on their thin-skinned necks, and we had single women who lived with brothers and sisters or took care of an elderly parent. Bess had comments on all of these: "They have eaten their anger and grown large," she would say. And there were the sullen ones who took care of men broken by the war, women who were hurt by the men's stories of death and glory but never told them to get on with living, like I would have done.

Bessie's own brother, J.D., had gone to the war and returned with softened, weepy eyes. He lived at the veterans hospital and he did office work there on his good days. I met him once and knew by the sweetness of his eyes that he had never killed anyone, but something about him reminded me of the lonely old shacks out on cotton farming land. His eyes were broken windows.

"Where do you think that young man is headed?" my mother asked.

Something in her voice was wistful and lonely. I looked at her face, looked out the window at the dark man, and looked back at my mother again. I had never thought about her from inside the skin. She was the mind reader in the family, but suddenly I knew how she did it. The inner workings of the mind were clear in her face, like words in a book. I could even feel her thoughts in the pit of my stomach. I was feeling embarrassed at what my mother was thinking when the stranger crossed the street. In front of him an open truck full of prisoners passed by. They wore large white shirts and pants, like immigrants from Mexico. I began to count the flowers in the wallpaper again, and the truckful of prisoners passed by, and when it was gone, the young man had also vanished into thin air.

Besides the young man, another thing I remember about the fair that year was the man in the bathroom. On the first day of the fair, the prisoners were bending over like great white sails, their black and brown hands stuffing trash in canvas bags. Around them the children washed and brushed their cows and raked fresh straw about their pigs. My friend Elaine and I escaped the dust-laden air and went into the women's public toilets, where we shared a stolen cigarette. We heard someone open the door, and we fanned the smoke. Elaine stood on the toilet seat so her sisters wouldn't recognize her shoes. Then it was silent, so we opened the stall and stepped out. At first the round dark man, standing by the door, looked like a woman, but then I noticed the day's growth of beard at his jawline. He wore a blue work shirt and a little straw hat. He leaned against the wall, his hand moving inside his pants. I grabbed Elaine, who was putting lipstick on her cheeks like rouge, and pulled her outside the door, the tube of red lipstick still in her hand.

Outside, we nearly collapsed by a trash can, laughing. "Did you see that? It was a man! A man! In the women's bathroom." She smacked me on the back.

We knew nothing of men's hands inside their pants, so we began to follow him like store detectives, but as we rounded a corner behind his shadow, I saw Aunt Moon walking away from the pigeon cages. She was moving slowly with her cane, through the path's sawdust, feathers, and sand.

"Aunt Moon, there was a man in the bathroom," I said, and then remembered the chickens I wanted to tell her about. Elaine ran off. I didn't know if she was still following the man or not, but I'd lost interest when I saw Aunt Moon.

"Did you see those chickens that lay the green eggs?" I asked Aunt Moon.

She wagged her head no, so I grabbed her free elbow and guided her past the pigeons with curly feathers and the turkeys with red wattles, right up to the chickens.

"They came all the way from South America. They sell for five dollars, can you imagine?" Five dollars was a lot for chickens when we were still recovering from the Great Depression, men were still talking about what they'd done with the CCC, and children still got summer complaint and had to be carried around crippled for months.

She peered into the cage. The eggs were smooth and resting in the straw. "I'll be" was all she said.

I studied her face for a clue as to why she was so quiet, thinking she was mad or something. I wanted to read her thoughts as easily as I'd read my mother's. In the strange light of the sky, her eyes slanted a bit more than usual. I watched her carefully. I looked at the downward curve of her nose and saw the young man reflected in her eyes. I turned around.

On the other side of the cage that held the chickens from Araucania was the man my mother had watched. Bess pretended to be looking at the little Jersey cattle in the distance, but I could tell she was seeing that man. He had a calm look on his face and his dark chest was smooth as oil where his shirt was opened. His eyes were large and black. They were fixed on Bess like he was a hypnotist or something magnetic that tried to pull Bess Evening toward it, even though her body stepped back. She did step back, I remember that, but even so, everything in her went forward, right up to him.

I didn't know if it was just me or if his presence charged the air, but suddenly the oxygen was gone. It was like the fire at the Fisher Hardware when all the air was drawn into the flame. Even the chickens clucked softly, as if suffocating, and the cattle were more silent in the straw. The pulse in everything changed.

I don't know what would have happened if the rooster hadn't crowed just then, but he did, and everything returned to normal. The rooster strutted and we turned to watch him.

Bessie started walking away and I went with her. We walked past the men and boys who were shooting craps in a cleared circle. One of them rubbed the dice between his hands as we were leaving, his eyes closed, his body's tight muscles willing a winning throw. He called me Lady Luck as we walked by. He said, "There goes Lady Luck," and he tossed the dice.

At dinner that evening we could hear the dance band tuning up in the makeshift beer garden, playing a few practice songs to the empty tables with their red cloths. They played "The Tennessee Waltz." For a while, my mother sang along with it. She had brushed her hair one hundred strokes and now she was talking and regretting talking all at the same time. "He was such a handsome man," she said. My father wiped his face with a handkerchief and rested his elbows on the table. He chewed and looked at nothing in particular. "For the longest time he stood there by the juniper bushes."

My father drank some coffee and picked up the newspaper. Mother cleared the table, one dish at a time and not in stacks like usual. "His clothes were neat. He must not have come from very far away." She moved the salt shaker from the end of the table to the center, then back again.

"I'll wash," I volunteered.

Mother said, "Bless you," and touched herself absently near the waist, as if to remove an apron. "I'll go get ready for the dance," she said.

My father turned a page of the paper.

The truth was, my mother was already fixed up for the dance. Her hair looked soft and beautiful. She had slipped into her new dress early in the day, "to break it in," she said. She wore nylons and she was barefoot and likely to get a runner. I would have warned her, but it seemed out of place, my warning. Her face was softer than usual, her lips painted to look full, and her eyebrows were much darker than usual.

"Do you reckon that young man came here for the rodeo?" She hollered in from the living room, where she powdered her nose. Normally she made up in front of the bathroom mirror, but the cabinet had been slammed and broken mysteriously one night during an argument so we had all taken to grooming ourselves in the small framed mirror in the living room.

I could not put my finger on it, but all the women at the dance that night were looking at the young man. It wasn't exactly that he was handsome. There was something else. He was alive in his whole body while the other men walked with great effort and stiffness, even those who did little work and were still young. Their male bodies had no language of their own in the way that his did. The women themselves seemed confused and lonely in the presence of the young man, and they were ridiculous in their behavior, laughing too loud, blushing like schoolgirls, or casting him a flirting eye. Even the older women were brighter than usual. Mrs. Tubby, whose face was usually as grim as the statue of General Pickens, the Cherokee hater, played with her necklace until her neck had red lines from the chain. Mrs. Tens twisted a strand of her hair over and over. Her sister tripped over a chair because she'd forgotten to watch where she was going.

The men, sneaking drinks from bottles in paper bags, did not notice any of the fuss.

Maybe it was his hands. His hands were strong and dark.

I stayed late, even after wives pulled their husbands away from their ball game talk and insisted they dance.

My mother and father were dancing. My mother smiled up into my father's face as he turned her this way and that. Her uneven skirt swirled a little around her legs. She had a run in her nylons, as I predicted. My father, who was called Peso by the townspeople, wore his old clothes. He had his usual look about him, and I noticed that faraway, unfocused gaze on the other men too. They were either distant or they were present but rowdy, embarrassing the women around them with the loud talk of male things: work and hunting, fights, this or that pretty girl. Occasionally they told a joke, like, "Did you hear the one about the traveling salesman?"

The dancers whirled around the floor, some tapping their feet, some shuffling, the women in new dresses and dark hair all curled up like in movie magazines, the men with new leather boots and crew cuts. My dad's rear stuck out in back, the way he danced. His hand clutched my mother's waist.

That night, Bessie arrived late. She was wearing a white dress with a full gathered skirt. The print was faded and I could just make out the little blue stars on the cloth. She carried a yellow shawl over her arm. Her long hair was braided as usual in the manner of the older Chickasaw women, like a wreath on her head. She was different from the others with her bright shawls. Sometimes she wore a heavy shell necklace or a collection of bracelets on her arm. They jangled when she talked with me, waving her hands to make a point. Like the time she told me that the soul is a small woman inside the eye who leaves at night to wander new places.

No one had ever known her to dance before, but that night the young man and Aunt Moon danced together among the artificial geraniums and plastic carnations. They held each other gently like two breakable vases. They didn't look at each other or smile the way the other dancers did; that's how I knew they liked each other. His large dark hand was on the small of her back. Her hand rested tenderly on his shoulder. The other dancers moved away from them and there was empty space all around them.

My father went out into the dark to smoke and to play a hand or two of poker. My mother went to sit with some of the other women, all of them pulling their damp hair away from their necks and letting it fall back again, or furtively putting on lipstick, fanning themselves, and sipping their beers.

"He puts me in the mind of a man I once knew," said Mrs. Tubby.

"Look at them," said Mrs. Tens. "Don't you think he's young enough to be her son?"

With my elbows on my knees and my chin in my hands, I watched Aunt Moon step and square when my mother loomed up like a shadow over the bleachers where I sat.

"Young lady," she said in a scolding voice. "You were supposed to go home and put the children to bed."

I looked from her stern face to my sister Susan, who was like a chubby angel sleeping beside me. Peso Junior had run off to the gambling game, where he was pushing another little boy around. My mother followed my gaze and looked at Junior. She put her hands on her hips and said, "Boys!"

My sister Roberta, who was twelve, had stayed close to the women all night, listening to their talk about the fullblood who had come to town for a rodeo or something and who danced so far away from Bessie that they didn't look friendly at all except for the fact that the music had stopped and they were still waltzing.

❖❖❖

Margaret Tubby won the prize money that year for the biggest pumpkin. It was 220.4 centimeters in circumference and weighed 190 pounds and had to be carried on a stretcher by the volunteer firemen. Mrs. Tubby was the town's chief social justice. She sat most days on the bench outside the grocery store. Sitting there like a full-chested hawk on a fence, she held court. She had watched Bess Evening for years with her sharp gold eyes. "This is the year I saw it coming," she told my mother, as if she'd just been dying for Bess to go wrong. It showed up in the way Bess walked, she said, that the woman was coming to a no good end just like the rest of her family had done.

"When do you think she had time to grow that pumpkin?" Mother asked as we escaped Margaret Tubby's court on our way to the store. I knew what she meant, that Mrs. Tubby did more time with gossip than with her garden.

Margaret was even more pious than usual at that time of year when the green tent revival followed on the heels of the fair, when the pink-faced men in white shirts arrived and, really, every single one of them was a preacher. Still, Margaret Tubby kept her prize money to herself and didn't give a tithe to any church.

With Bess Evening carrying on with a stranger young enough to be her son, Mrs. Tubby succeeded in turning the church women against her once and for all. When Bessie walked down the busy street, one of the oldest dances of women took place, for women in those days turned against each other easily, never thinking they might have other enemies. When Bess appeared, the women stepped away. They vanished from the very face of earth that was named Comanche Street. They disappeared into the Oklahoma redstone shops like swallows swooping into their small clay nests. The women would look at the new bolts of red cloth in Terwilligers with feigned interest, although they would never have worn red, even to a dog fight. They'd purchase another box of face powder in the five and dime, or drink cherry phosphates at the pharmacy without so much as tasting the flavor.

But Bessie was unruffled. She walked on in the empty mirage of heat, the sound of her cane blending in with horse hooves and the rhythmic pumping of oil wells out east.

At the store, my mother bought corn meal, molasses, and milk. I bought penny candy for my younger sisters and for Peso Junior with the money I earned by helping Aunt Moon with her remedies. When we passed Margaret Tubby on the way out, my mother nodded at her, but said to me, "That pumpkin grew fat on gossip. I'll bet she fed it with nothing but all-night rumors." I thought about the twenty-five-dollar prize money and decided to grow pumpkins next year.

My mother said, "Now don't you get any ideas about growing pumpkins, young lady. We don't have room enough. They'd crowd out the cucumbers and tomatoes."

My mother and father won a prize that year, too. For dancing. They won a horse lamp for the living room. "We didn't even know it was a contest," my mother said, free from the sin of competition. Her face was rosy with pleasure and pride. She had the life snapping out of her like hot grease, though sometimes I saw that life turn to a slow and restless longing, like when she daydreamed out the window where the young man had stood that day.

Passing Margaret's post and giving up on growing a two-hundred-pound pumpkin, I remembered all the things good Indian women were not supposed to do. We were not supposed to look into the faces of men. Or laugh too loud. We were not supposed to learn too much from books because that kind of knowledge was a burden to the soul. Not only that, it always took us away from our loved ones. I was jealous of the white girls who laughed as loud as they wanted and never had rules. Also, my mother wanted me to go to college no matter what anyone else said or thought. She said I was too smart to stay home and live a life like hers, even if the other people thought book learning would ruin my life.

Aunt Moon with her second sight and heavy breasts managed to break all the rules. She threw back her head and laughed out loud, showing off the worn edges of her teeth. She didn't go to church. She did a man's work, cared for animals, and chopped her own wood. The gossiping women said it was a wonder Bessie Evening was healthy at all and didn't have female problems—meaning with her body, I figured.

The small woman inside her eye was full and lonely at the same time.

Bess made tonics, remedies, and cures. The church women, even those who gossiped, slipped over to buy Bessie's potions at night and in secret. They'd never admit they swallowed the "snake medicine," as they called it. They'd say to Bess, "What have you got to put the life back in a man? My sister has that trouble, you know." Or they'd say, "I have a friend who needs a cure for the sadness." They bought remedies for fever and for coughing fits, for sore muscles and for sleepless nights.

Aunt Moon had learned the cures from her parents, who were said to have visited their own sins upon their children, both of whom were born out of wedlock from the love of an old Chickasaw man and a young woman from one of those tribes up north. Maybe a Navajo or something, the people thought.

But Aunt Moon had numerous talents and I respected them. She could pull cotton, pull watermelons, and pull babies with equal grace. She even delivered those scrub cattle, bred with Holsteins too big for them, caesarean. In addition to that, she told me the ways of the world and not just about the zodiac or fortune cards. "The United States is in love with death," she would say. "They sleep with it better than with lovers. They celebrate it on holidays, the Fourth of July, even in spring when they praise the loss of a good man's body."

She would tend her garden while I'd ask questions. What do you think about heaven? I wanted to know. She'd look up and then get back to pulling the weeds. "You and I both would just grump around up there with all those righteous people. Women like us weren't meant to live on golden streets. We're Indians," she'd say as she cleared out the space around a bean plant. "We're like these beans. We grew up from mud." And then she'd tell me how the people emerged right along with the crawdads from the muddy·female swamps of the land. "And what is gold anyway? Just something else that comes from mud. Look at the conquistadors." She pulled a squash by accident. "And look at the sad women of this town, old already and all because of gold." She poked a hole in the ground and replanted the roots of the squash. "Their men make money, but not love. They give the women gold rings, gold-rimmed glasses, gold teeth, but their skin dries up for lack of love. Their hearts are little withered raisins." I was embarrassed by the mention of making love, but I listened to her words.

❖❖❖

This is how I came to call Bessie Evening by the name of Aunt Moon: She'd been teaching me that animals and all life should be greeted properly as our kinfolk. "Good day, Uncle," I learned to say to the longhorn as I passed by on the road. "Good morning, cousins. Is there something you need?" I'd say to the sparrows. And one night when the moon was passing over Bessie's house, I said, "Hello, Aunt Moon. I see you are full of silver again tonight." It was so much like Bess Evening, I began to think, that I named her after the moon. She was sometimes full and happy, sometimes small and weak. I began saying it right to her ears: "Auntie Moon, do you need some help today?"

She seemed both older and younger than thirty-nine to me. For one thing, she walked with a cane. She had developed some secret ailment after her young daughter died. My mother said she needed the cane because she had no mortal human to hold her up in life, like the rest of us did.

But the other thing was that she was full of mystery and she laughed right out loud, like a Gypsy, my mother said, pointing out Bessie's blue-painted walls, bright clothes and necklaces, and all the things she kept hanging from her ceiling. She decorated outside her house, too, with bits of blue glass hanging from the trees, and little polished quartz crystals that reflected rainbows across the dry hills.

Aunt Moon had solid feet, a light step, and a face that clouded over with emotion and despair one moment and brightened up like light the next. She'd beam and say to me, "Sassafras will turn your hair red," and throw back her head to laugh, knowing full well that I would rinse my dull hair with sassafras that very night, ruining my mother's pans.

I sat in Aunt Moon's kitchen while she brewed herbals in white enamel pans on the woodstove. The insides of the pans were black from sassafras and burdock and other plants she picked. The kitchen smelled rich and earthy. Some days it was hard to breathe from the combination of woodstove heat and pollen from the plants, but she kept at it and her medicine for cramps was popular with the women in town.

Aunt Moon made me proud of my womanhood, giving me bags of herbs and an old eagle feather that had been doctored by her father back when people used to pray instead of going to church. "The body divines everything," she told me, and sometimes when I was with her, I knew the older Indian world was still here and I'd feel it in my skin and hear the night sounds speak to me, hear the voice of water tell stories about people who lived here before, and the deep songs came out from the hills.

One day I found Aunt Moon sitting at her table in front of a plate of untouched toast and wild plum jam. She was weeping. I was young and didn't know what to say, but she told me more than I could ever understand. "Ever since my daughter died," she told me, "my body aches to touch her. All the mourning has gone into my bones." Her long hair was loose that day and it fell down her back like a waterfall, almost to the floor.

After that I had excuses on the days I saw her hair loose. "I'm putting up new wallpaper today," I'd say, or "I have to help Mom can peaches," which was the truth.

"Sure," she said, and I saw the tinge of sorrow around her eyes even though she smiled and nodded at me.

Canning the peaches, I asked my mother what it was that happened to Aunt Moon's daughter.

"First of all," my mother set me straight, "her name is Bess, not Aunt Moon." Then she'd tell the story of Willow Evening. "That pretty child was the light of that woman's eye," my mother said. "It was all so fast. She was playing one minute and the next she was gone. She was hanging on to that wooden planter and pulled it right down onto her little chest."

My mother touched her chest. "I saw Bessie lift it like it weighed less than a pound—did I already tell you that part?"

All I had seen that day was Aunt Moon holding Willow's thin body. The little girl's face was already gone to ashes and Aunt Moon blew gently on her daughter's skin, even though she was dead, as if she could breathe the life back into her one more time. She blew on her skin the way I later knew that women blow sweat from lovers' faces, cooling them. But I knew nothing of any kind of passion then.

The planter remained on the dry grassy mound of Aunt Moon's yard, and even though she had lifted it, no one else, not even my father, could move it. It was still full of earth and dead geraniums, like a monument to the child.

"That girl was all she had," my mother said through the steam of boiling water. "Hand me the ladle, will you?"

The peaches were suspended in sweet juice in their clear jars. I thought of our lives—so short, the skin so soft around us that we could be gone any second from our living—thought I saw

Willow's golden brown face suspended behind glass in one of the jars.

❖❖❖

The men first noticed the stranger, Isaac, when he cleaned them out in the poker game that night at the fair. My father, who had been drinking, handed over the money he'd saved for the new bathroom mirror and took a drunken swing at the young man, missing him by a foot and falling on his bad knee. Mr. Tubby told his wife he lost all he'd saved for the barber shop business, even though everyone in town knew he drank it up long before the week of the fair. Mr. Tens lost his Mexican silver ring. It showed up later on Aunt Moon's hand.

Losing to one another was one thing. Losing to Isaac Cade meant the dark young man was a card sharp and an outlaw. Even the women who had watched the stranger all that night were sure he was full of demons.

The next time I saw Aunt Moon, it was the fallow season of autumn, but she seemed new and fresh as spring. Her skin had new light. Gathering plants, she smiled at me. Her cane moved aside the long dry grasses to reveal what grew underneath. Mullein was still growing, and holly.

I sat at the table while Aunt Moon ground yellow ochre in a mortar. Isaac came in from fixing the roof. He touched her arm so softly I wasn't sure she felt it. I had never seen a man touch a woman that way.

He said hello to me and he said, "You know those fairgrounds? That's where the three tribes used to hold sings." He drummed on the table, looking at me, and sang one of the songs. I said I recognized it, a song I sometimes dreamed I heard from the hill.

A red handprint appeared on his face, like one of those birthmarks that only show up in the heat or under the strain of work or feeling.

"How'd you know about the fairgrounds?" I asked him.

"My father was from here." He sat still, as if thinking himself into another time. He stared out the window at the distances that were in between the blue curtains.

I went back to Aunt Moon's the next day. Isaac wasn't there, so Aunt Moon and I tied sage in bundles with twine. I asked her about love.

"It comes up from the ground just like corn," she said. She pulled a knot tighter with her teeth.

Later, when I left, I was still thinking about love. Outside where Bess had been planting, black beetles were digging themselves under the turned soil, and red ants had grown wings and were starting to fly.

When I returned home, my mother was sitting outside the house on a chair. She pointed at Bess Evening's house. "With the man there," she said, "I think it best you don't go over to Bessie's house anymore."

I started to protest, but she interrupted. "There are no ands, ifs, or buts about it."

I knew it was my father who made the decision. My mother had probably argued my point and lost to him again, and lost some of her life as well. She was slowed down to a slumberous pace. Later that night as I stood by my window looking toward Aunt Moon's house, I heard my mother say, "God damn them all and this whole damned town."

"There now," my father said. "There now."

❖❖❖

"She's as dark and stained as those old black pans she uses," Margaret Tubby said about Bess Evening one day. She had come to pick up a cake from Mother for the church bake sale. I was angered by her words. I gave her one of those "looks could kill" faces, but I said nothing. We all looked out the window at Aunt Moon. She was standing near Isaac, looking at a tree. It leapt into my mind suddenly, like lightning, that Mrs. Tubby knew about the blackened pans. That would mean she had bought cures from Aunt Moon. I was smug about this discovery.

Across the way, Aunt Moon stood with her hand outstretched, palm up. It was filled with roots or leaves. She was probably teaching Isaac about the remedies. I knew Isaac would teach her things also, older things, like squirrel sickness and porcupine disease that I'd heard about from grandparents.

Listening to Mrs. Tubby, I began to understand why, right after the fair, Aunt Moon had told me I would have to fight hard to keep my life in this town. Mrs. Tubby said, "Living out of wedlock! Just like her parents." She went on, "History repeats itself."

I wanted to tell Mrs. Tubby a thing or two myself. "History, my eye," I wanted to say. "You're just jealous about the young man." But Margaret Tubby was still angry that her husband had lost his money to the stranger, and also because she probably still felt bad about playing with her necklace like a young girl that night at the fair. My mother said nothing, just covered the big caramel cake and handed it over to Mrs. Tubby. My mother looked like she was tired of fools and that included me. She looked like the woman inside her eye had just wandered off.

I began to see the women in Pickens as ghosts. I'd see them in the library looking at the stereopticons, and in the ice cream parlor. The more full Aunt Moon grew, the more drawn and pinched they became.

The church women echoed Margaret. "She's as stained as her pans," they'd say, and they began buying their medicines at the pharmacy. It didn't matter that their coughs returned and that their children developed more fevers. It didn't matter that some of them could not get pregnant when they wanted to or that Mrs. Tens grew thin and pale and bent. They wouldn't dream of lowering themselves to buy Bessie's medicines.

❖❖❖

My mother ran hot water into the tub and emptied one of her packages of bubble powder in it. "Take a bath," she told me. "It will steady your nerves."

I was still crying, standing at the window, looking out at Aunt Moon's house through the rain.

The heavy air had been broken by an electrical storm earlier that day. In a sudden crash, the leaves flew off their trees, the sky exploded with lightning, and thunder rumbled the earth. People went to their doors to watch. It scared me. The clouds turned green and it began to hail and clatter.

That was when Aunt Moon's old dog, Mister, ran off, went running like crazy through the town. Some of the older men saw him on the street. They thought he was hurt and dying because of the way he ran and twitched. He butted right into a tree and the men thought maybe he had rabies or something. They meant to put him out of his pain. One of them took aim with a gun and shot him, and when the storm died down and the streets misted over, everything returned to heavy stillness and old Mister was lying on the edge of the Smiths' lawn. I picked him up and carried his heavy body up to Aunt Moon's porch. I covered him with sage, like she would have done.

Bess and Isaac had gone over to Alexander that day to sell remedies. They missed the rain, and when they returned, they were happy about bringing home bags of beans, ground corn, and flour.

I guess it was my mother who told Aunt Moon about her dog.

That evening I heard her wailing. I could hear her from my window and I looked out and saw her with her hair all down around her shoulders like a black shawl. Isaac smoothed back her hair and held her. I guessed that all the mourning was back in her bones again, even for her little girl, Willow.

That night my mother sat by my bed. "Sometimes the world is a sad place," she said and kissed my hot forehead. I began to cry again.

"Well, she still has the burro," my mother said, neglecting to mention Isaac.

I began to worry about the burro and to look after it. I went over to Aunt Moon's against my mother's wishes, and took carrots and sugar to the gray burro. I scratched his big ears.

By this time, most of the younger and healthier men had signed up to go to Korea and fight for their country. Most of the residents of Pickens were mixed-blood Indians and they were even more patriotic than white men. I guess they wanted to prove that they were good Americans. My father left and we saw him off at the depot. I admit I missed him saying to me, "The trouble with you is you think too much." Old Peso, always telling people what their problems were. Margaret Tubby's lazy son had enlisted because, as his mother had said, "It would make a man of him," and when he was killed in action, the townspeople resented Isaac, Bess Evening's young man, even more since he did not have his heart set on fighting the war.

❖❖❖

Aunt Moon was pregnant the next year when the fair came around again, and she was just beginning to show. Margaret Tubby had remarked that Bess was visiting all those family sins on another poor child.

This time I was older. I fixed Mrs. Tubby in my eyes and I said, "Miss Tubby, you are just like history, always repeating yourself."

She pulled her head back into her neck like a turtle. My mother said, "Hush, Sis. Get inside the house." She put her hands on her hips. "I'll deal with you later." She almost added, "Just wait till your father gets home."

Later, I felt bad, talking that way to Margaret Tubby so soon after she lost her son.

Shortly after the fair, we heard that the young man inside Aunt Moon's eye was gone. A week passed and he didn't return. I watched her house from the window and I knew, if anyone stood behind me, the little house was resting up on my shoulder.

Mother took a nap and I grabbed the biscuits off the table and snuck out.

"I didn't hear you come in," Aunt Moon said to me.

"I didn't knock," I told her. "My mom just fell asleep. I thought it'd wake her up."

Aunt Moon's hair was down. Her hands were on her lap. A breeze came in the window. She must not have been sleeping and her eyes looked tired. I gave her the biscuits I had taken off the table. I lied and told her my mother had sent them over. We ate one.

Shortly after Isaac was gone, Bess Evening again became the focus of the town's women. Mrs. Tubby said, "Bessie would give you the shirt off her back. She never deserved a no good man who would treat her like dirt and then run off." Mrs. Tubby went over to Bess Evening's and bought enough cramp remedy from the pregnant woman to last her and her daughters for the next two years.

Mrs. Tens lost her pallor. She went to Bessie's with a basket of jellies and fruits, hoping in secret that Bess would return Mr. Tens's Mexican silver ring now that the young man was gone.

The women were going to stick by her; you could see it in their squared shoulders. They no longer hid their purchases of herbs. They forgot how they'd looked at Isaac's black eyes and lively body with longing that night of the dance. If they'd had dowsing rods, the split willow branches would have flown up to the sky, so much had they twisted around the truth of things and even their own natures. Isaac was the worst of men. Their husbands, who were absent, were saints who loved them. Every morning when my mother said her prayers and forgot she'd damned the town and everybody in it, I heard her ask for peace for Bessie Evening, but she never joined in with the other women who seemed happy over Bessie's tragedy.

Isaac was doubly condemned in his absence. Mrs. Tubby said, "What kind of fool goes off to leave a woman who knows about tea leaves and cures for diseases of the body and the mind alike? I'll tell you what kind, a card shark, that's what."

Someone corrected her. "Card *sharp*, dearie, not *shark*."

Who goes off and leaves a woman whose trees are hung with charming stones, relics, and broken glass, a woman who hangs sage and herbs to dry on her walls and whose front porch is full of fresh-cut wood? Those women, how they wanted to comfort her, but Bess Evening would only go to the door, leave them standing outside on the steps, and hand their herbs to them through the screen.

My cousins from Denver came for the fair. I was going to leave with them and get a job in the city for a year or so, then go on to school. My mother insisted she could handle the little ones alone now that they were bigger, and that I ought to go. It was best I made some money and learned what I could, she said.

"Are you sure?" I asked while my mother washed her hair in the kitchen sink.

"I'm sure as the night's going to fall." She sounded light-hearted, but her hands stopped moving and rested on her head until the soap lather began to disappear. "Besides, your dad will probably be home any day now."

I said, "Okay then, I'll go. I'll write you all the time." I was all full of emotion, but I didn't cry.

"Don't make promises you can't keep," my mother said, wrapping a towel around her head.

I went to the dance that night with my cousins, and out in the trees I let Jim Tens kiss me and promised him that I would be back. "I'll wait for you," he said. "And keep away from those city boys."

I meant it when I said, "I will."

He walked me home, holding my hand. My cousins were still at the dance. Mom would complain about their late city hours. Once she even told us that city people eat supper as late as eight o'clock P.M. We didn't believe her.

After Jim kissed me at the door, I watched him walk down the street. I was surprised that I didn't feel sad.

I decided to go to see Aunt Moon one last time. I was leaving at six in the morning and was already packed and I had taken one of each herb sample I'd learned from Aunt Moon, just in case I ever needed them.

I scratched the burro's gray face at the lot and walked up toward the house. The window was gold and filled with lamp-light. I heard an owl hooting in the distance and stopped to listen.

I glanced in the window and stopped in my tracks. The young man, Isaac, was there. He was speaking close to Bessie's face. He put his finger under her chin and lifted her face up to his. He was looking at her with soft eyes and I could tell there were many men and women living inside their eyes that moment. He held her cane across the back of her hips. With it, he pulled her close to him and held her tight, his hands on the cane pressing her body against his. And he kissed her. Her hair was down around her back and shoulders and she put her arms around his neck. I turned to go. I felt dishonest and guilty for looking in at them. I began to run.

I ran into the bathroom and bent over the sink to wash my face. I wiped Jim Tens's cold kiss from my lips. I glanced up to look at myself in the mirror, but my face was nothing, just shelves of medicine bottles and aspirin. I had forgotten the mirror was broken.

From the bathroom door I heard my mother saying her prayers, fervently, and louder than usual. She said, "Bless Sis's Aunt Moon and bless Isaac, who got arrested for trading illegal medicine for corn, and forgive him for escaping from jail."

She said this so loud, I thought she was talking to me. Maybe she was. Now how did she read my mind again? It made me smile, and I guessed I was reading hers.

All the next morning, driving through the deep blue sky, I thought how all the women had gold teeth and hearts like withered raisins. I hoped Jim Tens would marry one of the Tubby girls. I didn't know if I'd ever go home or not. I had Aunt Moon's herbs in my bag, and the eagle feather wrapped safe in a scarf. And I had a small, beautiful woman in my eye.

ROGER JACK

❖❖❖

The Pebble People

BEN ADAM sat outside his grandparents' weathered old loghouse.

He liked to sit outside and listen to the sounds of the forest. Especially after one of his grandma's famous chicken-and-dumpling dinners. And he liked to play one of his favorite games—making rocks war-dance. So he started looking for different-colored pebbles. Some were easily scraped off the surface of the well-worn path to the grandparents' loghouse, others he had to dig and scratch out of the earth.

Finally, he found the ones he wanted—black ones, white ones, red ones, yellow ones, and blue ones. Holding the pebbles on an open palm, Ben Adam talked to them. He spoke to the pebbles for a long time about the respect and discipline they should have while wearing the traditional clothing the Creator had given them. He talked of the symbols the old people said were in their dress. He spoke of how they should all try to conduct themselves with dignity. Ben Adam repeated the words of an uncle who had helped him dress for a war dance some time before.

After several moments of serious meditation, he placed the pebbles on the bottom of an overturned tin bucket, each according to its own size and color. He carefully placed the red, yellow, blue, white, and black pebbles into the circular grooves of the bucket in the formation of a bustle, the middlemost circle being the drum. Under his breath, he sang the ancient words of his favorite war dance song, but he didn't drum yet because he didn't want the dancers moved.

Ben Adam finished his silent song and again spoke to the pebbles. His message contained a prayer of thanksgiving that his people were alive to see another day and that they had chosen this day to come together in celebration of tribal customs. He thanked all the dancers, drummers, and spectators. He asked the Creator to bestow special blessings upon them throughout the evening and as they traveled back to their homes.

Ben Adam asked for blessings on behalf of people who were sick and could not attend the dance. He prayed for those imprisoned by steel bars and by personal weaknesses. And he asked the people to remember those people who had died since the last time they had gathered. Ben Adam's words were very well selected and delivered for an eight-year-old.

Following a moment of silence, he started singing a warm-up song. He drummed slowly on the bottom ridge of the battered old bucket and watched proudly as the pebbles began to dance. At first they moved slowly about the grooves of the bucket according to the rhythm of the song. "For this slow beat, the traditional dancers should be thankful," Ben Adam said.

The pace quickened. Ben Adam sang louder and drummed faster. The dancers hopped about fervently, like fancy dancers, their thunderous hoofbeats in tune with the drumming and their blurred colors lighting the air. Some of the pebbles began falling off the edge of the bucket to the ground. Ben Adam drummed and sang as long as there were some pebble dancers left.

After only a few were left, Ben Adam announced to them, "This will be a contest song!" He drummed faster and faster, harder and harder, until all the pebbles fell off the bucket. Then, carefully, he picked up those that were the last to fall. "Gee, that was a good contest," he said.

He thanked the dancers and said, "One day there will be a

big, big contest. Only those who are really good can come and participate in it." Ben Adam put the winning pebbles into marked jars to save. "The winners of the contest and my favorite dancers, I will take into the house and put away in my fishtank for the winter," he said to the pebble people.

MAURICE KENNY

❖❖❖

Wet Moccasins

SUPPER WAS COOKED and ready for the table when Mark came into the kitchen from work. He always enjoyed tuna fish casserole on fall evenings, and now the kitchen reeked of the scent of onions and peppers and the celery chopped and bubbling in the elbow macaroni and cream of mushroom soup. He sniffed the kitchen air, smiled and hung his tuke on the door peg. A husky man meant a husky eater, and the casserole dish was the largest in the cupboard. The kids were in school . . . Salli a sophomore at Oswego State and Danny a senior at Salmon River High. Dan that evening was off with friends, so the entire casserole was Mark's if he wanted to really gorge himself. Happily he marched off to washup in the bathroom, and it was time to put a salad together . . . a little lettuce, some late ripening tomatoes from the garden out back and a dressing. He and the kids preferred bottled French or ranch, but my old-fashioned tastes couldn't look at lettuce wilting under that sweetened gibberish called a dressing. What an insult to fresh vegetables. Oil and vinegar it was. Olive oil . . . a luxury, I know . . . in fact with some thyme and my personal favorite parsley and of course a good trouncing of garlic powder. With a side dish of peas and homemade banana bread-cake supper was completed, and I thought perfect for this late October evening meal. Behind me the bathroom door closed and I turned to observe Mark stroll leisurely through the kitchen his nose in the air like a beagle hound scenting game on the run. Foxy Mark took his place at the table, his elbows resting on the tablecloth, his plate forded between exposed flesh.

"I've always said your place is in the kitchen."

"Sexist."

He laughed big. Actually it was more like a howl.

"You howl like your hounds."

His laughter shook the table and the dishes rattled.

I poured water into two tumblers and purposely bumped against his shoulder.

"You should be a Mormon not a Mohawk. You could have three or four to cook and clean your kitchen."

"But they wouldn't know how to cook tuna fish casserole like you. They don't have tuna in Salt Lake."

"You know geography anyway." I couldn't keep a straight and serious face.

I carried the water pitcher back to the work table siding the sink. The outside view caught my eye and I stared out into the lowering night with early twilight coming down. Beyond the yard, clipped neatly by Danny, the apple tree, a translucent, seemed bare without those yellow apples hanging in the light. Picked. Some given to Mark's aging mother, some sauced and frozen, some in apple cake and many already in our deserving bellies. A clump of sumac, red berry tassels to the low horizon, stood firm against the background as though a fence to the yard. The leaves touched by autumn, maples reared up strong and tall beyond the sumac. Winter was out there somewhere. You could practically see it. Were the windows opened you could probably smell it on the night. Out of the corner of my eye I spotted something move. Probably Henna Tarbel's old grey cat hunting the last mice of summer. Maybe a skunk. Maybe . . . maybe a fox. There were lots of both burrowing the rez. Actually, it's kinda nice to think there are fox around the house and the old barn. I know. Fox take the chickens . . . but so do some house dogs. Nancy Montour lost lots of chickens this summer by her neighbor's sheep dog. Gave up smoking and the money she saved from cigarettes she bought chickens with. I buy her eggs. But foxes are such pretty things. Only a wolf is more magnificent, noble—my dad always said.

"Hey! We gonna eat. Or you gonna dream our supper to burn."

I turned with a big smile for my husky man.

"Just fox thinking."

"See one out there?"

"No. But I saw something move in the shadows. Probably that ol' grey cat."

Just then we heard Mark's hounds out back howl. A ferocious uproar as though a stranger walked through the yard.

"Henna's gonna raise hell again."

"She oughtta be happy. I've got those hounds to warn off any burglars."

"She isn't. You know how she goes to bed early."

"At six o'clock?"

"At six o'clock."

"Well, they'll quiet down in a second. Hey! Let's have some of that chow."

I looked across the yard again. Nothing stirring . . . not even a cat let alone a fox or skunk. In moments I had the salad and peas on the table. His dark face lit up like a Christmas tree when I placed the steaming casserole before him.

"You're the best, kid, the best. You know how to keep a man's belly happy."

"I try."

Mark's always enjoyed the news while eating supper. As I went to switch on the radio he called out . . .

"Turn the news on, would you, please."

"Please it is."

Some political nonsense in Albany with the governor as usual. A serial killing in Los Angeles. A defector from Russia. The sports . . .

"Hey! Oklahoma beat Nebraska . . . again."

"You're a real jock! I thought you wanted news."

By then I sat across the table from him. He took a huge portion of the casserole and shoved the dish toward me. With a mouthful of macaroni . . .

"Where's my son. I never seem to see him at the table any more."

"He's off with the Bentens. Lacrosse practice."

"He's good, isn't he?"

"He's good." I didn't need to assure Danny's father. He was confident in the lad's ability.

"Like his grandfather."

"Like his grandfather. Wait . . . yours or mine?"

"Both." How smart he is to patronize me.

The banter went back and forth across the table between forks of macaroni and peas. As I passed the salad bowl, Mark exclaimed. . . .

"OK. The NBA is safe. Now let's have some weather. What's tomorrow?"

"Sunny and crisp," I replied for the weather reporter.

"No, no, no. Not you. Him."

And at the stroke the reporter announced possible snow, possible sun and crispy air.

"I'll take the possible snow cover."

I was amazed. Mark really didn't like snow much. He was a summer person. Turtle Clan. He seemed always to actually enjoy not just summer itself but humid weather . . . moisture. True to a turtle.

"Feel the itch to hunt."

"Not my possible fox out back at the barn."

"No. Not your possible grey cat out back at the barn."

My husky eater taunted me. He enjoyed that like all upstanding Mohawk men. He had a comic or funny side. Could tell a good joke . . . not smut . . . and never forgot the punch line. Or made one up if he did. He was forty-five this November third. Held a minor position at the Tribal Council. Was a strong Traditionalist, a Longhouse man . . . would make a fine chief . . . I always thought, and gave us as good a living as he could.

Didn't drink. Didn't smoke, as both were non-traditional, and to the best of my knowledge didn't womanize. Of the latter I was particularly pleased. A mate knows. You know if the other is out doing what they shouldn't be doing. And he raised Salli and Danny the same. One reason why he's so proud Danny is really into Lacrosse and that Salli has taken up storytelling and art. Traditional. Gosh, how I missed him when he went to Viet Nam. It was horrible. Lonely. The kids are terrific and fun, but you can't go to sleep with the moonlight sitting on an empty pillow. He came home unscarred. Thank the Creator. Immediately went to work and commenced raising his family the way it should be raised.

"I'd like a little snow, a thin cover in the morning."

"Ohhhhh! Tomorrow's Saturday, isn't it. You've planned a hunt?"

"I'd like to with the boys."

"With the boys! You never ask me any more."

"That was when we were goin' around. I've got you here now. I don't have to take you to the woods any more to be with you. You're here."

"A . . ."

"Besides . . . I said before. Your place is in the kitchen."

"And cleaning, and making beds, and birthing your children, and ironing your shirts . . ."

"And gardening my vegetables, and picking my apples, and polishing my rifle."

"Never."

"I'd never let you."

"You don't think I could. Nor shoot."

"Nor shoot . . . either."

"Well, just let me go off tomorrow morning with you and I'll show you how I can bag home game. A deer, a quail, a moose if you want."

"Hey! Let's have spaghetti tomorrow night when I get home."

That's how he would end a discussion.

Actually he wasn't a sexist . . . or at least I never really considered him such, but . . . no; not really. As a traditionalist he couldn't be a sexist. Women had power with the people. Women made our chiefs, and took away the horns of power if the chief were delinquent, did not serve the people. Traditionally the women controlled the land, the garden and crop, the very house the men slept and ate in. No, he wasn't a sexist.

Munching down another mouthful of casserole he laughed so hard that he nearly lost his food off the fork.

How lucky can you be. He was near perfect. I thought of what his faults were. Well, yes, he did snore, loudly. Sneaked feet did have an odor. His paunch was gaining . . . a midline was developing . . . but then he was or is rather middle-age. What else. No, he did not like cutting the lawn. Against his traditional principles he claimed. Or laziness, I would barb. It should run wild . . . like kids. Naked and wild. Until it's six feet tall . . . like kids, I'd suggest. I couldn't wait for Danny to get big enough to mow the lawn. Must be other faults . . . someplace deep within the darkness of his being. What? Where? Not right, not normal for a man to be so pristine, exemplary. He didn't have any college like Salli. Neither of us did. Only high school. Some secretarial courses, a little business math. Certainly he wasn't brilliant . . . nor myself. But he could keep a checkbook balanced and as he always said . . . I know when to come in out of the rain so my moccasins don't get soaked. That was a warrior's oath. He was a warrior. And a hunter. A good one . . . both.

"Somethin' doing at the Longhouse tonight. Want to go?"

"A meeting?"

"Yes."

"Chiefs?"

"No, the community."

"I'll go with you tonight if you let me go with you hunting tomorrow."

To that I did not get an answer.

"Yeah! Spaghetti tomorrow night would be real nice."

We finished up supper with salad. I made coffee. He read the local paper.

"Good banana cake."

"Thanks."

"What did you do all day?"

"Went out and picked up hickory nuts. Made a little wild grape jam you like so much. That sort of thing."

"Oh! In other words a simple day. A nothing day." He laughed.

"A nothing day. Hey, you forget all the other things I have to get done in this house. Which I won't name."

"You're the best. The best. I've always said so."

"Thanks."

❖❖❖

We rose early. It had turned cold during the night. The morning sun was hazed but a sheen beamed off the roof of the barn. Looking out the bedroom window on rising, saw a thin cover of snow or frost. We were close enough to the mountains where winter truly comes early in the fall that cold winds could rush down from the Adirondacks and also up the river. Mark was still asleep. His thick black hair hung over his closed eyes. I stared. I was always fond of staring at him. He probably wasn't but I always thought of him as the handsomest man I had ever known. Good eyes. Still very good hair . . . not a strand lost yet. Good mouth. I reached out and touched his shoulder with my fingers. He stirred. Groaned a little. Rolled over. I touched his shoulders again and gave a slight shove, or push.

"Want some cold water on your face! Get up!"

"Go away."

Like Danny it was always hard, difficult for him to get up. Even when he had something to do he enjoyed.

"I'm going for the cold water."

Instantly he shot up like an arrow.

"All right, all right. I'm up."

Not long after we sat at the table having breakfast. Hot black coffee was on the table. Pancakes on the griddle. Syrup from maple trees out back and strawberry jam from last summer for his toast were there as well. As I now stood at the window pouring bacon drippings into an old soup can for future flavoring of some meal, or other, I noticed brown grass prickle up through the slight snow cover. There were tracks on the snow. Too far off for me to distinguish what creature had made the tracks. They were animal not human. I heard Danny call down from his room over the kitchen . . . "Coffee ready?" His father responded, "Get out of bed before I put a skirt on you." I giggled a little. That would be the last thing on earth Mark would ever do to his son. But it was an old reference back to the tribal days of the Iroquois/Mohawks when a man would not war or hunt. He was aproned or skirted and made a woman for life and never allowed to hunt or war again. About to turn back to the table, my glance caught a stirring in the low peonies/brush. An animal? Too much of a stir for a mouse, or wood rat. My fox? No, the grey cat. A porcupine?

"I'm going now."

"Without Danny."

"If he doesn't hurry. I'll start the car. Wrap him a cold pancake."

The boy stood in the kitchen doorway. Handsome as his father. Handsome as all heroes must be.

"Cold pancake like fun. I want a real hunter's breakfast."

"Then get it in the woods like all hunters should."

"Ma, you're a poet. It rhymes."

"Hurry up, Dan. Get something down fast. We got a date with the game."

Again my eyes were attracted to the window. There is something out there. A crippled bird? A strange puppy? I couldn't see that well in the peonies. Long past bloom and leaf, the leaves hung down in a wide spray, thick and yellowing. And the sunshine hit them just correctly so that view was impaired.

"Bye."

He was gone out the door. Danny behind him munching a cold pancake and gripping some cold but greasy bacon. I could hear his Datsun motor start, chug chug, sputter and then move down out of the driveway. He tooted his horn good-bye as he did every time he left the yard . . . a kind of kiss. Mark was not demonstrative. Passionate . . . well, at the right time, but not kissy . . . especially in front of others including the kids. It wasn't Mohawk. It wasn't male. Nor women going hunting . . . wasn't male. Wasn't Mohawk. Well, I certainly had other thoughts about that. There it was again. The peony leaves rustled soundless. Some creature had burrowed there. Not a puppy. Certainly. A skunk? A chipmunk? I turned my thoughts to the breakfast dishes. But before I could go collect the dirty plates and coffee mugs once more the thing stirred in the thick leaves. I could make out though barely a nose and a pair of lustrous eyes. Not a cat. Nor a puppy and definitely not fox or skunk. I was glued, naturally. Absolutely glued. Curiosity might have killed the cat. But confirmation brought it back. Something like that. Actually I think I was prepared to spend my entire day at the window until I could find out just what or who that creature was. To heck with the dishes. The dirty floor. Cooking Mark's spaghetti supper or whatever else I might have had to do in the house that morning. There. There . . . it moved again. A tiny ear slipped out from under the leaves.

"You rascal you."

❖❖❖

Mark has several shot guns. He probably took the twenty-two. The gun closet was in the hallway by the stairwell. No, no. He didn't. He took the high caliber 30.06 by mistake. That was his deer gun. I knew enough about hunting to know what gun was what gun. My grandfather, my father, Mark and my Dan all had guns around me all my life. I lifted the rifle from the closet. Odd. Mark had left it loaded. Very unusual. He had a law: no loaded guns in the house. We had children. Maybe Danny had loaded it and left it there. It came easily out the darkness of the closet. The barrel shining as light struck the black metal. Mark kept his guns clean and well oiled. Not a fingerprint to be found any place. In my own house, my own house, I crept down the hall back into the kitchen. The sun had melted the wisp of snow that had fallen on the grass. Now, truly it was brown and short. Growth had ceased for the year. Not until spring would it sprout green again. I'd wait.

I jumped out of my skin. Someone knocked on the front door. I didn't hear a car pull up. It must be Henna coming over to complain on the hounds. They were gone. Mark and Danny took them. They couldn't hunt without their beagles. Another knock. It must be Henna, or Peg Loy from down the road stopping for coffee. Maybe Jack, her husband, went hunting, too. I couldn't leave the window. It was too important. Utterly important. Henna could come back. Peg knew her way in. I'll shush her the moment she puts a foot on the kitchen floor. There it was. Finally. Big as all outdoors. Big as life. One of the biggest I've ever seen. I raised the window as quietly as I could. The sash went up slowly. I was most thankful Mark was a good man. Took excellent care of his things, especially his house and the windows. Like it was greased with bacon fat drippings, the sash rose. I took aim and fired.

❖❖❖

The men arrived back home at the house around five-fifteen. Their game bag was empty.

"I can't smell spaghetti!"

"No," I replied nonchalantly. As though I didn't give a darn about spaghetti.

"Supper's on, Dan. Not spaghetti!"

"No, not spaghetti."

He walked guiltily to the stove. Lifted the cover on a boiling pot.

"Potatoes," he shrilly exclaimed.

"I didn't promise you spaghetti. I expected to cook your game. And by the by, where is it. Your bag looks pretty limp."

"Well, it is. Ol' Daisey ran into a porky. Full of quills. James jumped into a creek and wrenched his front left paw. No dogs. No game. We stalked the woods without them. No game. And no spaghetti."

"What are we having?"

"Look in the oven."

"Dad, I smell powder. Ma, did you have a fire in here while we were gone?"

"In a word . . . you might say."

By then Mark was at the oven. He pulled the sprung door down and stared in.

"Holy jeeosaphat."

"That's right. My game bag is full. My moccasins are dry."

"Dan! A rabbit! Where the heck did you get a rabbit?"

"I shot it with your gun out in the backyard. You remember that grey cat you said was walking last night out back? Well, it wasn't."

THOMAS KING

❖❖❖

A Seat in the Garden

OE HOVAUGH settled into the garden on his knees and began pulling at the wet, slippery weeds that had sprung up between the neat rows of beets. He trowled his way around the zucchini and up and down the lines of carrots, and he did not notice the big Indian at all until he stopped at the tomatoes, sat back, and tried to remember where he had set the ball of twine and the wooden stakes.

The big Indian was naked to the waist. His hair was braided and wrapped with white ermine and strips of red cloth. He wore a single feather held in place by a leather band stretched around his head, and, even though his arms were folded tightly across his chest, Joe could see the glitter and flash of silver and turquoise on each finger.

"If you build it, they will come," said the big Indian.

Joe rolled forward and shielded his eyes from the morning sun.

"If you build it, they will come," said the big Indian again.

"Christ sakes," Joe shouted. "Get the hell out of the corn, will ya!"

"If you build it . . ."

"Yeah, yeah. Hey! This is private property. You people ever hear of private property?"

". . . they will come."

Joe struggled to his feet and got his shovel from the shed. But when he got back to the garden, the big Indian was gone.

"All right!" Joe shouted, and drove the nose of the shovel into the ground. "Come out of that corn!"

The cornstalks were only about a foot tall. Nevertheless, Joe walked each row, the shovel held at the ready, just in case the big Indian tried to take him by surprise.

❖❖❖

When Red Mathews came by in the afternoon, Joe poured him a cup of coffee and told him about the big Indian and what he had said. Red told Joe that he had seen the movie.

"Wasn't a movie, Red, damn it. It was a real Indian. He was just standing there in the corn."

"You probably scared him away."

"You can't let them go standing in your garden whenever they feel like it."

"That's the truth."

❖❖❖

The next day, when Joe came out to the garden to finish staking the tomatoes, the big Indian was waiting for him. The man looked as though he were asleep, but as soon as he saw Joe, he straightened up and crossed his arms on his chest.

"You again!"

"If you build it . . ."

"I'm going to call the police. You hear me. The police are going to come and haul you away."

". . . they will come."

Joe turned around and marched back into the house and phoned the RCMP, who said they would send someone over that very afternoon.

"Afternoon? What am I supposed to do with him until then? Feed him lunch?"

The RCMP officer told Joe that it might be best if he stayed in his house. There was the chance, the officer said, that the big Indian might be drunk or on drugs, and if that were the case, it was better if Joe didn't antagonize him.

"He's walking on my corn. Does that mean anything to you?"

The RCMP officer assured Joe that it meant a great deal to him, that his wife was a gardener, and he knew how she would feel if someone walked on her corn.

"Still," said the officer, "it's best if you don't do anything."

What Joe did do was to call Red, and when Red arrived, the big Indian was still in the garden waiting.

"Wow, he's a big sucker, all right," said Red. "You know, he looks a little like Jeff Chandler."

"I called the police, and they said not to antagonize him."

"Hey, there are two of us, right?"

"That's right," said Joe.

"You bet it's right."

Joe got the shovel and a hoe from the shed, and he and Red wandered out into the garden, as if nothing were wrong.

"He's watching us," said Red.

"Don't step on the tomatoes," said Joe.

Joe walked around the zucchini, casually dragging the shovel behind him. Red ambled through the beets, the hoe slung over his shoulder.

"If you build it, they will come," the Indian said.

"Get him!" shouted Joe. And before Red could do anything, Joe was charging through the carrots, the shovel held out in front like a lance.

"Wait a minute, Joe," yelled Red, the hoe still on his shoulder. But Joe was already into the tomatoes. He was closing on the big Indian, who hadn't moved, when he stepped on the bundle of wooden stakes and went down in a heap.

"Hey," said Red. "You okay?"

Red helped Joe to his feet, and when the two men looked around, the big Indian was gone.

"Where'd he go," said Joe.

"Beats me," said Red. "What'd you do to get him so angry?"

Red helped Joe to the house, wrapped an ice pack on his ankle, and told him to put his leg on the chair.

"I saw a movie a couple of years back about a housing development that was built on top of an ancient Indian burial mound," Red said.

"I would have got him, if I hadn't tripped."

"They finally had to get an authentic medicine man to come in and appease the spirits."

"Did you see the look on his face when he saw me coming?"

"And you should have seen some of those spirits."

❖❖❖

When the RCMP arrived, Joe showed the officer where the Indian had stood, how he had run at him with the shovel, and how he had stumbled over the bundle of stakes.

After Joe got up and brushed himself off, the RCMP officer asked him if he recognized the big Indian.

"Not likely," said Joe. "There aren't any Indians around here."

"Yes, there are," said Red. "Remember those three guys who come around on weekends every so often."

"The old winos?" said Joe.

"They have that grocery cart, and they pick up cans."

"They don't count."

"They sit down there by the hydrangea and crush the cans and eat their lunch. Sometimes they get to singing."

"You mean drink their lunch."

"Well, they could have anything in that bottle."

"Most likely Lysol."

The RCMP officer walked through the garden with Joe and Red and made a great many notes. He shook hands with both men and told Joe to call him if there was any more trouble.

"Did you ever wonder," said Red, after the officer left, "just what he wants you to build or who 'they' are?"

"I suppose you saw a movie."

"Maybe we should ask the Indians."

"The drunks?"

"Maybe they could translate for us."

"The guy speaks English."

"That's right, Joe. God, this gets stranger all the time. Ed Ames, that's who he reminds me of."

❖❖❖

On Saturday morning, when Joe and Red walked out on the porch, the big Indian was waiting patiently for them in the corn. They were too far away to hear him, but they could see his mouth moving.

"Okay," said Red. "All we got to do is wait for the Indians to show up."

They showed up around noon. One Indian had a green knapsack. The other two pushed a grocery cart in front of them. It was full of cans and bottles. They were old, Joe noticed, and even from the porch, he imagined he could smell them. They walked to a corner of the garden behind the hydrangea where the sprinklers didn't reach. It was a dry, scraggly wedge that Joe had never bothered to cultivate. As soon as the men stopped the cart and sat down on the ground, Red got to his feet and stretched.

"Come on. Can't hurt to talk with them. Grab a couple of beers, so they know we're friendly."

"A good whack with the shovel would be easier."

"Hey, this is kind of exciting. Don't you think this is kind of exciting."

"I wouldn't trip this time."

When Joe and Red got to the corner, the three men were busy crushing the cans. One man would put a can on a flat stone and the second man would step on it. The third man picked up the crushed can and put it in a brown grocery bag. They were older than Joe had thought, and they didn't smell as bad as he had expected.

"Hi," said Red. "That's a nice collection of cans."

"Good morning," said the first Indian.

"Getting pretty hot," said the second Indian.

"You fellows like a drink," said the third Indian, and he took a large glass bottle out of the knapsack.

"No thanks," said Red. "You fellows like a beer?"

"Lemon water," said the third Indian. "My wife makes it without any sugar so it's not as sweet as most people like."

"How can you guys drink that stuff?" said Joe.

"You get used to it," said the second Indian. "And it's better for you than pop."

As the first Indian twisted the lid off the bottle and took a long drink, Joe looked around to make sure none of his neighbors were watching him.

"I'll bet you guys know just about everything there is to know about Indians," said Red.

"Well," said the first Indian, "Jimmy and Frank are Nootka and I'm Cree. You guys reporters or something?"

"Reporters? No."

"You never know," said the second Indian. "Last month, a couple of reporters did a story on us. Took pictures and everything."

"It's good that these kinds of problems are brought to the public's attention," said Red.

"You bet," said the third Indian. "Everyone's got to help. Otherwise there's going to be more garbage than people."

Joe was already bored with the conversation. He looked back to see if the big Indian was still there.

"This is all nice and friendly," said Joe. "But we've got a problem that we were hoping you might be able to help us with."

"Sure," said the first Indian. "What's the problem?"

Joe snapped the tab on one of the beers, took a long swig, and jerked his thumb in the direction of the garden. "I've got this big Indian who likes to stand in my garden."

"Where?" asked the second Indian.

"Right there," said Joe.

"Right where?" asked the third Indian.

"If you build it, they will come," shouted the big Indian.

"There, there," said Joe. "Did you hear that?"

"Hear what?" said the first Indian.

"They're embarrassed," said Red under his breath. "Let me handle this."

"This is beginning to piss me off," said Joe, and he took another pull on the beer.

"We were just wondering," Red began. "If you woke up one day and found a big Indian standing in your cornfield and all he would say was, 'if you build it, they will come,' what would you do?"

"I'd stop drinking," said the second Indian, and the other two Indians covered their faces with their hands.

"No, no," said Red. "That's not what I mean. Well . . . you see that big Indian over there in the cornfield, don't you?"

The Indians looked at each other, and then they looked at Joe and Red.

"Okay," said the first Indian. "Sure, I see him."

"Oh yeah," said the second Indian. "He's right there, all right. In the . . . beets?"

"Corn," said Joe.

"Right," said the third Indian. "In the corn. I can see him, too. Clear as day."

"That's our problem," said Red. "We think maybe he's a spirit or something."

"No, we don't," said Joe.

"Yes, we do," said Red, who was just getting going. "We figure he wants us to build something to appease him so he'll go away."

"Sort of like . . . a spirit?" said the first Indian.

"Hey," said the second Indian, "remember that movie we saw about that community that was built . . ."

"That's the one," said Red. "What we have to figure out is what he wants us to build. You guys got any ideas?"

The three Indians looked at each other. The first Indian looked at the corn field. Then he looked at Joe and Red.

"Tell you what," he said. "We'll go over there and talk to him and see what he wants. He looks . . . Cree. You guys stay here, okay?"

Joe and Red watched as the three Indians walked into the garden. They stood together facing the beets.

"Hey," shouted Joe. "You guys blind? He's behind you."

The first Indian waved his hand and smiled, and the three men turned around. Red could see them talking, and he tried to watch their lips, but he couldn't figure out what they were saying. After a while, the Indians waved at the rows of carrots and came back over to where Joe and Red were waiting.

"Well," said Red. "Did you talk to him?"

"Yes," said the first Indian. "You were right. He is a spirit."

"I knew it!" shouted Red. "What does he want?"

The first Indian looked back to the cornfield. "He's tired of standing, he says. He wants a place to sit down. But he doesn't want to mess up the garden. He says he would like it if you would build him a . . . a . . . bench right about . . . here."

"A bench?" said Joe.

"That's what he said."

"So he can sit down?"

"He gets tired standing."

"The hell you say."

"Do you still see him?" asked the second Indian.

"You blind? Of course I still see him."

"Then I'd get started on the bench right away," said the third Indian.

"Come on, Red," said Joe, and he threw the empty beer can into the hydrangea and opened the other one. "We got to talk."

❖❖❖

Joe put the pad of paper on the kitchen table and drew a square. "This is the garden," he said. "These are the carrots. These are the beets. These are the beans. And this is the corn. The big Indian is right about here."

"That's right," said Red. "But what does it mean?"

"Here's where those winos crush their cans and drink their Lysol," Joe continued, marking a spot on the pad and drawing a line to it.

"Lemon water."

"You listening?"

"Sure."

"If you draw lines from the house to where the big Indian stands and from there to where the winos crush their cans and back to the house . . . Now do you see it?"

"Hey, that's pretty good, Joe."

"What does it remind you of?"

"A bench?"

"No," said Joe. "A triangle."

"Okay, I can see that."

"And if you look at it like this, you can see clearly that the winos and the big Indian are there, and the house where you and I are is here."

"What if you looked at it this way, Joe," said Red, and he turned the paper a half turn to the right. "Now the house is there and the old guys and the big Indian are here."

"That's not the way you look at it. That's not the way it works."

"Does that mean we're not going to build the bench?"

"It's our battle plan."

"A bench might be simpler," said Red.

"I'll attack him from the house along this line. You take him from the street along that line. We'll catch him between us."

"I don't know that this is going to work."

"Just don't step on the tomatoes."

The next morning, Red waited behind the hydrangea. He was carrying the hoe and a camera. Joe crouched by the corner of the house with the shovel.

"Charge!" yelled Joe, and he broke from his hiding place and lumbered across the lawn and into the garden. Red leapt through the hydrangea and struggled up the slight incline to the cornfield.

"If you build it, they will come," shouted the Indian.

"Build it yourself," shouted Joe, and he swung the shovel at the big Indian's legs. Red, who was slower, stopped at the edge of the cornfield to watch Joe whack the Indian with his shovel and to take a picture, so he saw Joe and his shovel run right through the Indian and crash into compost mound.

"Joe, Joe . . . you all right? God, you should have seen it. You ran right through that guy. Just like he wasn't there. I got a great picture. Wait till you see the picture. Just around the eyes, he looks a little like Sal Mineo."

Red helped Joe back to the house and cleaned the cuts on Joe's face. He wrapped another ice pack on Joe's ankle and then drove down to the one-hour photo store and turned the film in. By the time he got back to the house, Joe was standing on the porch, leaning on the railing.

"You won't believe it, Joe," said Red. "Look at this."

Red fished a photograph out of the pack. It showed Joe and the shovel in mid-swing plunging through the corn. The colors were brilliant.

Joe looked at the photograph for a minute and then he looked at the cornfield. "Where's the big Indian?"

"That's just it. He's not there."

"Christ!"

"Does that mean we're going to build the bench?"

❖❖❖

The bench was a handsome affair with a concrete base and a wooden seat. The Indians came by the very next Saturday with their knapsack and grocery cart, and Red could tell that they were impressed.

"Boy," said the first Indian, "that's a good-looking bench."

"You think this will take care of the problem?" asked Red.

"That Indian still in the cornfield?" said the second Indian.

"Of course he's still there," said Joe. "Can't you hear him?"

"I don't know," said the third Indian, and he twisted the lid off the bottle and took a drink. "I don't think he's one of ours."

"What should we do?"

"Don't throw your cans in the hydrangea," said the first Indian. "It's hard to get them out. We're not as young as we used to be."

❖❖❖

Joe and Red spent the rest of the day sitting on the porch, drinking beer, and watching the big Indian in the garden. He looked a little like Victor Mature, Red thought, now that he had time to think about it, or maybe Anthony Quinn, only he was taller. And there was an air about the man that made Red believe —believe with all his heart—that he had met this Indian before.

JUDITH MINTY

❖❖❖

Killing the Bear

SHE HAS STRUNG the hammock between two birch trees at the edge of the clearing. Now she drifts in and out of the light there and drowsily studies the pattern made by the rope's weaving and the flickering leaves.

When she had the dog, he stretched out beneath the hammock. Hackles raised, growling and nipping at flies, he'd meant to save her from shadows. In truth, he startled at noises, even at shifts in the wind, and she ended up more his protector than the other way around.

❖❖❖

There were wolves at the little zoo when she was a child. She heard them howling from her aunt's kitchen and went to see them up close.

And a bear.

Three times she visited, slowly circling the bear pen, but he was always sleeping. He looked like a bundle of clothes by the dead tree. His fence was electrified and posted with signs, and she was afraid to touch the iron bars.

The wolves set off a chorus of neighborhood dogs. Their calling floated back and forth all that summer vacation.

❖❖❖

She lies in the hammock every afternoon, her life in the rhythm of the woods. Up at dawn to the shrill pitch of bluejays. Logs tossed into the stove, match lit, breath steaming in the cabin's chill. Trip to the outhouse, coffee perking, bucket of water from the river. The rest of the morning, ping of nails driven into boards. Her porch is nearly done. One room and another room. Something inside and something out.

The afternoon silence and the sway of the hammock lull her and when she hears a low gutteral, she thinks, at first, it is the dog. Then she remembers the dog is gone.

She struggles to sit up and makes the hammock sway crazily.

A bear stands beyond the pines—small jets of eyes, heavy black coat. He snuffles, then drops on all fours and weaves into the forest.

Her hands lift to cover her breasts.

❖❖❖

Her favorite doll was a stuffed animal and she slept with it close to her heart. She was nine when her mother said, "Give me your bear for three months. Let's see if you can stop sucking your thumb."

She tried very hard to stop, and when the time was up, she asked for the bear again.

Her mother said, "Another month."

One day, as she sat in the kitchen watching a cake being stirred and poured into the pan and then put into the oven, it came to her that her bear was gone, that it had been thrown down the incinerator.

Only a few years ago, her mother told her, misspeaking even then, "I'm sorry for burning the animal in you."

Her hammer has stopped its thump and echo. The roof is laid. The porch smells of fresh paint. She has hauled the old sofa out and can sit there in the evenings, if she wants.

When the bear understood that she was alone, he came closer. The first time, she was reading in the hammock and heard something like a sigh. She knew it was him, even before she caught a glimpse of black gliding through the woods. The next time, he was so close she smelled him—a terrible, rancid odor. Without looking, she swung out of the hammock and walked to the cabin. Two days later, he stood next to the birch tree, breath rattling his throat. If she'd turned, she could have touched the bristles on his shoulder.

◆◆◆

The Gilyak tribe honored him. They put his head on a stake outside their doors and made offerings to it. On Yezo Island, the Ainus thought he was a man trapped inside the body of a bear. If a hunter found a cub, he brought it to his wife who suckled it.

In Lapland he was King of Beasts. The men lived alone, purifying themselves, for three days after the hunt. At the funeral, after they had feasted, they put his bones back together in the ground.

Once she spent an evening with two Swedes. At dinner, their wineglasses held the tint of leaves. Ole, the painter, said, "You live in green light." Gunnar told magic tales. "When a woman meets a bear in the woods, she must lift her skirt. Then he will let her pass."

◆◆◆

In the travelogue about Alaska, the Kodiak caught a salmon, his claws stretched out like fingers. When the second bear approached, he reared up. He looked soft and gentle, as if he were greeting a friend, until, with a sweep of his paw, he split open the head of the other.

In college, a classmate told about the summer he'd worked at Yellowstone and got too close. He never felt the nick, only knew when blood trickled down his forehead.

There was also the news story about the woman dragged from her tent in the middle of the night, crying, "He's killing me. Oh God, he's killing me." The bear carried the woman away, his claws tangled in her hair, ripping at her arm.

❖❖❖

When she drove to town for supplies, she bought a secondhand rifle. She keeps it loaded now, propped against the doorjamb inside the cabin.

The clerk at the hardware store showed her how to fire it, how to aim along the sights. He winked and told her she could get a man with it at twenty yards. She said she didn't need a man, just wanted to do some hunting.

She misses the dog. She carries the gun awkwardly over her shoulder when she goes to the woodpile, or to the river.

❖❖❖

Her calendar hangs on the cabin wall, each day of summer marked with an X, the rest of the year clean and open. She turns up the wick on the lamp and starts to brush her hair, staring at her reflection in the windowpane.

She is thinking about leaving. She is thinking about driving out of the clearing.

When the scream begins, it breaks against the walls. It shudders in a moan, then rises. Everything, even the wind, holds its breath.

It is over so quickly she almost believes it didn't happen and raises the brush again, and barely recognizes herself in the glass. She runs to the lamp and blows out the flame, then to the window, hoping she will not see what must be there.

❖❖❖

She did not shoot cleanly the first time. When he ripped the screen and tore the siding loose, she stood on the porch, gun leveled.

"Go away."

He was no more than ten feet from her when she fired. He spun around and fell to the ground, then raised himself up.

When she realized she had only wounded him, she ran into

the cabin and turned the lock and leaned against the door. She could hear him thrashing and bellowing in the bushes and against the trees.

She knew she would have to step onto the porch again, go to the ripped screen, with nothing but night air between them. She would have to take aim and shoot again. And if that didn't stop him, she would have to slip the bolt and reload the rifle and stand there and shoot him again until he stopped bawling and weeping and falling down and getting up and lurching against the trees.

When they began this, she never thought she would have to kill him so slow. She never dreamed she would have to hurt him so much.

It is nearly dawn when he dies, when she gets up from her chair, when his groans stop pricking her skin. She takes the flashlight and goes out on the porch. She shines the beam around in the gray light and sees the blood dried on the new screen and on the fresh-painted sill and spattered on the leaves around the cabin. She sees the trampled bushes and broken branches and where he crawled into the weeds.

She shines the arc out, light bouncing on tree and log, until it lands on a black heap, huddled in the middle of the clearing.

As soon as the sun rises, she begins to dig, and by midafternoon she is through with it—the rope tied to him, the car backed up to the hole, the rifle and box of ammunition remembered and dropped in next to him, the musty soil put back, and branches over that.

Then she bathes with the last of the water from the river and sweeps the cabin floor, thinking that rain will wash away the blood and that, soon enough, snow will fall and cover it all.

It is dark when she gets to the state line. Next summer, she will dig him up to take the claws.

N. SCOTT MOMADAY

❖❖❖

She is Beautiful in Her Whole Being

A REMARKABLE CHANGE came upon Grey, almost at once. She stood and moved and talked differently. Here, in her mother's home, she assumed an attitude of deep propriety, dignity. With Set she could still tease and joke and whisper words in her old diction, but now she spoke quietly, in a plain and simple way, and her language was made of rhythms and silences that he had not heard before. She put on the bright blouses and long pleated skirts of her mother's people. She combed out her long black hair and fashioned it in the old way, in a queue wrapped with white twine at the back of her head, and she adorned herself with silver and turquoise, old, simple pieces. She wore no makeup, except a pollen on her forehead and cheeks, which after days shone faintly, as from within, an orange-copper glow. Set observed her with wonder. She had been a beautiful girl—he held on to the vision of her in the buckskin dress, with feathers in her braided hair, her face painted—with a free and original and irrepressible spirit. And now, in a wholly different context, she was a beautiful woman, endowed with experience and purpose and grace. She ripened before his eyes. He felt almost boyish in her presence, and indeed, in keeping with the story, he must play out his part as Set-talee, Tsoai-talee, boy bear, rock-tree boy. But Grey had evolved from a girl into a woman, and he had been witness to it. And, fittingly, he began to attend her. One day, while looking at her as she played with Nanibah, it became clear to him that she belonged to him, and he to her. And he felt a happiness beyond anything he had ever known.

That summer they lived in the hogan beyond her mother's house. Little by little Set fitted himself into the rhythm of life at Lukachukai. In the night he went out to see, as for the first time, the innumerable brilliant points of light in the sky. Looking at them he thought he had never seen the night, and he wept and laughed and at last kept the silence of the stars. In the early morning he walked into the dawn's light, slowly at first, stiff with cold, but warming as the flood of light fell from the east, and he saw with wonder and fear and thanksgiving the land become radiant, defined by light and long, color-bearing distances. And when enough of his strength returned he began to run.

The boy ran. In the days he drew and painted, watching the light change and the colors turn and shift upon the earth, the shadows extend and deepen. His paintings were strong and simple, primary, like those of a child. He listened to the wind and the birds and thunder rolling on the cliffs; in the darkness there was the yip-yip-yipping of coyotes, and at first light the coyotes set up a din that was otherworldly, that was like an electronic music descending from every point on the horizon to the center of creation, to this place, this hogan. And he listened to the voices of Grey and her mother, of Antonia and Nanibah, of old men and women passing by. He listened to the turning of their voices in the element of *diné bizaad*, to the exotic words with their innumerable edges and hollows and inclines—*chizh, dlǪ́Ǫ́, tXízí, tódiXhiX.* And he began to understand and use very simple words and constructions in Navajo—*aoo', dooda, daatsʼí, hágoónee', Set yiʼniʼshyé, haash yiniʼyé?*

At first he did not know how to behave with Lela and Antonia, nor did they with him. But Grey was a good intermediary, and by and large all was well. Nanibah made a great difference, too. She was, like Grey, mischievous and undaunted in her spirit. She took a liking to Set, and she taught him very quickly how to get along with her. He had no experience of children to speak of, and so he walked on eggs. Nanibah adopted him.

One day, when Grey was working at the loom and Antonia had taken Nanibah to Chinle to buy hay and grain, Lela approached close to Set. He was drawing.

"She weaves well," Lela said, under an obligation to speak offhand.

"I think so too," Set said.

"She talks like a Navajo."

"I am glad," Set said.

There was a long pause, which to Set was uncomfortable, to Lela not. He made heavy strokes on the paper with a piece of charcoal.

"She has told us that you are Kiowa."

Set considered. Lela knew from the first that he was Kiowa. She, having been married to one, knew better than he what it was to be Kiowa. This oblique conversation would have frustrated him at one time; it did not frustrate him now. It was the proper way to proceed.

"I am Kiowa," he said.

"You have strong medicine," Lela said, as a matter of fact.

"Yes."

"Grey knows of this medicine." Again, not a question.

"She gave it to me," he said.

"Yes, so I have heard," Lela said. She was a large woman. She looked him in the eye for a long moment. Wisps of hair turned on the air at her temples. Her hands were at her sides. He could read nothing in her eyes. After a long time she said, "It is a hard thing to be what you must be, *daats'i*."

"*Daats'i*," he said. Perhaps.

There was another long pause.

"Do you think you will marry my daughter?" Lela asked. She spoke in a considered way, with measured breath. *Anachronism forwards,* he thought. Her face was shining, especially her forehead and cheeks, and was almost the color of copper. Her face was wonderfully round. She held hands with herself; it was a habit with her. She held them clasped lightly together and low on her abdomen. Her hands were brown and shapely; on three of her fingers were silver rings with bright turquoise stones. She stood with her feet apart. Her stance, and the lines of her body, suggested a fine and firm balance.

Puppies were romping and yelping in the shadow of the house. Butterflies were flitting and floating on the shine of the air. The walls of red rock in the distance appeared to vibrate in the rising heat. The spring had taken hold of the long valley. In looking out across the wide, warming land, Set could conceive of the summer—it was a conception like memory, the remembered summertime of his boyhood at the Peter and Paul Home or at the house on Scott Street; and he marveled to feel his senses awakening—as Lela had conceived of it days and weeks ago, in advance of the final snowfall, when the skies above the Lukachukai Mountains were still curdled and dark. He drew his gaze back upon the closer ground to see Dog standing beyond the hogan, his ears pricked, appearing to search the horizon, standing like some old granitic cairn on the plain, and closer, before the hogan, Grey, at three quarters, sitting, her fine brown fingers picking at the loom.

"I don't know," he said. He looked into her eyes and could see nothing devious there, nothing, unless it was the faintest glint of mischief, a humor so tentative that he dare not count on it. "But it is a thing I have in mind."

"You *want* to marry my daughter, *daats'i?*"

Then he heard himself say, "Yes. Yes, I do. I want to marry your daughter. There is nothing I want more than that."

Then he thought of her asking, You have told her this? And he was ashamed; he searched desperately for some plausible answer: No—not yet . . . I did not know. . . . I have not been clear in my mind. I am going to tell her now. But it did not come to that. Instead, Lela said, "My daughter is a beautiful woman, like me."

"Yes, she is."

"She is beautiful in her whole being, like me."

"Yes."

"She will bear beautiful children, like me."

"Yes."

Pause.

"But you, if I may speak in a clear way, you are sick. This I have heard. This I have seen. The bear stands against you."

"Yes."

"Yes?"

"Yes. I am sick. I have been sick for a long time, but I hope to be well and strong. I can be well and strong with Grey's help —she knows how to help me. I have become stronger since I have been here, because of Grey."

"*Aoo*'. Yes."

"*Aoo*', I have been afflicted. The bear stands against me."

"*Aoo*'."

"*Aoo*'. I am the bear."

"*Aoo*'."

❖❖❖

In the early mornings, when he inhaled the cold air that ran down from the mountains, and when he touched the earth through the soles of the moccasins Lela and Grey had made for him, he knew how glad he was to be alive. His skin grew darker, and his body began to grow hard, and his hair grew over his ears and shaggy at the nape of his neck. It seemed to him that he could see a little farther into the distance each day and that his legs were hardening and becoming more flexible at the ankles and knees, his stride longer and more regular and persistent. He ran until the sweat streamed on his body, and he tasted the salty exertion at the corners of his mouth, and he ran on until his breathing came in time with his stride and his whole body was fitted into the most delicate and precise rhythm. He entered into the current of the wind, of water running, of shadows extending, of sounds rising up and falling away. His life was in motion; in motion was his life. He ran until running became the best expression of his spirit, until it seemed he could not stop, that if he stopped he would lose his place in the design of creation—and beyond that, until his lungs burned and his breath came hard and fast and loud, and his legs and feet were almost too heavy to lift—and beyond that, deeper into the rhythm, into a state of motion, mindless and inexorable, without end. And when he returned to the hogan Grey bathed him while he stood naked, allowing his body to settle down. Then she gave him water to drink and a kind of gruel, made of crushed corn and goat's milk, piñons and dried fruit, and in the manner of old Najavo men a hundred years ago, he wrapped his loins in white cloth and lay down on a pallet in the shade of a juniper, near the loom, and Grey slowly kneaded the muscles in his shoulders and back and legs. She made a mild abrasive out of sand and oil and massaged his feet, and she sat beside him, singing softly, stirring the air over him with a grass broom, and he sank into deep relaxation. And in the afternoon he drew and painted and dreamed and set his mind upon marriage. He spoke Navajo to Lela as far as he could, and he was not offended when she laughed at him. He played games with Nanibah and put notions of the wide world in her head. He instructed her in painting, and in turn she gave him words, the words of a child, which are at the center of language. And he observed with deep appreciation, wonder, and respect Grey's return to the Navajo world.

In the late afternoon they convened at Lela's table. There was usually lamb or mutton, and dried corn and tinned tomatoes and beans, and dried fruit. There were wonderful breads: fried bread, corn bread, oven bread. Set liked best the dense, sweet oven bread, baked in an *horno* of adobe bricks and mud plaster; it was the bread of the pueblos; Lela had learned to make it when she was a girl attending the fiestas in the ancient towns on the Rio Grande.

At dusk Grey prepared a sweat lodge for him, a small conical hogan with an opening on the west. When the stones in the pit were hot and the flames had died down, Grey and Set entered the sweat lodge in breechcloths and sat next to each other. Grey poured water on the stones, and they hissed and let off steam. In the bare light of the embers, before they were extinguished, Set

looked at Grey discreetly, saw her smooth skin shining and glis-
tening, as bright beads of water appeared on her forehead, her
throat, her shoulders and thighs. The tips of her breasts were
nearly as dark as her hair. He watched as she leaned to pour the
water, her long side and flank shining, her toes flexing into the
sand. Discreetly he watched, the heat of the steam and of his
desire coming upon him. And for a time he became dull and
heavy, as on the verge of sleep, dreaming of the woman beside
him, dreaming longingly of her body, which was so anomalously
soft and firm, which was so exciting in its curves and lines and
hollows and folds, of the smell of her when she came fresh from
sleep, of her casual gestures, of her voice in the day and night
when she spoke of this and that with interest or excitement, or
with anger or frustration or sorrow, of the breathy cooing of her
ecstasy, of her singing softly, of her gentle breathing in the night.
And then the drowsiness and the dreaming dissolved, and he felt
suddenly refreshed and invigorated and clean and hot, and he
began to laugh, and Grey too, and they touched, and their hands
slipped over their bodies, describing desire, but yet discreetly, for
Lela and perhaps Antonia and Nanibah might be close by. All
things in their places. In this little house was peace and purification. Outside the evening air bit them with cold and was sharply
delicious. And they walked away from the house and hogan and
lay down on a dune, observing the night sky. And later, when the
moon was high, they rode horses into the arroyos, among shadows that were like pools of time and eternity.

❖❖❖

At the end of April a man came down from the Chuskas, bringing mountain earth. In the center of the hogan he constructed
an altar and performed a ceremony through most of the night.
Set and Grey sat side by side to the left of the priest. Coals were
laid upon the altar, and a firestick was placed in the coals just so,
on the east side, so that the pointed end smoldered and shone
like a brand. Crystals were placed here and there on the altar's
rim. The priest arranged his paraphernalia before him. There
were herbs and pollens, a gourd rattle, pots of liquors and teas,

peyote pastes, feather fans, a bowl of water, and an eagle-bone whistle. Nanibah slept on a pallet at the wall of the hogan. Lela and Antonia assisted the priest, keeping the coals alive, sprinkling sage and cedar, crushed with tobacco in their fingers, bringing water and coals as needed. Set and Grey glanced at each other occasionally, and sometimes they touched hands, but they were concentrated upon the ceremony. Smoke was fanned upon them, and when it was proper to do so they spoke of their visions. Their visions were very beautiful, and their words were the best that were in their hearts, and their voices were joined in the smoke to other voices, ancient and original. Their voices were soft and everlasting, and in them were laughter and wailing and reverence and awe, and they made stories and songs and prayers. And in the dark early morning, after they had gone out of the hogan to say themselves to the night sky and returned, they stood before the altar, holding each other close. In their honor the priest gave the firestick to the fire, and they knew, though it was not an explicit knowledge, that they were married. In ceremony, in tradition out of time, in a sacred manner, in beauty they were married forever.

DUANE NIATUM

❖❖❖

Crow's Sun

ALL MORNING Thomas had sweated over the verdict. Since yesterday he had known that he was sentenced to the brig. The usual bureaucratic red tape had prolonged his transfer until after lunch, much of which he could not eat. The ride in the jeep into the Naval Shipyard at Bremerton from Keyport had been completely silent. It was rumored his punishment had already begun. Since they had driven out of the main gate, the Shore Patrolman had not looked at him once. The many miles of silence had only made the air more suffocating. The challenge would be like a long flight through an unknown storm. Now in the Navy for a year, he was still unable to understand why servicemen, seventeen to seventy, lived by and for the test. It seemed the one thing they wanted to know about life, or all they were capable of knowing. He was never sure which. They always looked and talked like the same zombie, drone ant. He shuddered. It was to him a far worse prison than thirty days in the brig.

The Navy SP swerves the jeep into one of the designated parking areas, outside the Marine Brig, and orders Thomas to get out. They step briskly as they reach the door. While waiting for someone to answer the bell, Cook, the SP, forces a smile, and speaks.

"This hole'll be your home for thirty days, Thomas. And buddy, you'd better watch your mouth. Do your time with your trap shut, until you're running free. Don't act the wiseguy. I don't like your face, Thomas, but I don't think those hicks from the base were right. You're a punk, but who isn't at your age? They went too far. I believe burning a man at the stake's like what I left in Alabama."

Thomas wonders why Cook bothers to tell him this. Since they first met they have never liked one another. Cook, a career man with four hash-marks, is a spit-and-polish sailor married to the idea that blind obedience to orders is the only law. Thomas realized almost immediately after his enlistment that he had made a mistake when he had let his parents talk him into joining up. Since he was underage, they both had to sign papers before the Navy would take him. Very confused about what to do with his seventeen years, he let himself be pushed into it.

"You're not exactly what I call a friend, Cook, but you've never proven an enemy either. What's the lecture?"

"Well, a few of the guys you tangled with on the base called the brig warden and painted an ugly picture of you. I guess you know they told the warden he ought to break both your legs. So, if you got *any* sense in that thick skull of yours, you'll be careful. Very, very careful."

"Thanks for the tip, Cook. It's good to see you haven't given all your soul to that tin badge and forty-five. I may be Indian at heart, but I can appreciate a Negro soul."

With the tension somewhat released, Cook laughs.

"Sure, arrowhead, black is beautiful—all that jazz—but remember, you better be on your toes with these Marines. They don't play and most are mad-dogs from hell. Being a high-yellow redskin isn't going to help your ass in the brig. It might even add to the danger. You understand what I'm telling you? Don't be a goddamn hothead."

Thomas assures him he knows what they are like in the brig. Then with a grunt or two, a Marine private opens the huge steel door, and the two men enter. Everything glistens in the dim light, like an anesthetized tomb. In a room at the end of the brassy corridor, a man with a handlebar mustache sits at a desk. He seems to be checking a record or report and ignores or does not hear the men approach. Cook motions Thomas to stand at attention inside the door as he walks up to talk with the Sergeant at the desk: the Brig's Warden.

"Got another one for you, Sergeant. Name's Young Thomas."

The Sergeant glances at Thomas a moment, without looking at Cook.

"Yes, we've been expecting him, bosun. You can head back to the base; we'll take care of him real good for you. Don't worry about a thing."

"Right, Sergeant." Cook turns smartly. In passing Thomas, he slaps Thomas's arm lightly with his club, and goes out the door. With a quick nod, Thomas acknowledges Cook's way of saying good luck. Still, he wonders if a Black Panther or a Muslim will ever reach the older man before the State cancels him in retirement? He shrugs his shoulders when he remembers he has never believed in miracles or gods.

After glaring indifferently at Thomas for a while, the Sergeant returns to the papers on his desk. He grasps a pencil and rolls it back and forth rhythmically between his hands, ignoring the stranger standing like a statue at the door. The only sounds Thomas hears are the Sergeant's slow breathing and the pencil striking the different bulky rings on the Sergeant's fingers. From the corner of his eye, Thomas notices the other man swing back in his chair and look directly into his eyes. Thomas almost flinches. Realizing it is the first time the Sergeant has said a word to him, he breathes more evenly.

"You see that yellow line in front of my desk, boy?" The younger man looks down at the yellow line the Sergeant is pointing at.

"Well, get your ass in front of that line, boy. When I look down again, I sure as hell better not see your shoes touching it. Now, move!"

Looking triumphant, the Sergeant bends forward, flings his pencil on the desk, and begins thumbing through the papers stacked in front of him. He mutters about the fucking rat race he has chosen for himself and how many years he has to pass before he can retire to Dixie. He goes on mumbling of the endless duplication of junk and faces. How he would prefer to be any place but here.

At attention before the Sergeant's desk and yellow line, Thomas looks straight ahead. His friends have warned him of the prison; the men who run it. He focuses his eyes on a notice tacked to the wall behind the Sergeant's desk. It reads in bold-face type:

> A Marine has no friends.
> A Marine wants no friends.

Casually, as if just waking up, the Sergeant lets his eyes drift down to Thomas's shoes and the yellow line.

"What's your name, boy?"

"Young Thomas."

The Sergeant's jaws flush; grow puffy. He lurches from his chair almost knocking it over.

The muscles in Thomas's face tighten; his eyes thicken; narrow into tiny moons peering from behind a shield of fern. He sways slightly; stiffens his whole body, not sure what to expect from the man closing in. Grandson to Cedar Crow, Thomas feels his fingers change to claws, to a wing of thrashing spirit flying wildly inside his ear. (Be calm and steady now. This man's your enemy. Know his every move. Break him like a twig if he tries to harm you. Be the thunderbird in our song. I am Crow, your father.)

Suddenly, the Sergeant's short grunts of breath beat his face. Thomas searches for the owl spirit in the eyes of the man looming toward him; they are gray and crystalline. Death is not there. He relaxes as the blood returns to his feet; watches the Sergeant's mustache twitch around pockmarks and pimples. Words spit into his face, yet, the cell remains whole. Owl has not called.

"What did you say, boy?"

"I said, Young Thomas, Sergeant."

Nearly uncaged now, the Sergeant pants in a faster rhythm. His well-creased shirt is saturated with large sweat-patches, the wrinkles spread. He grabs the younger man by the neck, drags him to the wall. Thomas does not resist. A river bird builds a nest at the center of the storm in his heart; his thoughts run for the longhouse of Old Patsy at Hadlock village.

Mechanically, the Sergeant slams Thomas's head against the wall; kicks his shoes together. Reluctantly, he releases the young man's neck. After letting go, he steps back. He straightens his tie and wipes his brow to regain his composure; authority.

"Listen, punk. And listen hard. Down here, morning, noon, or night, when a Marine asks you to open that idiotic mouth of yours, you remember to say, sir. Sir! *Sir!* And you little bastard, you'd better not forget it!"

As if following an impulse, the Sergeant grabs Thomas's head and slams it against the wall again. Apparently satisfied, he returns to his desk and hollers, "Did you get that, boy?"

"Yes, sir."

Thomas hears his most pessimistic teachers and friends claim there is nothing but ashes in the forests of the Klallam people. Or nothing of value. Since his grandfather, his first teacher, had dropped among the cedars and pines to become another dead root, he had nearly succumbed to this belief himself, he heard it so much. Although his grandfather, the guardian of his zigzag path, had died a year earlier, the quiet man of the family had counseled him well. Young was convinced it was his grandfather who made the sunrise and sunset real and at anchor in his heart. Although the ancestral longhouse and fishing village was destroyed long ago by hordes of white settlers streaming into every inch of the land of the Seven Brothers, he had promised the old ones in his family to wear his grandfather's feather to the grave.

"Yes, sir."

"Now, get your ass in front of that line."

The Sergeant leans back in his chair, leaving two handprints on the glass desktop. The chair squeaks.

"Who in the hell are you, boy? What'd you say your name was?"

"Young Thomas, sir!"

"That's more like it. How old are you, boy?"

"Eighteen, sir."

"Just a punk, aren't ya?"

(Keep close to the winter fire, your family circle; join in the sing, little Crow)

"Yes, sir."

"Let me hear you say, 'I'm a fucking idiot, sir.' "

(Your life'll seem a waste; only a chain of wrong paths, little Crow. With these hoops you must seek the friendship of Courage; keep your eyes open until the cedars are a branch of your shadow. It's like dying, little Crow. So it is with me, so it'll be with you and your son and your son's son. Pain's the father, but the river's your guardian. Listen for our voices in each storm and wind.)

"You're a . . . I mean, I'm a fucking idiot, sir!"

The Sergeant smiles, takes the handkerchief from his pocket, systematically wipes his forehead and hands, and continues.

"Know just what you are, don't ya, boy?"

"Yes, sir."

"Say, mush face, a few swab-jocks from Keyport been tellin' me you're a real wiseguy. Read a lot of Commie shit. Think you're some kind of revolutionary. Are you a troublemaker, boy?"

"No, sir."

"Everybody been telling me a different story, boy. They tell me you're a tough guy. You look more like a bag of bones to me. Ha! Yes, sir, more like a coon man slipping down some tree. Ha! Ha! Well, can you dig a hole like a pig, boy?"

"No, sir."

"Christ, boy, can't you howl like a cat?"

"I guess so, sir."

"I guess so, sir. You fucking idiot! Don't ya' know nothing?"

"I guess not, sir."

"All right, stupid. What's your serial number?"

"Nine-nine five, five-seven, one-five, sir."

"Where were you born, punk?"

"Seattle, Washington, sir."

Slow and methodical, the Sergeant inches his way around the desk to stand in front of Thomas. He plans to bury the next questions in the younger man's soul.

"Who ya' trying to kid with a name like Thomas, boy? How's a wetback like you got a name like Thomas? Ain't it really Pancho Villa? Ha!"

"I'm not from Mexico, sir. I . . ."

"In my book, you're a fucking wetback. Shit, you're a wetback from head to toe. Who you kidding, boy?"

Thomas stares back into the two gray crystals. He watches the sweat roll down the Sergeant's temples. He feels it roll down his own as well. His clothes are a sweat-sponge. Yet, he says not a word. Silence is his shield. The Sergeant eases back into his chair, and turns a little. The leather snaps as if he had been glued to it. Thomas answers for someone else in the room. A man with blood darker than the forest of his people. A Klallam elder he has sworn to his ancestors to honor with his name and his life.

"My father's a white sailor and my mother an American Indian, sir."

Irritated and reflecting disappointment, the Sergeant shouts, "It's about time ya' answered, boy. But how many goddamn times I got to tell you to speak loud and clear. I'm deaf, ya' got to holler it out."

"Yes, sir! My mother's Indian, my father white."

"I can't hear a word you've said."

"Can't you, *sir!*"

"So, your father didn't swim the Rio Grande. Too fucking bad. He should'a. Down home where I come from, we fry niggers like ya' in chicken fat and feed the remains to the hogs. Ya' know that?"

Thomas calls secretly to Cedar Crow; the chant his grandfather gave him as a child.

(When the world's too broken for the heart, live in the cave inside your skull: follow hummingbird's flight through the yellow light to the center of our birth. Lie like a stone in the grass.)

"No, sir."

Thomas disappears into the notice; it is the mountain clearing of his mind. Although fear and anger make war inside his gut, he does not take his eyes from the wall.

"You can't tell me you're from this country, boy. Americans know how to obey orders. After thumbing through your records, this leaves you out of the ball game. Fucking up left and right since boot camp, from what I hear. All the time, making trouble, fucking up."

Thomas returns from the clearing; the sweat forms like oil beads and rolls down his forehead to his nose and lips. His eyes blink rapidly a few times, but never leave the wall. He sighs. He watches from behind the beargrass and giant ferns, the dancing at Old Patsy's last potlatch in 1891. Then his mind moves on to the sea. On a coastal beach he sees Killer Whale surface and fall back into the water.

"Yes, sir, I mean, no sir."

Once more the seated man fondles his pencil, pushes back his chair, and looks away from Thomas. Faint clicks echo off the walls. He heaves himself from behind the desk and abruptly exits the room. Almost immediately he returns, wiping cold water from his lips. He steps close to Thomas, smiling.

"You don't know what ya' mean, do you, boy? You're such a stupid retard, ya' probably couldn't find your way to the shitter, if your ass was chained to the stool. Shit, all ya' can say is yes sir and no sir. Isn't that true, boy?"

"Yes, sir."

"What? Somebody cut out your tongue? Those weren't words."

"Yes, sir! yes, sir!"

"All right, all right. Jesus Christ, give me a break. That's enough. So the cat ain't got your tongue. You're just a god-damned idiot."

"Yes, sir."

The Sergeant leans forward; he tries to look through Thomas.

"Now let me hear you say real loud, 'I'm the camp idiot, sir!' "

"I'm the camp idiot, sir!"

"Shit, I'm sick of looking at your ugly face, boy. I'm going to kick your ass into the hole. You bore the piss out of me. From here on out, you're not Young Thomas anymore; you're Thirty. And if you don't want to end up at Sick Call, you fucking well better answer to Thirty. Turnkey! Turnkey! Get this piece of shit out of my sight before I puke!"

A crow rises from a red cedar branch, upward to the mountain peaks, falling back to the river and its source. The change sweeps through Thomas. Thanking his grandfather, the people, and the dawn striking its feathers into the undulating coastal waters, he steps easily within the shadows of the room. The crow circles downwind into the clouds, and vanishes.

CARTER REVARD

❖❖❖

Never Quite
a Hollywood Star

IF YOUR SCALP ITCHES, it may be because I am temporarily controlling your mind. So don't try a dandruff shampoo unless you have already looked out the window for the Indian attack; we are hiding behind the trees and shrubs on your lawn. I myself am from the stars; and my Omaha friend Cliff works at the Army Arsenal here, where we have all the needed guns and grenades. But seriously, folks, these words popping out on the page as you read are pouring out of the constellation you call the Big Dipper. Like neutrinos they pass through everything until they just happen to get the right brain to interface: then they break into the word-hoards, put on English, and come marching out all together, clause left, clause right, wherever England was pink on the globe, and while you watch them take cover behind a yew hedge you can uncover the plot we are involved in. Their strength is your weakness—leaving a story unfinished is as hard as stopping in the middle of other acts to which our appetites drive us. Not to be obscene, I leave you to imagine that, but it may be said that thirst for water or love is not stronger than need to finish a story or remembering that can make you sure you are still you. I have used this story-sense to log into your mind, or as Cherokees say I am walking in your soul, my friend. Unless we *are* friends, of course, this is an Indian attack, and you will be trying to kill me, our story, if you don't trust me. But its corpse will nag: not truly American till you've been in an Indian attack, it says. So, shall we begin?

The story. Oh lord, I forgot to mention. It's aimed at you, but its words pass through you to others, one of whom you need to know is William F. Buckley Junior, a former Yalie. (I see you there, Billy Boy, on your Firing Line in the back of this reader's mind where I've set you. He doesn't really want you there like a ghost on his dark TV tube which he's trying to tune to Indian affairs. Go ahead, though, try to convince him that I am Sandinista. He of course will get very frustrated if I keep talking over his head to you, so please, sweet William, keep quiet for the moment and let my story begin.)

It begins in starlight: very dark, but in the clear night air of early spring stars are brilliant, even through branches thick with new buds here on the creekbank where the doe is poised, wanting to bend her head and drink but looking carefully round first. Now she plants her front hooves wider, bends the neck slowly, dips her muzzle slightly, jerks the head up and turns ears back, sniffs. She hears a rustle, flinches to leap but can't decide which way, hears the bow *thank* and gathering to jump is hit by the arrow behind her left shoulder, her head flies up, she springs, but a long-tailed shape flies through the air from the sycamore on her right and behind her, lands on her back with a grating snarling cry and fastens long teeth into her neck. She bucks, struggles, the mountain lion throws her off her feet and fastens teeth in her throat, throttles, growls, shakes her, has her pinned and subsiding. Again the bow *thonks,* an arrow strikes and pierces his chest entirely; he leaps free of the doe, turns and strikes and snaps at the arrow's feathered end, rolls on his back and screams and snarls, kicks, is on his feet and leaps for the sycamore tree, falls short of the branch and claws upward on its trunk. A third arrow drives into his back, splits his heart; he snarls, falls, thrashes briefly. The doe, ten feet away, is moving feebly, her head rising and dropping, beating against the ground. Now she and the cat lie unmoving, death throes over. And now a man stands up where he was kneeling among tall dead weeds to the left of the deer-trail down to the creek. He watches, listens as carefully as the doe had done, looks into our camera, an arrow notched and ready, does not see or hear us in this blind of time. He waits, a minute, two, three, looks carefully up into the sycamore. At last he moves one moccasined foot to a leafless grassy place, then the other, but freezes at a noise, a splash. He kneels, lowers himself to prone position, sights across the creek: an otter's head, swimming downstream, had made the splash. The man stands up. He looks up through the branches at the Big Dipper, checking the time: a meteor flashes down and fills the dipper with light as it vanishes. He speaks quietly to deer and mountain lion, takes out his obsidian knife. We kill him. He turns into a myth as we pour our words over him and he disappears, then rises like mist, takes human form again and walks down off the stage to the back of your mind. He sits down there beside William Buckley, who looks distinctly uneasy but is trying to hide it.

As the story continues, snow has fallen and bitter strong winds have drifted it. A pickup truck is carrying two young Indian men and a white reporter out from the church at Wounded Knee, now occupied by militant American Indian Movement warriors and their supporters from Mohawk, Chippewa, Ponca, Apache, other peoples. In the pickup truck is a rifle. Our story does not tell what kind of rifle it is, because we do not want the two Indians arrested; it is therefore an *alleged* rifle. They are going to kill a steer, allegedly, so this reporter can file a better story, indubitably. They drive out into a field where whitefaced cattle are gathered around a feeding station; some are eating hay from mangers. The reporter and the Indians look the cattle over, decide on one. It looks worried as they keep staring at it, turns broadside to them, looks alert and poised to run. None of the three has ever slaughtered a steer, but the Indians were taught to kill humans in Viet Nam. There is a report of one of them as having shot the steer in the chest. The steer, we are told, bellows and trots away. Again, reportedly, the rifleman shoots it, this

time from behind and to its right. The bullet is said to have
ranged into its flank and stomach and lodged behind a rib, causing the steer to stagger but not fall. The reporter is, on oath,
angry and guilty. The Indians, said one rumor, were embarrassed.
The reporter has taken pictures which are not only not admissi-
ble, but not interesting. Now the steer is weakening, drops to its
front knees—is that, the reporter wonders, really the right word?
—and goes over on its side. It lies suffering, rolling its eyes,
wheezing blood out its On the float suddenly the man in buckskin and warbonnet stands, looks, waves to her.

"Ponca Washtage!" he calls, loud enough for her to hear.

"Woody, look!" she cries, "look, it's Sugar Brown, remember
that great dancer—look, there's his boy! Hi, Elmer! Oh, for
goodness' sake!"

"Come see us at the circus," Sugar Brown is saying as the
float moves out of range. The tall blackhaired man and his Ponca
wife are grinning, could not be happier.

❖❖❖

"I'll be damned, right here in Maryville, California," the tall
man is saying, "what do you know. Jewel, let's get right over
there."

You feeling more at ease, reader, now the story has taken us
this far? That is, catching on to what I'm driving at, have you
begun regaining control of your mind, know where the brakes
are, accelerator and steering wheel in range again? I hope very
much that this is so, but remember old Billy Buckley back there
wants to be a backseat driver. He says even though all these
Indian attacks have been most contemptible, you should be
scared of them. One was merely expert savagery, another a savage fraud incepted by the media, the third an assault on your
bleeding heart, reader, Billy says. He is afraid of active unAmeri-
cans and every time he pops out of your TV, sees Indians everywhere he looks, in Nicaragua, West Germany (green Indians
there), in Yale, in Hollywood. Worst of all, they are spending his
money uncontrollably even as they accuse him of starving them
and taking their land, resources, rights away. It is, one thinks,

just short of impossible not to be impressed by such paralogisticism.

❖❖❖

But please join me, nonetheless, in this old car speeding down a stretch of U.S. 60 between Ponca City and Pawhuska, on the Osage Reservation. It is long after midnight, we are doing eighty and the asphalt road is dips and curves which our headlights shadow and highlight dizzily as we careen and thump over and round them. In the front seat are two Indian men. The man in the passenger seat is slumped down, may be asleep; the driver, like his passenger, is nodding. Now, though, he straightens, shakes his head, looks to his right and speaks loudly, asking for a cigarette. He gets no answer, and reaches over to shake the sleeper. "Hey. Elmer. Gimme a cigarette," he says. But Elmer does not wake, and the cigarettes are in his right shirt pocket. The driver tries to reach over across Elmer and fish them out. He has taken his eyes completely off the road, and as he leans he pulls the steering wheel right, the tires hit the soft grassy shoulder, the car lurches, the driver jerks round in panic, yanks the wheel back just as his right front wheel goes into the culvert and the car turns a twisting crunching somersault, lands in the ditch on its top and bounces onward, crashing over and over, windshield and windows shattered, driver thrown out and crushed under the rolling car as it makes a next-to-last headstand and tumble. The man on the passenger side, tossed like a rag dummy, is still inside as the car, one headlight impossibly shining, a taillight dully glowing, crumps once more and stands, tips, gently sags upside down on the barbed-wire fence at the top of the borrow-ditch. The front passenger door is open and Elmer hangs half out of it, head down, limp. He has been awake since the first screeching of tires but thinks in his numbness that it is a nightmare. He cannot move, or feel his body, but his open eyes see grass, prairie hay in clumps just above his head, and beyond it many twinkling lights. Then he finds he is looking at stars, but can't think why they are below him. The grass seems to be growing downward. Blacking out, he is thinking that he must be upside down. He hears himself breathing loudly. When he wakes up he is in a hospital and beside him sits a man he knows, who helped raise him, who in the Ponca way is his father-uncle, from whom he learned to be a great dancer. "Take it easy, Elmer," the man says. Elmer tries to sit up but nothing happens. "Gus, what's the matter?" he asks. "Johnny got killed," Gus says, "but they got you out. Doctors pulled you through." It does not take Elmer long to realize that he will not walk again, that he has very limited use of arms and hands, that one lung is ruined. He has been circus acrobat, Hollywood stunt man, champion wardancer on the powwow circuit. He will learn to use a wheelchair and be helped by others into and out of it.

Now through September drought and heat we are going to White Eagle for the Ponca Tribal Dances. You drive south out of Ponca City, through several miles of refinery stink: searing sulfur dioxide, rotten hydrogen sulfide, a sweetish warmth from the orange flares, creating the power you drive with. Presently you drive between wheat and oat fields, pass a beerjoint, then churches, come to a billboard announcing Ponca Powwow. You turn off right here, toward Salt Fork, wind around a little, turn off the asphalt after passing the Ponca Tribal Building and the medical clinic building. You can see trees and greenery down toward the river, and turning down that way you see some canvas tents ahead, olive green or khaki or blue, cooking fires in front of them, people with kettles and pans. But first, explain to one of the young Ponca guards here that you are one of us, not them. They want you to pay. You say you are Aunt Jewel's nephew. Finally you give them five dollars, because what the hell. It ought to go to the drum when you dance, but it is after all a contribution. (You see, reader? I have made you for the occasion one of us. Just keep Mr. Buckley down in the backseat there and have him narrow his Yale Blue eyes sufficiently.)

First time you've come here without an older member of the family to avouch you; firs' time for many years you've been here; the young men don't recognize you. Now ease this big old Dodge Polara down the dirt road, the knoll and sharp right down-turn, and here under the walnut tree are Aunt Jewel and the family.

Hey, here's cousin Buck, Carter and Linda, Craig and Stephanie, Kelly, Uncle Joe, the twins, after awhile Mike and Casey and the kids, Julie, Wesley, Suzeta and Huggy-bear in the green van with Shongeh-ska's name on it, then Darlena and her man come down from the house. Now there is catfish Mike caught down by Fairfax being fried here, lots of everything to eat, frybread, we feast. It is late afternoon, there has been gourd-dancing up at the arena already. Everybody sits around the fires in front of their tents, in the shade of trees along the winding dirt road that goes up toward the dance grounds, and Aunt Jewel's place here is not far from where the creek-bottom's underbrush and tall weeds begin. Some of the young men that will be wardancing are here to eat with Aunt Jewel. They do not know you and for a while they look less than friendly. After they listen to you talking with Aunt Jewel and Craig and Buck they relax a little. Craig gets you into some dominoes with him and three of them. One is heavy and muscular. Otoe, he says, looking as if that was not a good question. Craig introduces you to Elmer, who is sitting in his wheelchair near the fire with a beer in his right hand. Craig takes out a cigarette and puts it into Elmer's left hand, then when Elmer raises it hesitantly and puts it into his mouth, Craig lights it. Elmer blows out a stream of smoke and looks at you. He says it is good to be at the dances again. This is where he has always camped for the dances; Uncle Gus and the McDonalds have made this their place. He says, looking toward an open area between trees and creek, that he used to ride his horses here, racing the other men's best horses. It is darkening, and the dancers go back into their tents to put on fancy wardance gear. Presently we hear the bells, the jangling as they walk up toward the arena. It is the first night of the wardance competitions that Uncle Gus used to win for a long time, and that Elmer won. "Right here," he says, looking away, "I first raced my pony when I was just a kid. I saw this place when I was hanging there upside down from the car. I saw these trees and a cooking fire. They were right in the drinking-cup part of the Big Dipper."

When it is quite dark we go up under the stars to the arena, where the drum sounds and voices sing the wardance songs. Now

Carter and Craig push the wheelchair and Elmer in and along at the bottom of the bleachers, turn it so he has a front-and-center view of dancers and drum. We sit just behind on the front row. There is a break now before the finals; waterboys carry round to drum and dancers the buckets of cool water with their longhandled enameled dippers. Now the finals begin, drummers play the trickiest rhythms and fastest songs; the dancers must keep precise time, stopping exactly wherever the drum may suddenly end, anticipating so there is no slip, awkward pause, offbalance move. Only six are left dancing, and the crowd is happy; these are the best of the best. Then, as one dancer does a spectacular spinning and fast-stamping bit, the crowd goes *Ooooooh,* and I nod wisely. "He's really very good," I say. Elmer smiles, turns partly toward me, says very quietly, "That's the people that just lost money on him; he missed a beat." I sit and watch and do not say anything more. When the last song ends, the dancers walk round the circle in the sun's direction, all coming by to talk and laugh with Elmer while they wait for the decision. He congratulates winners.

You can come into my study now. It's pretty badly messed up, paper and books all over, but it does have three big south windows looking directly into the upper branches of this sweetgum, and the winter sun comes streaming in through its branches. Hundreds of seedballs hang from its branches, brown and burry, like geodesic stars. I am here among the stars, it appears. See, down on the ground the snow has appeared overnight, and it is dazzling. Now a sudden flight of juncoes sweeps into the tree. Immediately one of them flashes down to the untouched snow, hops neatly across it. Soon it will be Valentine's Day, when birds choose their mates, and I will be teaching Chaucer's *Parlement of Foules* about their gearing down of love from star-motions to birdsong to class warfare as they make their social contracts. Now,

> *Here's a junco neatly*
> *hopping, print print print*

in the brilliant snow, now
  he draws his feet up
into the white soft down
    of belly-feathers,
spreads wings to catch reflected
    warmth off dazzle, fluffed like charcoal
grey heatsink, "brooding
in the snow," Shakespeare said—
    no, warming his toes and thinking
      which seedball in the tree,
this sweetgum granary, he'll
fly up and hang by while he
        feasts,
              below zero
on a sunlit day, blue sky and
feathers full of sun, his crop
filled, his message
cuneiformed on snow:
      track me this far,
      see me brooding on this
        white death, then just
a blur where trackers say I
ended, but blue-eyed
              weasel looks up
where I feast on the round
      seedball under the round
      undying sun,
already turning north toward
      new leaves and flowers.

Now you can scratch your scalp if it itches; you see it's safe, we
all are among the stars, grenades only seedballs, this Indian just a
professor. Still, if you stick a junco feather in your hat and call it
macaroni, please be careful: it is a Federal offense unless you are
licensed to take part in Indian ceremonies involving feathers.
You see, we are different after all, we Indians; but, friend, it's
legal.

MICKEY ROBERTS

❖❖❖

The Indian Basket

HE YEAR WAS 1988, a bitterly cold morning in early winter. I held the small Indian basket, beautiful and artistic in the distinctive Native American tradition. It was clearly no copy of an Indian basket—it was the real thing and I did not have to be told that it was authentic.

The basket was laid out on a table at a garage sale and the ticket said it was for sale for $250. I inquired of the owner as to who had made the basket and was told it was made by "The Thompson River Tribe." The owner went on to say the basket was well worth the money for the Indians no longer made these works of art. I did not satisfy an urge to ask if tribes made baskets, for, being fair to the man, he could not have known the name of the Indian artist when it had never been asked for in the first place!

As I stood holding the basket, I remembered a bitterly cold day in the year 1939. It was the beginning of the winter season. We walked the streets of Bellingham—my mother, my great-grandmother, and me. We were selling Indian baskets. I was a very small girl and I kept saying I wanted to go home but my mother kept saying, ". . . just one more house."

We all carried baskets—large ones, small ones, round ones,

square ones. Some of them were rectangular, with perfectly fitted covers which were designed to be used as picnic baskets. How many hours of hard labor these baskets represented for my grandmother who could speak only in her native tongue. My grandmother had worked hard all her life and she had raised many children and had also raised my mother, who was her granddaughter. Somehow she had survived the changes that life had forced upon her with the changing life in a different culture.

At each house my mother would ask the occupant to look at the Indian baskets and suggest a price of a few articles of used clothing. If the woman of the house decided to look at the baskets and bring out some clothing she didn't want, the bargaining would begin. As in the case of our tribe's treaty, two generations earlier, the main decision would be at the discretion of the newcomer and many hours of labor would go for a few shirts or dresses.

These days the price of Indian baskets is very high and they are mostly owned by non-Indians. These treasures, obtained at less than bargain basement prices, are now being sold at premium prices, if they are obtainable at all. They are collector's items, but the name of the person who labored to make them is rarely known.

As we peddled our treasures in those early years, we probably appeared to be a pitiful people. We were, however, living in as dignified a manner as possible while selling a part of our culture for a few articles of used clothing.

We really hadn't much left to give.

MICKEY ROBERTS

❖❖❖

It's All in How You Say It

EVER SINCE I WAS a small girl in school, I've been aware of what the school textbooks say about Indians. I am an Indian and, naturally, am interested in what the school teaches about natives of this land.

One day in the grammar school I attended, I read that a delicacy of American Indian people was dried fish, which, according to the textbook, tasted "like an old shoe, or was like chewing on dried leather." To this day I can remember my utter dismay at reading these words. We called this wind-dried fish "sleet-schus," and to us it was our favorite delicacy and, indeed, did not taste like shoe leather. It took many hours of long and hard work to cure the fish in just this particular fashion. Early fur traders and other non-Indians must have agreed, for they often used this food for subsistence as they traveled around isolated areas.

I brought the textbook home to show it to my father, leader of my tribe at that time. My father was the youngest son of one of the last chiefs of the Nooksack Indian Tribe of Whatcom County in the state of Washington. On this particular day, he told me in his wise and humble manner that the outside world did not always understand Indian people, and that I should not let it hinder me from learning the good parts of education.

Since those early years I have learned we were much better off with our own delicacies, which did not rot our teeth and bring about the various dietary problems that plague Indian people in modern times. I was about eight years old when this incident happened and it did much to sharpen my desire to pinpoint terminology in books used to describe American Indian people and which are, most often, not very complimentary.

At a later time in my life, I had brought a group of Indian people to the county fairgrounds to put up a booth to sell Indian-made arts and crafts. My group was excited about the prospect of making some money selling genuine Indian artifacts. We thanked the man who showed us our booth and told him it was nice of him to remember the people of the Indian community. The man expanded a little and remarked that he liked Indian people. "In fact," he went on to state, "we are bringing some professional Indians to do the show!"

As we stood there in shock, listening to this uninformed outsider, I looked at my dear Indian companion, an eighty-year-old woman who could well remember the great chiefs of the tribe who once owned all the land of this county before the white man came bringing "civilization," which included diseases and pollution. My friend said not a word, but took the hurt as Indian people have done for many years, realizing outsiders are very often tactless and unthinking.

Of course, we all knew that the "professional Indians" were not Indians at all, but dressed in leather and dancing their own dances. And, anyway, how does one become a "professional Indian"?

I remembered my father's words of so long ago and said to my friend as my father had said to me, "They just don't understand Indian people."

GREG SARRIS

❖❖❖

How I Got to Be Queen

WATCHED JUSTINE across the street. I seen her from the window. Even with Sheldon and Jeffrey asking for lunch, I seen clear enough to know she was up to her old tricks. I said to myself, that queen, she's up to it again. This time it was a boy, a black boy whose name I'd learn in a matter of hours. Justine wastes no time. But just then I pulled away from the window, in case the two little guys might see what I did. Kids have a way of telling things, after all.

Nothing was unpacked. Not even the kitchen this time. I pulled a towel from boxes on the floor and dusted the paper plates left from breakfast. What food we had was on the table. Half loaf of Wonder Bread. Two large jars of peanut butter. Two cans of pie filling. Justine went for another loaf of bread, jam, and a packet of lemonade mix. She got far as the store, which is kitty-corner, just down the street, in plain view from the window.

She stood on one side of the bicycle rack, by the newspaper stand. She stood with a hand on her hip, her head lifted and tilted to the side. Like she was taking a dare, or fixing on some scheme. It makes people notice her. She draws them in that way.

She looked black as the boy straddling a bike on the other side of the rack.

I wondered what Mom would do if she seen her there. That's if Mom wasn't at the cannery with Auntie. I think it's bad the way Justine and Mom talk to each other when there's trouble. "Damned black-neck squaw," Mom says. "Dirty fat Indian," Justine says. "You don't even know which Filipino in that apple orchard is my father." On and on it goes. Of course, Mom don't say much any other time. And if Justine goes on long enough, Mom goes out or watches TV. Like nothing was ever started. Like she does with just about anything else.

I took the longest time setting two pieces of bread on each plate. I found things to look for: the aluminum pie tins, the plastic cups left over from Cousin Jeanne's party, the rolling pin. "I'm going to make a pie," I said to the boys standing at the table. "We'll have a party with pie and lemonade." They shifted on their feet with no patience. "All right," I said. "You act like starved rats and you look worse than pigs. Now wash up." I spread peanut butter on the bread, then sprinkled on some sugar. "I don't want no complaining," I told them when they came back.

❖❖❖

Justine came in about four, an hour before Mom.

"Now what good's that?" I asked. She put the bag of groceries on the table. "You might as well go back and get the burger and torts for dinner. And get flour. I got canned pumpkin for pies."

"Don't give me no shit, Alice," she said. Times like this she played older sister. She wasn't listening to me. She just shook that silky hair and said, "I'm in love. And he is fine. Ou wee, Sis, the boy is fine."

She was talking like a black person. It's one of her things. I don't mean talking like a black person. Justine does things so you notice. She goes for a response. Like what she started with Jack, the boys' father. Which is behind us coming to Santa Rosa. Mom said it's Justine's fault. I said Jack was old and his family would come for him sooner or later, anyway. Giving Justine credit just fed the fire.

It started with a Social Security check that wandered to the bottom of Mom's purse and stuck itself into something or other. Since a week went by and it didn't come up for air, Jack started to get edgy. "My money, where is it?" he kept asking. He was at the point if his dinner wasn't on time, you was trying to starve him. If a door or window was left open, you wanted him to die of pneumonia. It didn't surprise me he called Clifford, his son.

"What do you mean, you lost it?" Clifford said to Mom.

I heard Jack make the call, so I figured trouble. Clifford and Mom have a history, and Clifford was all along dead against Mom being conservator and signing for Jack. True, Jack wasn't in his right mind half the time, and his insides was shot. Like a sponge that doesn't suck water is what the clinic doctor said. But Mom wasn't no crook. I opened my huckleberry jam. I made toast and set the table. But Clifford, who's more stubborn than a ass and looks worse, seen none of it.

"What's the matter, Mollie, you start on the bottle again?" he asked Mom.

Mom was sitting next to Jack. I looked at the place mats and the food. Anyone could see the old man was cared for and fed.

"Cliff," I said. "Why not put a stop on the check? Go to the Social Security." I felt funny saying Cliff. For a while it was Dad.

"Yeah, and what's my father supposed to eat in the meantime? You kids is using up his money." Then he looked at Mom. "I'm telling you Mollie I'm sick of what's going on here."

He brushed past Justine, who stood in the doorway. I said the check would turn up. Justine said, "Who cares?"

But Justine seen how to use the situation to her end. She never liked Jack. "He nags Mom," she said. I said, "How can he give anybody else attention when he's half dead?" Justine didn't see my point. And it was Easter vacation, no school and no work in the orchards, which means you had nothing to do, no one to see. Or, in Justine's case, nowhere else to pull her stunts. So there was time for thinking.

All of a sudden Justine was dressed up. I mean dressed up

every day. She found clothes I never knowed existed in that house. She mixed skirts and blouses in different ways. She wore down her eyeliner pencil in a week. Each morning she worked her hair into a hive the size of Sheldon's basketball. And when that was done, she sat at the kitchen table painting her nails the color of a red jelly bean. Then, when Mom went to register at the cannery, she started on how she was going to buy a stereo. "I put down fifty dollars at the Golden Ear," she said.

That got Justine a response.

Clifford made it from the reservation in one hour. And he wasn't alone. His white woman was with him, the woman who opens her mouth only when her nose is plugged and she can't breathe. Her I wasn't afraid of. It was Evangeline, his sister, who just as soon spit than say hello. She hated Mom. She looked at me like I was Mom's bare foot and she wanted to smash it under her work boots.

I knowed the old man went into the bedroom and called someone. I figured one of his kids. I just never put two and two together. And neither did Justine. She never got the pleasure of being falsely accused of stealing.

Clifford left his woman and sister guard. Like we would lift the last penny from Jack's pockets. Then he came back with suitcases and boxes. "Come on, Dad," he said, "Evangeline is going to take care of you. She won't spend the money on *her* kids. Not like this lot of swine."

Mom wasn't legal with Jack. There was nothing she could do. It was agreed about the checks only because he lived with us. Since the car was Jack's, it was gone now, too. Even so, she walked to town, then took the bus to Santa Rosa, and canceled the check at the Social Security. Of course, three days later it floats up from the mess in her purse.

Auntie drove Mom to the res, but it was no use. Evangeline wouldn't let her see Jack. She didn't care about the check. I know what Evangeline said. I heard it before. "You screwed my brother, then went for my father. Dirty whore. I don't believe those two kids are my father's. Now get." I reminded Mom that we are from Lake County. "We're not from that res," I said.

❖❖❖

Justine unloaded what I first sent her for, then tore off for the dinner stuff. This time she was back right away. She kept the boys out of my hair. I got busy. My nerves pushed me. Rolling dough for pies, I thought of things. Which is a way I calm my nerves when working won't do it alone. I didn't like what I seen at the store and my imagination started to get the best of me. I thought of Jack. I guess because I hadn't made a pie since we left Healdsburg and came here. I thought how he'd settle down his griping when I cooked. Mom called me whenever he started screeching. He acted drunk, though the hardest thing he took those days was ginger ale. I rolled pie dough and didn't notice when he picked berries or applies or whatever it was out of the bowl. He was quiet. I thought that's what a grandfather would be like.

I set the pies in the oven. Then I got to work on dinner. I turned meat in one skillet and warmed torts in the other. I sent Justine to the store again, this time for cheese and chili sauce. The skillet of meat, a plate of warmed torts, sliced cheese and toast was on the table when Mom got home. Her place was at the head. It's where I put things, like the cheese and chili sauce which she likes on her meat, so you know.

She didn't say nothing. She was tired, I know. She finished eating, then cleaned up and went to play cards with Auntie like she did every night. "Tomorrow, we'll start on the boxes," she told me before she left. She was standing in the kitchen then, combing back her washed hair with Sheldon's pink comb. I kept on with the dishes. It has been two weeks, I thought to myself. Then, with my hands in the greasy water, I resolved to start unpacking myself, no matter what she said. We couldn't wait to see if we was going to stay here or not. Tomorrow, I told myself, first thing. I heard the front door slam.

I was still scrubbing, finishing the damned skillets, when I turned to tell the boys to take a bath before I gave them pie, which I had cooling on the sink. I thought Justine was behind me, seated at the table. But she wasn't. She was standing there with her friend.

"This is Ducker," she said.

First thing I noticed, the boys wasn't there. "They're taking baths," Justine said, seeing how I was looking at the empty seats.

She was referring to them not seeing Ducker. I never heard the door open since it slammed behind Mom. My ears pick up on those things. So I was caught off guard. Justine didn't have to embarrass me. "Close your mouth," she said. "You look like Clifford's wife."

I thought of the boys again. The bathroom door was shut. Then I thought this Ducker might think I'm stupid, or prejudice on account of him being black. My mind was going in several directions at once. I said what made no sense given the circumstances.

"Here, Mister Ducker, sit down and have some pie." I put a pie on the table.

Justine started laughing. I knowed she thought I was in shock seeing this black person in our house.

"It ain't *Mister Ducker*," she said. "It's Ducker. Ducker Peoples."

"Well . . ."

"We don't want pie," she said. She looked toward the bathroom, then to Ducker. "We're going for a walk."

"Nice to meet you . . ." he said, stopping when he got to my name.

"Alice," Justine said.

"Alice," he said.

I was still standing in the same place after they went out the front door. I tore to the window. Then I seen what he looked like. When they was across the street, almost to the store, I remembered who it was in front of me two minutes before. Funny thing about Ducker, he wasn't a man. Well, I mean grown. He was a kid, looked like. Bony arms hanging from flapping short sleeves. His face, shiny smooth, no hair. Like he should be chewing bubblegum and keeping baseball cards. Not holding on to Justine, who was sixteen and looked it.

"Who was here?"

I jumped around, half scared to death. It was Sheldon and Jeffrey out of the bathtub, drying their naked bodies.

"Now dry off in the bathroom," I said.

"Sound like a nigger."

"Hush up, Sheldon."

"Who was here?"

"Nobody."

❖❖❖

Next day something concerned me. Mom was in the kitchen, putting things in cupboards. I heard her even before I got up. Even then I didn't think she'd make a day of it.

"It's Tuesday," she said. "Day off."

She finished with the kitchen before I started breakfast. I had to open cupboards to find things. She was in the bedroom by the time I could help her. Her things she put in the closet first. I seen her red dress from where I was standing, opening the boys' boxes. It's crinoline with ruffles. She wears it with her black patent leather shoes with the sides busted out. Like at Great-Auntie's funeral. Or when she came home with Clifford. Same thing with Jack.

"I guess this means we're staying here," I said.

This move was a trial. Ever since we came to Santa Rosa seemed nothing worked for very long. First that house on West Seventh we couldn't afford. Then the one by the freeway which no one told us they was going to tear down for development. Got two months rent from us, anyway. And now this, which Auntie, whose idea it was for us to come here, got from the landlord she knows.

"What choice do we have?" she asked.

The way she said that matched her business putting things away. Like it was nothing. Seemed to me just then, anyway. Like I said, it concerned me. I was the one who most of the time put things away, after all. No matter what she said before or after. It was just this time she made such a big deal about the neighborhood. Then I guess we moved so much. Just three months in Santa Rosa, and three times already.

"Well," I said. "I like it here. It's a change."

"A lot of blacks," Mom said. "Auntie didn't say so much about that."

"Not everybody can be a Pomo Indian," I said. Since Mom had her stuff on the bed, I spread the boys' things on their sleeping bags, which I hadn't rolled up yet. I sorted underwear on my knees. I thought of reminding her that Justine is part Filipino, and that I'm part Mexican. But that is what Justine would do.

"It's nice having Auntie up the street," I said. I liked the way Mom called her cousin "Auntie," which she did for us kids. "I like hearing Auntie tell stories."

"Ah, don't listen to that old Indian stuff."

Auntie cooks good. She's got recipes. And she's classy. Slender-bodied, not like me and Mom. She knows how to talk to social workers, those kind of people.

I got up and put the folded things in the boys' drawers. Mom was hanging up me and Justine's clothes. "Is this okay?" I asked, seeing how she was putting things where she wanted.

"Your sister, I don't know what she'll do here. Run with them kids out there. Niggers, anything."

That made it click. My worries took form in a picture. Justine and Ducker. Still, I wasn't certain, I mean about Mom just then. Did Sheldon or Jeffrey see last night and tell? It's how Mom says things by not saying them. It puts you in a place where you don't know if she's saying something or not. That's far as she'll go. Unless it's with Justine in a fight.

I was caught, trapped, and bothered just the same. Mom kept working, her back to me.

"Don't worry about Justine," I said.

❖❖❖

We had a normal family dinner that night. I fixed chops and fried potatoes. I cut celery sticks and carrots. People need greens.

But this family don't eat them. Which is one reason there's so much crabbing. They're stopped up.

Mom stayed and helped with the dishes before she went to Auntie's. Of course while things looked peaceful I imagined a disaster. Like Ducker knocking on the door. I wondered if Mom was hanging around in case that happened. I saw loudmouth Sheldon saying, "It's him, It's him." But nothing happened. Even after Mom left.

The boys opened drawers, looking to find where I put their clothes. They kept bugging me about getting the TV fixed and hooked up. Justine moved stuff in the closet to her liking. Me, I only wanted a long enough couch in the living room. I was sleeping on the floor with the boys. I can't sleep in the bed with Mom and Justine. No rest, even with them out like a light.

Next day Mom went fishing to the coast with Auntie. Auntie's Mom and Uncle, they sat in the car when Auntie came in for Mom. The old lady stuck her white head out and said for me to come along. I stood on the front porch to say hello. "I can't," I said. Then she said to me in Indian what men used to say in the old days when they set out fishing. "Get the grill ready, then."

"Damn cannery's so cheap. Got illegals instead of working us extra days," Mom said when she came out.

"Don't think of work, Mollie," Auntie said.

Justine padded up and stood with me to wave good-bye. She was still waving after the car left. I thought she was nuts until I seen it was Ducker she was waving forward. Bold as daylight. He walked right up the front porch.

"Morning, Alice," he said.

I thought of my mouth this time. I kept it closed, not shocked. And I thought what to do. Already the boys seen everything. I got some bread in a plastic bag and headed for the park. I carried Jeffrey part of the way. Sheldon, I just about dragged by the hair.

"What's so big about seeing goldfish?" he said, whining like he does. A sure trait of his father. Proof I would have for Evangeline.

"Shut up," I said. "You damn ass brat."

"You just don't want us there with that—"

I slapped his face. Then he started crying like I tied him to a stake and burned him. Which I wanted to do. We was at the park by then. I put bread in the water for the fish. But nothing worked. Sheldon screamed so the whole park could hear. "I'm telling Mom," he said. Then I thought of the opposite of fire. Water. And I had it right there.

"Shut up," I said, "before I rub your face in dog shit. Now shut up, damn you." Then Jeffrey started crying. "Now see," I said. "Stop it, Sheldon. Please."

I threatened the police. Sheldon quit some, but I knowed what weapon he was harboring, that he'd use against me the minute he seen Mom. I looked at the soggy bread floating on the empty water.

"I'll get the TV fixed," I said. "But not if you act like that, Sheldon."

So I spent what was left in the tobacco tin. It's how I kept Ducker in the house and the boys quiet.

Ducker got to be a regular thing. And more—his friends. The only break I had was Mom's days off. Every night the party was on like clockwork. Soon as Mom was gone to Auntie's ten minutes. Then a worse deal. If Mom went fishing on a day off, the party was all day. I was never one for school, but I wanted this summer over.

Ducker brought his radio. I seen every latest dance. Imagine Justine. She was in her element. She knowed the dances best of anybody and showed it. The boys clapped. It was just boys coming to the house. "Why should girls come here?" Justine said when I asked. "We're the girls."

We had talks, Justine and me. I told her how we couldn't go on like this. She told me not to be so shy. "Don't be afraid to smile," she said. "Don't be worried about your weight."

Then she said how she had a plan for when school started. "I'll show them snobby white girls," she said. "I'll show them Indians from Jack's res, too." She pictured herself walking down the hall with Ducker. She was going to lose fifteen pounds. She was going to wear all kinds of makeup on her face. People would be shocked. They'd be scared of her.

"You already done that plan at Healdsburg," I said, reminding her of how it got her a white boy and a hassle with his family so she hit the mother, knocking her tooth out, and had the cops come and take her to juvee and tell the welfare to take us from Mom.

"Well, everything turned out okay," she said. "You have to see who you are, Alice. Look around and see what you see. See what you can do. How you can be queen. The queen is the baddest. She knows it all. That's how she's queen. Like how I walk at school. Don't be worried about your weight. Some boys like it."

Only thing I was worried about was her plan. I couldn't see the outcome to this one yet. I wasn't a queen. She tried to get certain of Ducker's friends with me. "The kids won't tell, if that's what you're worried about," she said.

This was true. It's not just the TV keeping the boys quiet now. It was Ducker. He took them to the school yard. He showed them all his basketball stuff. After that, I might as well disappear into thin air far as Sheldon cared. I had to get Ducker to make Sheldon mind.

If it was Mom's day off and she went fishing, I took Jeffrey to the park and left Sheldon with Justine. Not that I felt right about it. Another thing I must say, I had a friend. Anthony. Not a boyfriend, not in my mind. Anthony just made himself useful tagging along. "Now don't forget bread for the fish," he said, if we was going to the park. Sometimes we did that, on Mom's day off, all of us. What else Anthony and me talked about I don't know. I got used to him. I didn't even think of him being black. Until we run into Auntie's mom and uncle in the park.

I couldn't get out of it. The two old ones sitting on the park bench seen me five minutes before I seen them. The old lady was looking away the Indian style of looking away. Like you know she seen you and looked away so you don't have to see her. In them situations it's a sign to help yourself and keep walking.

I was hardly fifty feet from them. Anthony with me. He was

carrying Jeffrey on his shoulders. I knowed the picture they seen. I took the old lady's cue. I turned straight around, in the direction we came, and went behind the tall cypress trees, out of sight. It wasn't just that Anthony was black. I don't even think it was black people that bothered Mom so much. It was anything disturbing. It was what nobody talked about.

❖❖❖

I found the sheets that day. I remember. I had my senses. After what happened in the park, I was thinking. I knowed if I tried to wash the sheets in the sink anybody might see the blood. Anybody could walk in. So I burned them out back in the garbage can. Justine never mentioned a thing, even when I was cleaning up. "Me and Ducker had the most fun," she said, after Mom went to Auntie's that night.

Indians say blood is a sign of the devil. Where it spills will be poison everlasting. That's how a place gets taboo. Auntie told me a story once. It was at Great-Auntie's funeral. It was to explain why Mom didn't cry, why Mom didn't like Great-Auntie who raised Mom and didn't like having to raise her. Great-Auntie got stuck with Mom and her sisters after some man poisoned Mom's mom. But here's what I think of. How Mom and her sisters found their Mom in a puddle of salamander eggs and blood.

With Justine the expected worried me much as the unexpected. The expected, I worried when. The unexpected, what. When came like a straight shot, now that I look back at things. Mom came home early from Auntie's that same night. After the park, Justine's episode, and all my cleaning the floors and bed. Why that night? Why at all? I can't believe Mom didn't know what was going on before. Maybe she didn't want us to think she was dumb. Maybe she had to keep face for Auntie, if the old lady said something to Auntie. I don't know.

By this time our house was party central. It was Justine's party. She was queen. That's what the boys called her. Dance, Justine, dance. The neighborhood knowed Justine. She was dressing again. She was dressed up everyday. Mom saw the party.

She stood in the doorway half a minute, then turned around and left.

I unplugged Ducker's radio. I told everyone to get out. Must've been ten guys there. Something came over me so I was fierce. Justine said to shut up. The older sister, again. Usually, I ignored her, kept on about my business. Like Mom with most things. But this time I was Justine and more. I was going to floor her with the weight of my body. She must've seen because she was stopped cold. She tore out the front door with the guys.

Sheldon and Jeffrey, I put in the tub. Sheldon, I slapped in the mouth for no reason. He never made a peep. Neither one of them did. I put them to bed. No TV.

I finished the dishes and put them away. I wiped down the stove and refrigerator with Windex. I did the kitchen table too. Then I put together flour and water for torts. Torts by scratch. Mom's favorite. I was plopping them when Justine snuck past to the bedroom.

I finished. I set the torts on the clean table. I placed a fresh kitchen towel over the pile to keep in the warmth. Then next to a place mat made of paper towels I put a half cube of butter and the sugar bowl with a spoon next to it. Finally, I filled a glass with ice cubes and put it to the left of the place mat, opposite the butter and sugar.

Mom didn't come home until late. Around midnight. I was in the front room. I must've been dozing in the chair because when I opened my eyes, half startled, Mom was past me, turning into the bedroom. I thought of Justine and Mom in that bed together. I didn't hear a sound. Then I dozed again.

It was early morning I heard it. Like two roosters woke up and found themselves in the same pen. It started low in the bedroom, then came at full blast to the kitchen. Really loud. I thought of the boys. I pictured them hiding their heads for cover in their sleeping bags. I didn't move from the chair where I'd been all night.

Mom was hollering. "You're the lowest dirty, black-neck squaw. Chink . . ." And Justine. "Which one is my father? Tell me, you drunk slob, low-life Indian. Prove you're not the whore everyone says you are."

Then I heard the cupboard and something slam on the kitchen table. I couldn't believe my ears. I knowed without seeing what it was. Still, I didn't move. I don't know, it was strange. Then Mom comes out, her hair all wild from sleeping, and takes off, out the front door.

"Look how stupid," Justine said, nodding to the shotgun on the table. It was Jack's, what he forgot. I was still rubbing my eyes, just standing there. I picked it up and put it away.

"Fat bitch thought she was going to scare me with that," Justine said.

"Shut up," I said. "Just shut up."

I turned on the oven and warmed the untouched torts for breakfast.

❖❖❖

Mom might as well moved to Auntie's. We hardly seen her, except when she came back to sleep. She put so much money in the tobacco tin for me to spend. Like when she was drinking, only now we never seen her, and I didn't have to keep the money in my pockets for fear she'd take it out of the tin. Once, when she was drinking, she accused me of stealing the money. I'd spent it, of course, and gave her what I had left. Five dollars. She went berserk, hollering in the backyard. Just screaming, no words. Someone called the police. She stopped when they got there, then locked herself in the bathroom and cried herself to sleep. Later, to bug Mom, Justine said she called the police.

Mom strayed, like I said. It was me and Justine and the boys. And Ducker and Anthony and whoever else. Seemed nothing I could do.

We walked together, all of us. Who I mentioned. Justine didn't hang back at the house with Ducker so much anymore. She didn't say it, but I knowed she was anxious to try out with other boys what she tried out with Ducker. Certain things she said. The ways she talked to Ducker's friends and looked at them. Especially Kolvey, who was bigger, more grown, like a man. Signs Justine was up to something.

Anyway, I fixed the lunches. Most days we went to the park. Sometimes we walked other places. Like the fairgrounds where they was putting up the rides. Once we took a bus to the mall. Anthony would help me with things. He carried the Koolmate so we'd have cold pop. Another thing he did was the shopping. "What do you need?" he asked me. Like we was a pair. But there was nothing between us. In fact, lots of times at the park I went off by myself. I left him where Justine was pulling her stunts and where the two old ones sat and seen whatever they wanted. I took Jeffrey and went behind the cypress trees. He was the only one obeyed me. "Time to take a nap," I told him. It was cool there, away from everyone, and I pulled him close and slept.

It was Anthony who got me up. He told me something was going on with Justine. I was dead asleep on the grass there, and I felt Jeffrey slip from my arms.

"What?" I asked.

But by this time both Jeffrey and Anthony was looking through the trees. Then I seen it, too. Some skinny black girl and a couple of her friends, small and skinny like her, stood about twenty yards from Justine. Far enough so they was shouting and I could hear. The black girl was sticking out her hand, curling her finger like a caterpillar walking. "Miss Doris say for Mister Ducker Peoples to come right this minute," she was saying.

The boys was still on the ground, setting there. Justine was standing in all her clothes and makeup. Red lips. Nails. "What's this Miss Doris shit?" she said.

The girl shifted her weight to one side and put her hand on her hip. "Miss Doris say for Ducker to come right this minute if he knows what's good for him."

"Justine say Miss Doris eat shit," Justine said.

Then I grabbed Jeffrey. It happened fast. Justine crossed the line. She was face-to-face with that girl, and, with no words, just popped her one upside the head. The girl went over, like she flopped, hitting the ground on her side. Her two friends jumped back, like Justine would go after them next.

"Justine say to eat shit, Miss Doris," Justine said, looking down at that girl who was setting up now holding her face.

"I'm telling you, your sister shouldn't done that," Anthony said.

Something in the way he said that scared me. Like I knowed he told the truth.

"There's your grandparents," he said.

I looked to where Anthony was looking. With the commotion I hadn't seen the old ones on the bench, if they was ever sitting there. They was walking in the opposite direction, away.

"They ain't my grandparents," I said.

❖❖❖

It was in the air. Justine's doings filled the rooms of our house, in every cupboard I opened, every potato I sliced. Like you seen the white of the potato and seen Justine when you was doing everything not to. And it was outside. Like fog settling in the streets. It was between the houses, across at the store. You seen it in the way a bird sat still on the telephone wire.

I made macaroni and cheese and potato salad. Macaroni and cheese is easy. Just boil macaroni and melt the cheese. Potato salad, that takes time. Boiling the potatoes, chopping celery and onions. Mayonnaise. All that. I did it. And more. Two pies from scratch. And a cake, even if that was from a box. You'd think we was still on the reservation and I was putting up food for a funeral.

Mom knowed, too. After dinner, she didn't go to Auntie's. How could she explain herself being there when Auntie and them knowed about the trouble here?

I never sat, not once while the others ate. The pies and all that. And I started right in with the dishes. I frosted the cake and set it on the table with a knife and new paper plates. I folded paper towels to make napkins at each place. I put a plastic fork on top of each napkin. I thought of candles and ice cream, but it was too late for that.

I was scrubbing the pots when I heard the first noises and looked over my shoulder and seen the crowd collecting outside on the street. From the sink, if you turned around, you could look through the kitchen door and the front door to the street. I wanted to close the front door, but I didn't move. I mean I kept on in the kitchen. Mom was at the table, kind of peeking out. She had her hands on her knees. Straight arms, like she does when she's going to get up. The boys looked at the cake like they was waiting for me to cut it. I was just about to do that. I thought, what am I doing forgetting about the cake.

Then Justine came out from the bedroom.

She was in Mom's red dress. That's no getup for the occasion, I thought. Not that I lingered on that thought just then. Mom got up and went into the bedroom and the boys followed her. The bedroom door closed.

"Don't do it," I said to Justine.

I guess someone outside seen her, too, because the yelling and name-calling rose up. "Dirty whore. Come out and pick on someone your own size. Slut." All that. I looked once then, and the street was filled with people. Some was near the steps. Young people, old people, kids, filling the air. Shouting.

"You don't have to do it, Justine," I told her again. "Just tell them you didn't mean for them guys to go and say yes."

She looked at me straight. Not like she was mad, or even scared. Kind of like she had a plan. Like she does when she tilts her head and half smiles at you. "I told them, 'yes, I would fight that Miss Doris' sisters,' because I ain't scared of nobody. Not three big-ass mean nigger bitches, nobody. They'll see. I'm the queen, remember?"

That's when I took inventory of her getup. The red dress, too big for Justine, was cinched with a black belt, which matched her pump shoes. And she had nylons on and the delicate gold necklace she found in the girls' gym. Her hair was done up just so. Her face, it was a movie star's. This I was focusing on all the while the people outside came closer and louder. The house was surrounded. I thought girls fight in old clothes. Like the times in Healdsburg when Justine met in the park to fight someone.

"Anyway," I said, "you can't fight in them clothes."

She was still looking at me the same way. Half smiling like I didn't know a thing. And she kept that smiling and looking straight at me when she reached to the table and picked up the knife. She tucked it in the front dress pocket, her hand on the handle, and walked out.

When that many people is surrounding the house and screaming, everything is clattering. The walls, windows. It's like things was going to cave in or blow wide apart. It's where the first rip is you look. And I seen it. A rock through the front window. Glass shattering. A hole wide as a fist.

I was in the doorway between the kitchen and front room. That was far as I got, and when I looked out for Justine, after seeing that rock come through the window, she was gone. Just the crowd screaming and the empty house. Like the boys and Mom wasn't even there. Like they was rolling away, around the corner, out of reach. Everybody. It all just went so fast. The whole place blowing apart. Then I seen the hole again. I was in shock by this time, I guess. I turned around and started putting dishes away. I don't know what. I opened cupboards, and seen the gun. Jack's shotgun. I ran to the front porch and shot it.

❖❖❖

I didn't know nothing after that. Just colors. Everybody moving. Voices. People talking to me.

"Dumb ass, bitch. What'd you do that for?

"Alice, you're the queen now. Nobody's going to mess with you, girl."

"Dumb ass, bitch."

"Hey, Alice. You're bad, girl. Justine never got a lick in."

"Stupid, crazy bitch. Now the cops'll come. Dumb ass, bitch."

They said I just stood there with that gun. Like a statue or something. Like I been there a hundred years.

I thought of that and the other things I heard after, when I started to gain my senses. I was standing in the kitchen, against the sink. Auntie was there by that time, and a good thing. She was talking to two cops in our kitchen. She said the blast wasn't a gun. Some kids who throwed a cherry bomb at our window and made a hole. They believed her, because they never searched the house. She was in official's clothes, the kind that match her voice when she talks to social workers.

"It's a single-parent family," she was saying. "It's an Indian family just moved to town."

I looked at Justine. She was lifting a neat piece of chocolate cake to her mouth with a plastic fork. Her I'd have to reckon with on account I upset her show. I looked at Mom and the boys. They was eating cake, too. Auntie was still talking, painting that picture of us not capable of nothing. I seen the cops looking at the table while she talked. I seen what they seen, what Auntie was saying. But I seen more. I seen everything.

VICKIE SEARS

❖❖❖

Dancer

TELL YOU JUST HOW IT WAS with her. Took her to a dance not long after she come to live with us. Smartest thing I ever done. Seems like some old Eaglespirit woman saw her living down here and came back just to be with Clarissa.

Five years old she was when she come to us. Some foster kids come with lots of stuff, but she came with everything she had in a paper bag. Some dresses that was too short. A pair of pants barely holding a crotch. A pile of ratty underwear and one new nightgown. Mine was her third foster home in as many months. The agency folks said she was *so-cio-path-ic*. I don't know nothing from that. She just seemed like she was all full up with anger and scaredness like lots of the kids who come to me. Only she was a real loner. Not trusting nobody. But she ran just like any other kid, was quiet when needed. Smiled at all the right times. If you could get her to smile, that is. Didn't talk much, though.

Had these ferocious dreams, too. Real screamer dreams they were. Shake the soul right out of you. She'd be screaming and crying with her little body wriggling on the bed, her hair all matted up on her woody-colored face. One time I got her to tell me what she was seeing, and she told me how she was being chased by a man with a long knife what he was going to kill her with and nobody could hear her calling out for help. She didn't talk too much about them, but they was all bad like that one. Seemed the most fierce dreams I ever remember anybody ever having outside of a vision seek. They said her tribe was Assiniboin, but they weren't for certain. What was for sure was that she was a fine dark-eyed girl just meant for someone to scoop up for loving.

Took her to her first dance in September, like I said, not long after she came. It wasn't like I thought it would be a good thing to do. It was just that we was all going. Me, my own kids, some nieces and nephews and the other children who was living with us. The powwow was just part of what we done all the time. Every month. More often in the summer. But this was the regular first Friday night of the school year. We'd all gather up and go to the school. I was thinking on leaving her home with a sitter cause she'd tried to kill one of the cats a couple of days before. We'd had us a big talk and she was grounded, but, well, it seemed like she ought to be with us.

Harold, that's my oldest boy, he and the other kids was mad with her, but he decided to show her around anyhow. At the school he went through the gym telling people, "This here's my sister, Clarissa." Wasn't no fuss or anything. She was just another one of the kids. When they was done meeting folks, he put her on one of the bleachers near the drum and went to join the men. He was in that place where his voice cracks but was real proud to be drumming. Held his hand up to his ear even, some of the time. Anyhow, Clarissa was sitting there, not all that interested in the dance or drum, when Molly Graybull come out in her button dress. Her arms was all stretched out, and she was slipping around, preening on them spindles of legs that get skinnier with every year. She was well into her seventies, and I might as well admit, Molly had won herself a fair share of dance contests. So it wasn't no surprise how a little girl could get so fixated on Molly. Clarissa watched her move around-around-around. Then all the rest of the dancers after Molly. She sure took in a good eyeful. Fancy dance. Owl dance. Circle dance. Even a hoop dancer was visiting that night. Everything weaving all slow, then fast. Around-around until that child couldn't see nothing else. Seemed like she was struck silent in the night, too. Never had no dreams at all. Well, not the hollering kind anyways.

Next day she was more quiet than usual only I could see she was looking at her picture book and tapping the old one-two, one-two. Tapping her toes on the rug with the inside of her head going around and around. As quiet as she could be, she was.

A few days went on before she asks me, "When's there gonna be another dance?"

I tell her in three weeks. She just smiles and goes on outside, waiting on the older kids to come home from school.

The very next day she asks if she can listen to some singing. I give her the tape recorder and some of Joe Washington from up to the Lummi reservation and the Kicking Woman Singers. Clarissa, she takes them tapes and runs out back behind the chicken shed, staying out all afternoon. I wasn't worried none, though, cause I could hear the music the whole time. Matter of fact, it like to make me sick of them same songs come the end of three weeks. But that kid, she didn't get into no kind of mischief. Almost abnormal how good she was. Worried me some to see her so caught up but it seemed good too. The angry part of her slowed down so's she wasn't hitting the animals or chopping on herself with sticks like she was doing when she first come. She wasn't laughing much either, but she started playing with the other kids when they come home. Seemed like everybody was working hard to be better with each other.

Come March, Clarissa asks, "Can I dance?"

For sure, the best time for teaching is when a kid wants to listen, so we stood side to side with me doing some steps. She followed along fine. I put on a tape and started moving faster, and Clarissa just kept up all natural. I could tell she'd been practicing lots. She was doing real good.

Comes the next powwow, which was outside on the track field, I braided Clarissa's hair. Did her up with some ermine and bead ties, then give her a purse to carry. It was all beaded with a rose and leaves. Used to be my aunt's. She held it right next to her side with her chin real high. She joined in a Circle dance. I could see she was watching her feet a little and looking how others do their steps, but mostly she was doing wonderful. When Molly Graybull showed up beside her, Clarissa took to a seat and stared. She didn't dance again that night, but I could see there was dreaming coming into her eyes. I saw that fire that said to practice. And she did. I heard her every day in her room. Finally bought her her very own tape recorder so's the rest of us could listen to music too.

Some months passed on. All the kids was getting bigger. Clarissa, she went into the first grade. Harvey went off to community college up in Seattle, and that left me with Ronnie being the oldest at home. Clarissa was keeping herself busy all the time going over to Molly Graybull's. She was coming home with Spider Woman stories and trickster tales. One night she speaks up at supper and says, right clear and loud, "I'm an Assiniboin." Clear as it can be, she says it again. Don't nobody have to say nothing to something that proud said.

Next day I started working on a wing dress for Clarissa. She was going to be needing one for sure real soon.

Comes the first school year powwow and everyone was putting on their best. I called for Clarissa to come to my room. I told her, "I think it's time you have something special for yourself." Then I held up the green satin and saw her eyes full up with glitter. She didn't say nothing. Only kisses me and runs off to her room.

Just as we're all getting out of the car, Clarissa whispered to me, "I'm gonna dance with Molly Graybull." I put my hand on her shoulder to say, "You just listen to your spirit. That's where your music is."

We all danced an Owl dance, a Friendship dance, and a couple of Circle dances. Things was feeling real warm and good, and then it was time for the women's traditional. Clarissa joined the circle. She opened her arms to something nobody but her seemed to hear. That's when I saw that old Eagle woman come down and slide right inside of Clarissa, scooping up that child.

There Clarissa was, full up with music. All full with that old, old spirit, letting herself dance through Clarissa's feet. Then Molly Graybull come dancing alongside Clarissa, and they was both the same age.

MARY TALLMOUNTAIN

❖❖❖

Snatched Away

NEAR FOUR MILE summer camp, the Indians were nudging their fishwheel into calmer water. The Yukon was in a fierce, frowning mood. It tossed spray hissing skyward, hurled it back down like heavy rain into the weltering currents. Where stubborn little creeks shouldered out insistently, the river surged to attack, writhing up in silt-brown rapids. Accustomed to its tempers, the men kept tending the wheel, which alternately plunged two carved spruce arms into the current to rotate with the tide. An oblong wire basket at the end of the arm scooped up fish; on the next rotation, as the arm tipped, the fish slithered into a box nailed to the raft deck of the fishwheel; the arm loomed up again like a windmill blade, fell back, and turned with the force of the tides. The ascent of dog salmon heralded the coming of autumn; fish flowed in a stream of silvery rose.

Quick dark silhouettes against the greens of alder and cottonwood, the Indians were part of sky, river, earth itself: they wove dories through tumbling water, poled schools of darting salmon, strode like lumberjacks. Born rivermen, Clem thought with respect. Still, the river was a tough customer. In the seven years he'd been here, ten men and boys had drowned between Nulato and Kaltag.

Andy was the latest, and him only 22.

The day in 1916 when Clem had unloaded his gear at Nulato Garrison, he had met 15-year-old Andy on the riverbank, where the Army had barged the new soldiers upriver. A crooked tooth leaning into his wide white grin, the lad had offered to help Clem with his violin and banjo cases. Even then, Andy was the best there was: hunter, fisherman, trapper, nobody could beat him. Only the river could have beaten Andy.

Clem's boat chugged into the immense, misted expanses.

He wondered how Andy had felt, knowing himself caught, fighting. Did he see sky and trees flashing past? How long had he struggled, tumbled over and over in the fast rips out here where nothing existed to snag a man and hold him solid so he could keep his head above the deadly tides. Andy had never been found, though two months had passed. A cry had been heard on shore, but when the men got out and rowed toward the sound, only the voice of the river met them. Andy's empty canoe had floated in a gentle riff behind the island of silt growing in midstream.

Their friendship had stretched through the years. Clem had eaten with Andy's large family, gone with the men on hunting trips when he had leave from duty. He had thought the natives liked him as well as any *Gisakk,* the word they had for white men.

Clem thought of the afternoon he had spent talking on the riverbank with Andy and Little Jim. He thought Little Jim was related too, some way. Cousins, maybe? He couldn't find out how these people were hooked up together. Something about the families, how their forebears were related, the kinship among the whole Athabascan people, was dim and old as time.

Clem glanced over at Andy now and then. He had already discovered that these natives didn't like to be stared at; he tried to keep them from catching him. Andy didn't seem to notice. In the tall grass he lounged on his side, wearing a white man's wool shirt and store-bought overalls, chewing a grass stem, fur cap low over his eyes. He looked just like his father, Big Mike, the stubby Russian, the way Mike must have looked when he was 15 and a lot skinnier. Andy's eyes were fixed on the river. About 50 feet out, a small bundle came rolling down fast, something tied tight in a gunnysack.

"Hey what's that?" Clem asked.

"Yeah," Little Jim muttered.

"It's a baby," Andy said, following it with his gaze as it tossed and turned round and round downriver.

"What the hell?" Clem thought he'd heard wrong.

"Baby. Throwed away." Andy chewed fast, wagging the grass back and forth. "When baby come out, maybe he got bum leg, maybe no leg, or he come out wrong, head mashed. Women say he's no good, tie him up, dump him over riverbank." He appeared to draw in his breath, but Clem couldn't fathom any change in his expression. "They use to do it in old time," Andy said. "Things were worse then. They quit doing it, but sometimes women still throw them if they're too bad." Andy looked out over the river, barely rippling, shining, innocent. A flock of snowgeese, in formation passing south, announced their departure in ancient ceremonial voice.

Little Jim said, "Lots of babies die in old time. They get Gisakk disease. That mean white-man sickness. We got a doctor now, but when Grandfather was living it was real bad. The people name him Old Russian."

Clem asked, "How did Old Russian get here on the river?" Andy said, "Grandfather—well, he's really my grandfather's papa, you know, he come upriver with three Russians. We call them Gisakk too, like all white men. They talk-talk all the time, maybe we call them that name because they talk about Cossack, it go round, get to be called Gisakk. " Both men chuckled as if at an old joke. Andy went on, "But then came other Russians, buy furs from our people in our old hunting mountains, we call Kaiyuh. Those ones build big Russian kashim to live in, and trader's post store, on the river south of where Nulato sits now." He pointed the grass stem south. "Down there. That town is all gone now. Koyukuk warrior start war, burn down kashim, everybody die inside." *Silence followed while the men considered the ancient violence.*

"After they die, sickness come," Little Jim said. "First, it's smallpox. Old people say Gisakk bring it, who knows where it come from. No way to write it down. That's long time ago. Those people only talk, not read. Now we have this new sickness, this consumption, TB."

"That pretty bad?" *Clem asked.*

Little Jim frowned. "Yeah, no way to cure that when it get ahold. If they could go Outside, there's hospitals for it, but who could go Outside? Cost too much dinga." *He rubbed his thumb against his finger in the universal sign for money.*

Andy swept his arm wide. "Many other ways to die, though," *he said, crossing his legs, settling deeper into the grass.* "Sometimes a house catch fire, we fight it with river water, maybe people burn up anyway. Short life for some of us. That's why our people get married so young." *He laughed.*

Little Jim stared downriver. "Lots of people drown. The current play tricks, hide, next thing it's got you. Pretty near got me, couple times." *He grinned.* "We don't swim. Nobody swims."

"Jesus," *Clem said.*

With a heave of brown water, the river slammed a log into the bow of the boat, jolting Clem out of his flashes of reverie. Whew! No damage done! Seven years ago, he would have been alert to the river's tricks at a safe enough distance to get out of the way, he thought, steering away from the middle. The river hadn't been too tough for him back then; he was already a rugged fellow fresh from cavalry duty on the Mexican border, lean as a malamute, hair a sunbleached shock against perennially brown skin. His intent sea-colored eyes incessantly changed with the lights, focusing as if to X-ray everything he saw. His air was alert and confident. Seven years on the Yukon had converted him into a critter tough as walrus hide. It was his first taste of the wilderness: raising dogs, training them for sled work and distance travel; running search-rescue missions by dogteam in winter, by motorboat in summer. All around him stretched the stark and beautiful land. He tried to write his feelings in notes of music on scraps like the secret fragments of a poet, but they escaped him.

Away in a corner of his mind, an old piano tinkled, playing Mary Joe's favorites, "Yum Yum Waltz" and "Pitti Sing Polka." The notes echoed tinnily in his head. At Ruby, a red-hot boom town, he had been playing the tunes steadily for the past three days and nights. The miners and whores had hollered for dance music. He had rounded up young Charlie Wilson, a native banjo picker, and they went up by motorboat. Those wild rough folks had insisted on high jinks and kept Clem and Charlie playing day and night. Wouldn't let them rest, threw gold and dollar bills to them, yelled for them to keep going, offered bad bootleg he and Charlie waved away. The boys worked themselves so dizzy that Charlie had stayed on with kinfolks for a visit. Clem was dog-tired, he was homesick, he'd been away from Mary Joe too long already.

His biceps were numb from the kick of the tiller against him; that fast leaping current was deadly; he kept veering into it. Twenty- and thirty-foot trees tumbled up like matchsticks, roots clawing toward the sky. He swung over, pivoted the boat into still water. Even after he dropped anchor, the river kept grabbing, trying to yank him back. He knuckled his eyes. When his vision cleared, he saw tall green reeds in a slough 60 yards off. Suddenly a clump of ducks rose, bunched, started climbing. Shots cracked. Clem flattened fast. Four birds dropped; the flock fluttered south out of gunsight.

Who the hell is it? I didn't see a boat, he thought. Nothing moved. Then Floyd Tommy pried out of the reeds, holding a bunch of mallards. He ambled over. "Got a couple." He held up the birds. "I come down here early, before the sun. Sometimes a few duck stop here."

"Nice fat mallard," Clem said.

"Not so bad, been feedin' all summer." Floyd's gangling young body was wet to his waist.

"Scared them up, I guess," Clem said, climbing out of the boat, his red rubber Pacs plopping in the water. Ice tingled clear through the heavy rubber, the thick wool socks, on up the long johns.

"Feeding off of the bottom," Floyd said and grabbed a duck by its ringed neck, and a second. He dropped them on the grass. "Grub for the pot, anyways."

"That's swell. Thanks." Clem admired the birds, the green shine of their feathers.

"Nothing extra," Floyd said.

Clem fished out a tin of King Albert. "Take a smoke," he offered.

Floyd pocketed the tobacco. He coughed deeply and spit. The spit hung on a weed, a strand of pink swaying in the wind. He walked away and Clem saw his sharp shoulderblades, thin butt. Consumption, he thought. Kid shouldn't smoke. Sorry I gave him tobacco.

Clem crawled up the bank, lay flat under a tree. Fine here, let his whole body go quiet, he thought, let the stillness float into and around him while he stared at the scrambled pale blue sky.

Kid's cough made him think of Mary Joe.

Right after Clem had come to Nulato, he'd struck up an acquaintance with Cap Jaeger, the trader. They played fiddle and guitar for dances, with Freddy Kriska jingling and clinking away on his banjo. They practiced in Cap's store.

One evening Clem went outside to take a breath. Mary Joe was sitting on the porch step. He couldn't resist. He laid his hand on her gleaming, waist-long hair, bound with a bright purple band. "What a beautiful girl," he said. Once he'd seen her running through the village, hair flying, had seen that even in shapeless trousers and faded cotton shirt, she was lovely.

She got up; her smile seemed to glow in the dusk as she floated closer in a movement sensuous as a cat's; they faced each other. He smelled wind and furs, and something elusive like sweet grass.

They stood motionless, barely breathing. Then she broke the hush. "I'm about as tall as you, Clem Stone. You're my brother's friend. You know, Andy. I come and listen to you play music, but I always go away. This time, I risk it."

"That's no risk, girl. I'm not dangerous," he murmured. The very air felt electric with the closeness of her.

"Oh, yes, you are," she said. She pulled out a large white handkerchief, coughed lightly into it. A tingling—was it a foreshadowing of an unknowable sorrow?—shivered along his nerves. Somehow, he sensed, it broke an impasse.

She told him she'd just turned 21. She lived with her father, her brother Andy, and a younger brother, Steven. Her mother, Matmiya, two sisters, and a third brother had died of TB. Times were bad for the people. She did laundry for soldiers at the station. They wore "Alaska Warmies," a special Army issue of long johns, and the damned brown Army soap shrank them midget-sized. Mary Joe had a special way to wash them. It kept her busy, along with looking after her menfolk, getting in a little fishing, tending a few traps.

Just surviving, she had skills he'd never known existed. The traps and snares she so carefully laid, empty when the animals couldn't come out to tackle the howling cold. Wolves running hungry. Moose, caribou, galloping broomstick thin before the wolves.

And in the village, the hungry children.

Affection for her family was part of the whole business of hunger, he thought. It hadn't been like that with his folks, back in California. Hardly a time he could remember when Pa or even Ma showed their love for him and brother Jass, except when they were tykes, and then it was like he dreamed it. Becky, his mother, was always wrapped in thought, eyes far away, lips moving. How badly he wanted to get into her head! She kept her thoughts wrapped up inside, the way she wrapped her outside, in dark dresses and big white aprons with tails that tied round and round and hid her tiny waist. He hoped she was happy at last. She'd finally married Balch Jopson, the hired man, after she divorced Pa. Right away, Pa married that woman from Hoptown.

Pure orneriness. Pa had that terrible temper . . . suspicioned
Balch and Becky so hard he finally had to leave her. Clem
frowned. He'd never figured out why as a kid he'd been jealous
over Becky and Balch too . . . Vaguely, he knew he'd inherited
a trait of jealousy. He supposed he'd got it from Pa. When he
thought of Mary Joe and Taria, he got too mad to talk. She had
married that old man when she was 14, had a son the next year.
Not long ago, Taria had gone down to live in Kaltag and had
taken their son with him. Why had she let that boy go, and him
only five? When Clem tried to talk to her about it, she always got
him off the track with a funny remark or dinner on the table, or
lovemaking, anything to derail him.

Mary Joe was jealous too, in her secret way. There was the
day he'd been talking to young Talla and Mary Joe came along
the boardwalk, stalked right up to them, and walloped him a
good one on the jaw. She never mentioned it afterwards, but it
kind of lay there between them. Mary Joe had wanted one of
those little medicine sacks made of caribou hide, to hang on her
belt. He'd asked Talla to make one, and he'd been telling her
how the initials ought to be. Mary Joe thought he was sparking
the girl! Well, jealousy or no, Clem and Mary Joe had given
Lidwynne and Michael enough love to last a lifetime.

His mind magnetized to a worry that had been shoved back,
these few hectic days. He and Mary Joe were about to lose their
kids. She had found out from Doc Merrick that she had consumption, and he had offered to adopt them. Mary Joe had got
so worked up over that, he realized, she'd forgotten Clem's last
hitch was about up. Strange, but no use worrying yet. He'd just
have to let things take their course. Hell, like he always figured, it
would come out in the wash. . . .

A jay screamed from a lodgepole pine. Clem stood, whirled
his arms, kneaded his shoulders, took a fast run along the beach
and back. New energy shuttled through his blood. Kicking the
boat off, he noticed his tiller arm had eased up. He'd make it. He
had a damn good bulge of strength in those biceps. But his
calculation had misfired again. As usual, he had underrated the
river. The damned thing yanked him every which way. Time

blurred. No-Oy, as the natives called the sun, was well up the sky. Its light dazzled him and he centered in again on the tiller. God! that sprint of energy hadn't lasted! At last, through his daze, he saw Pete Slough alongside. Soft grayblue wings of a pair of teal flapped, rose. His eyes swarmed with blurs as he turned from the river glare, staggered stiffly up the bank.

Willy Pitka was netting whitefish in the ruffled water of the slough. He hauled in three fish, 10 to 14 inches long, threw them into a washtub. Willy looked as if he had always been there. He was strong, fierce-looking like most of the Ten'a Athabascans; good hunter, ten kids working every day, well fed. "Fishing pretty good today," Willy said, pointing to the nearly filled tub.

Clem pummeled his cramp-knotted arm. "Good big fish," he said.

"You come down from Ruby, yah?" Willy eased the handwoven net into the water. It flowed between his chunky fingers, barely rippling into the water.

"Been playing for a dance up there," Clem said, walking back and forth, the numbness inching out of his knees.

"River pretty fast, plenty wood coming down," Willy said.

"It was real bad a few miles. Got tired fighting it and stopped up yonder, below Tommy's camp. Floyd was getting a few mallard."

Willy nodded. "There's a few places up there, duck come every year about this time. Floyd knows them pretty good. Oh, yeah, you got to watch that river."

"Need eyes in back of your head. Easier in winter when she's frozen over," Clem said.

"You still got your lead dog Beauty?" Willy asked.

"You bet. She's my brood mother, pure malamute. I've got the best team on the river. Hey, you know Manuska built me a dogsled all spruce, not a nail, bound with walrus hide. Laid it around the joints wet, and it dried like iron."

"How much you pay him?"

"Couple sawbucks."

"Worth it. You take care of your team there at the station?"

"Yeah. Got a pot outside to boil their fish. I got three males, two females, out of Beauty. Bought my breeder, Moose, from old man Patsy, set me back fifty but he's worth every cent. Saved my bacon more'n once on the trail. He knows everything, even in the worst storms."

Willy chuckled. "Like you got money in the bank. Uncle Sam has to pay every time you use that team for Army business, yah?"

"Paid for itself a hundred times over." Clem pulled out a package of salmon strip and biscuit. The rich smoke made his taste buds water. He lay back and eased his shoulder muscles into the sunwarm padding of dry reeds. He looked up at the willows. They leaned nearly horizontal over the water. Fallen trees had been bleached to ivory skeletons, and lay crushed and scattered. Small waves slapped the sides of Willy's dory. The watery sounds soothed Clem to sleep.

"You got it made better'n three-quarters downriver to home now." The voice was just loud enough. Guess Willy figured I'd snooze too long, Clem thought. Time to get on. The voice continued, "You going to Nulato?" Willy's dense eyebrows almost grazed his straight soot-colored lashes.

"That's where I'm heading. Two, maybe three hours?"

"Three hours do it, I guess," Willy said, hauling net. He tossed another pair of whitefish into the tub, piled the net with great care into the dory. His teeth gleamed with good humor.

"Your camp downriver a ways?" Clem asked. He stretched and yawned. He thought, I'm rested now, maybe I can make it before dark.

"Yeah, we use the same old camp. Had that camp many years. Good run on kings this summer. Usually I come up here, get whitefish, let my boys handle the wheel."

Clem looked south. Away, faint in the clear air, the purple crest of the Kaiyuh range rested on the horizon. "Willy!" He pointed. "You think there's a Woodsman in Kaiyuh?"

Willy's face crinkled around the grin in tiny rolls of brown, velvety skin. "Oh, sure. Lotsa Woodsman over there."

"You ever see one?" Clem wasn't sure Willy was on the level. Probably joshing him.

"Yep. Mad like bear, bad like· bear. Steal babies." Willy's crinkles deepened and formed fans. They laughed.

"So long, Willy."

"See you."

Clem stepped into his boat and pulled the starter cord. The engine barked and on the next yank snapped to life. Almost at once, the boat kept trying to get out of his hands and pull out into the heavy rip. He needed all his wits just keeping her steady outside the churning middle river. A red horde of dog salmon thrashed upriver. They leaped against the edges of the riptide, fell back. He steered away, the tiller held hard against his body. It's a stampede out there, he thought, looking over his shoulder at the line of furious red dog salmon action. There's something besides fish alive, out in that river.

He had a sudden sense of repeated time, of some old and half forgotten grief.

He was carrying Lidwynne along a village path, and her frosty breaths puffed out on the windless· air. Mary Joe's boots padded behind him as his heavy steps angrily crunched the snow. He held the swinging lantern; its light bobbed in yellow winkings. His mind babbled. We will go on through the night snow and we will never come back. We will go to the hills, Mary Joe. They will never part us. She caught up with him. There was no sound as Mary Joe looked into the baby's face. The moon reflected roundly silver in her pupils. Snow drifted down out of the spruces. The silence was broken by a sighing sound, descending from an immense distance. His anger left him. Only weariness remained. He turned with Mary Joe and they went back. Inside the cabin, he laid the baby in bed and kissed the corner of her sleeping mouth.

At his shoulder, Mary Joe said, "You can't have her. She must go somewhere else." His breath was heavy; he heard the muffled beating of his heart. Her face was deep in the shadows. "Clem, I have a new baby in here." She laid his hand on her belly and they rested on the lynx-fur blankets. His mind played a small wandering melody; they drifted to sleep.

He did not know whether it was a dream or a strange, obscure knowledge; now it had come again to him in the fury of the river, the somber weariness of his body; he saw their faces in the aimless, enclosing mists of the Yukon, and he knew it would be so for all of his life.

He looked at his hands, rigidly white on the tiller. Needles of ice prodded them. The beaver-lined moosehide mittens he had forgotten to bring flashed into his mind. Mary Joe had sewn and beaded them.

Her face came toward him. The high flush of her flaring cheekbones. The gentle hollows beneath. The eyes he could never describe. The children, their laughter flashing white. Three faces together, wavering in the thin and growing mist.

Indian. Indianness. The words floated through his thoughts. He jerked his head, trying to flick away the daze. He shouted into the mist, "What difference now, how much the blood is mixed? Our kids are as much Irish or Russian or Scotch as Indian. What difference now?"

His words were snatched away by the wind.

CLIFFORD TRAFZER

❖❖❖

Cheyenne Revenge

1864

1

BUZZARDS FLEW OVERHEAD. A dozen or more of the large black birds circled above, perhaps a mile away. Their dark bodies appeared like irregular dots in the expansive blue sky. Death filled the air, wrapping the two Cheyenne riders in a deep chill of foreboding and warning them that something terrible had occurred. One of the young warriors had a vague sense of unease, which had grown throughout the day. He had said little about his feelings and he remained silent now. His companion spoke to him in the sign, fearing that someone might be close enough to overhear a spoken word.

Reining their horses, the two warriors communicated in silence, using their hands, head, and lips to speak with each other. Pointing to the sky, Tall Bear indicated to his young nephew that the buzzards were circling close to their camp. Tall Bear was sure that the camp had been attacked, but he could not say whether whites or Indians had struck the village of smoke-stained tipis, barking dogs, and spirited horses. Lone Wolf made no reply, but his face was drawn with worry and his muscles were taut as they urged the horses into motion.

The two men had left the village of Chief Black Kettle, located on Sand Creek in Colorado Territory, in search of buffalo. They had sought a herd large enough to ensure the village of Cheyenne men, women, and children a comfortable existence during the long, cold winter to come. Although they had set out as "wolves," scouting methodically for the great beasts, no sign of buffalo were to be found. The animals had been frightened away by white hunters. After two long days of hunting, the friends were returning home.

The night before, Lone Wolf had dreamed of tragedy and awoke shaking with the fear and dread instilled by the images of the night. Hesitantly, he described the dream to Tall Bear as they prepared to return to Sand Creek.

"I saw it so plainly, my uncle, in colors as real as the day," he had said, with emotion filling his voice. "I saw our camp, the tipis strung out along a tiny creek. I saw the Bluecoat soldiers, many of them, falling into our camp. They came from nowhere and we did not expect them. They fell on the people, killing everyone. I saw little children bleeding, and people dying, and those already dead. But I could do nothing to stop it."

Tall Bear had tried to console his nephew, blaming the dream on Lone Wolf's preoccupation with the hunt. But he understood the power of dreams, and the boy's dream had not been far from his thoughts during their ride back to the village.

As the horror of his vision swept over him once more, Lone Wolf feared that his dream had become a reality. He broke the silence, speaking to Tall Bear in Cheyenne.

"What do you think has happened, Uncle?" Feverishly, Lone Wolf responded to his own question without allowing his uncle a chance to reply. "Perhaps my grandfather has been blessed with buffalo. The men have made a large kill, I think, and the birds are waiting for their dinner." But the boy's voice was strained and unconvincing.

Lone Wolf laughed a faint, nervous laugh in a futile attempt to ease the tension. He tried to imagine that the buzzards had been drawn to the blood and entrails left by the women after butchering the mighty animals, desperately summoning the vision of the women cutting the hides from the meat, gutting the cows and bulls, and hacking off huge chunks of meat to transport back to camp. But the memory of his dream kept replacing these happier thoughts, and he could not believe his own tale. A voice deep inside of him whispered that there had been no buffalo hunt. The soldiers had fallen into the camp, just as the dream had foretold. The buzzards had come to feed on the bodies of dead Cheyenne.

2

A panorama of blood and gore unfolded below them, stretched out upon the plain beside Sand Creek where Chief Black Kettle's people had established their village. Lone Wolf's eyes narrowed, the lines of his forehead and temple growing deeper. He sat silently beside his uncle, taking in the scene below with pained disbelief. The rank smell of spent gunpowder and spoiled flesh filled the air, causing Lone Wolf's nostrils to flare. The young man closed his eyes tightly, hoping to blot out the nightmare of his slaughtered family and friends. But when he opened his eyes, the images reappeared again, and finally his mind registered the painful reality.

Dead bodies were scattered everywhere. They lay motionless on the ground amidst the hundred or so tipis, some of which were smoldering from fires set early in the raid. Bluecoat soldiers walked about the bodies, stopping now and then to pick up souvenirs. Soldiers had stripped the dead Cheyenne of their shirts, leggings, blankets, and beads. Lone Wolf numbly observed that some of the soldiers carried bows, knives, medicine pouches, and the like, stolen from the dead Cheyenne. Others had collected beautifully beaded moccasins, buckskin dresses, quivers, and the large leather pouches that the Cheyenne called "possible bags." Lone Wolf watched a group of Bluecoats scavenge for earrings, necklaces, and rings. When the rings failed to come off easily, because the fingers of the dead had begun to swell, the soldiers hacked off the fingers at the joints.

As Lone Wolf and Tall Bear continued to watch what had only a few hours ago been their peaceful, pleasant village, the enormity of the carnage became increasingly apparent. They watched in disbelief as soldiers removed fingers, feet, arms, and hands to keep as trophies. Some soldiers took the knives typically used to skin a hunted animal and split open Indian bodies, tearing out organs with their bare hands and leaving crimson-stained spots in the sand. One soldier, sporting a broad-brimmed hat, raced about the camp on horseback with the genitals of a woman dangling from the end of a stick. On the bank of Sand Creek, which was beginning to show the faint tint of flowing blood, three or four soldiers tossed about severed Cheyenne heads in a ghoulish game. Lone Wolf would not have believed that the heads of some of his beloved friends would one day wind up on desktops, becoming popular ornaments once the flesh had been stripped from the skulls.

Tears blinded Lone Wolf's vision, a product of the anger and pain which pierced his breast and created a tight knot in his stomach. Angrily, he wiped the tears away with the back of his hand. The nightmare continued to unfold in a gruesome pattern. Lone Wolf watched soldiers scalp some of the Indians, using sharp, uneven slashes to cut off the hair on their heads. Other Bluecoats scalped the pubic hair from some of the people, while still others had cut off or cut out the genital organs of the men, women, and little children. Lone Wolf noted bitterly that the soldiers showed no mercy—they indiscriminately killed young and old, men and women alike.

In his short life, Lone Wolf had killed men in battle. He had scalped his enemy, and twice he had counted coups. Tall Bear had even more experience and was considered the leader of the younger men. Still, neither had seen such wanton destruction. Lone Wolf was sickened by the massacre and he was most outraged by the murder of infants and their mothers. Some of them, perhaps the luckier ones, had been shot to death. The soldiers had smashed in the heads of others with a single blow of a rifle butt.

For the first time, Tall Bear spoke and his words were filled with bitterness and hatred.

"Your grandfather was a wise leader, at peace with the white man. This outrage, this act of mad dogs, was not provoked by our people." He gestured toward the village angrily. "See the flags, nephew?"

Lone Wolf's eyes strained to see through the smoke from nearby burning tipis, but he finally made out the flagpole which stood not far from Chief Black Kettle's lodge. The pole boasted an American flag which had been presented to Wolf's grandfather by Commissioner of Indian Affairs, A. B. Greenwood. Beneath it hung the limp form of a white cloth, a futile attempt by Black Kettle to convince the marauders that he was at peace with the white man.

Lone Wolf nodded, agreeing with his uncle's assessment that the attack was unprovoked. "What could have caused these Bluecoats to act so viciously?"

Tall Bear shrugged. "I cannot say. Your grandfather was expecting white visitors today, powerful men in the white man's world. But Black Kettle would do nothing to deserve this, this . . ." Tall Bear searched in vain for a way to describe the scene which the young men saw below them.

Lone Wolf and his uncle hunkered in some thickets, on a slight mesa located across Sand Creek from the village. They had carefully concealed themselves and their horses from the soldiers. From their position they had witnessed the scene across the creek, a scene that burned into their brains as if placed there by hot irons. As the numbness which originally immobilized them began to wear off, their thoughts turned to retribution.

Tall Bear studied the terrain and troops across Sand Creek, noticing a small detachment of Bluecoats who had separated themselves some distance from the others. He prodded his nephew gently with his elbow and directed Lone Wolf's attention to the group. Their concentration was interrupted, however, when a small child raced into the scene, sobbing for its mother.

One of the soldiers called out to his comrades, "Watch this, boys, you're in for some real shooting here!"

The soldier took quick aim, firing at the child before anyone could protest. A large portion of the child's skull blew off as the bullet found its mark. The impact of the bullet sent the child flying forward head first, its body rolling three times before landing face up in the sandy creek bed. Staring across the creek at the two Cheyenne were the large, wide eyes of the dead child.

As the echo of the rifle's report faded across the plains, the soldier shouted to his men. "The little son of a bitch rolled like a shot rabbit," he said. The soldier's remark brought a round of laughter from his cohorts. "You know, the more of 'em we kill this year, the fewer we'll have to kill next year," he added. The soldier's comments were cut short by the appearance of a superior officer.

"What kind of a man are you, Watkins?" admonished the officer. "You shameless son of a bitch. Only the lowest form of life on this earth would kill a child. I hope to God you burn in hell for this. Haven't you had enough killing for one day? My God, look around you." The officer drew his horse menacingly close to the soldier. "If you harm anyone else, and I mean anyone else, I'll hunt you down and kill you myself."

With that, the officer rode away. But his words had little effect on the men, who simply laughed at the rider and returned to their sordid deeds.

Lone Wolf's body tensed, his muscles tightening as if he was flexing them. The thick veins in his neck bulged blue and his heart pounded, sending adrenaline to every corner of his body. He pressed his lips, his mouth growing increasingly drier. Just at the point that Lone Wolf was ready to bellow his deep war cry and charge the soldiers, Tall Bear reached around his nephew's waist to hold him back. With his other hand, Tall Bear grabbed the reins to Lone Wolf's horse.

Quietly, but forcefully, he spoke to his nephew. "The time is not right," Tall Bear exclaimed, holding tightly onto the warrior and his mount. "Not yet, my young warrior, not yet."

Lone Wolf stiffened even more, the words of his uncle not

registering. Tall Bear persisted, repeating his words until Lone Wolf finally relaxed. The younger warrior calmed himself, releasing the air in his lungs. Tall Bear moved his hand to the young warrior's shoulder, firmly grasping his nephew while pointing upstream.

"Behold your enemy, Lone Wolf. We will have our revenge on these dogs who kill women and children. These dogs have separated themselves from their pack, and we shall destroy them."

3

Tall Bear turned his black stallion and rode swiftly away from the hiding place. Lone Wolf mounted his great silver horse and followed his uncle into battle. The two warriors rode recklessly down Sand Creek on their way toward the small detachment of soldiers who were busily scavenging on dead bodies. When the soldiers had first attacked, several women and children had fled downstream to hide. At a spot where the spring runoff had cut a deep swath into the bank, these Cheyenne women and children dug foxholes and made their last stand. The Bluecoats had found this place and attacked. Although the women had fought well, they were no match for the well-armed soldiers. The Long Knives killed every woman and child they found, sparing no one.

Tall Bear reined his horse, stopping less than fifty yards from the soldiers. Lone Wolf pulled his horse alongside his uncle. Through the low-growing mesquite trees that looked more like oversized bushes than trees, they saw the soldiers moving among the dead. The bloody scene included the dead bodies of several mothers holding their slain children. Directly in front of the two warriors some half dozen or so picked over the remains.

The desire for revenge caused Lone Wolf's blood to pump fiercely through his veins. The younger man prepared his mind for the battle to come, willing his heart to stop racing and his muscles to stop tensing. He waited for Tall Bear's signal, which did not come. Instead, Lone Wolf heard Tall Bear gasp, a weird sound more akin to that of an animal than a man. Unable to speak, Tall Bear raised an outstretched arm and pointed through the mesquites. Lone Wolf's eyes followed his uncle's finger and what he saw made his heart miss a beat. There on the ground lay the bodies of Tall Bear's lovely young wife, Morning Star, and his two small children. Three soldiers stood over the bodies, stripping them of souvenirs. One of the soldiers, a big man with his sleeves rolled up to his elbows, bent over Morning Star's body and took off her moccasins, beaded in the soft hue of Cheyenne pink. Tossing the moccasins to another soldier, he ripped a beautifully beaded pink necklace from her neck and quickly pocketed it.

Tall Bear and Lone Wolf watched in horror as the soldier tore Morning Star's buckskin dress from her limp body. The soldier's arm turned toward the hidden Cheyenne men, dangling the dress from his fingers and revealing a tattoo of a sailing ship on the man's forearm. The soldier unsheathed his knife and began to cut a line through the beautiful woman's midsection. Tall Bear's breathing became ragged, his eyes bulged, and his mouth contorted in rage. With great self-discipline and determination, he commanded his mind to channel all thoughts toward the battle to come. Tall Bear silently sang his war song, certain that this time it would also be his death song.

The Great Grizzly Bear had appeared to Tall Bear in his youth, during his vision quest. The Bear had given the young man power through the song, and now more than ever before, Tall Bear called on his medicine song to help him avenge the deaths of his wife and small children. Over and over the words ran through his head, and in the process prepared his mind, body, and soul for battle. Finally, the grieving warrior blurted the words out loud, singing in a deep voice and screeching the words in the Cheyenne language. Tall Bear's black stallion leaped forward as he dug his heels into the animal's side. He raced ahead at a breakneck speed to engage his enemy. The death song rang out for everyone to hear, and Lone Wolf listened in anguish to his uncle's plaintive cry.

The bear is my Power
He follows me into battle
With my bow in hand
With my lance beside me
I go into battle

The bear is my Power
He follows me into war
With my horse beneath me
With my body in motion
I go into battle

The attack caught the soldiers by surprise. They had been so engrossed in carving into the lifeless body of Morning Star that they had not seen Tall Bear and Lone Wolf. The big man with the tattoo had just begun to cut into Morning Star when he heard them coming. The charging Cheyennes raced toward the white men like two prairie fires fed by the wind. From Tall Bear came the sound of a cougar in pursuit of his prey, a sound which sent chills down the backs of the white soldiers. The big man with the tattoo stood up to meet Tall Bear's attack. Unarmed except for his knife, the Bluecoat picked up a fallen tree limb. He raced forward on foot and clashed in mortal combat with the mounted Cheyenne warrior.

Tall Bear met the challenge with his face contorted and teeth bared, taking on the appearance of an animal as he charged into combat. The soldier whirled the stick above his head, waiting for the right moment to swing it at the Cheyenne. Tall Bear raised his lance in his right hand and lunged at the soldier, grazing his side with the lance's sharp point and knocking the man to the ground. Blood spurted from the Bluecoat's torn arm as the lance ripped open the skin. The force of the lance and the fall jolted the wind out of the man's lungs. He lay gasping for air while one of his cohorts worked his way carefully to drag him to safety.

Meanwhile, Lone Wolf raised his lance in one hand and his shield in the other, simultaneously engaging two soldiers armed with swords and pistols. Lone Wolf killed the soldier grasping a pistol in his right hand without difficulty. The man had waited too long to fire, for by the time he pulled the trigger, the deadly thrust of Lone Wolf's lance had found its mark. The young but skillful warrior drove his lance in and out of his enemy's stomach. With lightning speed the lance entered the body without touching a bone which could have caught the lance and prevented Lone Wolf from retrieving it. The man fell to the ground as his hands grasped his midsection. His partner stood nearby, unable to help.

While the Cheyenne dispatched the man on his right, the warrior used his shield to defend himself from the other Bluecoat. As Lone Wolf's great silver horse rode past the soldiers on his first pass, the man to his left stabbed at the warrior with his sword. The point of the long knife hit Lone Wolf's shield first, but it did not penetrate the thick war shield. Lone Wolf had skillfully turned his shield so that it caught the long knife at an angle and deflected its point.

Furious that he had missed his prey and angered that his comrade had fallen under the lance, the Bluecoat chased after Lone Wolf. A string of obscenities tumbled out of the soldier's mouth as he ran after the silver horse.

"I'll kill you," he screamed, the sword-wielding arm flailing wildly before him. "You dirty son of a bitch," the soldier bellowed as he pursued Lone Wolf.

The Bluecoat caught up with the Cheyenne before the warrior could turn his horse. The soldier struck Lone Wolf with the sharp edge of the sword, splitting a large swath of flesh on the Indian's back.

"Take that, you goddamned devil," he yelled, pulling the long knife back to take another swipe at Lone Wolf. Blood poured from the long open wound, but the blade had made only a superficial cut. The blood flowed in a steady stream, bathing Lone Wolf's back in the red fluid.

The sword was at its apex when Lone Wolf wheeled about, turning his body and moving his lance over his horse's head to the left. In a single, fluid motion, Lone Wolf turned enough to thrust his war lance into the soldier. The lance sunk deep inside his enemy, but instead of penetrating the white man's stomach as Lone Wolf had intended, it pierced the soldier's heart. Blood spurted from the open wound onto Lone Wolf and his silver horse. The point became stuck between two ribs, and as the horse turned toward the Bluecoat, Lone Wolf lost his hold of the shaft. The man fell to the ground, face down, the lance lodged in the body. Lone Wolf began to dismount to retrieve his weapon when the sharp report of gunfire caught his attention.

While Lone Wolf fought the two soldiers, his uncle had engaged two others. After a few passes with his lance, Tall Bear faced two men with guns loaded. On his third ride past the Bluecoats, one soldier shot him in the back. Lone Wolf heard the crack of the gun and turned in time to see Tall Bear cringe as a bullet smashed into the warrior's spine. The other soldier fired a round, but it missed Tall Bear, finding its mark in the rear leg of his black horse. The animal tripped, falling backward. The horse crashed to the ground and Tall Bear was thrown some distance from the horse. He landed face down on the ground, where Lone Wolf could see the small black hole in Tall Bear's back where gunpowder had burned a patch in his uncle's leather shirt.

The tattooed soldier led the remainder of his band as they rushed to surround Tall Bear. One of the men picked up the wooden club and swiftly raised the club over his head. Tall Bear feebly pulled himself up some six inches from the earth. He tried to turn and meet his foe, but the gunshot wound had left him partially paralyzed. Lone Wolf acted quickly and instinctively, holding his bow in his right hand and arming it with an arrow.

But Lone Wolf was too late. The club was on its way before the arrow left the bow. The soldier smashed Tall Bear's skull, breaking bones and splattering brains upon the green earth. The arrow, however, found its mark, entering the white man's throat and lodging in his upper spine. The soldier did not die instantly. Both hands grabbed at his throat, tugging at the arrow. As the wounded soldier stumbled and gasped for air, the sound of gurgling blood came from his throat. The soldier vomited a small amount of blood and fell over dead.

Lone Wolf shot another arrow before the soldiers could react. The arrow struck another Bluecoat in the thigh. Crying out in severe pain, the man fell to his knees and pulled violently at the arrow. The head of the arrow remained firmly lodged in his muscular thigh. He screamed out in pain, rolling about on his back and side with both hands holding the bloody wound.

The Cheyenne kicked his silver horse with his heels and charged the last man standing, the big man with the tattoo and the flesh wound in his side. This time the soldier held a .36 caliber Colt Naval pistol. Although the gun was loaded and pointed at the Cheyenne, Lone Wolf acted without regard for the pistol. The white man fired once, then again and again. One of the rounds blew a hole into the warrior's arm.

Lone Wolf lost his balance as he grabbed for his arm. He tried to catch himself from falling by tightly clenching his knees together against the sides of his horse, but he was too late. He fell to the ground with a thud and looked up to find the white man towering above, the hammer of his pistol cocked and ready to fire.

"You goddamned little bastard," he said, slowly enunciating each word as he kicked Lone Wolf in the head. The white man's boot caught the warrior on the left side of his face, making the young man gasp. The heel of the leather boot then crashed into the back of his skull.

Dots swam momentarily before Lone Wolf's eyes, then everything faded into darkness. He dropped to the ground unconscious, his life in the hands of the big man with the tattoo.

4

Lone Wolf was roused by water splashing down hard upon his face. He dimly perceived figures above him, but at first he could not make out who they were. His face and head ached where he was kicked, and his back burned as if a thousand porcupine quills had been stuck into his skin. Slowly his vision cleared and his memory returned. He found himself cold and nearly naked, staked out on his back with his hands and legs spread wide. Above him stood several soldiers, including the big man with the tattoo, the one Lone Wolf had injured with his lance. The Cheyenne feverishly wished that he had killed the white man when he had the chance.

"He's awake, Sergeant," reported the man pouring the water on Lone Wolf's face. "What are we going to do now?" he asked, a slight grin on his face. He stepped aside as the tattooed soldier moved forward, stepping into the area between the warrior's legs. The big man untied his hunting knife, slowly sliding it out of its worn leather sheath. Holding it in his right hand and slapping the sharp metal blade against the palm of his right hand, the tattooed man spoke.

"I once heard of an Apache chief that got himself into quite a pickle down in Mexico." The soldier spoke to his men, unaware that the young Cheyenne had learned some English from his mother. "Seems that the Apache got himself captured by some soldiers who didn't cotton to Apaches one damn bit. Them folks cut that ol' boy up into small pieces, first flaying the skin."

The tattooed man wanted to be sure his words were creating the proper effect, so he paused a moment before continuing.

"You all know what flaying is, don't you?" he asked, waiting for the others to admit their ignorance. He then described in detail how thin, narrow cuts were made running in lines down the body. The skin was then lifted up and slowly torn from the body. The bleeding was minimal with this technique, but the victim would be in agony as each strip was removed. In short, the tattooed man wanted to skin Lone Wolf alive.

The soldiers cringed. Some quickly lost interest in the sadistic act and drifted away. Others remained to hear more. Encouraged, the big man continued.

"Seems that before the Apache went off to his reward, they cut off his limbs, one by one, till nothing was left. They cut off the hands and feet, then the legs and the arms." Again, the man paused. "That's what I have in mind for this filthy bastard. He killed four of our men. Now he'll twitch and jerk real good before he finally bleeds to death." A look of deep hatred had replaced the smug satisfaction on the soldier's face.

Kneeling down between Lone Wolf's outstretched legs, the Bluecoat cut off the warrior's leather leggings, exposing his muscular thighs. With the gleaming knife, the white man made several incisions down the full length of Wolf's right thigh. Blood began to trickle down the leg, making the separate cuts indistinct. With the point of his knife, the soldier dug just beneath the skin, lifting the skin and separating it from the muscle. As he progressed from one strip to another, it was apparent that this tattooed man relished inflicting pain in a way Lone Wolf had never known before.

The Cheyenne had understood from the beginning what was going to happen to him, and he had vowed to die bravely, without crying out. Although he withstood the initial cuts courageously, he could not restrain himself as his skin was peeled away. Despite his desperate prayer for a swift death, the torture and pain continued.

The tattooed soldier raised his knife to cut into Lone Wolf's left leg, but a bullet suddenly whizzed by, sending a spray of sand into the air. So great was his torment, the young Cheyenne did not notice. The shot had been fired by an army officer mounted nearby upon a roan horse. He looked sternly at the soldiers, vehemently barking his orders.

"Get away from that man and cut him loose. You've had your good time, now let him up." The officer still had his .44 Starr Double Action army revolver in his hand. The hammer was not cocked, but the weapon stood ready for use should its holder simply pull the trigger.

The soldiers, even the sergeant, were now standing. The big man spoke brusquely. "You don't understand, sir. This son of a bitch just attacked us. Hell, he killed Joe Merriwether and Sam Johnson and two others. He tried to kill me!" The soldier pulled up his shirt and pointed to the cut he had received from Lone Wolf's lance.

The officer spoke in a quiet but menacing tone. "Listen to me carefully, gentlemen. I'm giving the orders around here and not you. There's been enough bloodshed for one day. The first one of you who touches that Indian is a dead man." For a moment the officer and the man with the tattoo locked stares, but the officer prevailed as the other man dropped his eyes. "You all make me sick to my stomach. Now get out of here."

Slowly, the soldiers drifted away from the scene, swearing to themselves as they withdrew. The big man with the tattoo was the last to leave. As the others moved away, he slid his knife back into the worn sheath. He finally walked off, rejoining the others. The officer sat on his horse, one eye following the men as the left and the other eye fixed on Lone Wolf. His pistol, still drawn, remained ready until he was certain that the soldiers had left.

The officer dismounted and walked toward Lone Wolf with the gun in his right hand and the reins in his other. "You make a false move and I'll use this, understand?" he said in a stern voice, motioning to his pistol with his eyes and lips. "I know you can't speak English, but you sure as hell understand this."

As he spoke, the officer reached into his pocket and pulled out a two-bladed pocket knife. He began to cut the Cheyenne loose. Lone Wolf was too weak to stand, but the officer helped him to his feet and gave him a handkerchief to place over the leg wounds.

"Now get on this horse," said the officer in the exaggerated tones of one who thinks his language is not understood. Again, Lone Wolf needed the white man's help in mounting the cavalry horse. Taking the horse's reins in his hands, the officer led the animal away from the scene of the battle.

From the back of the horse, Lone Wolf absorbed the tragedy around him. Tall Bear's body and that of Morning Star lay close by. With grim satisfaction Lone Wolf noted the bodies of the men Lone Wolf and Tall Bear had killed. Dry blood and rotting flesh filled his nostrils. His body ached and he felt faint. Slumping painfully in the saddle, Lone Wolf was led off by a man he did not know and could not trust.

The officer's name was Silas Soule. Although a fine soldier and respected officer, he hated senseless killing and despised those who had prompted the incident at Sand Creek. He had stood by helplessly as the volunteer soldiers ignored the pleas of the peaceful Cheyenne and indulged in ruthless murder. He watched in stunned horror as Black Kettle ran out of his tipi, followed by the white governmental officials who were conducting peaceful talks with the tribal leaders. The volunteers took no heed of the situation, but instead began the vicious attack. In all his years as a cavalryman, he had never seen such debased and inhuman acts as those carried out on the shores of Sand Creek.

Perhaps he could not right the wrong done that day, but he could, he thought, at least save the life of one Cheyenne. He was a mere boy, he thought, and it comforted him to think that at least one of the children had been saved. Silas Soule led the horse away from the Cheyenne camp, away from the gore and carnage, along the bank of Sand Creek, until they had put at least several miles behind them. They finally stopped at a small grove of trees. Lone Wolf could barely hold on to the saddle, and the officer had no trouble pulling him off of the horse and laying him on the ground. He threw a wool blanket onto the boy's naked body and tried to make him as comfortable as possible.

Silas held the young Cheyenne's head as he poured a small portion of water down his throat. Lone Wolf took the refreshing liquid gratefully. Silas then removed some alcohol and bandages from his saddlebags and set about repairing the tattered legs. Although Lone Wolf knew the man intended to help him, the agony of the sharply stinging alcohol when applied to his wounds was more than he could bare and he lost consciousness almost immediately. The officer finished his work quickly and efficiently, then settled in for a long night's vigil by a small fire.

Lone Wolf tossed and turned in delirium through most of the night, but was greatly improved by morning. He woke to find Silas Soule asleep. The young man tried to move, but his leg and back were so stiff that he cried out in pain. The outcry roused Soule, who quickly jumped to his feet and brandished his pistol until he saw that Lone Wolf meant him no harm.

"I've got to get back to my outfit now, but I think you'll be all right. You may be a little sore, but you can hide out here for a few days until you are fit to move on."

Lone Wolf haltingly acknowledged the white man's words in a few words of broken English. The language seemed unfamiliar to him, although at one time he had been able to converse rather freely in his mother's native tongue. Soule looked surprised that Lone Wolf could speak English at all.

"You mean you've been able to understand what I've been saying?" the officer asked. When Lone Wolf nodded in reply, Silas let out a long, hearty laugh. "Well, good for you, boy. Listen, my name's Soule, Silas Soule. I'll leave you some jerky and hardtack to help you get through the next few days, but that's all I have in the way of food."

"Thank you, Silas Soule." The effort it took to speak those few words surprised Lone Wolf. He didn't remember ever feeling so weak. But he knew that if he were to survive, it was going to take all of his will and all of his cunning. Silas Soule had helped him all he could. Lone Wolf watched him saddle his horse.

"Listen, I wouldn't leave you if I didn't have to, you know?" The older man was obviously affected by the Cheyenne's dilemma. "You ever make it to Denver, you look me up, you hear? I'll be living there when I finish my stint with the cavalry soon." Before riding away, he reached out to touch Lone Wolf on his shoulder.

Lone Wolf lay quietly after Silas had gone. He repeated the name of the officer over and over so that he would always remember it. He owed his life to Silas Soule, and he vowed never to forget that fact. But he also swore that he would never forget what had happened at Sand Creek. One day, he thought, he would avenge the lives lost there. One day he would savor the sweet taste of revenge.

GERALD VIZENOR

❖❖❖

The Baron
of Patronia

LUSTER BROWNE shouted at the birch behind the parish house; he revered the bright woods, but not so white, and not so close to the missionaries. He bashed the weeds and threw his words at the white posse on the back porch of the mission.

Luster was there at dawn, a mixedblood at the scratch line, to disrupt the land allotment measures on the White Earth Reservation in northern Minnesota. He prowled behind the birch and sneered at the federal agents on the porch; later, tired and lonesome, he abided the distance with the mongrels and became a nobleman.

That comic moment reared a compassionate tribal trickster, nurtured his wild children and nine grandchildren, and overturned an instance in racial hocus-pocus on that woodland reservation, which was invented in eighteen sixty-eight by withered white men in cutaway coats.

Luster renounced the strict summons to mature in a base and possessive civilization, and he would never wait on a mission porch to have his mind mended by the government, even when his mind needed mending. The trickster seceded at dawn behind the bridal wreath; he pissed on the birch with the mongrels and countered the breach in communal tribal land. In response, he was handed a land patent that banished him to the wild outback on the reservation.

"Luster Browne, also known as Lusterbow, his callow moniker, son of a pagan mother and a mixed father, a common factor in the fur trade, comes hitherward for his allotment, the last holdover on this reservation roll," the government clerk announced in a taut monotone. "Howbeit, the halfbreed has lost favor with the mission and our agents."

The assistant secretary, braced high in a chair behind a bench overspread with a martial blanket, scorned the recalcitrant mixedblood when he issued a certificate in his name. The untamed land between the metes and bounds ascribed, the secretary believed, was impenetrable muskeg, as worthless as the peerage he pronounced that humid afternoon in the name of the president.

"Whereas, there has been deposited in the General Land Office of the United States an Order of the Secretary of the Interior directing that a fee simple patent issue to Luster Browne, a White Earth Mississippi Chippewa Indian, for a quarter west of the Fifth Principal Meridian containing one-hundred sixty acres in a Township named Patronia:

"Now know ye, that the United States of America, in consideration of the promises, has given and granted, and by these presents does give and grant, unto the said Luster Browne, and to his heirs, the lands above described, and the title, Baron of Patronia; to have and to hold the same, together with all the rights, privileges, immunities, and appurtenances, of whatsoever nature thereunto belonging, unto the said Baron Luster Browne, and to his heirs and assigns forever.

"In testimony whereof, I, Theodore Roosevelt, President of the United States of America, have caused these letters to be made Patent, and the seal of the General Land Office to be hereunto affixed."

The malevolent assistant secretary, however, was mistaken

about the worth of the land he had allotted to the mixedblood trickster; the baronage, intended to be a colonial hoax, became a virtue in one generation, and the heritable tribal noblesse has prevailed in various ancestral comedies, here and there, and on the reservation.

Patronia is a wild crescent on the White Earth Reservation northeast of Bad Medicine Lake. The shallow creek at the treeline carries the last rumors of glacial rivers that once tumbled the huge granite boulders down the hollows; there, the greens are tender in the spring.

A weathered hutment bears down behind the cedar on the west bank of the creek; white pine and a rush of paper birch hold between the boulders on the slow rise of the crescent. Thousands of moccasin orchids bloom in the moist summer shadows.

The sunrise widens on the other side of the creek, over emerald waves, blood hues, and wild blues, on a natural meadow; insects swarm in humid columns, and at night, fireflies leave their traceries in the moist weeds.

In a warm pond, on the northern brow of the wild crescent, mallards remain in winter; their green heads and brown bodies cross in the mist between the reeds, between the children on the luscious shore.

The Baron of Patronia camped behind the cedars that first summer and built a small cabin near the pond. When the rime turned the leaves and the blues withered on the meadow, he cut whitewood for the winter; later, when the mallards waited on the warm water, he married an orphan who lived in a wigwam over the meadow at Long Lost Lake.

Novena Mae Ironmoccasin was born premature in a wild snow storm on Advent Sunday. The unmarried mother died from exposure behind the mission. The Benedictine sisters at the White Earth boarding school cared for the child; when she recovered and opened her eyes for the first time on the ninth day of their prayers in eighteen ninety-two, the nuns named her for the novena. She was a dark and silent child, a serious student, and devoted to the sisters at the mission, but she turned down a summons to become a nun. Instead, when she was fifteen, she created a wild Stations of the Cross on fourteen wounded trees behind the mission, and then she retreated to the hardwoods.

She was sixteen when the second winter loomed on the mound and a lone trickster wandered close to her wigwam. Crows roused the red pine, wind rushed the cattails, beaver cracked the thin ice on the riverside; these motions she understood. But over these natural sounds that late autumn she heard several splendid wild human shouts.

The Baron of Patronia came over the meadow and buried his lonesome voice in seven panic holes; there, he believed, the overturned earth would nurture wild flowers with his words, in his noble name. He planted his voice, in this manner, with the seasons: in summer with the moccasin orchids, his solace bloom; on the meadow in spring and autumn; under the cedar in winter.

Novena Mae watched him move between shadows; she was hushed and courteous at the treeline. He was sudden; his breath was wild, blanched, blued on the tender rise. The mongrels raised their wet noses on the wind, sensed her presence, but the trickster was not aware that she had tracked him more than a mile back across the meadow to his baronage, down to his cedar cabin on the pond.

Lusterbow shouted and circled the pond, but she remained silent and held her distance. The mallards browsed on the warm water between them. He recited poesies on the weather, ducks in winter, rimes on the wild wind over warm water, and the moss down the crescent to the pond, and then he told trickster stories about hibernal bears and the colossus icewoman who consumed lonesome men in winter.

"Woman, come over here," he shouted and danced on the shore. The mongrels bounced in the weeds, searched in wild circles for new panic holes, and then barked at the baron. "The Baron of Patronia, he is me, and he welcomes you to live on his land, as long as the grass grows, the river flows." He laughed, waved his hands, and then silence. "Would you be the icewoman?"

Novena Mae remained silent; she smiled and rolled a shoulder when the crows and whiskey jacks responded to his loud voice. He shouted several more humorous invitations; the bewildered mongrels barked at his shadow, made their own panic holes, and then moved to the other side of the pond.

Later, when it was dark, he built a fire on the shore and announced that he would wait there for her response. When he leaned back, a solemn shadow in the weeds, she teased the mongrels and returned to her wigwam on the mound. There she touched a blue stone bear that her mother wore when she died in the storm; she listened and remembered the nuns at the mission, the wounded trees, and counted the months that she had been alone. She remembered each month in scent and sound: the harsh cracks on the lake ice, mice in the dried oak leaves, blue mire overturned in winter, black bears on the river boulders, water striders in a warm rain, lightning in the white pine, and her heart beat under moss, in cold river water. She would never be ruined with these memories; she would be mocked but never ruined by a tribal trickster.

Novena Mae untied the birchbark wigwam, packed several bundles on a small travois, and towed her possessions back across the meadow and down to the warm pond. Lusterbow snored low in the weeds; the cedar embers hissed, snapped, and danced over his head.

The mongrels were the overseers that night when she tied the larch poles and re-covered her wigwam with bark. She spread woven rushes and cedar boughs inside. The entrance opened on the creek and the best sunrise. She listened to the water resound over the stones and then made a small fire in the center of the wigwam.

The Baron of Patronia awakened with a shiver and stirred the cedar embers. Overhead, mythic hunters spread their scarlet pennons on the dawn; the autumn meadow shimmered and the paper birch on the crescent were rose-hued. He moved closer, mongrels in the lead, to the wigwam. When he peered inside, his shadow covered her head and chest. She was curled near the fire; thin, even smaller than he had imagined from the other side of the pond. She wore a leather blouse, laced under the sleeves and buttoned down the sides, wide cotton trousers, and leather leggings. He moved back to watch the dawn reach over her neck and cheeks; when her nose hitched, he retreated to his cabin.

Lusterbow leaned on the window sash and brooded over his isolation; then he marched down to the warm pond to bathe and wash his pungent clothes.

Chicken Lips, the most curious of the two mongrels, hopped around inside the wigwam; he sniffed her hair, her feet, and then pushed his wet nose into her crotch. When she awakened he sneezed and lost his balance, rolled over on the cedar boughs. Chicken Lips was mottled brown with three wide white paws; the right front paw had been severed in a beaver trap.

White Lies was seated at the entrance. She was white with brown blotches and with narrow bands on her stout tail; brown wisps shrouded her rear. She moaned, licked her sides, and snapped at a slow insect. The mongrels were more at home in the wigwam than on the rough boards in the cabin.

Novena Mae and Lusterbow never lived in the same house; he remained in the cedar cabin he had built near the pond, and she lived in the wigwam where she delivered ten children in twelve years. She was wild, generous, hushed; he was wild, bounteous, hoarse. He screamed the names of his children over panic holes on the meadow; she marked the birth of her children on the hardwoods and taught them to read from leaves. She wrote words and names on leaves and scattered them on the hard snow; the children collected the leaves and told stories with random words, their words, their voices on the rise.

Lusterbow told wild stories, trickster and creation stories, and coached his children to scream into panic holes when the spirit moved them. The meadow was covered with wild blooms, nurtured with screams; even the mongrels barked into holes and covered their sound with the earth. He was in motion when he told stories, never at rest; he worked with cedar, or he walked and talked, and waved his beaver stick between phrases.

Lusterbow built small cedar cabins for each of his children, an enormous barn near the pond, and several other buildings for sheep, mongrels, and dead machines issued by the government; when he worked he told stories about tribal tricksters who lived in compasses, clocks, watches, and church organs, where the best of them recast tunes, overturned time, and reversed magnetic directions in the manifest white world. The children learned apace to listen and then to imagine their connections to the earth; each child earned a characteristic nickname and a comic temper to endure the ruthless brokers of a tragic civilization.

The children learned that the old tribal tricksters turned "rose window malevolence" into comic beams and enlightened those who had lost their shadows on the concrete.

Shadow Box Browne, the eldest son, and his two unmarried sisters remained with their parents, Luster and Novena Mae, at Patronia. The other seven children moved to small communities on the reservation; two were reconciled in cities. Rain Browne and her brother Bones studied art and distinguished themselves as painters: he was a romantic and a tribal naturalist, she was a hard expressionist. Swarm, the eldest daughter, had vanished in a thunder storm when she was twelve; two sons, the smallest and the most intrepid of the children, had died in a cloud of mustard gas over a narrow trench in the Great War.

Shadow Box married Wink Martin, his cousin, who lived with her brother, Mouse Proof, at Bad Medicine Lake. Wink was silent but never solemn. She was stout and her breath was bad; she covered her mouth with one hand to hide her rotten teeth. She winked when she listened, and double winked when she smiled. Wink counted and measured words with winks; she even winked to count her children, the cabins, the mongrels, the mallards on the pond, and the crows on the blue meadow. She winked over the panic holes but never learned to scream.

Lusterbow built a cedar cabin for each grandchild, two more for Mouse Proof Martin, who would not leave his sister, and one cabin for Griever de Hocus, the avian trickster from Bad Medicine Lake. When his children and grandchildren were grown and the cabins weathered in silence, Lusterbow invited street tricksters, those with docked visions, mixedbloods from the cities, to live at Patronia. Three remained, learned his stories, and built their own cabins; the other mixedbloods screamed once into a panic hole and then braced their boredom at the Last Lecture, the nearest tavern, where they subscribed to new names and renewed indentities.

Mouse Proof Martin moved with his sister and established a new museum in the two cabins that the Baron of Patronia had built for him near the pond. Mouse Proof earned his nickname at a federal boarding school, where, on his hands and knees, he learned to read and write under an organ console. He waited, with one slack ear, at the narrow feet of his teacher when she played the organ in the classroom. There, on the bellows pedals, the two words of his nickname were pressed in metal. Mouse Proof turned under the organ and looked up her dress, into her dark crotch, as she perched on the stool. Then, with one finger, he traced the deep letters in the two words on the base of the pedals. He carved these words on his battered wooden desk, he wounded trees with his written name, and he painted his name on the new water tower.

Mouse Proof secured his name on the reservation, but he was better known as the trickster who collected lost and autographed shoes. His wild obsession with shoes started at the feet of his teacher; the smell of white flesh and polished leather. Later, when he found lost shoes at the roadside, he would remember his teacher, the scent of her crotch and shoes, and the unusual origin of his name. He owned thousands of lost shoes, each one catalogued, covered with a sock, and stored in his cabin archives. Once each season he scheduled tours to various institutions and museums with a selection of his rare shoe collection.

Mouse Proof and his wild shoe stories were popular on college campuses; he animated the lonesome shoes, moved them in uncommon pairs, uncovered their character and precise wear, and imagined in stories what happened to the shoes that never got away, the shoes that were never lost. The children adored his stories about lost and lonesome shoes.

Griever de Hocus roamed with Mouse Proof Martin and told stories about meditation and broken wheels to college audiences. Griever was born without a name, the child of a caravan called the Universal Hocus Crown. His mother told him that she met his father at three places on the reservation. Once in the birch behind the parish house, twice on the old government road, and three times in the ice barn near the lake; and then, "the caravan and your father, gone in less than a week." She never even learned his real name, never understood his peculiar language, but she remembers his tongue, his music, and she whistles his wild tunes at night; most of all, she remembers what he said about "griever time."

"Griever time meditation," he told her in the dark, "cures common colds, headaches, heartaches, tired feet, and humdrum blood." The caravan sold plastic icons with grievous poses, miniature grails, veronicas, and instruction manuals entitled How To Be Sad And Downcast And Still Live In Better Health Than People Who Pretend To Be So Happy. She owes her old age to "griever time meditation" three nights a week. Griever owes his name and humor to her compulsive lamentations, but not much more. Mouse Proof and Griever de Hocus met under the organ console and were close friends at boarding school.

Wink Browne covered her mouth with both hands, counted nine children, her husband, brother, and stopped on eleven winks. "No more," she whispered, "no more bad breath," and she uncovered an enormous cast of ceramic teeth. Mormons provided the teeth, an inducement to their religion. Wink smiled at the missionaries twice a week for three months, an estimate of the value, and then she returned to the old mission and the mean deacon with the winy breath; instead of winking she clicked her teeth. Wink was so pleased with her smile that she traveled with her brother, Mouse Proof, and his shoe collection to several museum shows.

Shadow Box counted cabins and names marked on the trees near the pond. China, he shouted, his first born daughter; Tune, his eldest son; Tulip, the detective; Garlic, the farmer; Ginseng, the root rustler; Eternal Flame, once a nun; Father Mother, once a priest; Mime, who imitated her mother; and Slyboots, the avian dreamer and microlight radical.

China was born when the clover and rue anemone were in bloom on the meadow. Shadow Box roared with the scarlet hunters that morning; the mongrels circled the cabin and barked at their loose shadows. Lusterbow shouted in a panic hole to celebrate the birth of his first grandchild.

Chicken Lips waited at the bedside and whined over the child. He mocked her babble, and then he licked her little pink feet. He pushed his smooth tongue between her moist toes; the more she moved her toes, the more he licked.

White Lies and Chicken Lips, namesake mongrels, inherited their names; seven mongrels barked into panic holes on the meadow, withered, and died, but their names were resurrected in each generation. Patronia children remember the same mongrel names in their tribal stories.

China Browne teased Chicken Lips when she was older; she would spread her toes to catch his smooth tongue. Later she pretended that her feet were bound, golden lotuses under blue bandannas, and the mongrels were her eunuchs. Lusterbow claimed that he heard the echo of her name when he shouted into a panic hole, down to the other side of the earth, to the other world.

China studied literature, the first child from the baronage to graduate from college, and she traveled around the world as a magazine writer. Chicken Lips came to mind whenever she was lonesome or insecure; she would remember the reservation and that warm mongrel tongue between her toes. Now, once or twice a week, she draws silk ribbons between her toes; an unusual meditation, and the certain origin of her nickname. . . .

GERALD VIZENOR

✦✦✦

China Browne

CHINA BROWNE waited with the privileged cadre in the new railroad station lounge. She trimmed her nails and looked over pictures in a news magazine; she would not touch her bare arms or neck to the couch because the leather was stained and smelled of garlic sweat.

Two men in uniform smoked and whispered at the counter near the entrance to the lounge; a man in a thin white shirt wheezed in a corner chair, his stout arms surrounded a plastic briefcase with a broken zipper. Enormous fans whirred near the door to the latrine and circulated the noisome stench of urine.

China smiled as she read the faded broadsides on the wall over the counter, travel legends overrun with advertisements and cautions: China, A Treasure In The Heart; See Tibet With Two Big Eyes; Make Wind On A Phoenix Bicycle; Chemicals Not To Travel The Trains; No Spit The Floor; Monkey King Opera; No Spit The Street.

Outside, in the main section of the train station, tired women hunkered over their children and cloth bundles; the men smoked and watched foreigners. Some families, in spite of the heat, cooked on charcoal braziers; elders heated water for tea.

The pollution beclouded the patriotic portraits high on the walls in the station.

An American couple, a mock blonde and her bearded husband, rushed into the lounge and collapsed, breathless, on the leather couch. She counted their parcels and suitcases, retied a carton wrapped with newspaper, and then she fanned her neck and measured the other people in the lounge. The two men in uniform moved closer to read the headlines on her carton, the folded pictures of four men convicted of rape and sentenced to death.

"Angel and me are teachers here, this is our second year," said the bearded man in a loud voice, "we thought it might be easier the second time around with some experience, but maybe not, who are you?"

"China Browne."

"Angel, this is China Browne," he said and dried his beard with a hand towel. "Well then, you must be part Chinese."

"Native American," she said with a smile and waited for the characteristic responses, the racial catechism, questions about reservations, religion, language, and tribal radicals in prison.

"Aren't we all?"

"Native American Indian."

"Like I said, aren't we all," said Angel.

"Make up your mind," he said.

"China like in China?" asked Angel. When she leaned forward her white thighs squeaked on the dark leather. "Where did you ever get a name like that?"

"From my father," whispered China.

"Cinch is my nickname," he announced.

"China is mine."

"My father said making me was a cinch, the easiest thing he ever did that ended up paid to travel and talk in a classroom," boasted Cinch.

"China comes to China," mused Angel. "Where are you going in this awful, awful heat?" She mopped her short hair and withered neck with a towel; rouge and other cosmetic hues were smeared on her cheeks.

China was prepared to respond when a woman in a blue uniform propped open the double doors and announced the departure of the train to Tianjin. China nodded to Angel and then shouldered her overnight pack.

Children churred in the wide corridor of the station; women washed their babies on the aisle, and toddlers pissed on the terrazzo. Cinch and Angel plodded through the crowd with their parcels.

"China, you're my kind of woman."

"How is that?"

"You travel light." Cinch carried three suitcases and a backpack. "There are no porters here, not since the revolution, you can be sure."

"Liberation here, burden there," mocked China.

"Where is your luggage?" asked Angel.

"Beijing Hotel."

"So, you've been here how long?"

"Three days, long enough to catch my breath."

"Here, carry this then, you need something in your hands to be with us." Angel handed her the carton wrapped with newspaper which was much heavier than the suitcases; the coarse rope cut into her fingers.

China pressed through the narrow turnstile behind an old woman with bound feet. The woman was dressed in loose blue trousers, a black blouse, and a brown shroud on her shoulders; she wore a visor cap with a red ceramic star on the front cocked back on her head like a soldier.

China was pushed down the stairs, butted with baskets and hard bundles. She slowed the press from behind so the old woman could hobble at her own speed down to the platform; there, when the woman stopped near the tracks in a patch of light and held a rail ticket close to one eye, China moved closer to her side, turned, and smiled. The woman covered the ticket with both hands, as if her destination were a state secret, and stared at the nose on the foreigner; then the old peasant woman lowered her head in silence.

China bowed, bundled her hands between her breasts and

spoke in Chinese: "China Browne is my name," she said in measured tones. "I am an American."

The old woman wobbled to the side on her golden lilies and dropped her cloth bundle. China reached down to retrieve the bundle, but the old woman shivered, waved her arms, and dropped her ticket; she moved over the ragged cloth, raised her head, and shouted, "Yang gui zi, yang gui zi," which means, "foreign devil."

China moved back when a crowd gathered around her on the platform. The woman shouted that the foreign devil had spied on her, tried to read her ticket and steal her clothes. The men smoked and watched the scene in silence; the women in the crowd repeated in whispers what the old woman had shouted.

"China, never mind, Mao's still on her mind," said Cinch. "There's nothing you can do or say, best to count your change and move on with the other foreign devils."

"Love that star on her hat," said China. She brushed her hair back, smiled, and pretended not to be troubled by the occurrence.

"We've been here a year and we still don't understand," said Angel, "so don't get your hopes up in three days. Best to ignore the old people unless they seek you out, nothing comes of trying to help people here, they won't even help each other."

"Estranged, and with no porters," muttered China.

"Right, that's the ticket," said Cinch. He moved their suitcases to cover a particular crack on the platform; there, he explained, "is where the soft seat coach will stop, right on the crack, right on time."

The old woman hobbled down the platform to a place she knew the "hard seat" coach would stop; crowded, unreserved, right on the mark. She waited with her head raised, her mouth puckered.

China would overturn mistrust and suspicion on the baronage, back on the reservation, with tribal trickeries; however, she was a foreign devil cornered in a hard-core diorama with no natural cues to the humor in the nation. Men stared at her breasts, that was not new, and the children watched her shoes;

the women whispered about the prominence of her nose and the criminals pictured on the carton that she carried. The locomotive thundered into the station and steam smothered the curious crowd on the platform.

Cinch sat on the aisle, sipped green tea, and commented on each crossroad, hamlet, lime mine, and new advertisement on the sides of buildings between Beijing and Tianjin. When the train arrived, he was on the platform in seconds; he maneuvered through the crowded station and onto the main street. Angel ran close behind and complained the whole distance.

China, meanwhile, waited in the station to see the old peasant woman once more; she hobbled alongside a couple with an automatic washer in an enormous carton tied to a bicycle. The old woman waited at the curb outside the station for a few minutes; she raised her head several times and then hobbled across the wide street, oblivious to the trucks and buses. She paused on the other side, raised her head, and turned down to the river. The bank was stepped with rough concrete. Children swam into the black water from the last tier; women spread their washed clothes on the concrete.

The old woman inched down the bank, side to side on her narrow bound feet. The tiers were crowded with people; hundreds were at the waterline to cool their bodies on the breeze over the river.

China leaned back on a tier high above the water and watched the children, the old woman, and the boats loaded with bales. She remembered the baronage, the cedar, and her grandmother, who lived in a wigwam near the river; the old woman invited the mongrels to lick her toes when she was a child. China whispered her name there on the stepped bank, "Novena, Novena Mae," and the names of the mongrels, "Chicken Lips," and "White Lies." She imagined that Chicken Lips pressed his wet nose on her toes, turned his tongue between her toes. China removed her shoes, spread her toes on the rough concrete, and prepared to meditate; however, when she drew the blue bandanna from her shoulder pack, the old woman stumbled over a seam on the last tier and bounced into the water. The woman was desperate, she held her arms and shoulders above water, but she was weak, her hands trembled on the concrete.

China was thirteen tiers above the river; she waited for someone to help the old woman. There were people near her, but no one seemed to notice. Her bound lotus feet bobbed in the dark water, stunted creatures from the imperial past.

China shouted and waved with her shoes to those below; when no one responded, she bounded down the tiers. She eased the old woman back from the water and rested her head on the shoulder pack. The woman shivered on the concrete; she moved to hide her feet, and her cloth bundle, under the shroud. The two women watched each other in silence; one smiled and then the other.

China raised the wet shroud and spread it on the concrete tiers to dry. She unbound the old woman, loosened the swathes, uncovered her feet. China opened the tender wizened toes like secrets and cleaned the pinched ocherous nails; the lotus toes were more erotic than she had imagined, more beauteous than the pictures of bound feet she treasured as a child. She dried the turned toes with her blue bandanna, the same cloth she drew between her own toes in meditation.

The cicadas roared in the broad leaves, and boat whistles sounded on the river; diesel engines bellowed over the bridge in the distance. China drowsed and children dabbled in the water on the tier below her head. She dreamed that her grandfather floated past on a boat and told stories about the mixedblood trickster who lived in a town clock. The trickster read the minds of those who looked to the tower for their time, and he set the hands back to calm their nerves. Lusterbow said that when the trickster moved the hands on the tower clock, the time in the whole town moved back; this, he mused, was the pleasure of a compassionate tribal trickster.

China awakened when the boat passed and the stories ended. The old woman had bound her toes and waited with her cloth bundle at her side. China shouldered her pack and the two women climbed the tiers together. China narrated the rise with the origin of her name and the baronage on the reservation. The old woman did not respond, she was out of breath and did not seem to hear the stories.

China ushered the woman to a wooden bench that overlooked the river. There, beneath a tree, she shouted into a panic hole and the old woman understood; she smiled, nodded, and bowed, and then she clapped her withered hands. China shouted a second time into the seared earth.

"Yang gui zi," she whispered, and then laughed louder than she had shouted earlier on the platform. The old woman leaned over and presented a small herb box and her cloth cap to the foreign devil on the bench beside her; she polished the red star, bowed twice more, and hobbled down the road. China watched the old woman cross the bridge; she vanished in the crowd.

Cinch was irritated that the time in his measured world had been disturbed by China. He marched to the back of the bench and shouted in her ear: "Where have you been? We've been looking all over the place for you, now we're late." She was taken unawares and twitched with his voice; when she turned he circled the bench. He pulled his beard as he marched, then he stopped and waited for her response.

"Two o'clock on my watch," she said. China had moved the hands back one hour; she leaned back on the bench and smiled at the tormented man. "Were you in a hurry to get somewhere?"

"Well, two o'clock," he muttered and looked around for confirmation of the time. "My watch is ten minutes fast, then."

"Where did you get that hat?" asked Angel. She complained about the heat from at least a block behind her husband. She had brushed her cheeks with a second coat of cosmetics.

"Remember that old woman on the platform?"

"No, you ran her down and stole it!" shouted Angel.

"Good for you!" shouted Cinch.

"No, no, she gave it to me," said China.

"Gave it to you?"

"Never!"

"Yes, she gave it to me."

"What for?"

"Well, she fell in the river and I pulled her out when no one else would help," related China. "We talked, she showed me her bound feet, and then she gave me the cap. Do you like the star?"

"Bullshit," snapped Cinch.

"These people never help each other," carped Angel.

"Come on, China, you either stole it or you found it on the bench," insisted Cinch. "Anyway, you look like a typical Mao mocker in a cap like that, with a Commie star no less."

"She gave me this little box of herbs too," said China. She opened the round metal box and raised the thick brown flecks close to his nose. The cover was decorated with bound lilies and pale monarchial portraits.

"What is it?"

"Some kind of herb," she said. China spread the contents on the palm of her hand. "The old woman showed me how to sniff it, open the nostrils wide and inhale in short breaths, but the herb smells rather musty to me."

"Those are not herbs," he shouted. Cinch pinched his nose closed and moved back behind the bench. "Keep that shit away from me."

"Don't tell me."

"What is it then?" asked Angel.

"Scabs."

"Sore scabs?"

"You have a sick sense of humor," said China.

"Diseased scabs."

"Spare me, please."

"No shit China."

"Cinch knows, believe me," pleaded Angel.

"Rich Chinese picked smallpox wounds," he explained from the other side of the bench, "and shared the scabs with relatives, sort of a token inoculation, a smell for good health."

China returned the scabs to the metal box; her nose creased and her muscles trembled. "Nice box," she said and pinched the cover closed. She placed the box on the bench and wiped her moist hands on her trousers.

"Box, box, where is our box?" shouted Angel.

"Shit, did you lose our juice extractor?"

"Was that a juicer?"

"What did you do with it? Where is it" Angel shouted and pranced on the hard earth behind the bench. She pounded her arms, and her neck blushed with anger.

"Forgive me, when I rushed down the steps to help the old woman I left the box behind," explained China. "A juicer, no wonder it was so heavy."

"Where did you leave it?"

"Cinch, you told me that China is not a nation of thieves," chanted China. "Unlike America, you said, people always return things here, so what's there to worry about?"

"Nice move, now where did you leave the juicer?"

"Down three tiers," said China.

"What time is it Angel?"

"Two-fifteen," she answered, "but I thought it was later than that? What was the big rush then?" Angel leaned back on the wooden bench and sighed. "Our marriage has been a timed event; we are ruled by the clock."

"There, the box is down one tier, right where I left it," said China. More than a dozen men circled the carton with their hands behind their backs to read the news stories about the condemned criminals. What was in the carton did not seem to interest them.

"Are you really an Indian?" asked Angel.

"Not really," mocked China, "you see, my grandfather was a nobleman, he was the Baron of Patronia, and we inherited the baronage."

"Really?"

"Yes, really."

"The Chinese love titles; you got it made China," she said. Angel turned and watched her husband climb the stepped bank with their juice extractor.

"Angel, please don't wrap our packages with newspapers next time," he said, winded. Cinch unwrapped the carton. "These people seldom steal, but they read anything, even instructions."

"In that case," said China, "you should cover everything you own with newspapers. Consider it insurance, crowd protection of the contents."

"China is a lord, did you know that?"

"Of course," said Cinch.

"Listen, how did you know that?"

"She travels lighter than the rest of us."

"That's my Cinch," said Angel.

"We got nothing to lose, so wrap the other packages with newspapers, but turn those capital punishment stories under this time." Cinch leaned back on the bench; he wiped his beard and watched the boats on the river. "China," he sighed, "who would name a child China?"

ANNA LEE WALTERS

✦✦✦

Bicenti

THINGS WEREN'T RIGHT.

Maya sat on the mattress and sank into its springs and lumps. She contemplated the squareness of the small room, sharpened by the afternoon shadows strewn across the floor. The angular walls, the floor and ceiling tiles cut impotently into infinite space and time, but the fragile structure confined her there indefinitely. She stared out the rectangular window to an identical house across the street, and closed her eyes tightly.

"I have this feeling that something is wrong," Maya said sheepishly to Wilma, when Wilma entered the room. Wilma was round and her circular shadow broke up the box space in the sparsely furnished room as Wilma gestured and moved around.

"Oh? What's the matter?" Wilma asked with concern. Her eyebrows lifted in a question.

Maya's oval brown face cracked slowly into a crooked smile. She asked, "Did you ever look at this room, Wilma? The squareness of our little worlds? The insignificant walls? Have you ever wondered if there were a futility and senselessness in these structures? Why are we so infatuated with squares? Are there squares in the real world?" Maya giggled at herself and pointed out the window with her last question.

As Wilma sipped her coffee noisily, she studied Maya's face. It wore a nervous frown that was there one minute and gone the next. "You didn't come here to ask me about this room," Wilma said matter-of-factly. "You didn't drive all the way from Albuquerque to Santa Fe, to question me about this room. Huh-uh."

Maya put down her own mug of coffee and looked into the eyes of her old friend intently for a few seconds, making a decision to tell Wilma everything. She dropped her voice to barely a whisper. Wilma had to lean toward Maya to catch the words Maya let go. The words visibly hung in the air between the two women for seconds.

Maya said, "Things have been happening to me lately. I've lost some things. Well . . . , actually they were taken, you know, uh . . . stolen." Maya watched Wilma's response. Wilma's face was blank. Maya continued, "Then, there have been accidents on the highway, traffic accidents, all occurring within seconds from me. Too close!"

Wilma was sipping coffee. Her shadow slipped under her and stayed a step ahead of her as she glided to a chair, one of three pieces of furniture in the room. Maya bent and leaned even closer to Wilma. The wooden chair holding Maya's weight made a little sound. Planes of light and shadow played over Maya's face as she asked Wilma, "Do you know what I am talking about?" The frown was laying over Maya's face again.

Wilma nodded her head decisively. "Yes . . . , oh sure. I was just thinking about things you can do about it. First, tell me about the items you've lost. Did you get anything back? Returned to you?"

Maya leaned forward and held her oval face in her long fingers. Her pointed elbows were on her knees. "Well, first two blankets disappeared. That pretty purple one with the tan and black stripes. Then I missed a red one with green fringes, both taken from the place I am now staying, in Albuquerque."

"Go on," Wilma encouraged. Maya looked thoughtful and far away. Maya's round figure stood before the rectangular window. Clouds floated on her shoulders and through her black hair.

"A purse was taken next. Everything in it," Maya said. She

waved her purse away with a soft bare arm. A streak of sunlight radiated under her arm.

"And the accidents?" Wilma prodded.

"Always to other people, just ahead, or just behind me, a split second from me. As far as you are to me. It's happened three times now, people died each time." Maya poured the remaining coffee into her mouth and sat back on the chair.

The room became quiet. The sunlight on the floor crawled from Wilma's feet to Maya's, half-way across the room. Maya's face went through a variety of expressions in this silence, while Wilma's face stayed blank, non-committal.

Then Wilma soothed Maya's prolonged frown. "Stay here tonight, you can —can't you? We'll talk and think this thing through. Okay?"

Maya nodded her head, though she did not speak. She went again to the window, staring beyond the house across the street, into infinite space and time.

"If we can't come up with any answers or solutions, then you go to Bicenti. You ought to anyway, to find out about your missing things. He will locate them for you. Okay?" Wilma asked while Maya nodded her head again. Their shadows had stretched longer by then, and the planes of the room were elongated, distorted by the hour at hand.

❖❖❖

The Sangre de Cristo Mountains loomed in the east, soft and rolling cones, under a melting orange and purple sky. This evening was cool, a gentle wind from the south played on the two women.

Maya and Wilma sat on the porch. Wilma hummed a tribal song as the two watched the mountains, and the sky and clouds dissolve into darkness.

Maya said, "Wilma, you've been listening to my problems all day. I didn't even ask you about the vandalism you have been experiencing out here. What's happening?"

Wilma answered, "Well, we are about ten miles from town. I guess distance may have something to do with it. But things have been quiet lately. If you don't count the weird incident that happened next door." She raised a finger and indicated her nearest neighbor's house. Then she continued, "It happened about a month ago. And Maya, you can't really call it vandalism. All that can be said about it is that it was *very strange*. Bizarre might be the word to describe it. That reminds me, Maya, you ought to park your car up here by the house."

"Well anyway," she went back to her story, "this lady and her husband next door, they're Spanish people . . . One evening they came home and parked their car out in the parking lot in front of their house. See? The next morning, *the car was upside down*. It was pretty strange. No one heard a sound during the night. But sure enough, the next morning there was this car sitting in the exact spot where it had been parked the evening before, but it was upside down!"

Maya laughed, "I guess so! I hope things like that don't happen too often. Are you afraid living out here by yourself?"

"Not at all," Wilma chuckled. "I usually enjoy it. I can't stand the thought of living cooped up in town. The houses are so close together. We're close here too—but it's different. Besides Raoul is here more often than not. You haven't met him but you'll like him, Maya, when you do meet him. He's mostly Spanish, but he's part Indian too."

"Is everyone here Spanish?" Maya wanted to know.

"Mixed, but mostly Spanish. There's a Taos family on the other side, and old Comanche woman down this street, and then there are *Dine*—Navajos." She laughed. "The rest are *Bilagaana* or *Nakai.*" As an afterthought, Wilma said, "Indians are everywhere, no matter where you go."

Maya smiled. "It's a nice, peaceful community," she said. "Too bad about the vandalism. As often as I've been here, I would never have known the problem exists out here—if you hadn't told me."

The two women sat there for a while longer until Wilma asked Maya if she were tired. Maya admitted that she was, stress had taken its toll. Before they retired, Wilma said, "Maya, why don't you move your car up here, beside the porch?"

Maya said, "Nothing's ever happened before. I'm sure that it will be okay. I'll just leave it where it is."

Maya stretched out on top of a sleeping bag in the middle of Wilma's square floor. Her eyelids soon twitched in a deep sleep.

Wilma stood over her friend for a long time that night, thinking of the words Maya had dropped in the next room. A frown creased Wilma's forehead now that Maya couldn't see. Wilma went to the only window in this room to close the drapes. She raised the window several inches to allow a breeze to circulate. She saw Maya's car sitting under a streetlamp that emitted a yellow circle of light around the car.

About midnight, Maya woke. Her eyes stared into the blackness of the square room. She was fully conscious. Her thoughts went immediately to her car. "They're doing something to it," she whispered. She rose, went to the window and looked out. The car sat safely under the high beam of the streetlamp. Maya breathed a sigh of relief. She sat in the rocking chair beside the window and kept a vigil over her car for a few minutes. Then, satisfied that for the moment it was safe, she lay back inside the sleeping bag. The breeze was stronger, billowing the drapes.

❖❖❖

At five-thirty the next morning, the alarm clock buzzed.

The Sangre de Cristo Mountains were a faint shape outside Wilma's house. A white line curved around the horizon of the mountains, sun streaks spread fan-like at one end of the range.

Wilma got out of bed and stopped the buzzing alarm. The house was all dark. She walked from her room to the one where Maya slept. She pulled the cord at the window. The drapes, like stage curtains, parted on the glowing horizon. A cold wave slid into the room. The window was still open. Outside in the parking lot, the streetlamps were dark. Wilma could see the faint blue mountains in the east, the silhouette of night in the west engulfed nearby houses.

Wilma went to the kitchen to put coffee in the percolator. She turned on the radio. Its dials were fluorescent when Wilma flipped off the light switch.

Then she went into the bedroom, stripped off her clothes, and went naked into the bathroom. In a few minutes, the shower could be heard.

Maya woke to a country and western singer moaning on the radio and the shower beating into the bathtub. She lay there a moment with her eyes closed listening to the music drift into the room. The odor of perking coffee followed the music.

When Wilma entered the room in a long white terry-cloth robe, Maya asked, "What time is it? I have to be in Albuquerque by eight. I have one of those awful early classes today."

"It's about five forty-five," Wilma answered drying her long hair with a red towel. "I set the alarm a half hour early, so we can visit a little longer. I have to go to work too. I hope you don't mind my getting you up so early."

"Oh no, I'm glad you did," Maya said. She sat on the sleeping bag and added, "Wilma, thanks for everything. I feel much better, refreshed and in a clean frame of mind. I'll go to Bicenti this weekend."

"Good, I'm glad that's settled," Wilma answered, shaking out her long wet hair that had fallen to her waist. She said, "Maya, I think the coffee's ready. You want some?"

But Maya held up a hand and said, "I'll jump in the shower first." She gathered her clothes and carried a small suitcase into the bathroom. The light in there escaped from under the closed door. The rest of the house was dark.

Wilma went to lower the open window in the room. Her wet hair had chilled her. While she was pulling the window down, she looked toward Maya's car. It was assuming a vague shape in the dawn. Wilma paused momentarily straining her eyes at the car. "Hmm," she said and went into the kitchen.

She poured a cup of coffee and looked at the radio when the female announcer came on and said in a seductive voice, "Good morning, sleepyhead. It's six a.m."

Not too long after, Maya's feet padded into the room. Her hair was wrapped in a towel turban-style. She wore blue jeans and a turquoise blouse. Her toes stuck out of her house shoes. She poured herself a cup of coffee and took a taste. That's when Wilma said, "Maya, it looks like there is something on your car."

"Oh?" was Maya's response. Her feet padded to the open window. The sun had not risen yet, but the mountains were purple and the sky above them was a delicate pink. Daylight was spreading tentatively toward Wilma's community. The community buildings however were still square silhouettes against the fingers of dawn. "It's a beautiful morning," was Maya's first observation. Then her eyes went to the car.

There *was* something on it, but she was near-sighted and without her glasses. She said, "Yes, Wilma, there does seem to be something on it. But I can't make it out that well." Her words made her remember the vigil at midnight.

Wilma stood at Maya's side. She said, "Let's go see. Maybe they punctured the tires, or something like that."

The two women walked out of the house. Maya carried her mug of coffee. They stood on the porch. Wilma pointed to her flower bed. The flowers were uncurling. They walked past the marigolds and down to the parking lot. None of the other houses were lit, not even the apartment complex at the end of the block. The local streets were empty of early morning traffic. "That's strange," Maya said. "There doesn't seem to be anyone stirring but us."

Wilma looked up and down the streets, her damp hair clung to her shoulders. "Yes, that's right, isn't it?" she agreed with Maya. The domed sky was turning a pale blue. Clouds skirted the mountaintops.

Maya's car pointed north. As she walked toward it, she noted that the windows were unbroken, the tires inflated. The car appeared to be unharmed, at least on one side. But what was that on top of it? A black shadow lay on the roof of the car. It stretched the entire length of the roof. Maya and Wilma stopped about ten feet from the car. Their eyes locked briefly. Then both women had the same thought, they gazed at the houses around them. The houses were mute and lifeless forms. Wilma pulled her wet hair over her right shoulder and looked southwest. The Sandia Mountains were now distinguishable in the dawn. A crescent moon glittered on Sandia Peak. A few cars on Interstate 40 still had their lights on. These lights zipped east and west without a sound.

"Strange," commented Wilma. Maya took a shaky step closer to the shadow on her car. Wilma followed. And when Maya stopped just at the left headlight, Wilma did too.

"What in the world?" Wilma asked in a breathy and perplexed voice.

Maya was frozen for a second, desperately sorting images that flashed before her eyes. She saw herself standing in front of the car, moving like an actress in a bizarre play, detached from herself but nevertheless affected. The only thing she could say was, "What?" and again, "What . . . ?"

The thing on the car grew into a foreboding shape in morning light. A large dog was draped over the roof of the car. The outline of its head was clearly discernible.

"What?" Maya repeated, "How . . . ?" She didn't finish the question.

The animal did not move. Maya half expected it to pounce on her or off the car. Again Maya's eyes zeroed in on the houses. Not a curtain in any window fluttered. She noted that Wilma too was studying the houses. When the dog did not move, Maya put her coffee mug on the hood of the car and took another step.

It was then that she saw the spray of blood covering the front window, on the passenger side. It had dripped down the side windows on the other side of the car. Dried pools of red stained the cement.

The jaws of the dog hung open and it looked as if this was from where the blood had gushed until the animal was thoroughly drained.

Maya tried to make sense of the scene. She went through a flood of emotion; anger, compassion for the dead animal, and resolution not to submit to fear.

"Let's go inside," she told Wilma. Wilma nodded, grabbed the mug she had placed on the hood, and involuntarily shivered.

Inside the house, Maya grabbed Wilma by the shoulders and asked, "What's happening?"

Wilma's eyes were round and her mouth was round too as she said, "Oh, Maya, I don't know. It's like that incident with the car. Weird as hell. What shall we do?"

"I don't know," Maya said. "Let me think." She kicked off her house shoes and slipped on leather sandals. While she did this, Wilma threw on the clothes she wore the day before.

"We have to get rid of it," Maya said. "Someone gave that thing to me. I don't want it and I refuse it. I'm taking it back to wherever it came from . . ."

"We'll have to clean the car," Wilma said. She ran to get a plastic jar of dish detergent, and she filled a Tupperware bowl with warm water.

"I don't get it," Maya said looking out the window once more. "Where is everyone? There used to be early morning traffic here, I remember that!"

"Don't try to figure it out now, Maya. Let's act, move, do something!" Wilma said. "This absence of the neighbors—maybe we can use it to our advantage."

"Yeah, okay." Maya nodded her head. She took a roll of paper towels Wilma handed to her.

Again, they ventured out. The sky was opaque, the sun had not yet climbed the lowest mountains. Not one car passed on this street, or down the side streets.

Maya and Wilma acted quickly and in coordination. The two women lifted the dead animal off the roof of the car. Its body was stiff and heavy. It must have weighed a good seventy pounds. They laid the rigid body just off the walkway in front of Maya's car. Again anger filled Maya as she poured soapy water on the dried blood. Wilma scrubbed the front of the car while Maya did the side, wiping the car clean and dry with paper towels. It took a few minutes. Wilma went back inside the house. Maya stayed to empty the remaining water on the pools of blood on the cement. The soapy water colored a pink tint and ran in rivulets down the street.

Then Maya noticed something she hadn't seen before. A trail of blood led to her car from across the street. She followed it and came upon another pool of blood just in front of the house opposite Wilma's house. From there the trail went down the block. Maya stood in front of that house for a moment. Then she quickly walked to the place where she and Wilma had carefully laid the animal, a few feet from the car.

She picked up the stiffened body by its front and back legs, and she carried it across the street, struggling with her burden and panting when she was done. She left the dog in the pool of dried blood there, stood defiantly and challengingly in front of that house. There were no signs of life in the neighborhood yet. She scooped up a handful of dirt from that yard and carried it to her car where she scattered it over the drying pools of water and blood. She rubbed the dirt over the cement viciously with her sandals. The blood darkened to brown spots.

"Now," Maya whispered, "we'll see what happens."

At that moment a light came on in a house on a corner. She heard a door slam somewhere. A quick look inside her car reassured her that nothing more had been done to it. The tires were in good shape. She retraced her steps to Wilma's house. Wilma met her at the door. Wilma's wet hair was tied with a rubber band and she wore a sweater.

"What now?" Wilma wanted to know.

"We wait and see what happens," Maya said. "No matter what does happen though, we don't know anything about that dog, okay?"

"It's the best way," Wilma said.

Maya unwrapped the towel around her head. "What time is it?" she asked.

"It's about six-forty," Wilma said, "You should leave before seven if you want to make that class."

Maya asked, "Will you be all right?"

Wilma went into the kitchen, searching for the coffee cup she'd put down someplace earlier. As she poured a hot cupful of coffee, she answered, "I'll go to work. No, maybe I won't. I have time I need to use for my leave anyway. But, I'll be all right."

Footsteps were coming down the sidewalk outside. Wilma came out of the kitchen and looked questioningly at Maya. The steps ended on her front porch. Someone pounded on the door.

Wilma opened it. Maya sat in the living room and listened. "What did you do with the dog?" a female voice asked in a huff.

Maya heard Wilma ask innocently, "What dog?"

The woman repeated the question. Wilma asked again, "What dog? What are you talking about?"

To this, the woman shrieked, "You're going to pay! Killers!"

Wilma then said, "Look lady, calm down. If I can help you in some way . . ."

But the woman interrupted the offer of help, threatening Wilma with curses and vile names. Maya heard Wilma close the door.

Wilma returned to Maya. She looked calm, but Maya saw her hands shaking. "Did she frighten you? Who was she?" Maya asked.

"I don't know," Wilma said, "but it wasn't the woman who scared me. It was the man."

"The man," Maya asked in surprise.

"Yes," Wilma said. "There was a man with her, standing behind her the whole time. He stood there in silence and made obscene gestures at me. His gyrations were so unnatural, not humanly possible. It scared the hell out of me!"

"You didn't show it, did you?" Maya asked in alarm. "Fear won't help us Wilma."

"No, I don't think it showed. I was just so startled. But it was the damndest thing!" Wilma gulped her coffee. Maya put an arm around her friend. "Are you okay?" Maya asked. Wilma shuddered, but managed a smile.

"Listen, I'm going to have to leave. I hate to just walk away like this, I don't understand any of this," Maya said.

"It may be that walking away is the only way to respond," Wilma said pursing her lips. "But I am convinced that you need to see Bicenti, now more than ever."

Maya nodded in complete agreement.

Footsteps were at the door again. Wilma looked at Maya and went to the door. "Killers!" the woman was screaming. "The state police are coming after you." Maya saw her lift a pudgy finger and stick it in Wilma's face. The woman was clownish in appearance, her face painted in brilliant hues. Maya stood behind Wilma.

There *was* a man with the woman. He was dark, possibly Hispanic or Indian. He bobbed up and down, as if there were springs in his legs and feet. He waved his arms imitating a grounded bird, and he contorted his face into grotesque masks that changed and flitted away as quickly as they settled over his features. Then his hands went to the crotch of his pants and he mimed an unearthly performance, contorting his body beyond the bounds of human ability. The woman with him blocking the doorway was unconcerned with his antics, she continued to shout obscenities at Wilma. They poured out in a torrent of stinging words.

Then Maya said to the woman, slowly and very clearly, "I don't know what's happening, or who you are—but you are not welcome here, and neither is anything that you bring with you." The words hung in the doorway for seconds.

The woman's eyes blinked surprise at Maya's words. For a moment, the woman's own stream of words stopped. She balanced her bulky weight on one foot. Her painted face became a frozen mask. The dark man behind the woman ceased his gyrations for a split second fracturing time and space after Maya spoke. He poised himself in the interlude, unnaturally immobile. The feat was startling. Maya was elated, felt a jab of tiny victory that her words had somehow paused his weird pantomime.

"Close the door," Maya said in Wilma's ear. Wilma pushed the door shut on the two figures. Outside, the woman again started her harangue, and then the din subsided. There were no sounds of departing footsteps. Only abrupt silence.

Wilma went to the window to observe the walkways and parking lot. "Nothing," she said in a low voice to Maya. "Nothing."

They gathered up Maya's things and prepared to go to Maya's car. Maya took out her keys from her pants pocket. They were ready to face whatever waited outside.

Before Maya opened the door, she said to Wilma, "Wait until I see if the car is going to start. Don't leave me until I know for sure. Then I'll wait until you're back inside before I drive away."

The streets were silent. None of the occupants of the dozen houses around them were visible. Wilma and Maya were completely alone. The orange rim of the sun was spreading up behind the mountains then.

"I'm sorry to have to leave like this," Wilma said. "But don't worry about me. I'll let Raoul take me to someone like Bicenti and learn something about this mess. I'll be all right. Now you just promise me that you'll see Bicenti as soon as possible. Promise."

Maya nodded and looked back toward Wilma's house. That dark man who had been on Wilma's porch a few minutes earlier now stood on the walk. Maya's head went up sharply and she sucked in a deep breath. Wilma turned to see what had affected Maya this way. The man seemed suspended there on a background of cumulus clouds. He was detached from the earth and everything that Wilma and Maya knew. He began to bob, spring up and down, a jumping-jack. Again, his hands went to his pants crotch and Maya turned away. So did Wilma.

"Is is possible that I am cracking up?" Maya asked Wilma. Wilma smiled a caring and trusting smile. "If you are, I am too," she told Maya. "Look, Maya—don't mention this, *what's happened here* to anyone. You know what I mean, other than the likes of Bicenti. Few people understand, have seen beyond . . ."

Maya looked again to where the dark man had been. He'd disappeared into Santa Fe's thin air. "Yeah," Maya said, "I know. I agree. Our people understand . . . this kind of fracture of space and time . . . But like you say, there's only a few who do. Don't worry, I won't say anything. Now you go inside as soon as the car starts." She unlocked the car, took her glasses from the glove compartment, and put the key in the ignition. The car started smoothly.

"Okay," Maya said to Wilma, "go on. I'll wait until you get inside." Wilma reached inside the car and hugged Maya, then she turned and retreated to the house.

Maya backed out of the parking lot slowly, noting that the

curtains in a few houses were moving. She turned on the radio and set the dial on the Santa Fe station. The woman's voice had not abandoned the seductive tone. And it was now 7:05.

❖❖❖

Wilma waited alone in her house all day, expecting something to happen but nothing did. About mid-morning, the neighbors showed some signs of life and activity. Cars cruised the streets.

Maya drove directly to Albuquerque, negotiating the tricky freeway traffic in time to make her 8:15 class at the university. But her mind played a reel of events that had happened to her recently; broken images of the dawning hours returned to her. By then, she was doubting her senses, asking herself if any of it had happened. In a university parking lot, she climbed out of her car, ambivalent about what she should do. She gathered her books from the car trunk and slammed it down hard. Then she went to put a quarter into the meter. Splotches of dried red blood on the car caught her eye. Suddenly her doubts vanished, her mind cleared. She set her jaw in determination, and she climbed back into the car. Bicenti was in Arizona six hours away.

It was nearly four when Maya arrived home. Her family met her at the front door. "What's wrong, Mom?" one of her children asked. "You're not supposed to be home yet. Are you cutting class?" The boy laughed and then he noticed Maya's strained face. He asked, "Are you all right?"

"No," Maya answered. "Let's talk."

In Santa Fe, Raoul knocked on Wilma's door. Wilma let him in. He hugged her, his white even teeth showing in a wide smile. "How's my girl today?" he asked.

Wilma answered him, "Raoul, how would you like to take me for a long ride today?"

"How long?" Raoul questioned.

"To Cañoncito, thirty miles from Albuquerque," Wilma told him. "I'll make it worth your while," she said with a wink.

"Okay by me, but why are we going to Cañoncito?" Raoul inquired.

"I have to see a man there," Wilma said.

Raoul smiled and teased, "Won't I do?"

Wilma laughed, "Afraid not, lover boy. The man we're going to see finds things, tells you what's wrong. Know what I mean?"

Raoul nodded. He understood.

At dusk, Maya and her man were riding down a treacherous road that wound through sagebrush and piñon trees. The Chuska Mountains were dark green behind them and Black Mesa was ahead of them some forty miles distant. A cribbed log *hoghan* and a house were in sight at the end of the road. Sheep were penned in a nearby corral, and their bleating sailed through the evening's space and time.

Maya's man went into the house and not long after came to get Maya, waiting in the pickup truck. "Bicenti is in the hogan," he said. He opened the truck door. Maya followed him inside the dark hogan.

Maya's man greeted Bicenti who sat on a sheepskin that covered the earthen ground. They touched each other's hands, then Maya touched Bicenti's hand, and took a place on the sheepskin beside him. Through the smoke hole, Maya watched the pink sky fade. In time Maya told him everything. *Things weren't right* she said intermittently while he sat and listened, not surprised at anything she said.

They left Bicenti's hogan over an hour later. The eastern sky was sprinkled with early stars and the world appeared as it should be. Bicenti would come to Maya's house the next night. He would quietly tell all. Then he would bind the tiniest fracture in infinite space and time. Then, he would go silently away, until the next time.

JAMES WELCH

❖❖❖

Fools Crow

IT WAS A SUNNY windless day, and the seven children pulling their blackhorn-rib sleds to a steep hill beyond the horse herds talked and teased each other. The two girls, at twelve winters, were the oldest. They had been sent to keep an eye on the younger ones, but they were not happy, for the five boys made jokes about the size of their breasts and the skinniness of their legs. One Spot, in particular, was cruel to them. He liked these times when he didn't have to follow his older brother around, and so he bullied the younger boys and made the girls chase him. He boasted of his hunting skills and rubbed snow in another boy's face. When one of the girls hit him with a small skin of pemmican, it stung his cheek but he didn't cry. He called the girl Skinny Weasel and he liked her, although she was a year older than he was. She liked One Spot's brother, Good Young Man, but he was more interested in hunting than girls. He was off hunting the bighorns with Fools Crow now near the Backbone. They would be gone for two or three sleeps. One Spot picked up a handful of snow and threw it at Skinny Weasel. His cheek stung but he liked her.

None of them noticed the wolf that had emerged from behind a clump of drifted-over greasewood until he was fifty paces to the side of them. He was large and gray and his eyes were golden in the brilliant sun. Snow clung to one side of him as though he had been lying down. As he walked, his tail drooped and dragged on the deep snow, and a sound, somewhere between a growl and a grunt, came up from his chest.

It was this sound that Skinny Weasel's girlfriend heard, and when she looked over she saw the animal's gait was shaky and listed to one side. He had his head down, his tongue hanging almost to the snow. Then she saw the whiteness around his mouth and thought he had been eating snow. Her first impulse was to turn and run, but then the wolf began to veer away from them. She watched him out of the corner of her eye as the wolf circled behind them. Then she said something to Skinny Weasel in a low voice and the girls stopped and turned. It was at this point that one of the boys let out a cry of fear, for he had just seen the wolf.

The wolf looked up at them and coughed and bared his fangs, making chewing motions as though he were trying to rid himself of a bone or hairball. He watched listlessly as the children ran, all but One Spot, who stood in the deep snow with his hands on his hips. He taunted the bigmouth with a war song that he had learned from Fools Crow.

The other children stopped near the base of the big hill and turned to watch. The wolf covered the thirty paces with such speed that they didn't have a chance to cry out a warning. By the time One Spot had turned to run, the wolf was upon him, knocking him face down in the snow, standing over him, growling, the hair on his back standing up and shining in the sunlight. The children screamed as they watched the wolf attack the bundled-up child. He struck repeatedly at the blanket, his low growl now a roar of fury. At last he found One Spot's head and sank his fangs into the exposed skin behind the ear. The child screamed in pain and turned over, only to feel a fang knock against his cheekbone, opening up the skin. Then the fangs were twisting and pulling at the cheek, gnashing into the soft flesh. One Spot felt the wetness and the hot breath. He saw for one brief instant a yellow eye and a laid-back ear—then he sank into the snow and the red darkness.

Skinny Weasel was crying as she watched the wolf stagger away. In his charge and attack, he had used up the last of his energy. Now his throat was swollen shut and the saliva hung in long strands from his mouth. He began a wide circle, veering always to his right, his eyes glazed, his breath coming in harsh barks, his tongue and tail once again hanging and dragging on the snow. Skinny Weasel watched him disappear behind a stand of willows near the river; then she ran to the limp form in the snowfield. When she rolled him over, she bit her lips to keep from screaming. A flap of ragged skin lay back over One Spot's eye, exposing the clean white bone of his cheek. One earlobe hung from a thin piece of skin and there was a large mat of blood in the hair. She thought she heard a rattle deep in the boy's throat. With a shudder, she placed the flap of skin down over the cheekbone. Then she and the others lifted him onto a sled. Skinny Weasel's girlfriend covered him up with her own blanket. Then the two girls pulled the sled through the deep snow back toward camp. The sun was high and the sweat was cool on the girls' bodies.

◆◆◆

By the time Fools Crow and Good Young Man returned from their hunting trip four sleeps later, One Spot was able to sit up and take some meat. But most of the time he lay in his robes and thought of the yellow eye and laid-back ear, the harsh breath and snapping teeth. Every time he closed his eyes, he saw the bounding wolf and cried out in his weakness and pain. Heavy Shield Woman had slept little, despite the fact that Red Paint and another woman had taken over the nursing of her son. Now she sat in a listless trance and thought of the many things that had happened to her family. She didn't really think much, but images of Yellow Kidney and Red Paint and Good Young Man entered her head and they all seemed far away, as though she had lost them all. Even when she looked down at One Spot, in one of his moments of peace, she saw the black pitchy substance that held his cheek in place and thought that he had gone away from her too. Only Red Paint was there to talk with, but Heavy Shield Woman didn't talk. She had begun to wonder about her role as Sacred Vow Woman at the Sun Dance ceremonies. Had she done something wrong? She thought she could not be a virtuous woman, for she felt no happiness or peace since her husband was returned to her. She felt a day-to-day barrenness of spirit relieved only by moments of pleasure at the antics of her sons and Red Paint's swelling belly. She knew she would never see Yellow Kidney again and that thought almost gave her relief, but then she would think of the happiness they had shared, the times they had lain together, the pride in his eyes each time she delivered him a child, and she would become consumed by a restless, quiet fury. Many times she thought of going to Three Bears and telling him what was in her heart and renouncing her role as medicine woman. In her mind she had already done so. Now when the girls looked to her for guidance, she averted her eyes and said nothing. She began to avoid them, for she was sure they would see in her eyes what she felt in her heart.

Fools Crow and Good Young Man rode into camp with the carcasses of two bighorns. Fools Crow had a set of horns for One Spot tied to the frame of a packhorse. He rode first to his own lodge and dumped one of the bighorns in the snow beside the entrance. Then he led the other packhorse to Heavy Shield Woman's lodge, kicking a black dog in the ribs when he became too curious. As he loosened the rawhide strings that held the animal down, Red Paint emerged from her mother's lodge. She came forward and squeezed his upper arm and smiled. She called a greeting to her brother, Good Young Man, who sat exhausted on his horse, ready to drive the packhorses back to the herd. Wearily he rolled onto his belly and slid off the horse. He had planned to return to the camp in triumph because he had shot one of the bighorns with Fools Crow's rifle, but now he felt the stiffness in his legs and butt and wanted only to lie down and sleep.

But Red Paint motioned him close, and then she told them about One Spot's encounter with the wolf. Even as she said that he was all right, her voice shook and she looked at the snow at Fools Crow's feet. Good Young Man ducked into the lodge.

Red Paint looked into her husband's eyes. "The children he was with think the wolf might have had the white-mouth. They say he was acting funny, walking sideways in a big circle. They think he had the foam on the mouth, but they couldn't tell if it was that or if he was eating snow."

"Did he breathe different?"

"Skinny Weasel said it was like a harsh bark in his throat."

"Maybe it was a bone stuck."

"Maybe," said Red Paint.

"Is your mother in the lodge?"

"She is out gathering firewood."

Fools Crow entered the lodge, with Red Paint right behind him. Good Young Man knelt beside his brother, holding his hand. One Spot looked at Fools Crow; then he grinned.

"I sang my war song," he said.

"But did you have your weapons?" Fools Crow got down on his knees and ruffled the boy's hair.

"No," the boy said sheepishly.

"Haiya! What warrior goes out empty-handed?"

"He would kill this bigmouth with his bare hands. He would be a great warrior," said Good Young Man.

"If I had my knife—"

"If he had his knife! Listen to him talk!" Fools Crow laughed. "And now you have your first battle wounds. Let me see." Fools Crow leaned over the boy's face. The patch of skin held by the black pitch looked a pale purple and was slightly swollen. He almost lost his whole cheek, thought Fools Crow. As it is, it will always be swollen and discolored, but it will at least be there. The earlobe was completely bitten off and would cause no trouble. But behind the ear, in a patch of cut-off hair, there were several puncture wounds. The whole area was an angry red, except for the small white circles around each fang mark. These were draining, but the area was swollen and tender-looking. It scared Fools Crow to look at these wounds, but he didn't say anything.

"He has nightmares," said Red Paint. "He gets very little sleep because of them."

"Sleep-bringer will visit soon. All warriors have bad dreams after battle. They will pass." Fools Crow looked down at One Spot. "You must not think of this wolf as your enemy. He did only what wolves will do. The bigmouth is a power animal, and if he visits you in your dreams, it is only because he wishes to help you. Someday he will become your dream helper."

"When I am old enough for my seeking?"

"Yes. Then he will come to you and give you some of his secret medicine. But for now, you must think of him as your brother and treat him with respect. Do you understand that?"

"But why did he attack me?"

"This one was—sick. I think he didn't know what he was doing. But wolves are unpredictable. It is best to leave them alone, even if they are our brothers—like the real-bear."

"Will I have a scar forever?"

"Do you remember the story of Poia—Scarface?"

"Yes. He came from Sun Chief and instructed our people in the Sun Dance. Afterward, Sun Chief made him a star in the sky, just like his father, Morning Star."

"But before that he was a boy just like you, with a scar on his face."

"But the people laughed and scorned him!"

"In those days, the people were not wise. Now we honor Poia. Of all the Above Ones, he is most like us, and so you must think of your scar as a mark of honor. You will wear it proudly and the people will be proud of you. And they will think highly of you because you did not kill your brother, the wolf." Fools Crow laughed. "We will tell them you took pity on this bigmouth."

One Spot thought for a moment, his dark eyes narrowed and staring up at the point where the lodgepoles come together. He heard some children run by but he didn't envy their freedom. Finally he said, "Yes, I took pity on my brother. Bigmouth will come visit me when I am older and I will welcome him. But if I had my weapons, I surely would have killed him."

❖❖❖

One Spot did not get over his dreams, but now, instead of attacking him, the wolf turned away or stopped, sometimes lifting his lip to growl, other times simply staring at the boy through golden eyes. But he always kept his distance, and One Spot, in spite of his fear, began to look forward to the wolf's visits, for he was memorizing every aspect of the animal, from his silver-tipped fur to the way his long ears flickered when One Spot shouted at him. For seven sleeps he dreamed of the bigmouth, and on the eighth day he was well enough to walk down to the river to throw rocks. Good Young Man stayed with him, never leaving the lodge to play with friends or even to visit Red Paint and Fools Crow. Together, he and his mother had skinned and quartered the bighorn. The meat was strong but good and would last a long time. Heavy Shield Woman also seemed to be recovering her spirit. For the first time in many sleeps she went to visit a friend who lived on the other side of camp. The friend was happy to see her, for she had been concerned about Heavy Shield Woman's misfortunes. They ate and talked until well after dark and the friend noticed that Heavy Shield Woman smiled and laughed more than she had in some time—since the days Yellow Kidney, then a whole man, and she had come to feast. When the friend's husband came home, with a fat blackhorn cow he had killed on the cutbank, Heavy Shield Woman remembered that she had not fed One Spot and Good Young Man. She looked up at the stars as she hurried along the icy path to her lodge, and the cold air was fresh in her chest.

When she entered, Good Young Man looked up anxiously. He was kneeling by his brother's side. "One Spot seems to be sick again. He seems to have trouble swallowing. He moves his jaws and is thirsty all the time but he can't drink."

Heavy Shield Woman ran to One Spot and sank to her knees. His forehead glistened in the firelight and his throat seemed to jump and quiver on its own. He looked up at her and his eyes were wide with fear. He tried to speak but the effort made him swallow and he cried out in pain. In panic he began to thrash around under the blackhorn robe. Heavy Shield Woman held him and spoke soothing words to him, but he didn't seem to hear or know her.

"Good Young Man, put on the water to heat—build up the fire first—then run for Fools Crow and Red Paint. Run fast."

One Spot had quieted down a little, but when Heavy Shield Woman looked down at him, she saw the saliva bubbling around his mouth. His eyes were dark and unseeing.

When Good Young Man returned with Fools Crow and Red Paint, Heavy Shield Woman was mopping the sick boy's face with a cloth dampened in the warm water. Suddenly One Spot began to tremble violently and make noises in his throat. He tried to kick the robe off, but Fools Crow held his legs.

"It is the white-mouth," he said. "The wolf has him."

"Oh, I feared it!" Heavy Shield Woman moaned as she remembered how a girlfriend had died of a fox bite. She had never forgotten it and now she was seeing it again.

"Red Paint! Hold his legs while I get Mik-api."

Fools Crow was gone for a long time. Red Paint helped her mother hold down the struggling boy. He did not recognize either of them, but the strange noise in his throat seemed a cry for help. Red Paint sank back on her heels once when her brother suddenly stopped and held himself rigid. She wiped the sweat from her forehead, and only then did she realize that she had been crying.

At last, Fools Crow entered the lodge. His chest was heaving and his face was crimson.

"Where's Mik-api?" Red Paint held her breath.

"I searched the camp. Somebody thinks he is visiting the Hard Topknots."

He looked down and Heavy Shield Woman was looking up at him with a blankness in her eyes. He suddenly thought that he had not looked at her this way since he had married Red Paint; nor had she looked at him. But now this taboo seemed far less important than the bad spirit in the boy they loved.

"We need a green hide," said Fools Crow. "Mik-api once told me how he did this."

Heavy Shield Woman looked down at her son, who was beginning to stir again. A trickle of blood from the crescent scab on his cheek ran down his neck. She wiped the saliva from his mouth. She looked up at Fools Crow and thought to question his ability as a medicine man—he was only an apprentice—but the dark shining in his eyes stopped her. He seemed to be somebody she had not known before.

"Morning Gun has just returned from his hunt," she said. "He brought back a blackhorn."

Fools Crow ran across a small icy field to Morning Gun's lodge. He told the hunter what he needed, and the two men began to skin the blackhorn. They worked quickly, not caring if they punctured the skin or left too much meat on it. When they finished, Fools Crow draped the skin over his shoulder and began to trot back to Heavy Shield Woman's lodge. He was surprised to see so many people standing around. They had been talking among themselves, but he hadn't heard a word.

The two women undressed the struggling, kicking boy while Fools Crow spread the green hide, skin side up, on the other side of the fire. Good Young Man helped him clear away the spot. Fools Crow clapped him on the shoulder and squeezed. Then he helped the women carry One Spot over to the hide. He was taken aback by the strength in the small body and understood how much effort it had taken the women to hold him down. But they managed to lay him on the smooth cool skin, with his arms pinned to his sides, and roll him up. Only his head stuck out of the shaggy bundle. Red Paint looked down and could not believe that the contorted face, the white foamy mouth which uttered such strange harsh sounds, belonged to her younger brother. But she knew that when a bad spirit entered one's body, the body no longer belonged to the person. And so, as she looked at the face she grew calm, for she felt that, now the spirit had been trapped, her husband would drive it away with the medicine he had learned from Mik-api. She helped her mother to the far side of the fire and squatted to watch.

Fools Crow, who had stopped by his lodge for his parfleche of medicines, took out a small bundle of braided sweet grass. He lit one of the braids and captured the smoke in his free hand. He began to chant and to rub the smoke over the out-of-his-body boy and himself. He chanted with his eyes closed, and the steady rhythm of his voice, like a heartbeat, seemed to place the boy under a spell. One Spot stopped struggling and the noise in his throat subsided. Fools Crow chanted:

> *"I take heart from the sacred blackhorn.*
> *Where I walk, the grasses touch my feet.*
> *I stop with my medicine.*
> *The ground where my medicine rests is sacred."*

Then he removed a burning stick from the fire and touched against the shaggy hide. There was a hiss and the lodge was suddenly filled with the stink of burning hair. Heavy Shield Woman started, but Red Paint held her close. Still chanting, Fools Crow burned off more of the curly hair. He did this several times until the hair was black and crinkly; then he turned the boy over. The movement made One Spot cry out. But now Fools Crow began to pass the burning stick over the green robe, lighting long strips of hair, and the smell made Red Paint feel faint. She looked beyond her mother to Good Young Man, but he was watching intently, mesmerized by the moving stick of fire. Again Fools Crow turned the boy over until he was lying on his stomach. The boy made no sound and Red Paint became frightened.

Fools Crow stopped to wipe One Spot's sweat-drenched head. He looked into the boy's eyes, but they were opaque and without recognition. Then he turned him again and burned off the last of the hair.

When he had finished, Fools Crow threw a bundle of sage grass onto the fire to purify the air. As he did this, he said a prayer to the Above Ones to take pity on the boy and restore him to health. He asked the Medicine Wolf to take pity on the boy and to forgive him. Then he instructed the women to unwrap One Spot and bathe him with warm water. While they did this, he took some sticky-root and tastes-dry and ground it up into a paste. The women placed the small limp body on a robe and

Fools Crow swabbed the paste on the boy's throat and mouth. They covered him with another robe.

Fools Crow sent the two women back to his own lodge, there to prepare some meat and broth. He said he would send Good Young Man to fetch them when they were needed. Heavy Shield Woman was reluctant to leave, but Red Paint talked her out of the lodge. The sudden draft of cold air swirled through the space and dried the sweat on Fools Crow's face. The lodge smelled of burnt hair and sage and sticky-root.

Good Young Man built up the fire and gave Fools Crow a drink of water. He dipped another cupful and looked questioningly at his younger brother, but the medicine man motioned the youth to sit on the other side of the fire.

For the rest of that night Fools Crow beat on his small neckhide drum. His stick was made of ash, rounded at one end, feathered at the other. He accompanied the slow beat with a monotonous song:

> *"Medicine Wolf walks with me.*
> *Medicine Wolf is my brother.*
> *Medicine Wolf enters me.*
> *Medicine Wolf is my helper."*

Fools Crow sang this song over and over and Good Young Man eventually fell asleep. Just before dawn he was awakened by a harsh growling and snapping. He sat up and saw Fools Crow, down on all fours, circling the body, swinging his head from side to side, growling and snapping his teeth at One Spot. He made three circles, sometimes feinting in to snap, other times growling low in his throat. Then Fools Crow wandered off to a bed near the tipi liner. He circled around and around four times, then lay down and curled up like a wolf. He closed his eyes.

Sometime after first light, Good Young Man awoke again and it was quiet. He threw back the robe and sat up. Fools Crow knelt beside One Spot, but now he was hunched over, his head down. Good Young Man watched his broad back move up and down with his breathing. Then he slid his legs from beneath the robe and tended to the fire. It was nearly out, but he coaxed a flame out of some dry twigs. When he had the fire crackling, he crept around and looked down at the face of his younger brother. In the half-light of dawn, the face looked pale and shiny, like the belly fat of a blackhorn. Only the skin on the cheek that had been torn away had some color. It was a dull purple, fading to bright pink along the scar. Good Young Man got down on all fours and looked closer. He looked at the chest beneath the robe. Nothing moved. He became frightened, and in his fear he blew on the face. The eyes seemed to move beneath the lids. He blew again, and this time the eyes opened and the brows came down in irritation. . . .

ROBERTA HILL WHITEMAN

❖❖❖

Summer Girl

FIFTEEN-YEAR-OLD Phoebe Cornelius dragged her brown suitcase past the long row of hedges bordering the Leeds' driveway. She followed Mrs. Helen Buffington who had picked her up at the Lake Forest, Illinois, bus depot twenty minutes earlier and was now escorting her to this new summer home. The scent of lily-of-the-valley blooming in the early June air rose to meet her. Her father had sent her to this three-story white colonial house in Lake Forest. A good experience, he said. Hobnob with the rich instead of powwows all summer, he said. Money for school clothes in the fall, he said. Feminine intuition, he claimed, as if she didn't already have enough. After her mother died when she was seven, he had raised her and her sister, and he worried about his attempts at parenthood.

In a white straw hat and flowered silk sundress, Helen Buffington rang the bell and smiled weakly at Phoebe. Shrubs squatted under the first-floor windows and green shutters framed every window but the attic. In an even more exotic place across the road, set off from the street, shrill pink azaleas bloomed in huge crocks. Tulips and daffodils fluttered near the walk of another house.

Even highways through Lake Forest had sidewalks. Phoebe

paced across the porch to look around. The porch was as big as
the deck of the ferry she had ridden to Detroit two years ago.
Stepping back to the door, she saw the two narrow windows on
each side, like doors in those magazines that show beautiful
rooms where nobody lived. When Mrs. Leed opened the door,
Phoebe thrilled at her thin figure and deep tan. Her wheat-
colored hair shook as she tilted her head to greet them. Her eyes
were the same blue as hollyhocks back home.

Phoebe lugged her suitcase inside. To the left of the large
white hall with its black marble floor was a sunken living room
furnished in golds and greens. Crystal vases sparkled on a long
oak sideboard, throwing shifting light against the ivory walls.
Behind the pair of white leather couches facing each other in the
center of the room, a breeze shook the iridescent curtains with
watery ripples. The windows on either side filled the room with a
playful sunlight, like that of a long-forgotten summer day under
cool, wet sheets drying on a clothesline. Across the foyer, a library with a huge rolltop desk held shelves of leather-bound
books. Not one paperback. A family Phoebe once knew lived in
about as much space—mom, pop, grandma, and eight kids. She
couldn't help hearing the women as they spoke in hushed voices.

"I know it's late to rearrange summer girls," Mrs. Leed said,
"but do you think Joyce would exchange? She said her girl came
from a farm town in Wisconsin. This girl will have trouble relat-
ing to my children."

Helen Buffington said, "Connie, these decisions were made
in May. You should have come to the last meeting we had. I
didn't know her, ah, heritage. I won't call Louise up north and
have her tell this girl's family she's in a different home. I can't
foresee trouble with the Club. You can let her swim a short time
after the pool begins to close."

Phoebe turned to the two women and then looked at the
floor. Where were the three children she was to watch?

"She'll do," Mrs. Leed said to Mrs. Buffington after a brief
pause. To Phoebe, she said, "Bring your things and I'll show you
to your new room." As Phoebe climbed the stairs, she wondered
if she'd get a closer look at the silver tureen in the china cabinet.

❖❖❖

In less than two weeks, whatever glow Phoebe felt about her new position had dimmed. At the Forest Country Club one day in early August, her new friend and fellow summer girl Alicia Davis agreed to keep an eye on the kids so she could sneak a call to her father. She had to tell him this job was not just baby-sitting like his friend Louise Ferguson had claimed. Yesterday, she had polished the silver tureen down to its scrolly feet and curved handles while the three-year-old napped. Mrs. Leed insisted that Phoebe stay out of the pool, even though other summer girls swam and played with their charges all afternoon. Now Phoebe wouldn't touch that water even if a little Leed went belly-up. Gregory rubbed his eyes as he sat in a little puddle twenty feet away. Phoebe carefully considered whether he'd be worth the humiliation should he drown. Then she realized how many times Mrs. Leed said, "in your spare time." Each day Phoebe couldn't figure out whether to watch the kids or clean the oven. Mrs. Leed took the position of employer seriously. Phoebe wasn't to play with the children or even sit down to eat for too long.

All she wanted now was her father to tell her to come home. Dashing down to the phone booth and dialing, she longed for that fatherly command. How she wanted to crawl through the lines and be with other Indians, getting ready for Menominee Powwow. Under the pines, down in the bowl-like arbor, the dancers would whirl like a living mosaic within the music of the drum and its singers. Under the clear sky, she would smell fry bread and smoke from camp fires, hear the laughter of friends greeting each other, the teases of lovers, and have time to watch midges careen toward the coming dusk.

Feeling her breath in the mouthpiece, she hollered into the mouthpiece to her sister, "Think about the time, Shirl." Tears welled into her eyes, but she struggled against them, twisting her long black hair around her fingers and quickly leaning from the booth to see if her employer was in the change room. She thought of her father, plunking down in his red chair. He grimaced in the glare of Saturday night fights, and often ducked and bobbed with the action. Sometimes, she would bet with him on a winner, but he rarely paid if she won. She heard Christina, the oldest of the three children she watched, shout from the change room.

"Get Phoebe to help you, dear." Mrs. Leed's voice rolled toward Phoebe like the chlorine waves in the pool beyond. Phoebe dropped to the floor, chin up to the receiver, drowning in gum wrappers and goo. The phone rumbled.

"Phoebe, is 'at you?" he teased.

"It's so good to hear your voice." she said, recalling his comforting darkness, his familiar smells of cigarette smoke, Aqua Velva, and brandy. What if something happened to him while she was gone? She remembered the moment her father told her that her mother had died. Every bit of lint on the sofa, the slant of light in the window, the tone of his voice, were indelibly marked in her memory.

"Ahh. I wish your sister felt that way. I shoulda sent both of yous off to Chicago. We haven't heard from you since the fourth. How's it now, anyways?"

"Dad, I tried to call you last week. Did Shirl tell you? I'm having some trouble."

"You're not pregnant, are you?"

"Heck no!" She started crying.

"You been working hard?"

"Sure, Dad, but this woman wears an alligator over her heart, like a badge. She and her husband aren't getting along. I feel like I'm in a war zone. We went to an estate and . . ."

"You got gumption like your aunt Pearl when she was young. She dazzled 'em in '29."

He coughed into the phone. She remembered the photo of her father's sister Aunt Pearl wearing a violet and lace chemise, looking like a summer moth that flitted through the woods back home. Dead of diphtheria at seventeen. A wood nymph clothed in the color of mourning.

"Your time is up," the operator broke in. "If you wish to continue, please deposit the correct amount."

"Dad, I'm so unhappy here." Phoebe sniffled into the receiver and prayed the black little holes would make him say, well, come back home then. "I gotta go, okay? Take care."

"Wellha!" he snorted. "Call us again soon and let us know your plans."

"Sure." He didn't hang up. She waited for him to say good-bye, but that was something he never did. He always breathed into the phone until the caller gave in and hung up first.

"Dad?"

"Hon?"

"Ma'am, if you're going to continue this conversation, please deposit two dollars and ten cents."

"I won't let you down. Bye now."

He didn't understand, she thought, pushing the quarters down the slot. As she raced through the green hall into the change room, she guessed which lockers had shirts with grinning alligators over the hearts. Three teens in silky, rainbow-colored bikinis twittered when she slipped past a bank of lockers. Phoebe wrapped a black journal and pen in her green beach towel. Even though her plain blue suit announced her summer girlhood like a loudspeaker, she forced a controlled gait through the conditioned air of the change room, out the double doors into the sunshine, past the olympic pool where lifeguards lounged under-red-and white umbrellas, over the painted THREE FEET DEEP sign. She glanced a moment toward the water where fifty rich children babbled and bobbed. On the other side of the fence, waitresses cruised with trays of amber Manhattans and mint juleps in frosty glasses, while the murmur of summer conversations drifted over the place like smoke. She tripped over a toy bucket and skipped toward Alicia, her chubby black friend of seventeen, who sat on a deck chair, rubbing her legs with Jergens lotion.

"Thanks for watching Gregory," Phoebe said.

"It's nothin'. What's another. kid anyway? They got some chairs over there." Alicia waved her hand to show the direction, her eyes sparkling with secret lights. She rubbed the lotion into her elbows and shooed one whiny blond boy toward the pool.

"B'Jesus, these white kids are dumb." She sighed. "They can't get along alone and they can't get along together. They'd never live past day one on the south side." She took a swig of her root beer. "Get a chair and sit awhile."

"I'll get one in a minute."

Alicia crossed one leg over the other and shook her head. "Girl, I've met Indians before, and you gotta be the most mixed up one I've ever met. Most of them are the easiest going people ever, but *you*. So wound up, you make me itch. I start to break into hives after we get to talking." She motioned for Phoebe to come close so she could whisper.

"Relax. Mrs. Leed can't fire you on the spot. She *needs* you. It's a status thing." Alicia smiled and patted Phoebe's arm. She stretched in the chair and laughed. Her cocoa-colored skin glistened in the sunlight. "B'Jesus, I hate getting a tan."

"This water's so unnatural-looking, inn't?" Phoebe said, sliding down to sit on the concrete nearby.

She looked at Alicia, who had been a summer girl for the past three years. "I bet some of these people think it's like the Caribbean."

Alicia squinted up at the sunlight and cupped her hands around her eyes to peer over both pools.

"Cassandra," she hollered, "don't you be treating your brother that way." She smiled at Phoebe. "Heck no, girl. These folks know better'n *you*it's not, but to impress poor suckers like us, they turn it bluer than any city pool around. This here's the Forest Country Club, and no otha' blue's as blue as this blue is."

She put her thin fingers across her eyes and squinted at Phoebe. "You been cryin'?" she asked. "It can't be that bad, unless the family you stay with gots a horny man chasing you around the table at night."

"No. The unicorn is rarely in the house. That's what I call Mr. Leed. I don't see him much, but when I do, he doesn't make me feel like I should be constantly doing work. He's not even bad-looking, in a pruned and treated sort of way. If you go for business types, that is. It's just . . ."

Phoebe took a deep breath, determined not to cry in front of all these white faces.

Alicia leaned closer and spoke as if they were planning a

heist. "Listen to me now. What you do on your days off? You pine away in the attic, or do you find some fun?"

"I don't know the freeways. Everything's so far. I've just been going down to the beach. For weeks now. I hate it here. Even the ten-year-old girl treats me like dirt. How do you manage?"

"The beach! The beach ain't no place to go! You might as well work anotha day as go down to the beach. You gotta get outa there. You gotta find your own."

"How can I?" She bit her nail, her deep-set eyes darkening with frustration.

"Take a bus, boat, walk ride. Catch a sailor on the tide." Alicia sang, waving her hands and smiling. "What about your boss? Why don't he take you? Mine does."

"I don't know who's the boss. I never ask Mr. Leed for anything. He's so *nice*, if you know what I mean, it's scary." Phoebe answered.

Alicia's full-bodied laugh filled the air. The nearby lifeguard turned to look to see if someone had lost a halter top. "You are such a green girl," she said, her black eyes squinting into Phoebe's as she slowly shook her head. "Ask the man of the house. You can handle him. Maybe he'll say yes, maybe no. You jus' haffta ask. If he says no, take an el and go to Lincolnswood. That's a big amusement park. All kinds of people there."

Phoebe untangled the long hair that fell around her shoulders, then she pulled herself up, using the deck chair for support. In a half hour, she would have to gather the children and meet Mrs. Leed for the trip home. "Thanks again. I mean it."

"Hey, forget it. I'll ask you for favors too. When's your next day off?"

"Tomorrow."

"Maybe I'll stop by and see if you made it to Lake Shore Drive one of these days."

Phoebe nodded yes. She picked up the towel and walked to where Gregory, the three-year-old Leed, splashed water down a small drain. When he saw her, he squealed, jumped into the baby pool, and began bouncing up and down, singing. She stood there checking for the other two children, feeling like a mud hen among swans in her faded suit.

Maybe Alicia was right. Maybe Mr. Leed would take her to the city tomorrow if she could get enough gumption to ask. When she first came to Lake Forest, she believed all people could be friends and get along. Now she wasn't so sure. The other teens she tried to meet threatened her. The boys raced their MG and Triumph convertibles around the town square. In their expensive shorts and T-shirts, the girls mocked her as she walked past them in the malt shop. Knowing a summer girl was as far from their reality as the ozone.

Mrs. Leed also regarded her distantly. After the first month, Phoebe had felt loneliness settle under her breastbone, as if she had swallowed a peach pit. In moments of confusion, it swelled, choking her. She searched for cues how other summer girls behaved, but because she was the only summer girl in the house, she was at a disadvantage in the daily decisions she had to make. There were no guidelines. She didn't know why she always felt threatened.

Thinking about times when she rode to town with friends back home, she walked long the fence that enclosed the shallow pool. Christina pranced on her toes through the water, a Pepto-bismol–colored dragon wrapped around her ten-year-old belly. Kelly, her seven-year-old sister, cautiously jumped off the pool edge onto a green inner tube. With a shift of her head, Phoebe noticed Mrs. Leed, leaning back in her lounge chair, her cleavage ripening in the sun. Every now and then, she adjusted her Polaroids. At a nearby table, a slender young man and an older woman chatted with her.

Phoebe found a deck chair, opened it, and curled her knees up so she could write and check on Mrs. Leed at the same time. A man, casually dressed in white shorts and a pale yellow sweater, came by them, brushing his martini glass against Mrs. Leed's bare shoulder. He had trousled gray hair with boyish bangs and laughed as he moved a chair close to Constance Leed. She brushed her upper arm against his thigh, then removed her sunglasses as if to search for Phoebe or the children. Phoebe quickly put the journal and pen on the chair and covered it with a towel. A child screamed directly behind her.

Kelly and Christina struggled across the concrete, a limp green-and-white inner tube stretched between them.

"You did too. You broke it on purpose," Christina shouted, jerking it back. "You jumped on it on the ground."

"I never did," Kelly shrieked, straining toward Phoebe. "You said I could have it, poopoo face, so it's mine." Kelly looked at Phoebe. "Tell her it's mine, Bee. Mom said." Kelly screamed to stop Christina from talking.

"Hush. Let me see if I can get it fixed," Phoebe said, trying to pry Kelly's fingers from the tube.

"We don't want it *fixed,*" Christina yelled, trying to jerk it away from both of them. With her pixie-cut hair flattening along her face and neck, she looked like a defiant water rat. "I want a new one." she said.

Phoebe leaned toward them. "If you both don't give me this tube right now and go play, I'm going to make you sit in the change room until we go back."

"You're too mean. I'm going to tell Mother on you." Kelly glared at Phoebe with her sparrow-sharp eyes, her red hair curling around her ears. Then she stuck out her tongue at her sister, and Christina pulled on it with her hand. *Schluck*—the tongue slipped back in Kelly's mouth. Both girls laughed. Kelly dashed around Christina in circles, sticking out her tongue, then her buttocks, then dashing a short distance away. Christina made a grab, but missed her.

"Don't run," Phoebe mumbled as they ran away. They almost tripped another summer girl who was wrestling a screaming four-year-old toward the showers.

Phoebe slouched back into her chair and curled her knees up for a desk. In a careful script, she wrote *I want to go home where the wind blows through the apple tree. Dad's probably sitting in the living room with Aunt Dovey and Uncle Roy, talking about how they weren't allowed into town when they were kids, except on Saturday and then they could only go to two stores. I must be going nuts, cause sometimes I hear dance bells coming from thun-*

derclouds. Dumpy Shirl and Dinosaur Dad, please don't let anything happen to you until I get home.

She eyeballed her three kids, then paged back through the journal, spotting a line about how rich the air smelled in Lake Forest, like tamarack on a sweet river. "Shit, you were dumb to come here," she said out loud, glancing up to discover Mrs. Leed had vanished and that it was time to gather up the kids.

She told Kelly to go in and change. Taking Gregory by the hand, she walked into the change room and helped him with his underpants. After he was dressed, she asked Kelly to help him with his shoes while she went to find Christina. She thought she saw her in the hallway leading toward conference rooms, so she walked into an unknown wing beyond the coffee shop. Then she heard girlish laughter and the slamming of a door. She ran down the hall and followed the laughter up the stairs. Opening the door to the second floor, she heard another door close. The green shag carpet hushed her footsteps, but she knew Christina must be in that room. Suspecting another chase if she knocked, she jerked open the door, ready for a tussle.

"Who told you I was here?" said Mrs. Leed, rising from the brown velvet love seat. Startled, the tall gray-haired man settled back into the cushions. He crossed one hairy brown leg over the other and smirked.

"I thought Christina was here," Pheobe said, startled by her own loud voice.

Mrs. Leed smoothed her tennis skirt and shook her head. The lanky man appeared perturbed as he rose and walked over to a carafe of wine on a nearby sideboard.

"I expect you to watch my children every minute, especially in this pool," she said.

"I am so sorry if I interrupted you. I thought I heard her laughing."

Mrs. Leed crossed her thin tanned arms. The man offered her a glass of wine. Her face glowed like polished wood, and the lashes around her eyes held thick coats of mascara. Sky-blue eyes coming from such a deep tan startled Phoebe as much as her first encounter with the Siamese cat her girlfriend Lucy once found.

"Never mind the excuses." Mrs. Leed's soft voice filled the room, and she took the wine in a graceful reach. "Find Christina and we'll meet where we usually do. Let's hope she hasn't gone outside or left with friends." She sipped her wine. "You should not allow the children run around like wild animals." She pressed her lips together and her jawline rippled.

Phoebe ran back down to the change room, her arms and legs shivering as if she had been in the pool. Christina was chasing Kelly in the change room while Gregory played with his shoestrings.

She led them to the parking lot and watched them snuggle in the small backseat of the white convertible. Constance Leed crossed the lot and slipped into the driver's seat. She turned to Phoebe.

"How old did you say you were?" she asked, her voice openly irritated.

"Fifteen, going on a hundred," Phoebe answered.

"Don't get smart. I only want to point out that I am twice your age, so I figure you should have twice my energy. Summer is *my* time." She put the key into the ignition. "I don't ask you to do any more than I do all winter. But you do things so sloppily and need such prodding. If I pay you for relief from childcare and housework, I don't expect to keep an eye on you or discover that you've lost the children. Do you understand?"

Phoebe nodded.

"Now, this afternoon, while Gregory naps," Mrs. Leed said, "cut some of the looseleaf lettuce growing in the backyard, with the pair of scissors from the kitchen. Cut it so it will grow back. Never pull it." She said, suddenly smiling, "Wash and dry it off, then leave it in the colander. We'll have it with dinner."

Phoebe bit her thumbnail down to the quick, every nerve on alert, and glared at the woman. She felt her chin twitching as she spoke. "Mrs. Leed, I'm supposed to watch kids, not clean ovens and harvest lettuce."

"That's nonsense. You will do as I say. Not only do I pay you thirty dollars a week, but I must pay for your room and board as well. You need more get-up-and-go, or you'll be one of those people, sitting in parks waiting for someone to toss you a quarter. Stop scribbling in the notebooks and reading romances." She revved up the motor, and wind blew around them as they headed back to the house.

"You won't even let me play with the kids," Phoebe said into the wind, feeling blood banging against her earlobes.

"You aren't a child." Mrs. Leed countered. "You are to be responsible and discipline the children. You take my place while I do other things."

❖❖❖

Phoebe snipped lettuce growing around the fence in a far corner of the L-shaped lawn. The shadows from a huge elm played along the ground. Although midges wheeled around her eyes, drowned in her sweat, and made her pause, she loved the smell of dirt and growing grass. She snipped a few more leaves and tucked them into the bowl. In the kitchen, she didn't feel her hands growing numb under the cold running water. When she turned off the faucet, she heard Mr. Leed's car pull up the drive. She peered out the window, careful to avoid moving the curtains. "Watch me, Wendell," Phoebe murmured to him through the windows above the sink. "I'll blow each leaf dry for us. Let us eat. Let us live." She imagined teasing him.

Christina and Kelly threw their Barbie dolls under the patio table as Mr. Leed pulled out his briefcase from the passenger's seat and shut the door of his blue Audi coupe. The two girls held hands as they walked up to their father and began to chatter. Phoebe remembered how she ran to her father with shrieks of joy and hugs. She would bound down the stairs and tumble into his arms. When she was younger, she would put her feet on top of his black workboots and he would whirl with her around the room. These girls didn't touch their father, didn't hug or poke or pull on his clothes. Her fingertips remembered the feel of her father's hair. She thought these girls sometimes acted like strangers with the ones they loved.

Mr. Leed vanished from her vision. In a moment, she heard him enter the back door. Phoebe whisked the colander from sink to countertop so she could see him if he walked past. He acted at times as if a genie had conjured his children and the summer girl in the kitchen. Placing a towel under the colander, she flipped it in the air. Water from leaves showered over her strong and supple body.

Entering the kitchen, he paused to watch. "Does doing it that way serve a particular purpose?" he asked.

"It doesn't smoosh 'em like a towel," she answered. "Cools me off too." She tilted her head to see if he was watching, then threw lettuce in the air one more time. When she caught his smile, she looked at the floor. He had a dimple in his left cheek, and his auburn hair had fallen over his forehead. Her face and groin grew warm. His gray eyes caught hers when she looked up. She imagined Chicago at five o'clock with a perpetual gray rain pounding storefronts, and red, yellow, blue neon winking in caverns of gray skyscrapers. Gutters were filling with water rippling into gray with swatches of color swirling as all of it got sucked down, down, down.

"Is this something you people do that's different?" he was asking, twisting one wrist against his cuff, his other hand still clutching the case.

Phoebe puckered her lips. "Oh no, sir. This I discovered all by my lonesome."

"I heard you whispering. I thought you were speaking to me. Are the children behaving?" he asked, walking closer to the counter and leaning against it, unbuttoning his suit coat. He seemed taller to her, like a man in an advertisement who had come to life, the woodsy aroma of cologne wafting around him.

"I was just telling the lettuce. Get ready. We're going to eat you. The kids, children, I mean, are doing good, whenever I see them." Phoebe moved back to the sink, a safer distance. She bit into a lettuce leaf for luck, looking at the bank of cupboards above his head so that she would not see "no" if it appeared in his eyes.

"Mr. Leed, I've been here almost the whole summer and haven't gotten downtown once. So I'd like to ask you, sir, if you could give me a lift to town and back tomorrow. It's my day off."

"I don't see why not. I could show you a good place to eat lunch."

"You would? Anything but leaf lettuce." She laughed.

"Nothing beats this lettuce, with its airy flavor," he said. "Unless it's a chocolate malt." He smiled broadly again, turned, and walked down the hall. Phoebe felt a pang of pity for him. She was sure the older man Constance met today was her lover.

❖❖❖

After supper, Mrs. Leed asked her to come to the library. Phoebe walked through the wide double doors and sat down in an armchair. Mrs. Leed's ruby ring trembled as she touched her hand to her forehead. The last rays of sun brightened the books and lit up her hair. She sat at the desk with a half-written letter before her. Aquamarine eye shadow made her eyes darker, almost the Prussian blue of the oriental rug on the floor.

"How many weeks have you left in our employ?" she asked.

"Three, maybe four, I guess," Phoebe answered.

Mrs. Leed leaned back in her chair and fidgeted with a silver letter opener. Phoebe noticed that although the tan made her look young from a distance, Mrs. Leed had a web of lines around her eyes. Around the corners of her mouth traces of frowns still lingered. Time was telling her the jig was up, but Constance struggled against the inevitable. Now she seemed to compose herself after each comment. She was taking an exceptionally long moment to speak. The sun brightened the red armchair across the room and lit the wall in the silence.

"I wanted to tell you we have a guest arriving on Monday. She is my husband's niece from Texas, and she'll be staying here for about three weeks." Mrs. Leed placed one slender hand under her chin and locked on Phoebe's dark eyes. "She has been used to a personal maid all her life, and since we do not have a maid here, I will expect you to perform that function." She dropped the letter opener on the desk. Phoebe thought for a moment that Mrs. Leed was testing her hearing.

"Mrs. Leed, three children are enough for me to handle all day. But you got me scrubbing your black marble floor every morning and cleaning ovens and cupboards and picking lettuce. Now you're saying I'm to be somebody's personal maid?" Phoebe tried to regain her composure, but a peach-pit lump was shifting its thorny edges up her throat. It felt like it would rip through her left lung any second.

"Our niece is your age," Mrs. Leed said, leaning toward Phoebe and speaking in an even tone. "Each morning someone has taken out her clothes for her. Every day, someone has picked up after her. She comes from a very wealthy family and we are happy she will be here to visit, but you will have to help out because that is why we are paying you. Right now, you do not do more than I do every fall, winter, and spring. I'm still young and expect to enjoy myself. You wanted to work, but it seems that you do not understand what that means." She tapped her lacquered finger on the desk to emphasize her last three words.

"Mrs. Leed, how can I pick up after someone my age?"

"You did expect to work for your money and not sit around lost in daydreams. I have never had such a lazy summer girl. You do not even make the beds correctly." Her prominent cheekbones glistened like polished teaspoons. Her slender body's power seemed to fill the whole room, and Phoebe felt so crushed by the invisible gravity of it that her thighs itched against the cushions.

"I'll think about it, Mrs. Leed," Phoebe said, wondering if she could handle being a maid, picking up the underwear of some girl her own age.

"I don't see what there is to think about. The decision is final as far as I can see," Mrs. Leed said, turning to the letter, a gesture that dismissed Phoebe as a presence in the room. The sun had set. In the purple twilight of the room, Phoebe could smell the sweet perfume of her employer, but her heart felt crazed with resentment. She wanted an edge of power, a sense that she too could call some shots.

"Mr. Leed is going to take me to Chicago tomorrow on my day off. I'll let you know whether I'm going to stay here when I come back from downtown."

"Truly?" Constance Leed answered, glancing at her.

"Very truly, if you know what truly means," Phoebe found herself saying. She could say something to the unicorn about the gray-haired man.

Mrs. Leed ran one hand through her soft curls. "Isn't it time to chase my little rascals to bed?" She reminded.

Phoebe rose to accept the that job, but flashes of color flared behind her eyelids and anger thundered in her ears as she left the room.

❖❖❖

She encountered Kelly running down the back stairs. Grabbing her by the shirt sleeve, she led her back to the bedroom she shared with Christina. It was almost her day off, she told them, and she was touchy. She opened the door to find Christina and Gregory in the midst of a trampoline tournament on the bed. "Enough, you guys." she hollered.

"I'm a girl, not a guy," Christina said, whapping one last bounce into the mattress, and stifling her giggles into the pillow.

"I'm not in the mood to argue. I'll drown you in the toilet if you don't behave."

"You can't. Mother would fire you like that," Christina said, trying to snap her fingers.

"You'll go to jail with other people like you," Kelly said. "People who call a davenport a couch." They pealed with laughter. Phoebe strutted slowly into the large bedroom, imagining how it might be to pick up after someone her age. "Ouch!" she shouted, grabbing her foot and pulling a jack from between her toes. From her perch on the bed, Kelly pealed with laughter again. Phoebe grabbed her by the arm and whisked up her legs so that she dropped to the mattress like a sack of cats. She shoved Christina's head toward the pillow. "Sleep," she said.

Gregory padded toward her from his spot near the bedpost. "Reeree, I need to go to the bathrung." She took him down the hall and helped him, then put on his pajamas with the blue and green clowns flipping over themselves. She sent him to his bedroom and stopped by the girls' room to flip off the light, warning them that it was her day off tomorrow. They cheered. "If I have to come back here, you'll be sorry," she said, wondering what she would do, even if she did have the strength to come back.

When she returned to tuck in Gregory, he asked for his men. She picked up the small toys scattered on the braided rug. She sat on the bed and pranced the macho men over the ridges of the blankets. His eyes widened and glistened in the light from the hall. His chin relaxed when he yawned and he sank back into his pillow. Such long lashes and dark eyes. Phoebe leaned over and kissed him on the cheek.

"Why'd you do that, Ree?" he asked, cupping his hand over the spot.

"For fun, Gregory Leed." She smiled at him before she shut the door.

❖❖❖

In her attic room, she cursed the ceiling, sloping like a thumb over her head, the dusty rose walls descending on her. She wished she had enough gumption to run full speed through the door, leap from the bed through the window with a crash and land in the treetops, like a diver might break through lake water to meet the startled carp below. Instead, she stood on the bed and looked down at the streetlight glowing in the leaves. When she opened the window, a delicious summer night blew against her hot cheeks. The texture of the leaves, the way they spun as night air washed them, softened her anger. She reached for her journal.

Almost Tuesday. The nerve of her to even think I would pick up after someone my own age. That is the limit. I gotta get out of here somehow. Downstairs, Constance Leed is riding her steed. Off goes the tennis dress. All teeth and eyes, she suggests Wendell to bed. He doesn't know that his former airline stewardess has been serving that dish to others. But tomorrow, I'll ride to the Loop with him, an ad man, add it up, man!

She wrote the next day's events with such certainty and in such detail it had to come true. Then she slammed the book shut and tripped down the back stairs. Suspended like a wave before it crashed on rocks, a shout was building in her chest. She snuck

out the back door and ran down the driveway. Elms cradled the
first stars in their topmost leaves. An occasional houselight went
on, while near other houses, the glow of cigarettes and the occasional sound of voices rose from the darkening patios. The smell
of barbecue hung in the air. Phoebe peered into the immense
homes and watched the man of the house before his television,
or cranky children being chased to bed. Her heart felt it could
leap any gap. It was a feeling she had last summer when her
friends Kaye and Karen and she had wandered until after midnight under the summer stars, flinging old underwear into trees
and telling the stories people would make up to explain them.
She danced along with blood so hot, her fingertips crackled. Under the porticos of elms, she skipped down the block.

A porch light flickered in a big stone house surrounded by
hedges. In the house next to it, a girl played the piano in rhythms
that reminded Phoebe of paddling a boat. The music blended
with the spicy scent of carnations and mums. After wrapping her
long hair in a single twist behind her back, she climbed through a
wall of lilacs. The girl played effortlessly, as if the talent and the
means to develop it had been a birthright. Although Phoebe
applauded when it was over, the girl did not hear.

When she stepped from the lilacs, the night no longer suspended her loneliness. It coursed fiercely through the lawns and
leaped from the now dark borders of street corners. She ran
gladly up the Leeds' driveway and opened the back door with
relief. She raced through the kitchen and up the back stairs.
When she reached the second-floor hall, she heard voices, one
deep, insistent, the other, quiet and terse. There was nothing she
could do but creep down the hall past the main landing to listen
intently for the mention of her name or words that might signal
an end to her plans. "Do you think you're any better?" Mrs.
Leed challenged. Mr. Leed shouted, "You have the nerve to suck
my dick and tell me you love me!" Phoebe thought she would
dash up to the attic, but she was drawn back by the voices. "How
can you be so crass?" Constance complained. "So shut me up,"
Wendell growled back. "You're the one wrecking everything."
The voices suddenly seemed just behind the door. Phoebe ran

down the hall and up to her attic room. She could still hear them as she got ready for bed, like a distant party out of control.

❖❖❖

She was ready in the back hall soon after six, and sat on those stairs, watching the ugly minute hand sweep away her free time. He had to come soon, because his Audi was in the drive and she had heard water running when she woke up. She moved her purse and checked her wallet the sixth time, then brushed off her jeans. She decided to wait in the car. The sun rose through trees on distant lawns. Wet with dew, the car door was locked, so she waited in a chair on the patio.

It was after seven when Wendell Leed rushed to his car. Phoebe sprang up when the door opened and darted behind the back of the coupe in order to slide into the passenger's seat. He didn't unlock the door, but rolled down the window after he started the engine. His eyes were hard as Formica.

"I can't take you today," he cried out, turning around and moving out of the driveway.

"But Mr. Leed, I've been waiting. I'm all ready," Phoebe shouted back, running around to the front of the car that rolled away from her. "I won't be any trouble," she pleaded, still hopeful as the car reached the last few hedges. She chased it to the road. "At least give me a ride to the el," she hollered, watching it cruise down the street.

The children chased back and forth through the upstairs hall as Phoebe climbed the stairs. She sat on her bed, stuffing her suit, towel, and journal into the familiar beach bag.

"Don't cry," Kelly said, sliding her back down the door frame to sit on the floor, her red shorts visible under her pajama top. "My last year's summer girl was Laura. She had lots of pimples. She said it was bad luck to cry on a day off."

Kelly slid across the floor and crawled next to Phoebe on the bed, an intent look on her tanned face.

"Too bad you got no friends." Kelly's hand lightly touched Phoebe's knee. "Laura knew lots of other summer girls. Are you sad to be here? Do you wish you lived in a bigger house, like my cousin from Texas, with maids and butlers to wait on you? I wish I did."

Phoebe looked at her. Kelly's face beamed with the desire to chat.

"I'm disappointed, okay? Leave me alone."

"You don't want us to bother you, right?"

"Please."

"Not on your day off, right?"

When Phoebe rose and looked out the window, the full summer morning was sweeping past. Kelly melted toward the door. Then she twittered to her sister as she stepped down the attic stairs. After washing her face, Phoebe headed toward the kitchen where Gregory sat, eating dry cereal. She left through the back door and headed toward her usual street corner. She boarded the same bus to the beach. After walking down the asphalt road and through the parking lot, she discovered too many kids with summer girls, too many woman rubbing Bain de Soleil into their darkened thighs. She longed for the blast of wind that quickened everything with the scent of alewives and lake weeds. She could almost hear Alicia chastising her—Don't you ever learn? She began to trudge north, the direction of her longing.

The beach narrowed to a rocky shelf along the water. Phoebe kept on. She smelled spruce trees. On the hill flashed purple patches of wild lupines and an occasional wild rose. The ridge extended into a beach. She trudged through the closely growing trees and thickets humming with crickets and honeybees. She longed to escape her life as it unfolded its dark wings.

She flapped her feet a little coming down the ridge where the shore leveled out into a cove. A large hurricane fence crossed her path and went out a hundred feet into the water. Struggling through the undergrowth, she pushed toward it and found a large white sign in bold black letters.

WARNING. JET BLAST AREA.

TRESPASSING FORBIDDEN BY LAW.

FORT SHERIDAN AIR FORCE BASE.

Beyond the fence sunlight gleamed more peacefully than where she stood. She scanned it up and down for an opening.

She wanted to go in, as she had wanted to be part of Lake Forest or to be home, but wasn't. She began to climb over, pushing her tennis shoes along the chain links. She threw her beach bag into the grasses below and slipped under the barbed wire at the top. Flinging herself through, she fell to the ground. Nothing happened. Only the slapping sound of the blue-gray waves, and the distant caw-caw of a crow. No dogs. No jet blast. No airmen with guns.

The lake flickered with familiar green and blue lights. The sand looked as if a thousand undercover caterpillars furrowed beneath the shore. She broke through the underbrush, stashed her bag near a mossy stump and wandered on, stumbling over rotting logs and willow roots. A pair of finches flitted through a beech tree. Crickets paused suddenly as she passed. Farther into the woods, weeds scratched her legs. She slapped mosquitoes, yet the wide arches of elms lightened her anguish. A deer trail unwound through the trees.

She followed it up and over a hill along the shore. The ravine formed a small canyon, with a creek rippling lakeward and crumbled foundation stones scattered beneath weeds. She didn't expect to find the bones of an old mansion on an Air Force base. Even the rubble of the fountain exuded magnificence. Earlier, a channel had flowed down the winding trough and had collected in a pool, not twenty yards from shore. Phoebe crawled up the trough to the top of the hill. There, covered with grapevines and trailing arbutus, two stone jaguars mirrored each other. They rested together on either side of a large basin. Although crumbled along the bases, their curved tails and snarling muzzles made her shiver. She tore the vines away from both and looked at the mottled bodies. Shadow and light played over them. Once they had formed a massive fountain. Crouching between them in the flickering light, she caressed their bumpy backs and swelling haunches where that twilight before the fountain stopped, a long stone stairs wound down to the nearby lake. A spring had once welled up around the jaguars, rippled through the basin and down the trough. She leaned against the left jaguar and rested her feet against the other, listening to the slapping waves.

A searing desperation overtook her. She had nowhere to go. Unaware of how long she sobbed, she looked up to find her tears had darkened the stone of the jaguar. How like the night sky with stars, she thought, smearing them. How like a jaguar, each coming night. She could only guess its approach, never the moment it arrived. She knew she had to accept and love the night filled with dizzy, glittering silences. She had to ground herself in her eventual death and pay attention to those lives wheeling around her in the sky and earth. Only by understanding and feeling her own relatedness could she live.

She pushed into the curve of the jaguar's side. The slow rhythm of her breath echoed in the stone. Through the treetops into the deep blue sky, she felt a rhythm that insisted on patience. She prayed as an ant crawled over the stone. Life inside trees suddenly astounded her. A shaggy-barked hickory surged near the top of the ravine. Underneath the wide leaves of a chestnut, clumps of prickly green nuts gleamed and an amber syrup oozed from the dark pebbly bark of a third tree. As the wind swept through and trembled the leaves, Phoebe told herself each tree gave its dreams to the wind, blossomed and grew, burst through its own bark. Another tree welcomed strangers, offered bits of dreams to parasites, oozed its life stuff out for ants. Some never blossomed, never broke through, but curled back into the same source, the Earth herself who listened. Phoebe wrapped her arm around the jaguar's neck and felt its cool weight against her forehead and cheek. Then she started back, a center of gravity deep in her chest, leading her on.

❖❖❖

Late in the afternoon, she walked to the back door of the large colonial house. She heard Alicia's voice before she saw her, standing in blue jeans and a red T-shirt. She had been talking to Kelly.

"Hi. Good to see you here. Have you met Mrs. Leed yet?"

"I do believe I have. Every bit the woman you say. I didn't know if you'd be around with all the talk of downtown."

Phoebe led Alicia through the kitchen and they climbed the

stairs. Gregory scrambled down the second-floor hall, shrieking for joy.

"See all these night lights?" Phoebe said, pointing at the stairs and hallway.

"B'Jesus, at night, I bet it looks like a bus depot. All she needs is arrows to your room."

Phoebe pointed Alicia toward the attic door. Alicia stuck her head inside and chuckled. "Painted the color of a dried-up pimple," she said, stepping inside. "I just know the same guy did both our rooms. Guaranteed to prevent masturbation."

Phoebe threw her suitcase on the bed, and gathered wads of clothes, cramming them into pockets, and then pushing them down until every piece fit. Alicia sized her up.

"Have you longed for company so hard, when it comes, you lose your mind?" she asked.

"Yeah!" Phoebe said, smiling. "I've lost my mind. I'm going home. Some kinds of work can't be worth it. That hallway will never look the same. I want to go to the bus depot tonight."

"I can show you. You gonna tell her? Or are you simply gonna be gone?"

Phoebe flopped back on the bed, stretching her long arms across the rose colored bedspread. "I'm gonna call her tonight, after my day off. I got some money and I'm going to the bus depot. Home! They can't keep me here against my will. Inn't there a law?"

"False imprisonment. She's gonna puff and blow, you know. If that's what you want, don't let her bluff you," Alicia said, her knowing eyes on Phoebe. "I think you're coming to life, girl."

Her suitcase ready, Phoebe pushed it to the door. "The last good guy I saw around here was the garbage man. I took out the trash last Monday and had to hand it to him. Little cap on his head. Chicano, I think. Fine brown eyes. I told him I slept too late. You know what he said? 'Maybe I should come and wake you up'. Believe it?"

"Did you chase him down the drive?"

"Almost."

"You and the garbage man on the patio, doing it. Dancing,

of course. Constance would be creamed!" Alicia grinned. "Have you taught her daughters how to light their farts?"

"A terrible oversight in their education," Phoebe said, motioning to go. "It's hot up here. After we go to the depot, show me some fun."

She dragged her suitcase down the two flights of stairs and lugged it down the sidewalk. When she got too tired, she switched it to her left arm. Although it did get heavy, she knew her arms were strong.

DARRYL BABE WILSON

❖❖❖

Diamond Island:
Alcatraz

ALLISTI TI-TANIN-MIJI
(rock)   (rainbow)

THERE WAS A single letter in the mailbox. Somehow it seemed urgent. The address, although it was labored over, could hardly be deciphered—square childlike print that did not complete the almost individual letters. Inside, five pages written on both sides. Blunt figures. Each word pressed heavily into the paper. I could not read it but I could feel the message. "Al tr az" was in the first paragraph, broken and scattered, but there. At the very bottom of the final page—running out of space—he scrawled his name. It curved down just past the right-hand corner. The last letter of his name, *n*, did not fit: *Gibso*. It was winter, 1971. I hurried to his home.

Grandfather lived at Atwam, 100 miles east of Redding, California, in a little shack out on the flat land. His house was old and crooked just like in a fairy tale. His belongings were few and they, too, were old and worn. I always wanted to know his age and often asked some of the older of our people if they could recall when Grandfather was born. After silences that sometimes seemed more than a year, they always shook their silver-gray heads and answered: "I dunno. He was old and wrinkled with white hair for as long as I can remember. Since I was just a child." He must have been born between 1850 and 1870.

Thanksgiving weekend, 1989. It is this time of the year when I think about Grandfather and his ordeal. I keep promising myself that I will write his story down because it is time to give the island of Alcatraz a proper identity and a "real" history. It is easy for modern people to think that the history of Alcatraz began when a foreign ship sailed into the bay and a stranger named Don Juan Manuel de Ayala observed the "rock" and recorded "Alcatraz" in a log book in 1775 (*Alcatraz, The Rock*, 1988, p. vii). That episode, that sailing and that recording was only moments ago.

Grandfather said that long ago the Sacramento Valley was a huge freshwater lake, that it was "as long as the land" (from the northern part of California to the southern), and that a great shaking of an angry spirit within the earth caused part of the coastal range to crumble into the outer-ocean. When the huge lake finally drained and the waves from the earthquake finally settled, there was the San Francisco Bay, and there, in isolation and containing a "truth," was Diamond Island (Alcatraz).

He told me the story one winter in his little one-room house in *Atwam*. It is bitter cold there during winters. I arrived late in the evening, tires of my truck spinning up his driveway. The driveway was a series of frozen, broken mudholes in a general direction across a field to his home. The headlights bounced out of control.

My old 1948 Chevy pickup was as cold inside as it was outside. The old truck kept going, but it was a fight to make it go in the winter. It was such a struggle that we called it "Mr. Miserable." Mr. Miserable and I came to a jolting halt against a snowbank that was the result of someone shoveling a walk in the front yard. We expended our momentum. The engine died with a sputtering cough. Lights flopped out.

It was black outside but the crusted snow lay like a ghost upon the earth and faded away into every direction. The night sky trembled with the fluttering of a million stars—all diamond blue. Wind whipped broken tumbleweeds across his neglected yard. The snow could not conceal the yard's chaos.

The light in the window promised warmth. Steam puffing from every breath, I hurried to his door. The snow crunched underfoot, sounding like a horse eating a crisp apple. The old door lurched open with a complaint. Grandfather's fatigued, centenarian body a black silhouette against the brightness—bright although he had but a single shadeless lamp to light the entire house. I saw a skinned bear once. It looked just like Grandfather. Short, stout arms and bowed legs. Compact physique. Muscular —not fat. Thick chest. Powerful. Natural.

Old powder-blue eyes strained to see who was out there in the dark. "Hallo. You're just the man I'm lookin' for." Coffee aroma exploded from the open door. Coffee. Warmth!

Grandfather stood back and I entered the comfort of his jumbled little bungalow. It was cozy in there. He was burning juniper wood. Juniper, cured for a summer, has a clean, delicate aroma—a perfume. After a healthy handshake we huddled over steaming cups of coffee. Grandfather looked long at me. I think that he was not totally convinced that I was there. The hot, coffee was good. It was not a fancy Colombian, aromatic blend, but it was so good!

We were surrounded by years of Grandfather's collections. It was like a museum. Everything was very old and worn. It seemed that every part of the clutter had a history—sometimes a history that remembered the origin of the earth, like the bent pail filled with obsidian that he had collected from Glass Mountain many summers before, "just in case."

He also had a radio that he was talked into purchasing when he was a young working man in the 1920s. The radio cost $124. I think he got conned by that merchant and the episode magnified in mystery when he recalled that it was not until 1948 before he got the electric company to put a line to his home. By that time he forgot about the radio and he did not remember to turn it on until 1958. It worked. There was an odor of oldness—like a mouse that died then dried to a stiffness through the years—a redolence of old neglected newspapers.

The old person in the old house under the old moon began to tell the story of his escape from "the rock" long ago. He gathered himself together and reached back into a painful past. The silence was long and I thought that he might be crying silently. Then, with a quiver in his voice, he started telling the story that he wanted me to know:

"Alcatraz island. Where the Pit River runs into the sea is where I was born, long ago. *Alcatraz,* that's the white man's name for it. To our people, in our legends, we always knew it as *Allisti Ti-tanin-miji* (Rock Rainbow), Diamond Island. In our legends, that's where the Mouse Brothers, the twins, were told to go when they searched for a healing treasure for our troubled people long, long ago. They were to go search at the end of *It A-juma* (Pit River). They found it. They brought it back. But it is lost now. It is said, the 'diamond' was to bring goodness to all our people, everywhere.

"We always heard that there was a 'diamond' on an island near the great salt water. We were always told that the 'diamond' was a thought, or a truth. Something worth very much. It was not a jewelry. It sparkled and it shined, but it was not a jewelry. It was more. Colored lights came from inside it with every movement. That is why we always called it (Alcatraz), *Allisti Ti-tanin-miji.*" With a wave of an ancient hand and words filled with enduring knowledge, Grandfather spoke of a time long past.

In one of the many raids upon our people of the Pit River country, his pregnant mother was taken captive and forced, with other Indians, to make the long and painful march to Alcatraz in the winter. At that same time, the military was "sweeping" California. Some of our people were "removed" to the Round Valley Reservation at Covelo; others were taken east by train in open cattle cars during the winter to Quapa, Oklahoma. Still, others were taken out into the ocean at Eureka and thrown overboard into icy waters.

Descendants of those that were taken in chains to Quapa are still there. Some of those cast into the winter ocean at Eureka made it back to land and returned to Pit River country. A few of those defying confinement, the threat of being shot by "thunder sticks," and dark winter nights of a cold Alcatraz-made-deadly by churning, freezing currents, made it back to Pit River country, too.

Grandfather said, "I was very small, too small to remember, but my grandmother remembered it all. The guards allowed us to swim around the rock. Every day, my mother swam. Every day, the people swam. We were not just swimming. We were gaining strength. We were learning the currents. We had to get home.

"When it was time, we were ready. We left at darkness. Grandmother said that I was a baby and rode my mother's back, clinging as she swam from Alcatraz to solid ground in night. My Grandmother remembered that I pulled so hard holding on that I broke my mother's necklace. It is still there in the water . . . somewhere." With a pointing of a stout finger southward, Grandfather indicated where "there" was.

Quivering with emotion, he hesitated. He trembled. "I do not remember if I was scared," Grandfather said, crooked, thick fingers rubbing a creased and wrinkled chin covered with white stubble. "I must have been."

When those old, cloudy eyes dripped tears down a leathery, crevassed face, and long silences were between his sentences, often I trembled too. He softly spoke of his memory.

Our cups were long empty; *maliss* (fire) needed attention. The moon was suspended in the frozen winter night round, bright, scratched and scarred, when Grandfather finally paused in his thinking. The old cast-iron heater grumbled and screamed when I slid open the top to drop in a fresh log. Sparks flew up into the darkness then disappeared. I slammed the top closed. Silence, again.

Grandfather continued, "There was not real diamonds on the island. At least I don't think so. I always thought the diamonds were not diamonds but some kind of understanding, some kind of good thought—or something." He shook a white, shaggy head and looked off into the distance into a time that was so long ago that the mountains barely remembered. For long moments he reflected, he gathered his thoughts. He knew that I "wrote things down on paper."

❖❖❖

The night was thick. To the north a coyote howled. Far to the west an old coyote rasped a call to the black wilderness, a supreme presence beneath starry skies with icy freedom all around.

"When first I heard about the 'diamond,' I thought it might be a story of how we escaped. But after I heard that story so many times, I don't think so. I think there was a truth there that the Mouse Brothers were instructed to get and bring back long ago to help our people. I don't think that I know where that truth is now. Where can it be? It must be deep inside *Axo-Yet* (Mount Shasta) or *Sa Titt* (Medicine Lake). It hides from our people. The truth hides from us. It must not like us. It denies us."

The One-as-Old-as-the-Mountains made me wonder about this story. It seems incredible that there was such an escape from Alcatraz. Through American propaganda I have been trained to believe that it was impossible to escape from that isolated rock because of the currents and because of the freezing temperature as the powerful ocean and the surging rivers merged in chaos. I was convinced—until I heard Grandfather's story and until I realized that he dwelled within a different "time," a different "element." He dwelled within a spirituality of a natural source. In his world, I was only a foreign infant. It is true today that when I talk with the old people I feel like *nilladu-wi-* (a white man). I feel like some domesticated creature addressing original royalty—knowing that the old ones were pure savage, born into the wild, free.

In his calm manner, Grandfather proceeded. "We wandered for many nights. We hid during the day. It is said that we had to go south for three nights before we could turn north (My people landed at San Francisco and had to sneak to what is now San Jose traveling at night with no food until they could turn northward.) They (the U.S. Army) were after us. They were after us all. We had to be careful. We had to be careful and not make mistakes. We headed north for two nights.

"We came to a huge river. We could not cross it. It was swift. My mother walked far upstream then jumped in. Everybody followed. The river washed us to the other shore (possibly the Benicia Straights). We rested for two days eating dead fish that we found along the river. We could not build a fire because they would see the smoke and catch us so we must eat it (fish) raw. At night we traveled again. Again we traveled, this time for two nights also.

"There is a small island of mountains in the great valley (Sutter Buttes). When we reached that place one of the young men climbed the highest peak. He was brave. We were all brave. It was during the sunlight. We waited for him to holler as was the plan. We waited a long, long time. Then we heard: "Axo-yet! Axo-yet! To-ho-ja-toki! To-ho-ja-toki tanjan" (Mount Shasta! Mount Shasta! North direction!). Our hearts were happy. We were close to home. My mother squeezed me to her. We cried. I know we cried. I was there. So was my mother and grandmother."

Grandfather has been within the earth for many snows now. The volumes of knowledge that were buried with him are lost to my generation, a generation that needs original knowledge now more than ever, if we are to survive as a distinct and autonomous people. Perhaps a generation approaching will be more aware, more excited with tradition and custom and less satisfied to being off balance somewhere between the world of the "white man" and the world of the "Indian," and will seek this knowledge.

It is nearing winter, 1989. Snows upon Axo-Yet (Mount Shasta) are deep. The glaring white makes Grandfather's hair nearly yellow—now that I better recall the coarse strands that I often identified as "silver." That beautiful mountain. The landmark that caused the hunted warrior 140 years ago to forget the tragic episode that could have been the termination of our nation, and, standing with the sun shining full upon him, hollered to a frightened people waiting below: "Axo-Yet! Axo-Yet! To-ho-ja Toki, Tanjan!"

Perhaps the approaching generation will seek and locate *Al-list Ti-tanin-miji* within the mountains. Possibly that generation will reveal many truths to this world society that is immense and confused in its immensity. An old chief of the Pit River country, "Charlie Buck," said often: "Truth. It is truth that will set us free." Along with Grandfather, I think that it was a "truth" that the Mouse Brothers brought to our land from Diamond Island long ago. A truth that needs to be understood, appreciated, and acknowledged. A truth that needs desperately to be found and known for its value.

Grandfather's letter is still in my files. I still can't read it, but if I could, I am sure that the message would be the same as this story that he gave to me as the moon listened and the winds whispered across a frozen *Atwam*, during a sparkling winter night long ago.

PHYLLIS WOLF

❖❖❖

White-Out

N THE PENNY POSTCARD she sent home, she was pictured standing in a white high-collared waist. Twenty-five buttons could be counted down the front. The rest were lost in a voluminous skirt that skimmed her ankles.

—Do you remember this?

—No.

—This was taken when you were at school.

—Was it?

—Do you remember knitting dishrags?

—Oh, hell, I do. That's all we ever did was knit dishrags. That's why I don't like to knit. Go to school to knit dishrags.

She looked out the window and saw something no one else could see. She held her stomach delicately as young women hold theirs when it is first filled with life, smoothing hands over rounded curves. Her stomach wasn't gently rounded but protruded sharply to one side, yet she smoothed it with her hands. She held the contorted stomach as she stood to move toward the window. It was heavy and pulled at the intestines. The pain had made her cheeks hollow and she stood bent, waiting.

—Do you want to go outside?

—It's cold out.

There were only a few inches of snow on the ground but clouds the same color of snow had come. In the distance, she could not see where the earth ended and the sky began. Her hands moved over the stomach gently and caught it up from underneath. She thought of the babies, the bastard babies she buried. Her daughter was looking through a box of old letters.

—Who's this you're with?

—I don't remember.

—You're not even looking.

She turned toward the picture her daughter held up. It was a man in an ill-fitting suit two sizes too small. His hair was split down the center and greased flat to his head. His ears stood out.

—I don't remember.

She turned toward the window. She could hear cries being muffled. Infant cries muffled by dirt. She stood in front of the window and wiped her hands against her dress. Her stomach pulled. She looked down at it. Her cheeks had become even more hollow. No, she didn't remember and what she did she didn't want to remember. Small mouths filled with hard dirt. And the days would be like this where the sky was indistinguishable from the earth that she would pour dirt into those mouths. The mouths would be open and they would cry, but the crying would stop after a while. She only heard the cries now when her stomach pulled at intestines and then she would have to cradle the stomach in her hands to make the crying stop. She cradled the stomach now but cries still came from outside the window. Infant cries that pierced the stomach where she stood looking out to swirling white clouds that rose up from earth.

ELIZABETH WOODY

❖❖❖

HomeCooking

THE FLAT TEETH of the morning sun chew at the blisters of the old, tar-papered house. In the garden that thrives under a cloak of sagging cheesecloth, the grasshoppers pose on the promise of a meal. Gránma is framed in the kitchen window as the tongues of curtains remain out from the morning breeze. Even with the hollyhocks' colorful bonnets, up tight against the wall, the house can appear as barren as a piano without ivory. There is a swarm of colors about the screendoor, of calicos, tabbys, sylvesters and blackies. They mew for their meal, in a chorus. As I turn back the covers from my floor bed, I hear humming and a spoon scratching the sides of a pan.

Watching the swill of leftovers sop up the milk, Granma turns to take the pan to the cats, twenty-some wild ones. She is pleased to see me up so early and smiles a toothless greeting. "Hi honey, got to feed my livestock." She sings her good-morning, almost, in the sweet, high-voiced, rhythmic, dialect of Warm Springs English, that sounds Indian. She is no bigger than five feet and no more than ninety-eight pounds. I see her hook the cats in her path expertly with her toes to flip them aside, with a dancer's grace, a certain harmless precision. I once had balked at Granpa's joke about putting up little goalposts in the yard, for

Granma to improve her "cat-punting." That was some years ago. Now, I am oblivious to her harmless way of walking through the fur mass of cats that stay for the one meal, and all the mice and grasshoppers they can eat in the garden.

As I settle at the table I think of the music my grandmother makes, that evokes some aspect of the world I had forgotten since the last visit. Like toads slurping up great moths at night, or the ripple and tumble of water over the rocks in the river, that is how her songs sound to me. I breath in the sweet smell of old age that lingers after my mother's mother. The Nivea, the cleanliness of air-dried cotton, the oiled hair. I notice two rainbow trout on the counter and move to clean them.

She returns quietly, upon seeing me work to clean the plump trout, tells me, "You can fry up those fish. Someone brought them over real early. One relative, I don't know at all. All these kids look like strangers to me. I guess it's just old age that makes me forget how many of all you kids, there are." She laughs a little as she looks to my response out of her eye-corners, sitting behind her coffee at the table.

"Oh, Granma," I say, catching her mood, tease back, "I know you have to remember me. If not for my family resemblance, but just for the trouble you took to wind me, catch me, to make me come inside from playing." I eye her, likewise with cornered eyes. I see her catch her coffee in her lips, in her effort to keep from spitting the liquid and by laughing encourage me. She responds quickly by saying that my mother could outrun her. Usually, she ends this comment on my mother's great speed in childhood, by saying that "she was just too tired to whip her for her naughtiness." Listening to the house groan in the ceiling, Granma changes the subject, to the building of our ranch house up Tenino Valley.

"Your Grandfather's people made that old ranch house over there. All from one tree. All the people came to do what they could. Pound the nails. Split the wood. The women butchered and barbecued the steers. Everyone helped then. They drug the tree there by horse team. Those days our people knew how to do everything for themselves. Not like nowadays, where we have to hire big shots to come in and boss us around."

The pan snaps from the wet skin of the fish as I begin to fry them up. I know that she did not witness the building of this ranch house. She has only merged her stories with my grandfather's, a merging they wanted, symbolized by the two cedar trees that they both planted, side by side, when they married. Saying to one another, that these trees would grow together, like they would, intermingle their roots and branches as one, while still letting the winds of life blow between them. I say, to bring her back to the moment, "These are pretty trout, Granma. About as good as the ones we used to catch, that made Granpa so mad, when I was a kid."

Granma reaches up to arrange the folds of her navy blue western bandanna on her head. It is folded, tri-cornered and knotted on top. She tilts her chin upward. "Oh, how he would get mad. He always said I had more luck than sense. I had a good dream about him last night. That he and I and Baby were fishing. Baby and I caught a fish and we were screaming, and then we were jumping up and down around it, squealing. Granpa said we were scaring away his fish: He always wanted the fish to just jump on his hook."

I laugh, "Granma, I must have been that baby. Sometimes, I wish that we had some poles, so we could fish. But then, we never did learn how to tie a good knot for the hooks. Oh, how we chased the grasshoppers for bait. You laughed so hard at me, jumping as hard as the bugs. We just had to sit down in the cheat grass and hold our sides and our dresses close to our legs, so the grasshoppers wouldn't jump on them. But what really got Granpa, was the fish we caught and you would just flip them up in the air behind us. He said that was no way to treat a fish."

Granma, nodding her head, retorts, "We only used a pin and bait. He had to spend our money on the fancy lures, the steelhead poles. He had his science and some notion that he treated the fish better when he made some big game out of it. We just needed fish for our table, not the fireplace. Your Granpa was a good man, even though he had a soft heart about killing things, like the deer."

The heat intensifies outside and the "hotbugs" sing their legs into a zzzing without pause. Granma sips her coffee, intermittently stirs the spoon in her cup. She eyes the spiral and begins to dream, like she dreams during the day, between words.

These stories of old days are magical. I'm gullible and young enough to still believe in magic. The magic is this soft rumble of blood-life, laughter, our great heart under the land. I hear that great tree and the cedars breathe through this house, too, on occasion. Up the valley, I can see the mountain hold a cap of a cloud. That mountain is as storied as our lives. He walked, lived, and lusted after a young woman mountain, fought with Wy-East, for her, in a time way before the Changer came to have all this chaos beaded up into some monstrously big Dreamer design. The design I only sense from the perspective of a bead. Sometimes I dream of this. I see segments of this power hanging from the hands of old ladies as they dance at gatherings. When I told my boyfriend this, he just said I was too way-out for him. That's how he seems to be anymore. Despite all his singing, sweating, he's too heavy with war and struggle to see the story. Yet, love always seems to knock men down to drag them back to these houses of magic. Just like love knocks us down and pulls us out to the sticks, to follow that guy anywhere he wants to go. Keep an eye on him, just in case something might take him away by terrible magic. Yes, the age of the Changer has passed, but the bloodline is still with us, and the inspiring thread of women's labor, the beads, the Great Transformer and the talk of love. The Beautiful Woman in Earth still whispers into the ears of her children.

"Owwww-witch!" I holler, as the grease sizzles on the skin of my hand. The fish get one last bite on me.

"Watch your cooking. You might just get as bad as me. I never got the hang of cooking on electric stoves. I always cooked on wood stoves or campfires, especially the first days I was married to your grandfather. We lived in a tent to put his brother through college, you know."

"Yeah, Gram, but I think it isn't your cooking abilities, I

inherited, but the old Dreamer brain. I wasn't thinking about the fish in the pan."

At this point she chuckles deeply, bobbing her head, which turns her bandanna a nudge-worth out of place. A meadowlark tinkles a song from the yard. She tilts her head, so her bandanna looks correct, and says, "He sings about the rain that will come soon. Of course, in Indian, he makes his song. That's why it is so beautiful." She taps her finger on the neck handle of her eternal coffee cup. She waits, as she always waits, in a meditation. She waits through her chores. She waits as she waters the lawn with her green hoses, thumb holding the spray over the grass and shadows of juniper. She waits for her children to come and visit as I visit, answering her call for company.

As I pull out the enamel, shallow-bowled dishes, I remain quiet so as not to interrupt the thoughts I see about her, probably a prayer. She responds to me out of courtesy, since her thoughts linger over her long life, and the memories that are so rare and necessary.

I again think about the music I hear. I hear songs in my dreams. Which is unusual, since I do not know any songs, or even know Indian. I think of it as this, the music comes from the tapping of her finger, beating out the occasional soft song. The way a river sounds while we fish, and the sound of the life—dragonflies whirring, singing to me—the music mingles and makes these songs that sound through my dreams. Maybe I catch the hum of the mountain over there too. He's waiting, you see, to get involved with that fiery young woman he sees at the corner of his eyes. Mountain love is a real shaky, fired-up affair. They push up great hilly ranges, bed over the lakes, rub up against one another so wildly, that it takes years to cover up all that passionate rumbling and love talk. Once my grandmother said that her great-grandmother and aunt had to run their horses into a lake to cover themselves with wet hides to keep from getting burned. The water was so hot, it took all their courage to stay put. I believe that was the last rumble before the mountains curled up for a good sleep.

When I told one of my science teachers about this, he said

that these stories are just myth, not fact, and that mountains don't love or even erupt anymore. I believed him until Mount St. Helens erupted. It erased all innocent belief in the fable of absolute science for me. Thank goodness, I had heard some "fact" about those mountains way before I entered school.

I give my grandmother her share of the fish, and she says as she always says, "Oh, honey, that is too much. Put some back. I'm not company."

"Eat, Granma, we have plenty for many lifetimes over." I settle my "husky" body down to savor the fish. "You know I sure miss Granpa. I miss his whistling in the mornings. When you and him would cook together. You remember that?"

Granma retorts, "I have spent half of my life cooking for all of you. But it was your grandfather who could cook the best. He knew all the dishes of this and that. Just like he knew all that wild music. High-wy-ahn, I think it was called. He was a great singer as well as a great jokester. You tell a story as tall as he could, but I always thought you hung around him too much."

I smile, then say, "You both, were pretty wild examples for me to follow. I think a lot about how you two would play in the kitchen, while you cooked, what you called a farmer's breakfast, the potatoes, ham steaks, eggs. Between flipping over the food, you would dance to western music on the transistor radio, the jitterbug, the Charleston. Yeah, I remember how you two carried on while you thought I was still asleep." I smile thinking of how agile Granma was, dancing, diaper pins on her dress, blue tennis shoes toeing in and out. Granpa, twirling her around, in his sleeveless white undershirt, pants always neatly belted with a smile wide in pleasure, watching Granma's face spin like a light in the morning dawn. Granpa had a grin so wide, it was as if it could go halfway around his head, especially when he had Granma going, or getting her aggravated from his teasing. Then he'd grin all the more while he sweet-talked his way back into her good humor.

"It seemed that you always ended up your dancing with a good fight, boxing, with your dukes curled over. You always won with your 'Appalachian apple cut' half a wind up, a quick strike to Granpa's 'glass jaw.' Then you'd grab his pants seat and have him in your mercy. He'd holler, 'I give up honey! I give up, I'll marry you!' "

We both laughed a great laugh at the memory. Granma tucked the trout meat into a pooch in her soft cheek, tilted her chin toward me, and said in a quiet, matter-of-fact tone, "Your grandfather didn't marry me for my homecooking. I thought you always knew that."

BIOGRAPHICAL NOTES

Paula Gunn Allen

Paula Gunn Allen (Laguna Pueblo/Lakota) is a professor of English at UCLA. A poet, writer, and scholar, she's published seven volumes of poetry, most recently *Skins and Bones* (West End Press). Her prose and poetry appear widely in anthologies, journals, and scholarly publications. She was awarded the Native American Prize for Literature in 1990, and that same year her anthology of short stories *Spider Woman's Granddaughters* was awarded the American Book Award, sponsored by the Before Columbus Foundation. She also won the Susan Koppleman Award sponsored by The Women's Caucus of the Popular and American Culture Associations. She received a postdoctoral Minorities Scholar Fellowship from the National Research Council–Ford Foundation for research and was appointed Associate Fellow for Humanities at Stanford University, both in 1984.

Gloria Bird

Gloria Bird (Spokane) attended the Institute of American Indian Arts majoring in creative writing and received her BA in English at Lewis and Clark College in Portland, Oregon. She is one of the founding members of Northwest Native American Writers Association and has received a 1988 writer's grant from the Oregon Institute of Literary Arts to continue her work in poetry. She is the co-author of *A FILMOGRAPHY FOR AMERICAN INDIAN EDU-CATION* (1972). Her poetry has appeared in *Fireweed*, Native Women (1986); *The American Indian Reader* (1973); *Mr. Cogito* (American Indian issue, 1988); the *NWNAW Broadsides Collections* (1988, 1990); *High Plains Literary Review* (1989, 1990); and in *Caylx* and *Dancing on the Rim of the World:* An Anthology of Contemporary Northwest Native American Writing, 1990).

Beth Brant

Beth Brant (Bay of Qunite Mohawk) is the editor of *A Gathering of Spirit,* a collection of writing and art by Native American Women (Firebrand Books, 1989). She is the author of *Mohawk Trail*, prose and poetry, and *Food and Spirits,* short fiction, both by Firebrand Books. Her work has appeared in numerous Native and feminist anthologies, and she has done readings and lectures and taught creative writing throughout North America.

Joseph Bruchac

Joseph Bruchac (Abenaki) lives in the Adirondack foothills in the same house where he was raised by his maternal grandparents, with his wife and two sons. He and his wife are the co-directors of The Greenfield Review Press and Literary Center. His poems and stories have appeared in more than 400 magazines and anthologies. He is the winner of an NEA Creative Writing Fellowship, and the Cherokee Nation Prose Award, and his work has been translated into numerous languages. GOING HOME won the PEN Syndicated Fiction Award.

Elizabeth Cook-Lynn

Elizabeth Cook-Lynn (Crow Creek Sioux) is an associate professor of English and Indian Studies at Eastern Washington University. She is a poet and fiction writer whose work focuses on a particular geography and culture. She has published two chapbooks of poetry and a collection of short stories. In addition to teaching a wide range of literature and Indian Studies courses, she is a founding editor of *The Wicazo sa Review,* a Native American Studies magazine that has achieved a national reputation for excellence. *The Power of Horses and Other Stories* was published by Arcade Publishing (Little Brown) 1990.

Michael Dorris

Michael Dorris (Modoc), a professor of Native American studies at Dartmouth College, is the author of several nonfiction books, including *The Broken Cord* for which he received the National Book Critics' Circle award in 1989, and two novels, *A Yellow Raft in Blue Water* and *The Crown of Columbus,* written in collaboration with his wife, Louise Erdrich. He has also received the Indian Achievement Award in 1985.

Debra Earling

Debra Earling (Flathead) is currently a student in the M.F.A./Ph.D. program at Cornell University. She was published recently in *The Last Best Place: A Montana Anthology.*

Ed Edmo

Ed Edmo (Shoshone-Bannock) is a poet, playwright, traditional storyteller, and lecturer on Northwest tribal culture. His poetry has been published internationally, and *These Few Words of Mine,* a chapbook, was published by Blue Cloud Quarterly in 1985. Edmo works with the Artist in Education Programs throughout Oregon. He teaches poetry, legends, and creative writing, and discusses Native American political issues with students of all ages in schools and colleges. He often does special workshops on cultural issues and values for youth, church, senior, and civic groups as well as human services personnel.

Anita Endrezze

Anita Endrezze (Yaqui) has a master of arts degree from Eastern Washington University's Creative Writing Program. Her poems, short stories, and paintings have been published in many countries. A collection of poetry, translated into French, will be published in 1991 by Rougerie. She is also a professional oral storyteller and teacher. Previous publications include: *Anthology of 20th Century Native American Poetry* (Harper and Row); *Poesie Presente, The Chariton Review, Willow Springs, Yellow Silk, Poetry Northwest, Zyzzyva, Words in Blood,* and several dozen other anthologies.

Louise Erdrich

Louise Erdrich (Turtle Mountain Chippewa) is the author of three novels—*Love Medicine, The Beet Queen,* and *Tracks*—and two collections of poetry: *Jacklight* and *Baptism of Desire.* Her latest novel, written in collaboration with her husband, Michael Dorris, is *The Crown of Columbus.* Her awards include the National Book Critics' Circle (1984), and the *Los Angeles Times* prize for fiction.

Tina Freeman-Villalobos

Tina Freeman-Villalobos (Modoc) lives in Oregon with her son, Adrian, eleven years old and her daughter, Jasmine, thirteen years old. *The Way It Was* was written for Jasmine and Adrian so they would know.

Diane Glancy

Diane Glancy (Cherokee) received her MFA from the University of Iowa. She teaches Creative Writing and Native American Literature at Macalester College in St. Paul, Minnesota. She has published four books of poetry: *One Age in a Dream* (Milkweed Editions); *Offering* (Holy Cow! Press), *Iron Woman* (New Rivers Press), and *Lone Dog's Winter Count*(West End Press). Her first collection of short stories, *Trigger Dance* (The University of Colorado and The Fiction Collective) won the Nilon Minority Fiction Award. Glancy is also the recipient of a 1990 NEA and Minnesota State Arts Board

Fellowship. Her forthcoming book, *Claiming Breath,* has received the University of Nebraska Press Native American Prose Award.

Rayna Green

Rayna Green (Cherokee) is currently the director of the American Indian Program at the National Museum of American History at the Smithsonian Institution. She is the editor of *That's What She Said: Contemporary Fiction and Poetry by American Indian Women* published by Indiana University Press, and numerous works for print, visual media, and interpretations on American Indian history and culture.

Joy Harjo

Joy Harjo (Creek) graduated from the Institute of American Indian Arts and the University of New Mexico. She received her MFA in Creative Writing from the Iowa Writer's Workshop at the University of Iowa. She also attended the Anthropology Film Center in Santa Fe. She has published four books of poetry including *She Had Some Horses* (Thunder Mouth Press) and her most recent, *In Mad Love and War* (Wesleyan University Press, 1990). She is now an associate professor in the Department of English at the University of Arizona, Tucson, and is on the Steering Committee of the En'owkin Centre International School of Writing (for Native American writers). She travels extensively around the country giving readings and workshops and is the recipient of a 1989 Arizona Commission on the Arts Creative Writing Fellowship and a 1990 American Indian Distinguished Achievement Award. She is also a dramatic screenwriter and has produced works including *Apache Mountain Spirits* for Silvercloud Video Productions. She is at work on several other projects including a fifth collection of poetic prose, *The Field of Miracles,* an anthology of Native women's writing from North and South America, and plays saxophone with her band.

Kathleen Shaye Hill

Kathleen Shaye Hill (Klamath) has spent most of the past five years working for her Tribe. She also served as an elected official of the tribal government for two years. She is returning to the University of Washington this fall to pursue a concurrent J.D. and MPA degree program at the Law School and Graduate School of Public Affairs. A single parent for fourteen years, she married Joseph Dupris and they expected their first child in 1990.

Linda Hogan

Linda Hogan (Chickasaw) is an associate professor at the University of Colorado. She is a poet, novelist, and essayist of international recognition. She is the author of several books of poetry, and a collection of short fiction. Her book *Seeing Through the Sun* received an American Book Award from the Before Columbus Foundation. Her most recent book, *MEAN SPIRIT,* was published by Atheneum. Hogan is the recipient of an NEA grant, a Minnesota Arts Board Grant, and a Colorado Writer's Fellowship, as well as the Five Civilized Tribes Museum playwriting award. She has served on the National Endowment for the Arts poetry panel for two years and is involved in wildlife rehabilitation as a volunteer.

Roger Jack

Roger Jack (Colville Indian) holds an associate of fine arts degree in creative writing from the Institute of American Indian Arts in Santa Fe, New Mexico, and a bachelor of arts degree in creative writing from Eastern Washington University in Cheney, Washington. His work has been published in a number of journals and anthologies, including the *New York Quarterly, Spawing the Medicine River, Earth Power Coming, The Clouds Threw This Light,* and *Dancing on the Rim of the World.* He has also written a one-act play, *Buckskin Curtains.*

Maurice Kenny

Maurice Kenny (Mohawk) is the author of some eighteen collections of poetry and fiction. His work appears in more than seventy-five magazines and journals. He is the publisher of Strawberry Press and the co-editor of the poetry journal *CONTACT/11* in New York City. He has received the prestigious American Book Award, the Hodson Award, and the National Public Radio Broadcasting Award, and has been nominated for the Pulitzer prize twice. St. Lawrence University cited the poet in 1987 for Distinguished Service to Literature, and he has been honored by the New York Council on the Arts.

Thomas King

Thomas King (Cherokee) teaches Native literature, American studies, and creative writing at the University of Minnesota. He is a novelist and a short story writer. He has edited several volumes of fiction by Canadian Native writers titled *All My Relations,* and co-edited *The Native in Literature,* a collection of critical essays on the Native in Canadian literature. His poetry and short fiction have appeared in journals and magazines throughout North America.

Craig Lesley

Craig Lesley is the author of two novels, *Winterkill* and *RiverSong.* His work has received the Western Writers of America Golden Spur Award for Best Novel of the Year, the Medicine Pipe Bearer's Award for Best First Novel, and the Pacific Northwest Booksellers' Association Award. His short stories have appeared in such publications as *Massachusetts Review, Northwest Review,* and *Seattle Review.* He has been the recipient of a National Endowment for the Arts Fellowship, a Bread Loaf Fellowship in the Novel, as well as two National Endowment for the Humanities Fellowships to study Native American literature. Lesley has been fiction editor of *Writers Forum* over the past eight years and was associate editor for *The Interior Country: Stories of the Modern West* (Ohio University Press). He has taught English and creative writing at the college level for fifteen years and makes his home in Portland, Oregon, with his wife and their two daughters.

Judith Minty

Judith Minty (Mohawk) teaches at Humboldt State University in Arcata, California, and is the author of six books of poetry, most recently *Dancing the Fault.* Her first book, *Lake Songs and Other Fears,* received the United States Award of the International Poetry Forum in 1973. She is presently working on a novel. *Killing the Bear* was awarded the PEN Syndicated Fiction award in 1984.

N. Scott Momaday

N. Scott Momaday (Kiowa) is Regent's Professor of English at the University of Arizona. He has received the Pulitzer Prize for his novel *House Made of Dawn.* His other works include *The Ancient Child, The Way to Rainy Mountain, The Names, The Gourd Dancer,* and *Angle of Geese and Other Poems.* He recently received the *Premio Letterario Internazionale "Mondello" Award.*

Duane Niatum

Duane Niatum (Klallam) currently is doing his doctoral dissertation research on contemporary Northwest Coast American Indian art. He also publishes short fiction and essays, which have appeared in magazines and anthologies. His poems, stories, and essays have been translated into more than twelve languages. He edited *Carriers of the Dream Wheel,* an anthology of contemporary Native American poetry, and its sequel, *Harper's Anthology of 20th Century Native American Poetry* (both by Harper and Row). His volume of poetry entitled *Songs for the Harvester of Dreams* (Washington Press) won the Before Columbus Foundation American Book Award. His latest collection of poetry is *Drawings of the Song Animals: New and Selected Poems.*

Carter Revard

Carter Revard (Osage) attended the University of Tulsa, Merton College in Oxford on a Rhodes Scholarship, and Yale. He is now a professor of English at Washington University in St. Louis, Missouri. He is published in numerous scholarly journals and literary anthologies including *Voices of the Rainbow* (Viking); *Harper's Anthology of 20th Century Native American Poetry; Earth Power Coming* (Navajo Community College Press); *New Worlds Literature* (Norton); and *The Riverside Reader* (Houghton Mifflin) and has a collection of poetry entitled *Ponca War Dancers.*

Mickey Roberts

Mickey Roberts (Nooksack) is a graduate of Western Washington University in Bellingham. She was an executive secretary and is now a free-lance writer. She is also a researcher and collector of historical facts on the history of Washington State and the Nooksack Indian Tribe. She is the author of several short stories and *A History of the Nooksack Tribe of the State of Washington.* She is also the originator of the effort to make the Nooksack Indian Tribe a federally recognized tribe.

Greg Sarris

Greg Sarris (Pomo-Coast Miwok) is assistant professor of English at UCLA. His articles and essays have appeared in numerous journals and magazines, including *MELUS, College English, National Women's Studies Association Journal, American Indian Quarterly, Studies in American Indian Literdture, Decolonizing The Subject: Race and Gender in Women's Autobiography, The Ethnography of Reading,* and *Stanford Magazine.* Currently he is completing the story of his life with Pomo basketweaver and medicine woman Mabel McKay in a book entitled *Prayer Basket.* He received his PhD in Modern Thought and Literature from Stanford University.

Vickie Sears

Vickie Sears (Cherokee) is a writer, feminist therapist, and teacher. Her poetry and short stories have appeared in several journals and story collections. Her most recent publications appeared in *Spider Woman's Granddaughters* (Beacon Press) and *Simple Songs: Stories by Vickie Sears* (Firebrand Books). Her essay has appeared in *Changing Our Power: An Introduction to Women's Studies* (Kendall/Hunt)

Katheryn Stavrakis

Katheryn Stavrakis received her M.F.A. in creative writing at the University of Massachusetts, where she also received a Harvey Swados Award. Her short fiction has appeared in numerous literary magazines, including *Writers' Form* and *Grover*. Of Russian and Greek extraction, she is a first generation American and specializes in teaching English as a second language and creative writing. Currently she is completing a novel.

Mary TallMountain

Mary TallMountain (Koyukon Athabascan) writes from the Native American viewpoint, positing on the theme *In Our Ancient Heritage Is Our Strength.* Much of her work deals with social justice issues in the United States and with the state of the environment. She writes for the Way of St. Francis in a column called "Meditation for Wayfarers" and has been published in *The Animals' Agenda, The Alaska Quarterly* and many other anthologies. She appeared on Bill Moyers's poetry series, *Power of the Word.*

Clifford Trafzer

Clifford E. Trafzer (Wyandot) is a professor of American Indian Studies at San Diego State University. He is an author of several books and articles on Native American history, culture, and literature. He is a member of the California State Native American Heritage Commission. His book *Renegade Tribe: The Palouse Indians and the Invasion of the Inland Pacific Northwest* won the Governor's Book Award in 1987.

Gerald Vizenor

Gerald Vizenor (Chippewa) is a professor of literature at the University of California, Santa Cruz campus. He has written numerous books, including Bearheart, Griever, and The Trickster of Liberty. His autobiography, *Interior Landscapes,* was published in 1990 by the University of Minnesota Press.

Anna Lee Walters

Anna Lee Walters (Pawnee and Otoe-Missouri) works on the Navajo Reservation, where she teaches and publishes books. She also lectures on contemporary American Indian life, American Indian literature, and other topics. Walters writes to an Indian audience first of their common historical and tribal experiences. Her most recent work is *The Spirit of Native America: Beauty and Mysticism in American Indian Art* (Chronicle Books) and the novel *Ghost Singer* (Northland Publishing). To date she has contributed to about forty-five other publications, including scholarly journals and news magazines. Her newest book, The Sun Is Not Merciful (Firebrand Books), is a collection of short stories.

James Welch

James Welch (Blackfeet/Gros Ventre) is the author of four novels, *Winter in the Blood, The Death of Jim Looney, Fools Crow,* and *The Indian Lawyer,* as well as the poetry collection, *Riding the Earthboy 40. Fools Crow* received the *Los Angeles Times* Award for Best Novel.

Roberta Hill Whiteman

Roberta Hill Whiteman (Oneida) works at the University of Wisconsin, Eau Claire, where she has taught courses in creative writing and American Indian literature. She is currently completing her doctorate in American Studies at the University of Minnesota. Her first collection of poetry, *Star Quilt*, won the Wisconsin Writers Award in 1985. Her work has recently appeared in *Northeast Indian Quarterly, North American Review,* and *Amicus.*

Darryl Babe Wilson

Darryl Babe Wilson (Pit River) lives in California, where he went to school, became a marine, and worked in a logging camp. He has received the President's Undergraduate Fellowship for Poetry, has participated in the Minorities Undergraduate Research Apprenticeship in Letters and Science for two years, and has been on the dean's honor roll for three years. He is now finishing his last year at University of California, Davis. He has been active in many Native American rights issues and has had recognition for his poetry in Europe. He is now writing a book about the struggle of Native Americans in northeast California.

Phyllis Wolf

Phyllis Wolf (Assiniboine/Ojibway) was born in northeastern Montana on the Fort Peck Reservation.

Elizabeth Woody

Elizabeth Woody (Wasco–Navajo) majored in creative writing at the Institute of American Indian Arts in Santa Fe, New Mexico. Her work has been widely anthologized, and publications include national and international magazines. *Hand into Stone,* her first volume of poetry, was published in 1988 by Contact/II Press and won an American Book Award from the Before Columbus Foundation. Her poems have appeared in *Songs from This Earth on Turtle's Back, The Clouds Threw This Light, A Gathering of Spirit, Bearing Witness/Sobreviviendo, The Native American Today, Fireweed, Tyuonyi, Akewon, Contact/II, Greenfield Review,* and *Sur Le Dos La Torture: Revue Bilingue de Litterature Amerindienne* (France). In

1985 she won a poetry contest and was published along with seventeen other poets in *Image,* a project of the Seattle Arts Commission, and was juried into the Literary Readings series of the National Women's Studies Conference at the University of Washington.